... THE THING INSIDE BAKER
WAS HUNTING AGAIN

"I'm gonna hurt you bad, man. I'm gonna cut your heart out," snarled the one called Jace.

He had a knife. And he had Sumo to back him. But he was afraid.

Because Baker was changing.

Biaggi, watching from deep shadow, held his fire. They had told him about Baker. Until now, he had never quite believed it.

The change was subtle and yet it was total. Baker's body did not expand, exactly. It was more of a coiling. The eyes, the movements, were now those of a stalking animal. Baker's lips had flattened against his teeth, baring them. The eyes were shining.

Then Biaggi heard the voice. It was not Baker's voice. This one hissed and spat like escaping steam. It was the voice of the one they called Abel.

"You're not going to hurt me, Jace," came the words through a terrible smile. *"I'm going to hurt you. And then I'm going to hurt your friend."*

"Satisfyingly sensational ... a first-rate thriller."
—Publishers Weekly

Abel/Baker/Charley

John R. Maxim

BANTAM BOOKS

NEW YORK • TORONTO • LONDON • SYDNEY • AUCKLAND

*This edition contains the complete text
of the original hardcover edition.*
NOT ONE WORD HAS BEEN OMITTED.

ABEL/BAKER/CHARLEY
*A Bantam Book/published by arrangement with Houghton Mifflin
Company.*

PUBLISHING HISTORY
*Houghton Mifflin edition published 1983
Bantam edition/November 1993*

ISBN 0-553-29773-2

Published simultaneously in the United States and Canada

*Bantam Books are published by Bantam Books, a division of Bantam
Doubleday Dell Publishing Group, Inc. Its trademark, consisting of the
words "Bantam Books" and the portrayal of a rooster, is Registered in
U.S. Patent and Trademark Office and in other countries. Marca Reg-
istrada. Bantam Books, 1540 Broadway, New York, New York 10036.*

PRINTED IN THE UNITED STATES OF AMERICA

RAD   0 9 8 7 6 5 4 3 2 1

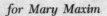

for Mary Maxim

The first beast was like a lion, and the second beast like a calf, and the third beast had a face as a man . . . and they were full of eyes within; and they rest not day and night.

—REVELATION 4:7–8

1

The tall man walked more slowly now, avoiding street-lights where he could, merging with the night shadows that lined the park wall. He was listening . . . feeling.

Fifth Avenue was dark and all but lifeless. No cabs had appeared in the fifteen minutes since he'd turned back to his hotel. A fine mist of rain seemed to hover more than fall, daubing a soft haze across his tinted aviator glasses. He stopped beneath a single low sycamore and wiped them dry against the suede of his jacket. Through flat green eyes that had a sadness about them he scanned the street he'd come down, probing one block at a time as he followed the receding wink of traffic lights.

There was nothing. Only the pull of the park, and it was getting stronger. The man who'd been following him, the young man in the gray raincoat, was gone. At least Baker could not feel him. He must have gone ahead, Baker decided, to where gray raincoat's partner waited. Back to the hotel where Baker had left one suitcase as an animal leaves its scent. Baker would not return there.

He turned south once more. Ahead of him by several yards was Seventy-second Street. There, the black maw of the park entrance opened wider as he approached. And he felt the pull. He thought he felt it. Slowing again, he weaved across the sidewalk and back, probing, like a dowser searching for a hidden spring. Although he felt no pain yet, he was almost sure. The thing inside him was hunting again.

"What's in the park, Abel?" He asked the question in his mind.

"safety."

"Central Park is not safe. Not at night." Even his inner voice was tired.

"safe for you. trust me baker."

Trust me! Three times now he'd heard it. Three times he'd heard Abel's warning, if that's what it was, since the airport taxi took him to that first hotel. Leave this place, it said then. Someone will hurt you here. Someone is saying your name here. Leave your smaller bag and go. No, Baker. Not through the lobby. Through the kitchen. Go. Trust me, Baker.

And then once more at the second hotel, where he'd given a new name. There the voice tugged at him as he sat at the bar nursing the single drink that he'd allowed himself. There'd been a woman sitting there alone. She'd looked at him twice since he entered and each time lowered her eyes to the near-empty glass in front of her. Baker almost spoke to her. He wanted to. She might have taken the edge off his loneliness. They might even have spent the night together. Baker knew that he was not good at that sort of thing. But it does happen. And it might have been nice. Not so much for the sex especially, but to feel the warmth of another human body where no one could find him.

Baker sighed. It was wishful thinking. He knew that he was so out of touch with single women that he would probably stammer like a schoolboy and make an ass of himself. Then there was the problem of keeping Abel leashed and quiet. Abel didn't like him getting close to people. Not even his own daughter. Well, you can go to hell, Abel. That's where the line gets drawn.

But he did leave the bar because Abel had said trust me. Walk awhile, Abel said, through the quiet streets so that I can listen. And now here he was. Standing outside Central Park on a damp night listening to another trust me. Closer to an obey me, which it damn well better not be.

"Abel?"

"the park."

"Who's in there, Abel? Who will I find in there?"

"*i've kept you safe . . . the park is safe . . . the park is darker.*"

Yes, Abel. You've kept me safe, for what that's worth. For what any of this is worth. But you're not worth it, Abel. Not you or Charley either. Not if the two of you are all I have.

"*go into the park, baker. safe.*"

For now, Abel, we'll do it your way. This close, we'll do it your way.

A tiny pressure behind his right eye, barely there and not yet building into pain, relaxed abruptly. Baker jerked his head to shake off the thread that remained. Then, with a grunt of disgust, he passed between the stone pillars into the park.

A city block to the east, the man in the gray raincoat breathed heavily into the mouthpiece of a sidewalk telephone. "Come on," he urged as he counted the number of rings. They stopped at eleven.

"Sir?" he inquired of the silence at the other end. "This is Michael, sir. Do you know my voice?"

"May I hope that your telephone is secure?" It was a low, rich voice that hinted at a lifetime of privilege.

"It's an open pay phone on Madison Avenue, sir. It doesn't figure to be dirty, and anyway this is the only time I could have called you."

"Madison Avenue in New York City?"

"Yes sir. He's here. Jared Baker is here."

There was a long silence on the distant end. Michael Biaggi could hear the older man swallowing.

"Jared Baker is where, exactly?" the voice asked finally.

"Right now he's taking a slow walk down Fifth Avenue. Mr. Harrigan is covering his hotel from the street and Kate Mulgrew is inside. She tried to pick him up in the bar but he didn't bite."

"Which hotel?"

"The St. Moritz, for now," Biaggi answered. "He checked into the Warwick first but that was a dodge. The name he's using is Harold Mailander."

"Humph!" The voice sounded approving. From his Virginia bedroom he could almost hear Marcus Sonnenberg's voice instructing Baker on the choice of assumed names. Pick a name that is easily mispronounced or forgotten. No names that reflect self-image, no names that are easily retained, such as Jared Baker, and no names matching your initials. Jewish and foreign names serve well unless you happen to be in a place where there are few Jews or foreigners. Harold Mailander. A good name. For the St. Moritz, a very good name. "Is there any sign of Dr. Sonnenberg, by the way?"

"Not so far, sir. Mr. Harrigan thinks he'll turn up, but I'm not sure Baker's even here to see Sonnenberg. Baker could have gone straight up to Westchester in the time it took him to get to midtown Manhattan."

"He'll see Sonnenberg. To Midtown from where, incidentally?"

"He came into Kennedy on a flight from O'Hare. Harrigan seemed to know that."

"And chose not to report it," the other man added icily. "You may assume the Chicago origin is another piece of misdirection. You may also begin to see, young man, why this arrangement between us was thought necessary."

"Yes sir." Biaggi hesitated.

"You are troubled, Michael?"

"Sir, it's Mr. Harrigan. He'd kill me if he knew. And there are times when I almost think he does."

"You've been listening to too many Connor Harrigan legends, Michael. Legends he does nothing to discourage. The man is hardly psychic. What he is is an extraordinarily perceptive man and a tenacious one. His perceptiveness should move you to caution but not to paranoia."

"Yes sir."

"Consider our relationship inviolate, Michael. Before long, you may find your position in life greatly improved. And I want to know of any unusual developments regardless of the hour."

"There might be one now, sir. Mr. Harrigan spotted some of Domenic Tortora's muscle hanging around the Warwick. It might be coincidence . . ."

"Or it might be disaster. Baker cannot fall into anyone's hands but mine, Michael. He is the most dangerous of Sonnenberg's experiments, and more than that, he has become Sonnenberg's right hand. I want him alive, Michael. Incapacitated, if necessary, but alive. No one must interfere with that. Do you get my meaning, Michael, in the event a quick decision must be made?"

"Even Harrigan, sir?"

"Anyone, Michael."

"Yes sir."

"Do you have doubts, Michael, whether you are up to this task?"

"No sir," Biaggi answered quickly. "It's just—just that I have to get back on him. I had to let Baker out of my sight to find a phone."

"You had to— Then fly, young man. Fly after him. Reassure me at your first opportunity."

"Goodbye, sir."

Michael Biaggi slammed the phone clumsily onto its hook, in the same motion bursting into a run toward Fifth Avenue. The receiver rocked and dislodged as he hit his stride. He heard it clatter against the cupola but he did not look back.

In a small study off the bedroom of his home in Alexandria, Virginia, Duncan Peck listened to the clap of receding footsteps and the sway of the dangling phone against its stanchion. It reminded him of a hanging man.

"Welcome home, Jared Baker," he murmured. He broke the connection and began to dial another number.

A hundred yards into the park, Baker stopped and turned. He saw that the thick trees of late summer had closed in behind him. It was only an illusion, he knew. A trick of the curving road. But it seemed that the park had sealed him in.

Oddly, the notion did not unnerve him. It intrigued him mildly that he felt no urge to flee a place where no prudent man would walk after dusk, but on the other hand Baker had always been comfortable here. He knew the park. Often, when his office was quiet, Baker would spend the noon hour here with his sketchpad. Up ahead was a favorite spot, a knoll popular among artists and especially among photographers of liquor and fashion advertisements. From it he could look out over the famous pond and footbridge and see the Plaza Hotel framed against the sky. Every issue of *The New Yorker* seemed to carry an ad with a model using that scene as background. That, or the Wollman skating rink, off to the right. Or the Central Park Zoo down to the left. There the models were usually children in jeans and jumpers. Tina had posed once. A photographer picked her out of the crowd one Sunday morning and gave her twenty dollars to be in a Buster Brown clothing ad. Tine was so proud. She was so tiny then.

That might have been the last time he was here with her, Baker realized. It was the year before she was to start school. Sarah had looked at the city through new eyes and saw that a place that had seemed exciting up to now had become dangerous and dirty. At least for Tina. Sarah found a house, their first house, in what she hoped would be the gentler surroundings of Connecticut. Baker shook away the thought.

He stepped off the main road, which snaked like a moonlit jungle river through the darkness. There was a footpath. He knew it would pass close by the zoo.

Comfortable! He chewed upon the word. He wondered how comfortable he would have felt a year or so ago. Strolling through this park after midnight. Not comfortable at all. A year ago, he'd have been hearing footsteps by now. He'd be sweating and struggling against an urge to run, looking for the shortest route to where there were lights and people. A year ago, he'd never have entered the park at night. And that woman at the St. Moritz. A year ago he'd never have given her a second look, nor would he have been in a bar drinking alone. It would have been too soon after Sarah. But then, a year ago he wasn't Baker either. Not exactly.

Baker moved off the rutted pavement and onto the grass, then on toward the red glow to the south. The grass was more silent and the foliage there kept him in deeper shadows. There was no reason for doing this that Baker knew.

"Abel?" He called the name in his mind. *"Why the sneaking around, Abel? Do you hear something? . . . Abel?"* There was no answer.

A quarter-mile farther, Baker knew by the scents in the air that he was passing the zoo. He would hear the animal sounds in a minute. That would put him only six blocks from his hotel.

"Charley? What about you? What am I going to do about the one sitting outside the St. Moritz? Do I ignore him until morning? Do I spend the night on a bench? Come on, Charley. If you can receive, you can also send. Why don't you call ahead and see if the Essex House has an empty room?"

Still no answer.

The hell with it, he thought. Maybe that woman is still in the bar. Except something about her bothered him.

The sounds came. They were grunting guttural sounds that he supposed were the equivalent of a man snoring. He heard a single heavy splash that might have been a sea lion falling out of bed. The splash was answered by the peevish chatter of a tropical bird and then a squealing sound that ended in a cough.

Baker froze.

The squeal had not risen from the zoo. It had come down, down the steep slope ahead of him and to his right. He cocked his head and waited. Nothing. Only the whisper of leaves and the roar of a bus on a distant street. He had just leaned into a step when it came again.

There was a thrashing of branches and then a sharp slap that could only have been flesh against flesh. A gasping sound.

Baker eased forward toward the slope, his movements slow and measured. Pressing his body close against the hill, he climbed on all fours, aiming toward a small stand of dogwood at the summit. He could hear words now. They were frightened, pleading words in a woman's voice. Its sound was despairing, as if she knew the words were useless.

He reached the crest and he could see them. There were two men, bent or kneeling low within a copse that bordered the bridle trail. Baker could not see the woman. She was pinned beneath them, lost in the shadow of their bodies. One man, a shadow much larger than the other, appeared to be pinning her arms outstretched above her head while the other knelt astride her. The smaller man held a knife with a blade that was long and thin. He raised it for a long moment and held it aloft, rolling it between his fingers so that she could see the flash of faraway park lights along the blade. Then his arm came down slowly and he pointed the knife at where her eyes must have been.

"Come on, man," Baker heard the other shape say. "We don't have all night for this."

"Shit, we don't," the knife answered. "Look what we got here. We ought to take her someplace for a week."

"Oh, hey, please," came the woman's voice again. "You don't have to hurt me." Her voice was stronger now. Baker knew that she was talking about the weapon. About being cut. Her tone said that she'd accepted whatever else they might do to her. If they just wouldn't mark her. If they wouldn't kill her.

The smaller man understood. With his free hand he tore slowly at her upper clothing. She tensed but did not move as his fingers ran over her skin, not until he found some part of her flesh and twisted at it. The woman's body bucked and heaved. A desperate flash of rage pushed through her fear. "You little bastard!" She sucked in her breath and spat full in his face. Once more she drew the breath of a scream, but a hand slashed hard across her face. Again it struck, backhanded, and the scream became a cough. Her body sagged and was still.

"See that?" he hissed. "I just saved you from yourself. You were going to scream, and I told you if you did that I was going to let your air out with this knife." He pressed the blade against her throat, and once more her body arched beneath him. But she made no further sound.

"That's better," he said. "You have to learn to be nice. Me and my friend here are your fans, you see. You have to be nice to your fans. But you, you cunt, you don't know about being nice, do you? You didn't want to come party with us, you called me bad names, you even scratched me here on my neck."

"And she tried to knee me in the balls," the big one complained.

"See? Even him. You don't know how to be nice at all."

His left hand did something. He must have grabbed her hair and twisted it because her face jerked into what light there was. "Miss Burke? You're not answering me, Miss Burke."

Baker had straightened to his full height. He'd begun to move forward, but the name seemed to stop him. A look of confusion crossed his face and he lowered his head to peer more closely through the hazy light. He tried to think. He squeezed his eyes shut and pressed his fingers against his temples in an effort to block the shove that was starting to build. Abel was back.

Baker tried to ignore him, turning his thoughts instead to the whirl of his own emotions. There was hatred. And there was a stab of fear that caused his heart to break into a runner's pace. The men had knives. And Sonnenberg or no, he was still human enough to fear them. And too, there was a small shock of recognition. He knew that name and that face. Twice that name had touched his life, and now it was here and it should not be here.

"*Abel? What is this, Abel?*"

Abel pushed again but he did not answer. Baker shook him off and his own rage returned.

The rage came because he knew the men. He knew them in a different way than he knew the woman, but he knew them. He knew their kind. They were not what he expected when he first heard the woman's cries. They weren't park people. Their clothing looked like Bloomingdale's. Their hair, even in this light, had a blown and sculptured shape, expensively barbered. Yet Baker was barely surprised. It was as if he knew what he would find. What Abel would find. And he'd found him. The one with the knife, the talkative one. The sadistic little shit who affected a kind of evil logic when he spoke. He was another taker. A destroyer. This one, Baker thought, was very much like that other. (You son of a bitch. You drunken son of a bitch. You killed them . . . Jesus, look at my bike. Stupid fucking broads made me bust up my bike . . . Your bike? Your bike? I'll kill you, you— Hey, back off, asshole. Why don't you keep them off the fucking streets where they . . .)

Baker dashed the picture from his mind. Just in time. The memory was becoming too fresh and the pain was too real, and it almost made him say Abel's name aloud. *It is you, isn't it, Abel? You found this one like you found all the others.*

The pain stabbed at him.

"Not yet, Abel. Maybe not at all this time."

The pain came harder.

"Abel, there's something different here, isn't there. Why is Tanner Burke here? And these two. How did you know they'd be here, Abel?"

No answer.

But Baker could feel Abel pacing inside his brain while the soft one with the blank face sat silently in his corner. If there was any furniture in there, Abel would be kicking chairs and tables out of the way. Kicking. Smashing. His eyes locked all the while upon the steel door that only Baker could open. Baker could feel the door shaking, bulging. Abel had his shoulder against it now.

"No, Abel. Not this time. These are mine."

"Don't!" The woman choked. More cloth was tearing.

A bolt of pain seared Baker's eye and tears flooded over it.

"No, Abel. All by myself, without you. I'm more than just your legs. More than just a stable boy who's here to let you out every time you snort and kick."

The shape of the one with the knife changed. His buttocks raised higher as he reached to his underside and tugged at himself, pulling loose his clothing. Baker tossed his head violently.

"That's it, dirt bag," Baker heard his own voice explode through the park as he stepped forward into a slant of light. "Get your filthy hands off—"

A battering ram struck from inside his head and both eyes erupted in a wash of salt water. *"Oh, damn you. Damn you, Abel. I can't see . . ."*

The one with the knife made a spinning leap and then scrambled to his feet. The big one rocked sideways on his knees, fumbling at his pocket.

"Who the fuck are . . ." The voice of the smaller man trailed off into silence. He saw at once the anguish on Baker's face and the gleam of tears and now he caught a scent of fear. Confidence sprang back. He stretched to his full height and breathed deeply. A smile came as he let it out. With deliberate slowness, he reached for the zipper of his trousers and pulled it shut. Next he fingered his belt buckle as if deciding whether to clasp it, then he let it fall undone. His message to Baker was clear. This would not take long.

"They have knives," the woman shouted. She tried to rise as the bigger man eased away from her, but he seized her hair and slammed her head against the grass.

"And look what we have here," the shorter one said almost pleasantly. "We have a concerned citizen." As he spoke, he circled to a spot between Baker and the bridle path. Baker's back was now to a thick wall of privet.

"Concerned citizen," the young man said through his teeth, "I want to explain this problem you have." But his eyes had still not focused fully on Baker. They darted around and past him, not yet ready to believe that one man alone would have faced them. Not without a weapon already aimed. But this one was alone. "Your problem is you have only two ways to go." He raised his knife for Baker to see. "If you come at me, or run, or anything like that, I'm going to cut out your fucking heart." He raised the index finger of his other hand. "However," he said brightly, "it happens that you have another choice." The young man slowly tilted the raised finger and pointed it at the base of the nearest dogwood. "If you'll just ease over to that little tree there and sit down, what I'll do is strap you to it with your belt. Your pants will get a little dirty, but the good part is you don't die. The even better part is you get a front row seat while we play with Hollywood over there."

Baker's fingertips brushed across his eyes and returned to his temples, keeping his face in shadow. He heard few of the young man's words as he struggled painfully to will Abel back and away from the door. It was no use.

"Hey Jace," the big one called, "this guy's cryin'."

Baker's head was pounding so badly he could hardly think. He had only to lean forward an inch or two and the battering ram would crash against the door. Abel could not get out unless he let him out. He knew that. But now he knew that Abel could stop him too. Abel would not let him fight.

Baker cleared his throat.

"I'm going to give you one chance," he said hoarsely. "Leave now, and no one will stop you." Baker knew as he said the words that they were useless. These two would not leave. He said them to spite Abel, but he knew in his heart that that was just as useless.

The face of the shorter man clouded in confusion. "What is this 'leave'? You got a gun? You're a karate freak? What?"

"Something like that," Baker answered wearily. "Please get out of here."

The young man threw up his hands in pretend frustration. "See that?" he said toward the sky. "I tried to be reasonable. Hey, Sumo. Didn't I try to be reasonable? But he took advantage. He got me remembering things. Things like him coming in here without saying excuse me. And he called me a bad name, just like Miss Hotshot did."

Crouching again, the knife swaying lazily from side to side like a cobra's head, the man advanced on Baker.

Baker only shrugged. He let his hands fall to his sides.

The young man hesitated, again confused. His eyes danced over Baker's body as if looking for some sign that would explain how this man could not be afraid. He was tall but not that tall. Close to forty, the young man would have guessed. Beneath his brown suede sportcoat and sweater, behind the pilot's glasses, there was no hint of particular power. But the fear was gone. There wasn't anything. Not excitement. Not worry. Not even confidence. The man was just looking at him in a tired way, as though he was something the man had picked up on his shoe. To his mind, the tall man's lack of fear could only mean that he had a stronger weapon or that he was not alone. He knew this must be true when he saw Baker's lips part again to say the words: "Abel. He's all yours, Abel."

"Hey, look out, Jace," the one called Sumo whispered. "This guy's got somebody with him."

Jace's eyes darted to the shadows behind Baker and then back to the bridle path. He kept the knife pointed at arm's length toward Baker's chest as if to pin him in place while he searched the darkness.

"You got a friend, citizen? Where's your friend?" His eyes had still not returned to Baker. "Maybe your friend will come out if I cut you up a little."

"Come and get it, pig."

The voice had come from Baker, but it was not the same man's voice. Jace backed away a full step when he saw the face that now moved into the light. The sound coming from it had started deep within the chest. It hissed and spat like escaping steam. The face seemed broader and more deeply lined and the lips were spread flat across the teeth. But it was the eyes that frightened him most. They were an animal's eyes. A stalking animal.

Jace, on impulse, took three quick steps to his left and then backed away. In part, to be closer to Sumo. In part, to give this man room. To let him leave. But the man also moved, turning his back to the open bridle path.

"You're going to make me hurt you, man," Jace blustered, backing still farther.

"You're not going to hurt me, Jace," came the words through a terrible smile. *"I'm going to hurt you. And then I'm going to hurt your friend."*

On Central Park South, the balding man in the blue Oldsmobile cursed as he rolled down his window and extended an antenna into the light drizzle. He slapped his transceiver uselessly and cursed again at the atmospherics that scattered the voice struggling to get through it.

A police cruiser drifted into his peripheral vision. Barely moving, Connor Harrigan allowed the radio to slide onto his lap and collapsed the antenna as it cleared the Oldsmobile's rain gutter.

The two policemen took no notice of him. Their attention was on a pair of hookers who tugged at the businessman between them as he waved for a westbound taxi. The hookers were gesturing toward the park. They preferred to transact business there.

"Don't you do it, bucko," Harrigan muttered. "Not if you want to see Des Moines again."

A taxi slowed and stopped, inviting the out-of-towner and his companions. The streetwalkers exchanged looks, shrugged, and climbed in behind the businessman. The police cruiser made a U-turn and followed.

"Good lads." Harrigan nodded. "At least the old rascal will make it to his hotel lobby. And speaking of rascals . . ." Harrigan tried again to raise Michael Biaggi and again he failed.

*   *   *

Inside the park, Michael Biaggi angrily folded his own transceiver and jammed it onto his belt. He cupped an ear, searching for the sounds he'd heard before. It had to be Baker. There was no time for him to be anywhere else but in the park. Except that the sound was like a woman's voice. He followed it anyway, gambling that this new voice and Baker would come together and that Baker would not simply pass it by. That he would not lose Baker.

A new sound, a squeal, cut through from his right. It came from over a knoll past what smelled like a horse trail. Staying low beneath the dogwood branches, he ran silently toward the dim outline of a boulder that topped the hill. Reaching it, he ducked quickly as the weak glow of a distant streetlamp washed across his face. But he'd seen them. Four of them. Even in the bad light, he could see the terror on the woman's face as her head was twisted toward him by the heavyset man holding her. There was something familiar about the woman, but he put that thought aside. Baker was there. Not twenty feet away, he calmly faced another man, who held a knife at the end of an outstretched arm. The man with the knife was looking beyond Baker, into the black underbrush. From his position behind the rock, Biaggi could not see what attracted him there, so his attention remained on Baker. What he saw caused his mouth to fall open. Baker was changing. He was changing in ways that were indescribable because they were so subtle. His body seemed to expand in all directions, and yet it filled no greater space. It was more of a coiling and bracing and a slow sucking in of air. His shoulders curled forward and his arms drifted out from his body in almost a wrestler's stance. It reminded him of . . . he wasn't sure what. The more remarkable change was transforming Baker's face. The mouth broadened, stretching across his lower teeth, and his eyes took on a shine that hadn't been there before. They locked upon those of the man with the knife as he turned back to Baker. *He sees it too,* Biaggi realized. *He sees the change and he's stunned by it.* Biaggi saw the rush of fear that clouded the younger man's face. He knew the fear was there because he felt it too. In that instant Biaggi understood, at least in part, the interest of Duncan Peck and Connor Harrigan. The man was a monster.

"You're going to make me hurt you, man," he heard the one with the knife say. The words were spoken without confidence.

"You're not going to hurt me, Jace. I'm going to hurt you. And then I'm going to hurt your friend."

The voice shocked Biaggi. It was not the voice he'd heard on Baker's wiretaps. And the words themselves carried no glimmer of bluff or doubt. Biaggi believed them. He believed them as he knew that the sun would rise in the morning.

Baker raised his right hand with an almost mocking slowness to the level of his shoulder, then reached inside his jacket at his chest. Jace flicked the knife toward the hand nervously but did not move forward. Baker ignored his feint. The hand came free again, holding a plastic, felt-tipped pen. This Baker held up for Jace to see. Confusion clouded Jace's face and he lowered himself into a wary crouch. Baker smiled. Still slowly, he twisted off the cap and snapped it in place on the pen's butt, then displayed the result for the man with the knife. The smile widened.

"Cut him, Jace," came the big one's voice. "He's gonna stick you with that." Jace's shoulders trembled once and he lunged, bringing the blade in low toward Baker's abdomen. In the same instant he snapped back violently, like a tetherball at the end of its string. He gave a short cry of surprise, and his free hand pressed hard against his cheek. What had happened was almost too fast for Biaggi to follow. Jace dropped his hand and stared at his palm. There must have been blood there because the agent could see two black punctures, one just beneath each of Jace's eyes.

Rage and pain blunted Jace's fear, and with a scream he leaped forward, slashing backhanded at Baker's chest. Baker barely moved. It was more that he sucked in his body as the blade flew past. Easily, he snatched the passing wrist with his left hand and jabbed twice more with the right. Baker's left hand gave a twist, and the smaller man slammed heavily to the ground.

He looked up at Baker, disbelieving, helpless, waiting for the attack that would follow now that he had fallen. An attack with feet and knees. That's what he would have done, he knew. No one ever got up once he put them down. But his hand made no move. Jace backed away slowly, crablike. Then, out of reach, he scrambled to his feet. With both hands, he brushed over the holes on his face. There were four of them now, and they neatly bracketed his eyes.

"*Do you begin to get the picture?*" asked the man who was Baker.

"Hey . . . Hey, shit, man" was all Jace could manage. The truth struck him like a blow from an ax. This man meant to put out his eyes. This man could have put out his eyes already. But he was toying with him. Jace felt his bowels go flaccid. He wanted to break and run but he couldn't. Not with Sumo watching.

Abruptly the man tensed and straightened. The animal eyes fluttered shut and his lips quivered at the edge of forming words. "*Stay there*" is what Jace thought he heard among the whispered sounds that came. "*Stay there, Baker,*" came now more clearly. Baker. The young man's eyes widened. Baker! He knew that name. But this couldn't be . . .

"Baker?" he whispered.

The tall man seemed startled. Jace saw the man's body sag, bewilderment on his face. The face and the body had softened. For the briefest moment, the man had the look of prey again, and Jace attacked even as another word was forming on his lips. The knife lanced up between arms that hung still. He had him. The tall man had blown it, and now he was going to be the one who took Jared Baker and he was going to do it by himself. Jace had time for a cruel grin of triumph to curl at his mouth before a bear trap crushed down on his wrist. He did not see the pen that slid up through his nostril and tore it away from his face. The scream rising in his throat became a fractured squawk as the pen rammed through the tissue of his cheek and pinioned his tongue against his upper jaw. Jace heard a dim snap somewhere below. He knew it was the wrist of his knife hand even before the message of pain reached his brain. He knew that hands had seized the thick hair at his temples, forcing his head down without effort, and he knew that something was rising toward his face. He remembered nothing more.

Biaggi watched as the man turned toward the one called Sumo. Sumo seemed stricken. He was standing now, above the woman. One foot lay heavily across her neck and pressed her face into the wet grass. The man, once more in his wrestler's crouch, advanced on Sumo. One hand snatched Jace's knife from the grass as he swayed past it. He stopped then and seemed to make a show of examining the knife thoughtfully.

"It's a pig-sticker, Sumo," came the voice that hissed. *"And you're a pig. Does that suggest anything to you, Sumo?"*

"Stay away, man." Sumo's voice was hoarse. He turned his own knife in his hand and held it by the blade in a throwing position.

Biaggi reached beneath his gray raincoat and groped for his pistol. Drawing it free, he raked its barrel across the plastic of his radio case, making a soft zipping sound. No more. Baker seemed to hesitate and half-turn. Biaggi lowered himself farther. He was sure the sound could not have been heard. It was barely a whisper, which would have been lost amid the rustle of wet leaves. With both hands he sighted the pistol on Sumo's chest, sweating, trying to blot out all other fears except his fear of Duncan Peck if he allowed Baker to die this way.

He waited too long. Sumo threw himself to his knees and with one hand dragged the woman's body against his own. She gasped and looked pleadingly at the shadow that was Baker, then went rigid as Sumo's knife pressed a spot beneath her breast.

The man stopped. He seemed first to be studying her face and then for a long moment he studied Sumo.

Sumo is about to panic, a voice told him. One stupid impulse and the woman could be dead. But the man with the animal eyes didn't care. The woman was the woman and Sumo was Sumo. He wanted Sumo. But he could not shake the voice away this time. All right, Baker. We'll give him some room. We'll try it your way, but do not stay long, Baker.

"Try it, Baker," he said. The woman heard the words and she too glanced around her, looking for the man who had been called.

"Sumo," came the new gentler voice. "I want you to pay attention."

"Wha . . . ?" He swallowed.

Baker held up Jace's knife and tossed it far to one side. "I have no knife, Sumo."

The big man breathed heavily but said nothing.

"Sumo, I want you to let her go and then back away. Go away and wait until we're gone and then come back for your friend. Do that, Sumo, or you'll be hurt just as terribly."

Sumo rocked as the words sank in. He seemed to consider running, backing off. But he was feeling better too. He was not afraid of this man now. He didn't know why he'd been afraid of him at all. It's the guy who's afraid, not him. He wouldn't try to deal if he wasn't afraid.

"I saw what you did to him, you bastard." It was something to say.

"The woman, Sumo. Let her go."

"You want her?" Sumo's voice was becoming shrill. "How bad do you want her?"

"Now, Sumo. There's no more time."

The big man turned his knife again so that the cutting edge rested on the underside of the woman's breast. "How about one piece at a time? How about if I cut off one of her tits for you, you want her so much." Sumo tightened his forearm viciously across her throat as he said this. The woman went limp against him.

Once again, Baker studied the woman. Her breathing was slow and labored. She would see nothing.

"Abel," he said.

The man in the gray raincoat watched a second time. He watched across the sight of his pistol until it began to shake. He was trembling almost to the point of spasm. Biaggi pressed the gun flat against the grass with both hands, and he heard this different Baker say, *"Recess is over, pig."*

Sumo went white. Making animal grunts, he staggered backward to his feet. The woman's torso fell heavily to the ground. Off balance, he whipped the knife cross-handed toward Baker's body. The knife spun once and hit. It stuck, he realized hysterically. He could see it dangling from the flesh of the man's hip below his open jacket. In almost joyful relief, he realized that the man was crippled. And he had no knife. Not even the thing he used on Jace. He could take this man, he realized. He could rip the arms off almost anyone who fought him barehanded. Then he'd pull the knife out of this fucker's hip and cut off his pecker with it and leave it in his mouth. Jace would like that. That would make Jace feel better except . . . except . . . Something felt wrong with his face . . . so fast . . . something hit his face . . . all numb and wet, and he was falling backward against a rock and someone was holding him . . . turning him around and . . . ooohhhh, he heard a faraway scream when the kidneys on both sides exploded inside of him and . . . my ass . . . what's the matter with my ass . . . Sumo fainted.

Biaggi could not stop the shaking that had spread across his shoulders and down his back. It was all he could do to keep his breathing soft enough to blend with the sounds of the park. He watched through blades of grass as Baker stripped off his jacket and wrapped it, indifferently, he thought, around the body of the unconscious woman, then lifted her onto one shoulder with astonishing ease. With his free hand, he knelt to gather bits of cloth and then, without pausing, stepped fluidly across a low stone wall as if he carried no burden at all. Biaggi put away his gun and fumbled for the radio on his belt.

"Harrigan," he whispered as he fed out his antenna. He did not bother with a call signal. "Harrigan, come in. Come in."

"Got you" came the broken voice from the box. "Where . . . hell are you?"

"He's headed your way from near the zoo," Biaggi panted. "There's trouble here. Park muggers. This guy Baker took them both out with ease. Except I think one of them knew him. And he's got a woman with him."

"What was . . . damned thing? Say again."

"He's coming your way. He just ripped the shit out of a couple of punks."

" . . . can't get . . . stay on him. You read?"

"I'm on him. Out."

Biaggi collapsed his radio as he pushed to his feet. He moved several steps in the direction Baker had taken and then hesitated, glancing toward the shape of the one called Jace. Baker would keep, he decided, for the few seconds it would take to see if these two were alive. He'd be slowed by the weight of the woman, and he could only be heading south to the exit nearest his hotel, where Connor Harrigan was waiting.

He knelt at Jace's side and bent over the ruined face but chose not to look at it. The gurgling, mewing sounds it made were enough. He stripped off Jace's watch and patted for his wallet. Both of these he dropped into his raincoat pocket. Almost as an afterthought, he placed his fingertips on the carotid artery of the unconscious man. Jace could live. Given attention, the bum could live. Biaggi stood and walked the fifteen yards to where the big one lay draped over the boulder. He lifted Sumo's wrist, feeling for a pulse as he worked loose a heavy chronograph. This pulse was weaker than the other. Biaggi studied the watch curiously, ignoring Sumo, who slid like a flow of mud from the rock and settled to the grass. Funny, he thought, for junkies to own watches. The big one's clothing, both their clothing, were good quality and they fit. They must have bought them new. Dressed like this, he wondered, and they're working the park?

He bent over and felt for Sumo's wallet. His hand

brushed over something wet and hard. Biaggi drew a penlight from his pocket and cupped his hand over the beam as he sought what he already knew was there. Again he turned his head away. A befouled and dripping bit of chrome gleamed obscenely in the light. The knife was rammed a full ten inches into Sumo's colon.

"Jesus," he whispered.

He fell backward into a sitting position and stared after Baker through the darkness. What the hell was going on here? He shuddered again at what he'd seen, and at the thought that had he not seen it, he might have tried to take Baker himself. Who wouldn't have? The guy was nothing. A commuter. Or he used to be. Just one more grunt who took the train to work and played golf on Saturdays and jogged with his dog on Sundays until it was time to light the charcoal. Sonnenberg could take a lump like that and make *this* out of it? What for? Who the fuck would want him? But you want him, don't you, Mr. Peck? You say, do you have doubts, Michael? Are you up to this task, Michael? We can't let him fall into the wrong hands, Michael. Not Domenic Tortora's hands, not Connor Harrigan's hands, not a couple of punks working Central Park . . . Wait a minute.

Biaggi patted his raincoat pocket and located the wallet that belonged to Jace. He drew out the soft leather billfold. It was expensive, he realized, even before he snapped on his penlight. Dunhill, maybe. The light made a circle the size of a half-dollar, and it quickly found the likeness on a driver's license of the one who seemed to know Baker. The name printed there seized Biaggi by the throat.

He was Baker again.

He had started south, then doubled back when he was beyond the hearing of the man who'd stayed hidden. His arms had begun to burn under the woman's weight, and the muscles of his back were tightening. Perhaps he'd sent Abel back too soon. No, she was beginning to stir. Abel might have . . . He wasn't sure anymore what Abel might have done.

Beyond the zoo, he found a bench that was deep in shadow and sat the rousing woman there, wondering if it might be best to leave her. The one in the gray raincoat might help her. The one who followed and watched. But he was far behind. He had a gun, Baker realized. Why did he have a gun in his hand this time? No matter. He was getting farther away. If she were left here now, someone else might find her. Maybe someone like the two he'd crippled. Or she'd wake up screaming before he was safely gone. Besides, he had to know first . . . *"Charley?"*

"yes?"

"This is Tanner Burke. Did you know that?"

"you did so i did."

"How can it be that she's here? Does she know me?"

"doesn't know jared baker."

"Why was she in the park, Charley? And how did Abel find her?"

"i don't knowwww." Charley lapsed into an irritating singsong that he used when he chose to be vague. The voice in Baker's head was softer than the other and higher pitched. Childlike. Baker despised this one sometimes.

"You do know, Charley. And the other one back there, the one called Jace. He knew me. He said my name. Who was he, Charley?"

"ask abel."

"I'm asking you, Charley. What has Abel done?"

"abel says go now. go to the hotel."

"Answer me, Charley. I'll bring you out if you don't answer me."

"You can't. she'll see."

The woman coughed and one eyelid fluttered. It opened slightly and then closed again, but her breath was coming deeper and faster. Baker waited until he could feel her body start to tense against his and then he closed his hand firmly over her mouth. Her eyes opened wide and she sucked in air through his fingers.

"Don't scream," he said as gently as he could manage. "You're all right now but you can't scream."

Her hands braced against him, fingernails biting, and her eyes turned to his. They were wide with terror.

"Do you understand?" he asked, whispering. With his head, he gestured toward a deeper part of the park. "I'm going to get you out of here. But you have to be quiet."

She flicked her eyes in the direction and nodded quickly. Baker drew back his hand but kept it hovered near her mouth.

"Where are they?" she croaked, peering into the damp blackness. Baker let his hand fall away.

"They can't hurt you. Do you think you can walk?"

"I think so." She felt her legs as if to measure the strength that remained in them. "Please, let's get out of here."

"Fifth Avenue is right past those trees." Baker pointed. "I stopped so you could . . . pull yourself together first." Baker touched the bulging pocket of the jacket he'd made Abel wrap around her. Abel would not have covered her. He would have carried her into the street the way she was. "Your things . . ." He faltered. "They're in that pocket. They're torn but they might be better than . . ."

Baker knew he was stammering. He was talking of clothing recently torn from her body, and he was talking to a face that had grown to mean much to him. A shyness seized him. She noticed. Or at least she sensed his discomfort and it seemed to ease her own. The woman reached into Baker's jacket and drew out the light, crumpled clothing. She fingered first the hooks of her bra. They were bent and twisted. The thin shoulder straps had been sliced through with a knife.

"The blouse isn't so bad," he suggested. "It's just torn near one button. I can walk back into the trees while you put it on."

"No," she snapped, digging her fingers painfully into his thigh. "Please." Her voice softened. "Please don't go anywhere." She pressed his thigh more gently and then rose to her feet. The woman shrugged off Baker's jacket and, making no effort to cover herself other than turning her back to him, she carefully slipped her arms into the cool fabric of her sleeves. It chilled her. Baker stood and stripped off his sweater, offering it to her as she buttoned her blouse. She took it, thanking him with her eyes, and slipped it over her head. Once more, Baker covered her shoulders with his jacket. Closing it across her chest, she hugged herself and stared into the darkness. He knew she was remembering.

"They had knives," she said, her voice dull.

"Yes." He drew the suede lapels together at her throat. "But don't worry about them now. They can't hurt you."

"But how did you . . . There were two of them and they were afraid of you. You don't seem . . ."

"I don't know. We'd better get going."

"The big one. He was going to cut me if you did anything."

Baker took her arm and steered her toward the east-bound path. He held her until he was sure she could walk steadily.

"We should call the police," she said.

"There's no need." Baker listened hard for some sign that she knew their names. At least the one who knew his. But he heard nothing. Felt nothing.

"But look what they . . . They could hurt somebody else."

"They won't," he promised. "Not for a very long time. It might help you to remember that."

She stared for a long moment into the darkness. "It still doesn't seem right," she said finally, a swell of anger pushing through the fear. "They grabbed me. Right out on the sidewalk they grabbed me and they pulled me in here. Goddamnit, they should go to jail."

Baker felt himself relax. She didn't know them. And she didn't know him either. Whatever was happening, whatever Abel was causing to happen, she need not be a part of it any longer.

"Put it behind you," he urged gently. "If you call the

police, you'll feel better for only a little while. But you'll spend years answering useless questions about tonight."

Her eyes clouded. It seemed as though there was another reason for calling the police. That other man in there. The one who hurt them. There was something terrible about him. This man? No, not like this one. He was like this one, but . . . The picture danced away from her.

"Let's just get out of here," she said.

She was silent as they walked slowly down the east side of Fifth Avenue, a street width away from the black stone walls of the park. By the time they reached the Frick Museum she was trembling. An aftershock was setting in. She would seize one shaking hand with the other and the quiver would leap at once to her elbow. Baker listened.

Approaching a streetlamp, Baker saw the wet line gleaming across her high cheekbone and curling down her throat. He stopped and fumbled, patting for a handkerchief he knew he didn't carry. Then, with his fingertips, he wiped away one welling tear and held her, drying her face against his shirt.

"I feel so cheap," she sniffed.

"Don't you dare."

"You don't . . . you don't know what I mean."

"You were remembering their screams," he said. "You were remembering the way they must have hurt. It made you feel better and you don't like that in yourself."

For a moment, she didn't move or speak. Then, not looking up: "How did you know that?"

I've had the feeling is what he almost answered. "I don't know" is what he said.

They were near the Pierre Hotel. Baker gestured with a thumb. "The bar will still be open if a drink might help. You can use the ladies' room to . . ."

She shook her head. "I don't want anyone to see me."

"Does that matter? Except for wearing my clothes, you don't look bad at all."

"People will recognize me."

Baker affected a shrug, pretending not to understand. "There are other places. Or I'll take you home. Tell me where you want to go."

She looked up at him, through his tinted glasses, into eyes that were a soft gray in that light. She saw no recognition in them. It bothered her. Not so much that he didn't know her, but the flash of intuition that told her he didn't want to know her.

"My home is in Idaho but I'm living in California. I'm mostly a skier."

Baker remembered, but he did not react.

"Except now I'm mostly an actress. I've made two movies and I've been on TV a lot. Maybe you've seen me in something." Oh damn, she thought, why did I say all that. He'll think I'm a perfect . . .

Baker smiled. "Now that you mention it," he said. "I didn't place you before."

It was a lie, of course. Baker had heard when Jace called her by name and when he called her Hollywood. And he knew the face. He'd seen it many times. He saw it a hundred years ago with Sarah at his side, watching her hand out trophies for a junior girls' slalom meet in Stratton, Vermont. Tina especially knew her. Tina had finished third. And her reward from Baker was a parka like the one Tanner Burke wore. Her reward to herself was to fix her hair in the long, layered cut of Tanner Burke and to ski like her and walk like her in that confident, striding way she had. To toss her long, loose curls when she laughed and to tilt her head when she grinned. Now Baker grinned to himself. He imagined Tina's eruption if he ever told her that he'd met Tanner Burke . . . Oh, Daddy, you actually talked to her? What did she say? Weren't you nervous? Is she like she is in the movies? Don't tell me if she's isn't nice. She is, isn't she? Did you tell her I still have her picture? Did you tell her she's my absolute most intense favorite?

And he'd seen her since. During the endless lonely hours of what Sonnenberg called his pupation, he'd seen her on the television screen. He'd looked for her there. By that time, she'd become more than Tina's idol in Baker's mind. She'd become a link that held him just the smallest bit closer to Tina when he could not be with her. For that reason, or for another, she grew on him. He saw her face often in television movies and in Clairol commercials. And once he even left one of Sonnenberg's sessions to watch her on a celebrity ski tournament.

Baker knew her. And someday he'd tell Tina. But for now, he thought, this particular night had better pass without their lives being further linked, except in memory.

"My name is Tanner," she said, looking at the sidewalk. "Tanner Burke."

"Hello, Tanner." He took her arm again to start her walking. "You're staying at a hotel then. The Plaza?"

Tanner Burke nodded. "Well?" she asked.

"I'm sorry?"

"You haven't told me your name." She paused with him on the sidewalk of the General Motors Building before crossing toward the Plaza.

"It's . . . Harry," he answered. "Harry Mailander."

"Harry?" Her eyes flicked up. "You hesitated just then."

"Just thinking," he said. "You should be all right from here if you don't mind walking through the lobby in my sweater. I'll watch you until you're inside."

Her pulse in the arm he was holding took a hitch. He felt it through his fingertips. She hesitated, then put a hand on his and held it. For reasons she could not yet sort out, his suggestion startled her. It was true that she was safe enough. The hotel entrances on Central Park South and on the fountain side were brightly lit and each would have a doorman near. But she'd be alone. He'd let go of her arm and the awfulness of what had happened would come flooding back, and he would not be there to blur it. The trembling would return, and if she turned back toward him he'd be gone and she'd wonder whether he had ever been there at all . . . There was that too. It hadn't struck her until now and it came with a shudder. Those screams. The gagging terror of the one who'd sat on her, and the horror she could feel in that huge and vicious man who'd held the knife against her breast . . . This man had caused that. This tender man. Harry?

"Harry Mailander," she repeated. "Why do I think that name doesn't fit you? Why do I think it isn't even your name?"

Baker couldn't help but smile. Her perceptiveness pleased him. He knew, of course, that she might have some dim memory of him speaking Abel's name or of Abel speaking his, but it was more than that. He could feel it. And he knew that she could sense something real beneath whatever name he chose to use, and knowing that made him feel less the invention of another man.

"It's nice to see you smile, though." She answered with a tentative grin of her own. "Another feeling I have is that you don't smile very often. But you should."

Baker flushed, but the grin remained.

From inside Baker's jacket, she drew out an American Airlines ticket envelope she'd seen when he placed it over her shoulders. "If I look at this," she asked, her own smile fading, "will it say Harry Mailander?"

"I'd rather you didn't."

She stopped again and faced him as he gently took the envelope from her hand and returned it to its place. Her eyes showed hurt and then anger.

"Well, Harry or whatever-your-name-is, I want to know why not." Her hands went to her hips. "I mean, I don't want to sound full of myself, but most men I meet want me to remember them. You don't even want me to know your name."

Baker touched her cheek. "I'll remember you," he said softly, "and I'll think about you. And yes, I'd very much like you to remember me."

"As Harry Mailander? Why not John Doe?"

"Tanner." He took her hand in his. He thought her eyes softened when he spoke her name. "Tanner, there are two very badly hurt men in the park. The bigger one might even die. I don't know why any of that happened, but I'm going to try to walk quietly away from it. I hope you will too. There are other reasons why I can't say or do what I'd like, but that's a big one. I can't get involved with . . . that park business."

Tanner Burke studied him, trying to absorb him. She opened her mouth to speak, to say to him that she'd never tell his name. Not even if all she had depended on it. But she said nothing. She knew that a promise would never be enough. Not for him. There was something surreal about him. Something shadowy. As if he was one of those creatures who existed only after dark. But that wasn't right. There was the airline ticket. And it made him real. If not here, then in whatever place he came from. Someplace where he said good morning to the neighbors and where he had friends and where anyone who knew him could talk to him anytime they wanted. But she couldn't. Once again, it struck her that if she turned away or shut her eyes, he might well be gone when she looked up again. She reached to touch him so that could not happen. So that he couldn't leave. Being with him, his gentleness, his touching and warming her, had thrown a cloak across the horror of the park, and now he was going to pull the cloak away.

He couldn't leave her.

"Can you stay with me awhile longer?" she asked, her voice small.

She saw him hesitate and blink. Something caused his right eye to water, and she saw his body lean away from the hand that she raised. Tanner stood for a moment, awkwardly, almost hating him in that brief moment. She turned in silence toward the hotel.

He watched her as she walked from him. He saw Tina in the way she walked. And he wondered if Tina would ever walk that way again. He wondered when the pain would end. And how many more lives would be torn apart. But one of them didn't have to be Tanner's. Let her go, Baker.

"Tanner." He heard his voice call her name.

She had already half-stopped, trying not to turn and

look. But she did turn and she walked slowly back to him. "At least to my door." She took his arm. "Stay with me at least to my door."

Tanner eased him toward the green-carpeted steps of the Plaza.

2

It was a day two full summers earlier. April. The rain then had stopped too. The first sun since midweek was slanting down through trees that were beginning to thicken, and children were emerging onto shining streets. Tina was the first. She had a Frisbee in her hand.

There had been a television program the day before about dogs who caught Frisbees. Some seemed to leap ten feet into the air, vaulting and somersaulting with a gymnast's skill, plucking the Frisbee in its flight and then soaring awhile before tumbling to earth in a happy heap. One of the dogs had been a golden retriever. He wasn't the best. The mutts always seemed to do better. But the retriever could do it, and if he could, Macduff could. Tina's golden retriever could do it too.

"Stupid dog!" Baker heard her voice from the front lawn. He stepped away from a harbor scene he was trying in watercolors—it was a mess, anyway—and looked out through the window of his den. He saw the Frisbee first. It sailed vertically upward, perhaps twenty feet in the air, then he saw Tina run under to snatch it. She caught the plastic disk with her hands, but she kept the hands close to her face, pretending to catch it in her mouth. "See, Macduff?" she called. The dog came into view, smiling foolishly. He pranced at her feet, hoping to show that he was willing to play, more than willing, and that he would try to understand what she wanted of him.

Tina showed the Frisbee to Macduff and, after faking twice to show him its direction, tossed it on a short and shallow trajectory. Macduff watched the disk until it landed, then leaped forward triumphantly, pinning it with his paws. Tina tried again, this time sailing the Frisbee directly toward the big golden's snout. He watched its approach and barely blinked as it bounced off his face.

"Dumb!" Tina shouted.

Baker smiled at his daughter's frustration. From two rooms away, he heard Sarah laugh. She too had been watching. Now she was going outside.

For several minutes, Baker watched Sarah try her luck with Macduff, who was by now thoroughly confused. Sarah had tried to reason with him just as she reasoned with lawnmowers that wouldn't start and checkbooks that wouldn't balance. Again the dog watched the Frisbee's approach, and again he allowed it to carom off his head. Baker wondered what the dog thought. Perhaps he'd decided that that was the game. It's called, stop that white round thing with your face and then chew on it until they pry it away.

Sarah and Tina gave up. They moved into the street, deciding that a simple game of catch would be more rewarding. Macduff watched them from the edge of the lawn. Their game didn't look nearly so interesting.

Still smiling, Baker returned to his canvas. The smile vanished. Really pretty lousy, he thought. After three years of adult education art classes, you'd think I could paint a lobsterboat that doesn't look like a bathtub toy. He took the canvas and put it aside, picking up instead an almost-finished oil portrait of Sarah.

Her warm, soft eyes looked back at him. At least it was supposed to be Sarah. The likeness wasn't terrific, but it wasn't bad either. Not bad for a Sunday artist. Not too terrible for a third attempt at portrait painting. The shape of the face was almost perfect. The high cheekbones, the auburn hair, and the line of the chin were just about right. And the eyes were close. One was just a trifle lower than the other, but no one would notice that.

The mouth was wrong, though. It was a wider, more sensual mouth than Sarah's. Not that Sarah wasn't sexy, but her mouth just didn't have that fullness. And the coloring was a little too dark. The face was almost closer to that of the actress whose photograph hung on Tina's wall by her trophy shelf.

The distant racket of a motorcycle engine cut through the morning quiet. The low, snarling sound changed its pitch, coughed, and changed again. Too fast, Baker thought. Too fast for these streets. He felt his jaw tighten and a rush of sudden anger swelled inside him. He turned his head toward the receding noise and felt his fingers flex in anticipation of grabbing the son of a bitch who . . .

Baker shook his head violently and blinked. Stop that, he told himself. What's the matter with you lately?

He was calm again almost at once. The rage was gone. But still, it troubled him; these feelings had been coming upon him too often in recent months. Maybe for the past year. The motorist who cut him off and then gave him the finger when Baker honked a complaint. Baker felt it then. He wanted to tear the finger off the man's hand. And there was the rude store clerk whose face Baker almost smashed and the drunk who jabbed his finger into Baker's chest. Baker might have hurt them too if he'd been less in control. Or they might have hurt him.

He did not understand these feelings because they were not like him. He liked to think he was a gentle man, that there was no meanness in him. But something was happening and he didn't like it. He didn't like the flashes of rage that came from nowhere, and he didn't like the other feelings he was getting. Feelings that he was being talked about. Almost hearing what was being said. That bothered him. Was he becoming paranoid? Or schizophrenic? He wasn't even sure what either term meant until the persistence of the feelings made him look them up. Neither fit exactly. The paranoid person felt threatened by thoughts he imagined, but Baker felt no threat. He simply knew that thoughts were of him.

Sometimes. Nor was there the withdrawal from reality of the classic schizophrenic. Or any behavioral change. There were just these feelings. Harmless, probably. Just a build-up of pressure. An edginess. A vacation would help. Maybe they shouldn't wait until ski season. No. It was nothing. Not as long as he kept it inside where it didn't show and where Sarah couldn't see it. She'd worry. She'd make him take a few days off. And Tina would worry. Tina would worry even more than Sarah, he thought. Because Tina seemed to know sometimes.

The motorcycle sound was coming back and it was louder. The anger came with it. Or tried to. Baker walked away from it. He laid down his paints and walked to the basement, where, with the water running, he washed the pigments from his hands and watched them blend into a weak beige as they circled down the drain.

Drains. That was another thing. There was something about drains lately. He had no idea what. Only that they made him feel . . . He didn't know that either.

Except this drain screamed. There was a roar and a banging and then a scream, and he felt a piece of himself tear away, and he felt it floating for a moment before it withered and dispersed.

My God, he thought. Baker, you worry me sometimes. Come on, knock it off. You've been indoors too long. Get out of here, grab Sarah's hand, and go take a long walk someplace before you . . . Baker reeled suddenly. He had to grab the edge of the sink. Sarah? Sarah? Why did he think there wasn't any Sarah? Baker stumbled up the basement stairs and smashed through his front screen door, shattering it.

He screamed her name.

Sam Willis saw it. He'd been staking tomato plants knocked down by the rain when he heard the insolent roar of that goddamned motorcycle. This time he'd call the cops.

He saw Tina first. He saw Tina running beneath a Frisbee that was curving back upon her and he saw Sarah

Baker, her eyes now fixed on the oncoming machine, running toward Tina, her arms waving angrily toward the motorcyclist. Willis could not hear the words, but he knew that she was shouting. The motorcyclist saw her. He saw the woman reach her daughter's side, and he saw one hand ease her toward the grass while the other hand, the fist, shook at the gleaming black helmet. The biker did not slow or turn. My God, thought Willis, the guy is aiming at her. He's playing chicken with her and she's not backing off. Now he is. He's trying to pass close with one foot up to kick at her, but his rear wheel is moving sideways. He's skidding. And Sara Baker's slipping. She's slipping down on the wet pavement and Tina is reaching back from the grass toward her mother. Oh God, no! Sam Willis shut his eyes.

At the crunching, sodden sound of impact, he shut them tighter.

Baker would remember seeing the Frisbee first. Rolling slowly on the gentle slope of the street, it caught his eye and held it. It was turning, tighter now and faster, finally into a spin that spiraled into a small white blur before it sputtered to a stop. But he was also seeing Tina with another eye. And she was crawling. She crawled right through the spinning blur and one foot seemed to bump along behind her; she was dragging it toward a pile of rags that were heaped at the base of Sam Willis's tree. Sam Willis was running now to the pile of rags. But something was wrong with Tina. Why wasn't Sam running to help Tina?

Another man was coming to help, but Baker didn't look at him. He felt himself floating toward the rags. They were white and they were red. The red part had hair on it and it must have been a head, but it didn't look like a head.

"Hey," a voice said, "I couldn't help that."

Baker was on his knees, holding Tina. He was cradling Tina's head so she couldn't see.

"I mean, hey." The voice was becoming more urgent. More desperate. "They shouldn't have been on the damned street. Streets are for cars and bikes, you know?"

Baker's left arm lashed toward the voice and it stumbled backward.

"Hey . . ." The voice was slurring and it was wilder. "Hey, back off, asshole. I could have got killed. Look at my bike. Look what they did to my fuckin' bike."

"Your bike?" Baker whispered. He saw his own hand after it had gripped the younger man's throat and he saw his other arm swinging a fist against the biker's face. The arm lashed forward a second time, but now the head twisted away and Baker's knuckles smashed painfully against the helmet's visor. A numbing shock shot up through Baker's elbow and he snatched at the lacerated fist with his good hand. Seeing Baker helpless, the younger man attacked wildly with fists and boots. One or more of the blows stunned Baker. He felt his world flash white and the pain became distant. He could feel the other body near his own and he knew that blows were being struck. Baker was dimly aware that the younger man must have been hitting him, but he did not feel the impact. Sarah . . . He had to help Sarah. Baker could hear Tina crying and shouting and he turned to her. He must have been holding the man who rode the motorcycle because that man fell to the street when Baker turned away. Baker didn't care. He wanted to hold Tina. He took her and pressed her against his chest with one arm while the other gathered the still body of Sarah Baker.

The police found him that way.

"Mr. Baker?"

The older man sat next to him on the green vinyl couch. A second man was standing. The older one spoke several times before Baker looked up.

"Mr. Baker, do you know where you are?"

"Hospital," he murmured.

"Mr. Baker, I'm Detective Sergeant Kinney and this is Detective Gurdik. Are you able to tell us what you saw?"

"Sarah's dead."

"I'm terribly sorry about that, Mr. Baker. But your daughter's alive and she's going to need you. We're going to need you too. Did you see it happen, Mr. Baker?"

"No." Baker ran his fingers slowly over his bandaged hand. "I heard something. I didn't see . . . till after."

"Sir, did you know the operator of the motorcycle?"

"No."

"You didn't recognize him?"

"I hardly saw his face."

The two detectives exchanged looks.

"Well, we'll pick him up soon, Mr. Baker. Your neighbors say he's busted down that street before. Also, Mr. Willis says you marked him up pretty good, so we shouldn't have much trouble finding him."

Baker seemed not to understand. "I what?"

"You recall striking him, Mr. Baker?"

Baker gestured with his throbbing hand. "I think I hit him once. After that I hit his helmet." He stared into space as if trying to remember. There was someone else there. Someone was fighting while he was looking at Sarah. And he remembered the one in the helmet lying in the street holding his face and trying to get up. And he did get up. He kept falling down, but he did reach his motorcycle and then he was pushing it down the street. Who else hit him? Sam, maybe.

"But Mr. Willis says you . . ." Detective Kinney stopped himself when a doctor, an older man named Bruggerman, entered the waiting room. He nodded to the detectives and extended a hand toward Jared Baker's shoulder. He seemed annoyed that Baker was being questioned.

"Tina's out of surgery, Jared," he said. "You'll be able to look in on her in about ten minutes."

"How is she?" Baker had trouble focusing. He was almost dozing from the effects of a Demerol injection.

"She came through fairly well. We'll have to do some touching up later but, with any kind of luck, she ought to have full use of her leg." Tom Bruggerman turned to the detectives. "Mr. Baker is heavily sedated, as you can see. You really ought to hold off any questions."

Detective Kinney shrugged and snapped his notebook shut. "I guess we can make sense out of it later. We'll give him a ride home after he sees his daughter."

"No." Baker waved his arm drunkenly. "I'm staying here."

"Go home, Jared," Bruggerman said firmly. "Tina won't even know you for at least twelve hours. When she does, you're going to want to be fresh. She'll need you very much, Jared, but not the way you are now."

He could not bring himself to enter the bedroom he and Sarah had shared. He was not even sure he could climb the stairs. Someone knew that. Peggy Willis, maybe. Peggy steered him to the couch in the living room and put a blanket over him. It didn't seem as though he slept, but the dreams started coming. Except they couldn't have been dreams. He'd be having them, but he could still open his eyes and see his fireplace and the brown leather chair beside it. He could count the seagulls in the watercolor above the mantel and he could hear Sam Willis's voice in the kitchen. Who else was out there? Oh, yeah. Jane Carey from next door. Sarah's friend. Trying not to cry. But Baker started to cry and then suddenly he stopped. He was dreaming again about the one on the motorcycle and that one was talking about him. Baker knew that. The one on the motorcycle was going to get Baker for what Baker did no matter what else happened. What Baker did? What *I* did, you miserable bastard?

Macduff barked outside.

Baker heard the man's voice louder now. He was talking about fire. Burning. He was talking about burning Baker's house.

Macduff was snarling now.

Sam Willis was saying something. Yelling something. Baker could hardly hear. Then how come he could hear Willis whispering just before if now he could hardly hear him yelling out loud. Yelling about what? Stop, Macduff.

Macduff screamed.

But that wasn't anger. That was pain. And now there was an orange light that danced across his living room wall. For a moment, the sky behind the seagulls turned red. A bolt of pain seared the back of Baker's eye, shocking him to his feet. Another orange ball roared across his bay window and blackened it before dissolving into tongues of flame. Off balance, Baker fell backward across a coffee table and his body crashed heavily to the floor on top of his bandaged hand. Half-blinded by tears and pain and clutching his screaming hand, he clamped his eyes shut and rolled to a sitting position. He wanted to leap up but could not. Yet he was up. When his eyes opened again, he saw that his body was moving toward the door. He was with it, but he was not of it. He followed it, like a passenger, through the door that he couldn't remember opening and onto the lawn and toward the man there whose face was scarred and torn and who held a baseball bat in his hands. And there was fire. And crying out. Willis and his wife were shouting. And Jane. And the one with the bat was screaming, except that half the bat was split away and the bottom half looked like a dagger. The dagger floated in front of him and his bandaged hand was holding it. Then the dagger was gone and the man who killed Sarah was leaping and shrieking and flapping like a scarecrow on the end of someone's arm. The hand on the arm was bandaged.

Baker saw the fire. A part of the house was burning and there was another pool of flame in the driveway. Macduff was in that one. He was in it and he was frying, and his hind legs were only now ceasing to kick. Oh, Macduff. Oh, God. Look what you did to Macduff, you bastard. Take a good look. Look close. Put your face right in there and look.

They found Baker at the hospital. In Tina's room. He was stroking her hair while she slept. The detectives watched as he paused to brush away a bit of charred gauze that had fallen on her pillow. Tina twitched once and winced as her leg stabbed at her from under the tent that covered it. But she did not awaken.

Baker wished the detectives would go. They seemed afraid, he thought, and that might frighten Tina. But Detective Kinney asked about Tina and that was nice. The other one didn't. What was his name? Gurdik. Gurdik stood off to one side, just watching.

Detective Kinney wanted to ask questions, but they were hard to answer. The questions were about a dream he'd had and the dream was fading. What's the use, Baker wondered, in talking about a dream? He put his fingers to his lips to hush them.

The detectives wanted to talk more, but not there. Could they go to Detective Kinney's office and talk awhile about the man who threw the gasoline and how Mr. Baker made him stop? Yes, Baker nodded, but only until Tina wakes up. Would he mind wearing handcuffs just until they got there? It was a rule. Baker nodded again. Detective Gurdik began reading something from a white card, about remaining silent. But why should I remain silent, Baker wondered, after I said I'd talk to you in your office? Kinney told Gurdik to put away the card.

Baker thought he remembered other men in the corridor. He thought he remembered flashbulbs and questions. But he wasn't sure. He did remember that his hand had stopped hurting.

3

There was another dream. Baker dreamt he was in jail and the devil was standing outside the bars, watching him. There was hatred on the devil's face and he wore a black suit. A devil with white hair and eyes that burned. The devil hissed some words at him that Baker couldn't hear but that made his eye hurt, and Baker felt himself moving closer to the bars. That seemed to frighten the devil, but it didn't stop the hating. The devil spat at him and then walked away.

"Mr. Baker?" The guard called his name for the third time, tapping now against the bars with his club.

The man in the cell did not look up. He was unshaven and his shirt was torn. He sat on a cot, staring down at a newspaper spread at his feet. Baker saw himself there, much as he looked now except somebody had washed the black soot from his face. Maybe he'd done it himself. He didn't know. The last two days were lost to him. Baker saw his house in the paper. There was a scar of black and blistered paint that rose up from one bay window and mushroomed out beneath the roofline. Even the house looked dead. Like Sarah.

Near the picture of his house was the face of the young man who threw the gasoline. He barely recognized the face. It was a high school picture, more than four years old, and the name under it was Andrew Bellafonte. Baker studied the photograph more closely. It was there. The same mocking cruelty and arrogance must always have been there. But not anymore. The paper said he no longer had a face. It said that Baker had done it. It said that Baker had impaled him. Impaled him? And it said that Baker was insane.

"Mr. Baker."

More on page 5, it said. Baker turned the pages and he saw the devil looking back at him. The same devil. But this one had a name: it was Lawrence Bellefonte and the devil was a judge.

Baker heard the cell door opening and looked up. The guard seemed reluctant to step closer.

"I'm sorry," he said, "I didn't know a lot of this." Baker waved his hands toward the open paper.

"You had a tough time," the guard answered. "Tough break, Mr. Baker. Anyway, your lawyer's here to see you."

"What lawyer?"

"Name's Meister. You have to see him here in your cell. I'm going to bring him in, okay?"

"I didn't call a lawyer."

"Somebody did. Talk to him, Mr. Baker. You're going to see a judge soon."

Baker picked up the paper at his feet and held it up for the guard to see. "This man." Baker pointed. "Has he been here?"

The guard made a face. "He came by. It's the kid's father." The guard looked around him and leaned closer to Baker. "Listen," he said softly, "that kid was a shit and he ran up a pretty good bill before he finally got his. The old man ain't much better. I'm not saying everything you did was good, but you better start protecting yourself. See this guy Meister. If you don't, the court's going to appoint someone else anyway."

Baker thanked him with a nod.

The lawyer was a fat man who seemed to be about fifty. It was hard to tell. He wore a youngish gray poplin suit and his shoes were by Gucci. His hair was light brown, probably dyed, with a few wisps of gray at the sideburns.

The eyes were at once sharp and mirthful. It seemed to Baker that they should have been baggy, but they were not. The lawyer carried a briefcase in one hand and a canvas garment bag in the other.

"Benjamin Meister, attorney," the man said. He jiggled the garment bag. "I brought you some clothes for court."

"Court?" Baker rose to his feet.

"Arraignment's in less than two hours. You don't want to look like a wild man when the judge hears me ask for bail." Meister held out the bag until Baker took it. "There's a comb in there and an electric razor. Wash up while we talk."

Baker saw that the clothing was his own. There was a dark three-piece suit and a soft blue shirt. The suit had been freshly pressed.

"Your neighbor across the street got them for me. What's his name?"

"Sam Willis?"

"Yeah. Pal of yours?"

"We get along pretty well."

"That's good. The guy's going to be a witness and he'd better be our witness."

Baker studied him. "Your name is Meister, you said?" Baker seemed to place emphasis on the name.

The lawyer rolled his eyes upward. "You're going to make some Meister the Shyster crack, right? Go ahead. Get it out of your system. We got work to do."

Baker had to smile. "No, it's just that I don't know you."

"You have a friend," Meister answered. "For now, he wants to keep his name out of it. But your friend has retrained me and has authorized me to post bail if they'll grant it."

"I can pay for my own lawyer."

"Don't argue with Santa Claus, Baker. In the first place, I'm not one of your local hacks who does divorce cases and real estate closings. My bill would cost you your house. In the second place, you're in reasonably deep shit. The charge is atrocious assault with intent to maim. Guess who you maimed."

"I read." Baker gestured toward the newspaper. "It says his father is a judge."

"Not just any judge, Baker. Andrew's father is Lawrence Bellafonte and he's a judge in the Stamford Superior Court. Guess where I have to go asking for bail."

"I'm appearing before the father?"

"No, they can't do that. But I have to tell you that Bellefonte has clout with the others. The guy knows whose hand has been in whose pockets because Bellafonte's hands have been in most of them. The way to bet is you won't find a friendly judge and the prosecutor will try to nail you with a felony rap no matter what your plea is. Your plea, by the way, is not guilty by reason of temporary insanity."

"I wasn't insane." Baker's face darkened.

"Then you'll do five years."

"If I was insane, they'll still put me away."

"Temporary, Baker, temporary. You acted under extraordinary stress while your judgment was diminished by prescribed medication. The guy, Bruggerman, pumped some Demerol into you. When the jury hears all that, they have to let you walk."

Baker rinsed his hands in the small stainless steel basin and watched the water run down the drain. There was something about the drain. He couldn't remember. But whatever it was, it was making him angry.

"They won't let me see my daughter," he said.

"You'll see her. First we have to get a judge to set bail. You want to call her?"

"Can I?" Baker brightened.

"Get dressed. There's a phone in the Attorneys Room."

She knew who it was. Even before the muted ring pushed through the narcotic fog that kept her body heavy and warm, Tina knew that her father was calling.

The phone stopped ringing and she heard a woman's

voice. It didn't sound like her mother. A nurse, maybe. No, it couldn't be her mother. Her mother was sick too. She was someplace else in the hospital.

". . . keeping her sedated, Jared," the voice said.

See? It is Daddy. I know why he isn't here. He's visiting Mom first.

"No, Jared. No one's talked to her. I don't think she knows."

Oh, Tina thought. That's Mrs. Carey. I remember. She's been sitting here since . . . since I don't know when.

"There's a priest coming over this morning from St. Paul's, Jared. Father Lennon . . . Well, she's asking, Jared. Someone has to say something . . . All right, Jared. We'll wait until you can get here."

Jane Carey held the phone against her breast and looked down at Tina, who was watching her sleepily. Jane's eyes were damp.

"It's your dad, honey. Do you think you can just say hello?"

Tina smiled and nodded. Jane placed the receiver on Tina's pillow against her ear. Then she turned her head away.

"Hi, Daddy. Where are you?"

"I'm with the police, babe. There are a lot of questions about the accident. How are you feeling?"

"Tired," she answered. "But it's a kind of yummy tired. Have you seen Mom?"

Jane could not help but watch Tina's face as she asked the question. Tina blinked. Her eyes narrowed and her lips pursed into an expression of confused concentration. Slowly, Tina's head began to move from side to side and color rose toward her pale cheeks.

"No," she whispered, and the first tear came.

"No no, Mom, oh, no." she cried less softly. Jane Carey shuddered and reached for Tina's hand. Tina's nails dug at her and her head turned away. The phone fell away from Tina's cheek. Jane paused, unsure, then took the phone and put it to her ear. Baker was still talking as if to Tina.

"It's me, Jared." There was a chill of anger in her voice. That was stupid, she thought. A stupid and cruel way to blurt out to a child that her mother was dead.

"Jane, what happened there?" Baker's voice was anxious.

"She's crushed, naturally. What did you think would happen?"

"Jane, I don't know what you're talking about."

Jane Carey dropped her voice even further and stepped as far away from the bed as the cord would permit. "Jared," she asked, "didn't you just tell her about Sarah?"

"All I said was that Sarah's pretty sick. That's all I said. Then all of a sudden she wasn't listening to me. She was listening to someone else."

Jane clamped her eyes shut and placed her fingers against her forehead. "Jared," she said, shaking her head, "then I don't know what happened." Tina was sobbing now. "Jared, I have to go to Tina. Please get here as soon as you can."

Jane hung up the phone and climbed into Tina's bed, holding her, kissing her, now in tears herself. Jared must have said something, she thought. He must have told her something. "Honey? Your . . . your dad told you?" she asked.

"He said . . ." Tina's chest heaved against her. "He said she was only sick. The other man said it."

Jane lifted her head to look into Tina's eyes. "What other man, honey?"

"I don't know." She sniffed. "Just some man who was talking while Daddy was talking. And why do they have Daddy locked in jail?"

Jane Carey suddenly felt cold.

Baker held the telephone for several moments before laying it down. He could still hear Tina's soft cry of "No!" as he choked on the lie that Sarah was only sick. It must have been his tone. There must have been something in his voice that told her the truth about her mother.

"Meister," he asked, not looking at the lawyer, "did you hear me say anything about my wife just now?"

Ben Meister had been studying him. The mirthfulness of his expression was gone and his eyes seemed to bore through Baker. "That she was sick," he answered. "You said that she was sick."

"That's all?"

"That's all, son."

"Can you get me out of here?" Baker whispered.

"I think so," he said. "Let's go see what kind of judge they give us."

The hour that followed was a blur to Baker. And throughout that hour, he wondered for the first time whether he was indeed insane and whether it was temporary.

First, there were the reporters again. A swarm of them waited on the sidewalk outside police headquarters, cameras clicking and flashing, microphones thrust at his face, voices calling questions. There were so many. Far too many for this town.

Meister's big hand was on Baker's neck, bending his head low and pushing his body toward a waiting car while the lawyer's free hand held a briefcase across Baker's face and his own. Baker struggled to shake off the hand, but the fat man held more tightly. He winced as a thumbnail bit into his neck, and he felt a sudden flash of rage and the coiling of his own body as well as the odd floating sensation he'd felt twice before. He might have struck out at Meister had not the wave of voices crashed upon him. So many voices, shouting, calling, whispering. A trim black woman caught his eye. In her hand she held a microphone with a network news emblem on it. Her lips moved as her eyes met his, but her words had already started before that, Baker was sure. He was hearing her before she spoke.

The lawyer's hand clapped across his cheek and the black woman was gone. But the rage was coming again. He cocked an elbow to drive it hard against Ben Meister's stomach. Too late. The big man's weight was upon him and the detective named Gurdik was holding a car door open and his body was going there. Wait, Baker wanted to shout. He wasn't there yet. For the briefest part of a second, Baker thought his body would leave without him.

Now the car was moving. The voices and the shouts were fading and storefronts were whipping by. The rage he had felt was gone and the floating sensation was draining away. His body and his mind were coming together. He felt, he thought, like two images being brought together in the focusing lens of a camera.

Meister's hand patted his knee.

"Forgive me, Jared." His voice was low and he was breathing hard. "I didn't expect all that either."

Baker didn't answer. He wanted to tell Meister not to shove him that way again and not to seize his neck like a schoolchild being rushed to the principal's office, but he was not angry enough even for that. Besides, he thought he understood. Meister was protecting him. Meister was keeping his face from the pages of newspapers and from evening news broadcasts. He was almost thankful when he thought of the television set in Tina's room.

There were more reporters at the courthouse. This time, though, they were kept at bay. Even then, Ben Meister shielded Baker with his own body as telephoto lenses were snapped on distant cameras. Again, Baker noticed, Meister seemed to be hiding his own face as well.

"Not a word," the lawyer said. "When we get into the courtroom, you're to say not a word. You're to show no emotion except sadness. Look beaten. Show utter surprise when you hear the charges read. No anger, Jared."

"Anger?" Baker answered uneasily.

"Do not let the judge see anger. Do not, moreover, be surprised at anything I might say, and for God's sake, don't argue."

Baker nodded.

*   *   *

The charges did surprise him. They were read from a folder by a short, bald man who glanced once at Baker and then not again. Nor did the judge, a bored and sullen septuagenarian named Toomey.

And Baker felt anger rising in him again. It was a different anger from what he had felt toward the biker with his gasoline and different from what he had felt briefly toward Benjamin Meister. This was his own anger. An odd thought. But it seemed a true thought. He was hearing words that described him as vicious, dangerous, bestial, senseless. He heard his own actions spoken of as horrible, inhuman, cruel. But he heard no mention of Sarah's name. Or of Tina's. He heard only "the wife" and "the daughter" and "the accident" and other words about carelessness and playing in streets. My God, he fumed, they're saying it's Sarah's fault. Sarah's lying dead and Tina's foot is crushed, and they're brushing those off as minor events in the sequence that led to his arrest.

"I'm prepared to enter a plea, Your Honor." Ben Meister's voice boomed in Baker's ear. Baker turned his head and saw the lawyer glowering at him. He struggled to relax his expression.

"Let's have it." The judge looked at the ceiling.

"Not guilty."

The prosecutor, an owlish man named Bloom, waved his manila folder. "Your Honor, we assume the defendant will be basing his defense on a claim of diminished capacity. In that case, the State asks that—"

"No diminished capacity," Meister interrupted. "Not guilty, period. He didn't do it."

"He what?" The prosecutor seemed genuinely surprised. "Well, does counsel happen to know who did? There are three witnesses who—"

"A witness is not a witness until testimony is given. In any case, that testimony will hardly support these charges. Until the State is able to assemble anything resembling a case against Mr. Baker, he's entitled to immediate release on bond. Since Mr. Baker is an established resident of this community, since his surviving child is here, and since he has no criminal record whatsoever, a cash bond should not be necessary."

"That's ridiculous, Your Honor. The man's clearly dangerous."

"Dangerous?" Meister shouted. "This man isn't the perpetrator. He was the victim. The man was attacked and he defended himself. The attacker, who has a long history of preferential treatment and quashed charges—"

"Be careful, counselor," Judge Toomey said through his teeth.

"I'm sorry, Your Honor. I realize that the horrid conduct of Judge Bellafonte's son is not . . ."

Judge Toomey fumbled for his gavel. He missed and it clattered to the floor. Reddening, the judge's eyes swept the row of reporters who stood inside the courtroom door.

"I'll jail you, sir," he seethed, "if you say another word on that subject."

"Yes, Your Honor." Meister shuddered innocently. The judge glanced at the prosecutor, Bloom. Baker thought he saw a look of helplessness.

"The State strongly advises against bail in this matter, Your Honor." There was an edge to the prosecutor's voice, as if a warning were being given. Toomey dropped his eyes.

"Perhaps a substantial bail," the judge muttered. "I'm thinking two hundred thousand dollars' cash bond."

"That's outrageous," Meister blurted. "Even if Mr. Baker could beg and borrow an amount like that, he'd be held in jail at least two weeks until he could raise it."

The judge cocked his head toward the prosecutor and raised one eyebrow. Baker watched for a reaction. Bloom's face showed nothing. But the hand that held the manila folder curled into a partial fist, leaving two fingers showing. The judge looked away and sat back in his chair.

"Well," he said, straightening, "the fact is that there's been extreme violence committed here, according to the charges. This court feels a greater obligation to protect the community than to give any special consider-ation to Mr. Baker because of the loss he suffered. I'm going to set bail because law and precedent provide for it. But I'm prepared to revoke it at any time, given any hint of violent behavior." The judge slapped his palm against his desk. "Bail is set in the amount of two hundred thousand dollars. The defendant is remanded to custody until he can post that amount."

The prosecutor smiled his thanks. Baker felt himself wilt. He thought of Tina and the weeks that might pass before he would see her. He thought of Sarah's funeral. The rage was building again. He could feel it pushing from inside his head. Baker took a step forward.

"I can post it now, Your Honor." Ben Meister stepped with him, one hand reaching to grip the back of Baker's jacket. Baker stopped. He saw the judge's mouth move and hang open. And he saw the prosecutor's face. Bloom's gaze was fixed upon the envelope Meister had drawn from his pocket. Its contents were already in the lawyer's hand. He counted off eight slips of paper. At least that many remained. "Your Honor, I'm holding eight cashier's checks in the amount of twenty-five thousand dollars each. My client is prepared to make bail."

Toomey recovered from his surprise, but slowly. "I thought I understood you to say that your client could not raise that amount, Mr. Meister."

"He could not, Your Honor. I was moved by a sudden impulse to post bail from my own resources."

Toomey's expression blackened. "This court does not take kindly to being bamboozled, Mr. Meister. I would feel entirely justified in rescinding that order and finding you in contempt in the bargain."

"My arguments and my offer are made in good faith, Your Honor." Meister dropped his voice to a stage whisper. "We all share the hope, Your Honor, that this matter will not be tainted by any talk of your relationship with the father of the Bellafonte boy."

Bloom, the prosecutor, coughed aloud, then closed his file. The judge, Meister knew, had been signaled.

Toomey's skin flushed angrily. He drummed his fingers on the bench. "See the bailiff on your way out, Mr.

Meister. Take your client and go. We'll look forward to an early trial date."

"God's grace be upon you, Your Honor." Meister smiled.

"I'll be seeing you again, Mr. Meister."

"Always a pleasure, Your Honor." Meister bowed deeply toward the bench and again toward Bloom. He was entirely pleased with himself. He had, after all, won the first battle. And if Toomey, as he expected, got himself assigned as trial judge, Meister had virtually assured that he would now lose the war. Baker would have little chance. And that, he told himself, was not a bad morning's work at all.

The courthouse was well behind them. Benjamin Meister had led Baker to the bailiff's office, where he counted off and endorsed checks totaling two hundred thousand dollars. Then, release papers in hand, the two men found a side exit and passed unnoticed through the section where divorce cases were heard. They walked slowly, lost among the chain-smoking men and women who stood about the corridor avoiding each other's eyes and among the lawyers who riffled through thick folders and whispered to nervous clients.

A taxi, called by Meister, waited outside. The lawyer directed the cab driver to Greenwich Police Headquarters, where his rented car was parked.

"He can drop me off at home," Baker said. "I want to get to the hospital."

"I'll take you there, Jared." Meister patted his knee. "We have things to talk about."

"You're damned right we have."

Meister silenced him with a wave of his hand a finger pointed at the driver.

Baker stared glumly out the window as the cab passed familiar streets and stores and drove onto a stretch of the New England Turnpike that Baker had traveled a thousand times. Everything looked different than it did three days ago. Three days ago it was a road that led home. Now there was no home.

"I have to find a place," he said. It had not struck him before. He could not stay in his house. Baker could not bear to stay there.

"We'll work it out, Jared. Trust me."

Meister worked his body into the seat of a Pinto that seemed much too small and too modest for him. Everything else about the man looked expensive. Baker noticed that the car had New York plates.

"I want to know who you are," Baker said as the engine coughed into life, "and why are you doing this."

"All in good time, Jared. You can trust your attorney."

"You keep saying that. Bullshit." Baker turned in his seat.

Meister feigned hurt feelings. "If I'm not your friend, Jared, who is? I thought I just did very well by you."

"What you did was antagonize that judge, to say nothing about the prosecutor. I know enough about law to realize that most of it is what a judge says it is. But you went out of your way to openly sucker a man who might be hearing my case."

Meister stiffened slightly. He had expected only blind gratitude from Baker. "What else is troubling you?" he asked.

"For openers, what happened to the diminished capacity plea?"

Meister raised an eyebrow. "Where did you hear that phrase? I don't recall using it."

"I watch television," Baker snapped. "And I'd also like to know why you happen to be carrying two hundred thousand dollars in your pocket."

"I'm carrying half a million." Meister smiled. "Isn't that the hospital up ahead?"

Meister steered his Pinto into the circular driveway

leading to the main entrance of Greenwich Hospital. He stopped near the twin electric doors, but Baker made no move to get out. "Whose half-million?" Baker asked.

"I can't tell you that yet, Jared," he said softly. "I hope to soon, but not now."

"Then why?"

"To get you out, naturally," Meister answered, "and at any cost. Your benefactor has an interest in you, and I give you my word that it's not a sinister interest. As for the plea of not guilty, if I'd said what the prosecutor expected, the judge would have had an excuse to bind you over for psychiatric examination. He could have denied bail on that basis but not so easily otherwise. Still, we were lucky. Old Judge Toomey was forced to think uncharacteristically quickly with all those reporters watching. I suckered him, as you put it, into setting a very high amount, never dreaming that you could come up with it. As for antagonizing him, the man is out to hang you anyway, Jared. The more I irritate him, the more appealable errors he's likely to make. For the moment, however, you are free and are about to visit your daughter. I expect a modicum of appreciation for that, at least."

"Thank you," Baker said. But the look he gave Meister said that he knew he was being massaged. "Why is he out to hang me?"

"I told you. You maimed the son of a judge. You can hardly expect dispassion from one of his colleagues."

"What about a change of venue?"

"Who's going to grant it? Toomey?"

"There are other judges. There has to be one who's impartial."

"Not for you, Baker. You're up against more than you know," Meister told him. "I'll pick you a decent jury, but the sitting judge will restrict me every way he can."

Baker shook his head. Appealable errors. Restricting judges. Meister was talking like a lawyer who expected to lose. Or, at least, that if he might win, it would be sometime in the distant future. Baker could not believe that. He could not believe that a jury would convict him

for defending his home against the man who had destroyed it. Meister sensed that disbelief.

"You've entered a new world, Jared," he said. "You
can't go back to the old one, and nothing in your life will
ever be the same again. Does anything seem the same to
you, Jared? Anything at all?"

"No," Baker admitted.

"Adapt, Jared. Adapt or you'll be swept away. And
for God's sake, learn who your friends are."

"The man with the money?"

"Go see your daughter, Jared."

Tina opened one eye just a crack, then closed it. The
man was still there. He was there yesterday too. She
thought then that it was Father Lennon from St. Paul's
because of the way he was dressed. But this one wore no
collar. Just a black suit and black eyes with bags under
them. And he never said anything. Not yesterday either.

"My father's coming," she whispered. Maybe that
would make him go away. Tina didn't like this man. She
liked the other one, though. She liked the one with the
spinning toy who said she could call him Grandpa. He
made everything seem not so bad. He made her feel not
so afraid and helped her not miss Mom so much. Maybe
not quite so much. But still a terrible lot.

"No." The man in the black suit shook his head.
"Your father will not come."

"He is," Tina answered. "I know he is."

The man didn't answer.

Baker was waiting at the elevator when he noticed the
lobby gift shop. He patted his pockets, knowing they
were empty. Meister had not thought to bring him his
wallet. Baker retraced his steps to the area where the
volunteer receptionist sat and he found the lawyer riffling through a pile of magazines. Meister loaned him
twenty dollars.

It was more than enough for the large, stuffed koala

bear that he'd noticed among the menagerie that covered one wall of the shop. With the change he bought a jigsaw puzzle, a tiny plant, and a Doonesbury paperback. Baker tucked the paper bags under one arm and rubbed his eyes with his free hand. He hoped that he looked more rested than he felt.

There was a rest room near the elevator bank. Baker wet his face with cold water, dried it, then straightened his hair with his fingers. Not too bad, he thought, except for the strips of singed and dirty tape wrapped around his knuckles. Tina can do without seeing that.

Baker peeled away the bandage and dropped it into a trash bin. Next he washed the hand, rubbing off the thin lines of adhesive with his fingertips. The hand looked fine, he thought. Very fine, considering how ugly it was three days ago. There remained only a faded bruise across two knuckles.

Baker stepped back into the corridor and found an elevator waiting. He entered it and pressed the fourth-floor button. As the doors slid closed, he saw Meister in the gift shop examining an embroidered pillow.

"What are you doing here?" Tina was alert now. She raised her upper body on both elbows.

"I have a son here." The old man's voice was flat.

"Now, you don't. This is my room."

"He's above you." The man lifted his eyes to the ceiling. "Intensive Care. If you listen hard, even here you can hear him screaming." His eyes met hers again. "How is it that you don't scream?" he asked.

Tina looked toward the door. There was no sound out there. Not even nurses walking past. She felt herself becoming frightened.

"Listen, would you please not stand there? I'm sorry that your son is hurt, but I think you should be with him and not here. Anyway, I told you my father is coming."

"It was an accident, you know. My son would never have harmed that woman." The man seemed to be talking to no one in particular.

"What woman?" Tina's color began to rise. She was afraid that she knew what woman.

"But what your father did"—these words were to her—"that was no accident." The man in the black suit stepped toward Tina's bed and lifted the sheet that covered her tented leg. Tina braced her hands and jerked her body backward, gasping at the bolt of pain that shot to her hip.

"You get out of here!" she cried out.

"Now!" Baker's voice hissed from the doorway.

"Daddy!" Tina called, but her father did not look at her. His eyes bored into the older man from a face that seemed on fire, and the sight of them caused him to stagger backward. Baker's hands opened and the bags they carried fell.

"You!" the old man whispered, the word dripping with hatred.

Baker saw his hand reached forward. For a heartbeat, it seemed to have a life of its own. He knew that it was reaching for the old man's throat and that it was flexed to tear the throat away from the retreating body. Baker knew the man. It was the devil he'd seen through the bars of his cell. He willed the hand down. It was his own hand again when it clamped down on Judge Bellafonte's arm and nearly lifted the old man's body from the floor. Baker half-dragged him toward the corridor.

Outrage at being handled replaced fear, and the judge found his voice. "Get your butcher's hands off of me," he choked as he flailed at Baker, slapping him hard across the face. Baker blinked back a tear from his smarting right eye, but he did not break his stride.

Heads appeared in doorways. The sounds of grunts and scuffling feet reached the duty nurse, who rose from her station and padded toward them. "Judge Bellafonte!" she called, horrified.

"Stop this animal," the old man shouted, his feet splaying now across the slippery floor.

Arms waving, the nurse fell in behind Baker as he danced the judge toward the elevator bank. Baker stopped and pressed a button. Once again, Bellafonte swung at his face. Baker caught the hand and twisted it, spinning the judge so that his chest was forced against the wall, then locked both the older man's wrists behind him.

Baker turned to the nurse. "You know this man?" The tone of his voice made her back away.

"It's . . . Judge Bellafonte," she stammered.

"It's the father of the punk who killed my wife and put my daughter in the hospital," Baker growled.

"You're Mr. Baker!" Her eyes widened with recognition and with a rush of fear that surprised Baker.

"I'm Tina Baker's father," he said, as if correcting her. "I want this man kept away from her. If I see him again in her room or even on this floor, I'm going to . . ."

The elevator door opened. Baker pulled the judge from the wall where he was pinioned and shoved him full into the astonished face of Benjamin Meister.

Meister caught him, blinked, but recovered instantly. "Where was he?" he asked. "Tina's room?"

"Frightening her," Baker answered. "She was backing away from him when I walked in."

"How is it you're not in jail?" the judge gasped at Baker.

Meister ignored him and turned to the nurse. "Was this man authorized to visit Tina Baker?" he asked.

"N-no." She wrung her hands. "Only family. Except for Mrs. Carey and clergy."

"And Mr. Baker escorted this man from a room where he was not supposed to be?"

"I guess . . . Yes."

"Were any blows exchanged?" Meister saw the redness on Baker's cheek.

"No . . . well . . . the judge slapped Mr. Baker."

"The hell with this," Baker snapped. He took the judge's arm once more and forced him deeply into the elevator. Baker pressed a button and stepped back into the corridor.

The judge raised both his hands in a clawing gesture

and he found his voice. "I'll break you, you butcher," he rasped. "I'll break anyone who . . ."

The doors closed on his words and the churning whine of the elevator muffled them.

"The rest of that threat would have been interesting to hear," Meister said, reminding the nurse that a threat had been made.

"Not to me," Baker said, straightening his suit jacket. "I came to see my daughter." He left the nurse and Meister standing there.

"I'm sorry, Daddy." She held out her arms as he entered the room. He shook his head and closed his eyes as if to say that she should not be sorry and that it was nothing, but he found he could not speak. Carefully, he set his gifts down on her bed and then leaned into her, holding her lightly while she squeezed him.

"That's not a hug." She sniffed. Baker shuddered and swallowed a sob. Then he crushed her body to his. There was no need to speak for many minutes.

"That was stupid, Baker." Meister glowered at him as he pulled back into traffic. "You're lucky you're not back in a cell already."

"He was scaring Tina." Baker rubbed his eyes. "You'd have done the same thing."

"I'd have done almost nothing the same," Meister retorted. "I'd have achieved a like result, but I'd have done it without manhandling a judge an hour after posting bond on an assault charge. And certainly not in front of a witness, God save us."

"That was almost two hours ago," Baker said disinterestedly. "If he was going to call the cops, they'd have been here by now. Thanks, by the way, for hanging around. And thanks for Tina's pillow. That was nice."

"Pretty girl." Meister nodded. "Smart for her age. The story she told those nurses might keep you out of jail yet."

"Story?"

Meister shrugged. "That he was off the wall. Scaring her. Still, it's hard to believe that His Honor intended physical harm to a little kid."

Baker cocked his head. His left eye had now begun to drift and he blinked it back into focus. "He came to see me too," Baker said.

"He what?"

"At the jail. He was staring at me the same way when I was asleep in that jail."

"When was this?" Meister slowed the car.

"Last night . . . this morning . . . sometime. I woke up and walked toward him and he . . . backed away. He almost ran away." Baker squinted and rubbed a hand over his jaw as if trying to remember something distant.

"He's going to try to hurt her, Ben." Baker's eyes narrowed. He did not quite know why he said that. But it was coming. Yes. It was what the old man said in the elevator. "He said he'd break me and he'd break anyone who helped me . . . and . . . you must have heard him."

"What did I hear, Jared?"

"He said that he's going to hear Tina scream like his son screams."

Meister took a very long breath. He had heard no such thing. But he believed upon his life that Baker had heard it.

"Where are we going?" Baker asked. Meister had turned onto the southbound entrance ramp instead of going north toward Baker's house.

"It's time you met another friend," he answered.

"No." Baker had been almost dozing. "I have a lot I have to do. Nothing's been done about Sarah's funeral. And Tina needs some things from home. And my office. I never even called my office."

"Father Lennon is making arrangements about your wife, Jared. As for Tina, I'll have you home in an hour."

"Arrangements," Baker repeated. A word he'd used all his life had a bad taste suddenly. You make arrangements to have your trash picked up or your car fixed. You don't just make arrangements for Sarah. Sarah had been alive and laughing for thirty-four years. Sarah made love and she cried and she made flowers grow. Sarah moved like a cat when she played tennis and she danced the same way. A hundred children can play the piano because Sarah taught them. Sarah was every nice thing that ever happened. Sarah gave him Tina. How much of this did Father Lennon know? He ought to be told. He ought to be told what should be said about her and who should hear it.

Meister's friend would have to wait.

Baker shut his eyes. He would tell Meister to turn around at the next exit. He would tell him in just a minute.

"The guy is a volcano waiting to blow." Meister spoke softly into a pay phone at an Exxon station off the Mamaroneck exit of the turnpike. A lumpish teenager stood whistling as the hose pumped a few unneeded gallons into the Pinto. Meister silenced him with a wave of his hand, pointing to the sleeping man in the passenger seat. The teenager scowled but fell quiet.

"If you want to see him," the lawyer continued, "it better be now. Bellafonte might still decide to put the dogs on him. The old guy's not playing with a full deck, by the way. If Baker catches him near the daughter again, he just might tear him apart."

"But are you encouraged, Benjamin?" The voice on the other end was eager, excited. "Have you seen anything?"

"Are you kidding? By you, the guy's like Disneyland. I saw it almost happen twice. In the hospital, he looked like he could have twisted off that judge's neck like he'd open a bottle. Then, when they were taking pictures, I forced his head down and squeezed his neck good and hard. Baker's neck turned like a rock and his pulse must have tripled."

"Pictures?"

"That's another problem. The wire services and two different networks had cameras outside the jail. I think I covered Baker, but they might have some clean shots of me. If any of Duncan Peck's people see one, you know he's going to be up here taking a look."

The voice was silent for several beats. "What about Baker?"

"I cleaned out his house of all the snapshots I could find. Six photo albums, a yearbook, and a few framed pictures if he was in them."

"No, no. I meant the man. Does he seem stable?"

"Wait." The pump attendant approached Meister. The lawyer fished for his wallet and selected a credit card, which the teenager took with a grunt. Baker had not moved.

"Well, he's not your garden variety psychopath," Meister said with a shrug. "Decent enough guy. No dummy either, by the way. But he hears things no one else hears, and I don't believe he's hallucinating. Have you seen that before?"

"Once."

"Also, he seems to have a special thing with his daughter. They're tuned in, somehow. You want my opinion, I think you hit the mother lode."

"Did young Tina speak of my visit this morning?"

Meister's eyebrow arched. "That was you? Grandpa?"

"I thought I'd better relax her if I could. Baker will need to know that she's at peace."

"You get around, don't you, Marcus?"

"Don't we all, Benjamin," the voice answered. "But come. Let us have a look at your Jared Baker."

4

The car had stopped moving. It had stopped once before, it seemed, but this time was longer. It had come to rest and rocked sideways once, and Baker thought he remembered the sound of a door being closed gently. He didn't care. The sleep was good. It made his body feel heavy and warm, and if he sank into it deeply enough, there would be no pain of remembering. And he could still feel Tina's touch against his cheek and around his neck. It made her seem close by.

A part of his mind seemed to detach itself from the rest. It formed a thin and wispy ball and it floated among thoughts of Tina while the rest was left to seethe and boil by itself. They were not troubled thoughts of Tina. He saw her in a Christmas play when she sang "Edelweiss" for all the parents, terrified that she might miss a note and only relaxing when she did. He saw her the first time she watched kittens being born, and when she first sailed his small boat by herself. He saw the letters from schoolteachers telling him how proud he ought to be. He saw her diving, which came easily to her, and he saw her skiing, which came hard. But she tried. Tina always tried. She even won that trophy. Baker had an odd notion that Tina was remembering that too just then.

Another thought intruded. Another wisp from his brain licked up and began lashing about. The ball of good thoughts seemed to wilt and retreat. That annoyed

Baker. He tried to shake the new wisp away, but it began prodding at him, probing, he felt, for a spot behind his right eye. He felt no touch, but it seemed that someone was trying to wake him. He resisted because now Tina was leaving, except that Tina didn't seem to mind. She called from far away that Grandpa was coming. That was a dream. Tina never knew her grandfather. Baker blinked, then opened one eye.

He knew at once that he was alone, even before the left eye followed and took in Meister's empty seat. The bright sky made him wince. It was a hot whitish blue and there were thin silver columns reaching into it. Dozens of them. Baker rubbed his face and sat up straight.

It was a marina, he realized. A boatyard. He focused now on the tall silver masts and the white decks at their feet. Where was Meister? He scanned the parking area, but the lawyer was not in sight. There was only a small boy struggling to launch a windsurfer, a fat woman sunning herself on the stern of a Chris Craft, and an older man with a fishing rod who limped down the dock in his direction. A steep gangplank blocked Baker's view of the fisherman's body, but Baker knew by the rhythm of his shoulders that he walked with a cane. Did he know the gray-haired man? He didn't think so. Yet a part of him thought he did.

He could not make out the face. It was framed in shadow between the visor of a red baseball cap and a trimmed Edwardian beard. His body too had the thick and substantial look of that period. And Baker liked him. He had no idea why, nor did he dwell upon it. He simply liked the man and wished they might talk.

The man in the red cap rested for a moment at the top of the gangplank. Baker saw the cane now. That, and an old wicker creel that hung from his shoulder. The man smiled toward Baker before coming on.

"Good afternoon, Mr. Baker," the bearded man said pleasantly. There was a flicker of pain on his face as he reached down to rub the leg that he favored. Baker stepped from the car.

"Maybe you should sit down," he offered.

"Walking is better." The older man forced a smile. "At my age, one cannot expect to dangle his legs from a pier without some complaint from them. The body complains, however, no matter what I do. So I go right on spiting it and it goes right on getting even. An impasse, you see."

He motioned for Baker to walk with him back toward the dock and extended his free hand. "The name is Sonnenberg," he said.

Baker took the hand and pumped it lightly. Sonnenberg held the grip just a moment overlong, glancing in that time at Baker's knuckles.

"I'm Jared Baker," he answered unnecessarily, once more scanning the parking area.

"If you're looking for Benjamin Meister, he'll be back presently. He said something about a glass of beer and a plate of fried oysters. Would you believe that he puts mustard and sugar on them? Disgusting." He shivered.

"Meister works for you?"

"On occasion." Sonnenberg nodded. "And yes, it was I who provided the wherewithal for your release."

Baker hesitated, not sure of what to say.

"You are, no doubt, curious as to my motives," Sonnenberg acknowledged easily. "This is natural. We don't live in an age when one can readily believe in fairy godfathers, do we."

Baker waited. It struck him that the older man's voice had a foreign cast to it. There was no accent, but his diction was precise in the way of one who has learned the language. Sonnenberg tried another opening.

"I am most sincerely sorry, Mr. Baker, about the loss you have suffered. I'm assured, however, that young Tina can hope for a full recovery, given correct treatment. Quite a courageous young lady, isn't she?"

Baker stiffened inside, vaguely irritated at this stranger's knowledge of his daughter. "She's holding up well," he answered.

"And a perceptive child." There was a sudden spark of excitement in Sonnenberg's eyes. "Do I understand correctly that she sensed her mother's death while in conversation with you?"

"Look, Sonnenberg . . ." Baker's own eyes flashed.

The older man seemed stricken, as if suddenly aware that he had plunged too far and too fast. His body rocked. Baker reached to steady him.

"I am so terribly sorry," he said, mortified. "That was unforgivably clumsy of me." Sonnenberg jerked his head toward a row of slips and eased Baker with him in that direction. His manner suggested that he needed a moment to recover from his embarrassment. Baker could not know that he was furious with himself. He had moved much too quickly.

"In any event," he said, keeping Baker's arm in his, "it's *Dr.* Sonnenberg." He steered Baker to a finger where the largest pleasure boats were berthed.

"Physicians develop a habit of asking intimate questions," he offered by way of apology. "We sometimes forget that all the world is not a patient."

He stopped Baker at the stern of a large moter sailer. "Can I offer you some wine? Perhaps a spot of lunch? My housekeeper is on board with me today."

Baker could hear movement below. He looked across the cockpit and caught a glimpse of another gray head moving inside the hatchway near what must have been the galley. "This is yours?" he asked. One hand reached involuntarily to touch a huge self-tailing winch of gleaming chrome. Two of those, he knew, would buy a whole boat like the one he owned.

Sonnenberg nodded. "Comfortable, isn't she?"

The boat distracted Baker, as Sonnenberg hoped it would. Baker had not seen her before on the Sound. Nor one quite like her. The boat's length, he guessed, was fifty-five feet. Big, but not a giant. Not even especially pretty because of lines that were squat and square and functional. But the boat looked like she could reach any harbor in the world. She was basically a trawler in design, made to maneuver and even cruise under power, but fitted with a short mainmast and a mizzen that would carry her even faster under sail when the wind was right.

Below, he imagined, the craft would be like a small house. The galley would be of a size that some apartments would covet, and there would be a three-quarter bathtub in the head. The captain's berth would hold a queen-size bed, and the main cabin would pass for the living room of a summer cottage. Baker knew that he was looking at a four-hundred-thousand-dollar indulgence. The amount of his bail seemed not so great anymore. His eyes fell on the transom.

"*Chimera?*" There was no port of registry lettered beneath the name.

"Yes, *Chimera*. Do you know the word?"

"Greek mythology." Baker nodded.

"A spectacular beast that was three creatures in one." Sonnenberg seemed pleased that he knew. "Came to grief, you might recall, at the hands of Bellerophon and hasn't been heard from since. An apt name, I think. This *Chimera* is part motor yacht, part sailboat, and part domicile. It's more of a retreat, actually. Come aboard, Jared." Sonnenberg eased him forward.

Baker held back. "I really would like to get home, Doctor."

"Twenty minutes," Sonnenberg assured him. "There's some excellent wine on board. Already chilled."

"A cup of coffee, maybe. I'm having trouble staying awake."

Sonnenberg's housekeeper, a middle-aged and gothic-looking woman he identified as Mrs. Emma Kreskie, passed a plastic coffee service from the hatchway. She followed with a sardine sandwich that Baker had not heard Sonnenberg request. He did not resist it. Baker could not remember when last he ate.

"Mr. Baker." Sonnenberg clapped his hands lightly in a small nervous gesture. "I am going to explain my interest in you as forthrightly as I can. I'm unable to answer every question you might ask, but assuredly I will not lie to you. Does that seem fair enough?"

Baker's mouth was full. He indicated that he was listening.

"Might I ask first if you consider yourself a violent man?"

Baker shook his head as he swallowed. The question chilled him. Sonnenberg had touched at once upon the single aspect of his behavior that most troubled him. What he had done to the judge's son, what he had fought against doing to the judge himself, was simply not like him. "No," he said finally. "I don't think I've even spanked Tina since she was four years old."

"Have you ever before struck an adult of either sex?"

Baker felt a flash of resentment over the last part. He was probably referring to Sarah. "Not since college. A fight over a girl we were both dating."

"Nothing more? What about violent impulses?"

"There are people I've wanted to belt."

"Often?"

"Maybe once in two or three years."

"Nothing more recent? No sudden flashes of anger? No sense that you're not fully yourself, particularly in annoying or stressful situations?"

"Yes," he admitted. "For the past several months, at least. What kind of doctor are you, by the way?"

"Not a psychiatrist, Jared. My field, broadly speaking, is behavioral modification. My interest, of course, is in your behavior."

"Two hundred thousand dollars' worth of interest?"

"Yes." Sonnenberg raised a hand while he sipped from his cup. "But we're getting ahead of ourselves and I've exhausted half your twenty minutes. Do you mind that I call you Jared, incidentally?"

Baker shook his head.

"Jared," he began, "I wish to offer my assessment of your situation, which I'm afraid will depress you. At the end, I will offer a solution and then invite you to consider my proposition at your leisure. As for the bail I've posted and the services of Benjamin Meister, I consider that you've repaid me by coming here today."

"Well . . ." Baker did not dismiss two hundred thousand dollars so readily. "Anyway, thank you. I'll make sure you get it back."

Sonnenberg smiled and made a gesture of dismissal. He cared nothing for the reassurance, but he was counting on the expression of gratitude.

"Here, Jared, is the depressing part. Even beyond the tragedy of your loss, your life has been shattered beyond reasonable hope of reclamation. Your home, as I know you've considered, is lost to you. No amount of fresh paint will make it a home again. You will discover that most of your friends are also lost to you. Some will fear you. Most will drift away because you no longer blend comfortably into their lives. Your business career, the job to which you commute each day, will also be put behind you. You'll have no stomach for it.

"The choice, however, is not yours entirely. You are facing a serious criminal charge. Due to its . . . forgive me . . . barbarous nature, you should expect some period of incarceration. A prosecutor will present you to a jury as a man who has done a monstrous thing. Your firm, you may depend, will wash its hands of you as soon as is decently possible and certainly upon a guilty verdict whether a jail term is involved or not. If Benjamin Meister does his work artfully, the jury may acquit you on the basis of temporary insanity. You might escape imprisonment. You might even escape consignment to a mental institution. But in the eyes of the world, Jared, and in the eyes of all prospective employers, you will be a man to be feared and shunned. Young Tina, I'm afraid, will bear that burden with you.

"Perhaps the worst part of your situation, Jared, is this. Your . . . victim . . . is the son of a superior court justice. But Judge Bellafonte is not just any judge. He is what used to be called a power broker. He is venal, corrupt, a dealer in favors, and, above all, vindictive."

Baker shrugged and looked away. His movements indicated that he had stopped listening.

"Jared," Sonnenberg asked, "do you question Judge Bellafonte's capacity for vengeance?"

"I question his capacity to do much about it, other than to try to frighten a little girl."

"On what basis, Jared? That this is America? That we live in a nation of laws? That we live in a world where evil is punished and virtue is rewarded and the innocent are protected? I pray you, do not look to the legal process for protection. Or your salvation. And certainly not for justice."

"We're not talking about the world," Baker answered. "We're talking about one hack judge in one Connecticut county who may or may not peddle his position. We're also talking about a man who's flying on one wing because of what happened to his son."

"We're talking about power. He has it and you don't. We're talking about ruthlessness, which you don't have either. This is not a man to cut his losses, Jared."

Baker sighed wearily and rose to his feet. Sonnenberg saw the disbelief on his face as well as scorn. Baker didn't bother to reply. Instead, he looked out across the Sound and the scattering of boats that coasted lazily in all directions. Now we're talking killers, he told himself disgustedly. Another cup of coffee and we'll be talking Mafia. Christ! A week ago, he thought, he was just like everybody else out there in those boats. Now he was in more trouble than he'd ever dreamed of and he had Meister and then Sonnenberg telling him it was even worse. Damn, how he'd love to climb on one of those boats and never stop until he hit Liverpool. Oh, lordy, would that be nice. Sell the damned house, buy a boat, grab Tina, and go. The minute Tina can walk, I'll—

"You'd like to walk away from it all, wouldn't you, Jared?"

Baker turned and stared.

"No." Sonnenberg smiled. "I'm not a mind reader. Flight is an altogether human impulse. Particularly among friendless felons who stand in boats gazing at the horizon."

Baker didn't return the smile. "You're about to tell me why I need you. Is that right, Doctor?"

"I'm about to suggest a solution."

*   *   *

Sonnenberg poured a second cup of coffee.

"What if you really could walk away from it, Jared? All of it."

Baker's face showed he did not understand.

"You read the papers," Sonnenberg said offhandedly. "You know that there are people who have left old lives behind and started new ones. People with far less reason than Jared Baker have cast off their old worlds the way a snake sheds its skin. Surely you've heard of such things happening."

Baker nodded slowly. "I've heard of it being done with government witnesses. Mobsters, mostly, who've agreed to testify."

"A drop in the bucket, Jared." Sonnenberg brushed those aside with what Baker took to be a look of contempt. "For every private detective who specializes in finding missing persons," he went on, "there's another who teaches people how to be missing. Very often, they're the same private detective. Beyond those, think of the Vietnam draft evaders and the network that delivered them to Canada and Amsterdam and later provided them with false papers that permitted their untroubled return. Add to these the many thousands who obtain a poor man's divorce by running away, or the women who vanish to escape abuse and neglect, or even senior citizens who seek an escape from the humiliation of a dependent existence. The rankest amateur, Jared, can make an adequate new life for himself and be rarely seen again. A few, a very few, are able to create new lives that are satisfying beyond their wildest dreams."

Baker sat down slowly. "Is that what you do, Dr. Sonnenberg?" he asked. "You put people in new lives?"

"Among other things, but yes."

"Why?"

"Because I can, Jared."

"That's not a reason."

Sonnenberg met his eyes. "The truth is often simple." The doctor clasped his hands and leaned toward

Baker. "Except this, perhaps," he said. "I don't much like
the world we live in, Jared. The power, including such
power as Judge Bellafonte's, is too much in the hands of
a few. Most men exist to serve them, to be exploited, and
to be crushed if they become troublesome. If you doubt
that, try refusing to pay your annual tribute to the government. But until they are either needed or troublesome, they live under the happy illusion that they are
free men. I could not have said this to you, Jared, even
one week ago. You would have called me a cynic at best
and a lunatic at worst. But one week ago, you hadn't yet
become bothersome, had you, Jared?"

Baker stared at him in silence for several moments.
It was all preposterous. He knew that. The thought of
leaving all that was familiar, all evidence that he had
made a life, friends . . . yet people did it all the time. Ordinary people. Career people who got uprooted every
couple of years. Military families. But they didn't change
their names and pretend to be somebody else. Except
what if they did? They'd still be the same. They'd still be
who they were. And they'd be left alone. Baker's right
eye began to water.

"Imagine it, Jared." Sonnenberg rubbed his hands.
"Imagine yourself running a ski lodge in Vermont, or a
charter boat on St. Croix, or living in a lakeside cabin
painting landscapes and even selling them. Just you and
your daughter, Baker, in a world of your creation. A
world of almost unlimited freedom and fulfillment . . .
and of peace."

Baker didn't have to imagine. Sonnenberg had just
named the most persistent of his dreams. Except, perhaps, for the part about painting. That was more fantasy than dream. Baker knew that he hadn't the talent.
Still . . .

"You know a lot about me, Doctor." Baker wanted to
be angry at the intrusion but he could not manage it. He
was fascinated. And a part of him was thrilled. Eager.
Baker wiped away the moisture from his eye and tried to
blink that part away. There was no reason for that feeling.
This was stupid. Impossible. A stranger comes from no-

where and says he'll help me walk away from all the sorrow and pain out of the goodness of his . . . "Why, Doctor? Why me?"

"Was I correct, Jared? Did I touch upon your
dreams?"

"I think you know damn well you did," he answered. "I think you know me inside out."

"I know pieces." Sonnenberg spread his hands in a
show of candor. "After all," he pointed out, "I'd never
heard of you until yesterday's newspapers. But there are
files on you here and there. Credit bureaus, executive re-
cruiters, and the like. I admit that I've had access to
them. The rest is largely guesswork. And a little insight.
I'm a behaviorist, you see, Jared. I teach certain people
to understand their behavior, to adjust to it, and sometimes to alter it. You, Jared, are a more interesting subject than most. And that, sir, is the long and the short of
my interest in you."

"There's nothing special about me."

Sonnenberg smiled at him. Baker saw his eyes drift
toward the moisture on his right cheek and linger there
a moment before they fell.

"You don't really believe that, do you, Jared Baker?"

Sonnenberg watched him leave. He watched Baker walk
slowly through the maze of the dock like a man in deep
thought. He watched him climb a gangplank steepened
by a falling tide toward a waiting Benjamin Meister. He
heard a clatter of plastic behind him.

"What do you think?" he asked, not turning. The
clatter stopped and he heard Emma Kreskie's feet shuffle
to his side. They watched until they heard the growl of
Meister's engine. The woman turned toward him and
nodded.

"I think so too," Sonnenberg answered. "I think it
will work this time."

Look at him, Sonnenberg said to himself. A tormented man trying desperately to make some sense out
of what has happened to him. Of what he's become. Of

what he is. But you'll know the answer soon, Jared. You'll
know what I know already. I have found my Chimera.

Who'd have thought it, Jared? Who would have
looked for a Chimera in this . . . suburbanite, this mower
of lawns and rider of trains. Who would have thought
that you were three totally different men? But you are,
you know.

You are only the host, but the others are there. They
are there in everyone. The almost beings that float un-
formed within every human brain. The shadow creatures
kept unwhole by the brain's own division. The stunningly
different visages that are evident in the separate halves of
every human face.

But in you, they became incarnate, Jared. Somehow
the pieces stopped floating and like attracted like and the
Chimera was formed. The horror that shattered your
gentle life seems to have thrown an arc across the neuron
soup inside your skull and called forth at least one of
them. The primal one.

"You know," he said distantly, "this would all be so
much tidier if there were no daughter."

The woman's eyes blazed at him.

"No, no. Just an idle thought." He raised a hand in
appeasement. "I would never harm the child. But she
may very well do violence to Baker's concentration. On
the other hand, her death might devastate him to the
point of uselessness. No, Mrs. Kreskie. I'm quite convinced that the daughter must be protected. And most
immediately from any extravagant behavior on the part of
the bereaved Bellafonte person."

The woman nodded.

"Bellafonte!" His expression was distant again. "Has
it struck you, Mrs. Kreskie, that the judge's surname
sounds remarkably like Bellerophon?"

She looked blankly at him.

"Bellerophon," he repeated. " 'And Bellerophon rode
Pegasus there to find the Chimera and there did slay the
beast.' " Sonnenberg chewed on that awhile. "A troublesome thought," he said at last.

Mrs. Kreskie nodded.

*   *   *

Ben Meister signaled a right turn onto Baker's street. He nudged Baker, who was lost in thought, when the white colonial house came into view.

"Looks like someone's been tidying up," Meister said.

Baker sat up in his seat. The burn marks on the outside wall, which he'd dreaded seeing again, were almost gone. The charred paint had been scraped away and a coat of white primer covered all but a grayish outline. Two boxwoods and a tall juniper had been trimmed to remove all evidence of the fire. The driveway had been coated with a layer of blacktop sealer. The marks were gone where Macduff had died and where he had destroyed the face of . . . Baker bit his lip. Looking away, he saw Sam Willis's ladder lying on its side against the foundation.

"You have nice neighbors." Meister took in what must have been a solid two days' work by more than one person. "What'll you bet there's a tuna casserole in the kitchen?"

Baker didn't answer immediately. His throat felt hot and he did not trust his voice. "Are you hungry?" he managed finally.

"I'll grab a steak up the road. You said you wanted to get to the hospital."

Meister stopped the car past two empty sealer cans that blocked the driveway. Baker made no move to get out.

"What happens next?" he asked.

"We get ready for trial. You start soon on a round of psychiatric testing, first with their shrink and then with my shrink. I start interviewing the witnesses to make sure they remember it right."

Baker nodded. "In court, you said their statements wouldn't support the charges. What did that mean?"

"They're on your side." Meister shrugged. "They tried to put the best face on what happened. You won't look so good under cross-examination, though, unless I drill them pretty good." Meister squirmed in his seat to fish an object from his hip pocket. "Listen, I'll be in touch. In the meantime, Sonnenberg wants you to have these." He held out a set of silver keys.

"They're for Sonnenberg's boat. He says to tell you it's stocked with provisions and it's yours to live on any time you like. Go down there if being here gets to you or if anyone bothers you. There's a radiophone on the boat. If you want to talk to Sonnenberg, just flip on the radio switch but don't touch the dials. He'll know you're there."

"Am I allowed to leave the state?" Baker asked doubtfully.

"Don't worry about it." Meister placed the keys in Baker's hand.

Baker hesitated as if making up his mind, then dropped them in his pocket. "Ben?"

"Yeah?"

"How long have you known Sonnenberg?"

"We go back a few years."

"Is he straight?"

"Compared to what?"

"Come on, Ben." Baker sighed. "You know what he wants me to do. You were setting me up for it all day."

"I was preparing you, Baker. Setting up isn't the same thing."

"What Sonnenberg was suggesting . . . Is it possible?"

"You mean about you and your daughter walking away from all this and never being touched? Yeah, it's possible. It's even easy."

"Do you know people who've done it?"

"A few, yeah."

"He said something about me making a living as an artist. That part can't be possible."

"Why not?"

"It's a hobby. I'm just ordinary at it."

"You don't know Sonnenberg."

Something in Ben Meister's voice made Baker turn his head. It was in Meister's eyes too. The breeziness that was part of the big man's manner was gone, only for a moment. "I'll give you a hint," Meister said, looking deeply into Baker. "You could even make a living as a lawyer if you wanted."

It was a few minutes past sunset. The streetlights had not yet blinked on. A Ford sedan drifted silently down the dark street by Baker's house. The driver could see without slowing that Baker's car was gone. The house was unlit. A single bulb burned inside the open garage. He nodded, satisfied, and the Ford coasted on before turning right at the end of Baker's street.

"That was the guy's house?" the other man asked. He was younger than the driver and half again as large. He spoke through thickened lips and his eyebrows had been torn and stitched a dozen times until the skin had a glassine shine to it. His mouth was twisted in a street tough's sneer and it hung partly open even as he chewed noisily on a wad of gum. Stanley Levy despised being with him. He nodded once but said nothing.

"I fought a guy named Baker once," Vinnie Cuneo said, squinting.

"Maybe you'll get to fight this one." God should be so good, Levy said to himself.

"I think his name was Ronnie." Cuneo's brow wrinkled into tight folds. "No, Randy. Randy Baker. A southpaw."

The homely little man wasn't listening. Ahead of him, his lights picked up the edifice of a church. The parking lot would be around to the side. It didn't seem right, he thought, doing this near a church.

"We were the featured undercard before a Joey Giardello fight out in Sunnyside Gardens. That was only three fights before Giardello took the title from Dick Tiger. I beat the shit out of him." He poked an elbow at Stanley Levy.

"Giardello?" Levy asked absently.

"No, Randy Baker. We had an all–light heavy card that night except for two spics fightin' bantam. I ruined him. Closed up both his eyes with my laces before I really went to work. In those days, the ref didn't jump in as fast as now."

"I'm sure you were a credit to your race," Levy droned.

Vinnie Cuneo turned his head toward the smaller man and stared for a long moment through hooded eyes. "What was that? Was that some kind of crack?"

Levy did not reply. He guided the car into the deepest shadows of the parking lot and shut off the motor. Vinnie reached toward Levy's arm and poked it.

"Why do you always treat me like I'm nothin'?"

Levy rolled his eyes. "Just an observation, Vinnie," he said. "No offense intended." He looked away and tried to ignore the sounds of air being forced through the bigger man's ruined nose. He wished he had a book to read.

"Don't talk to me no more like I'm nothin'," Vinnie pressed. He swatted Stanley's shoulder with the back of his fingers. Levy turned to the hoodlum and smiled. Perhaps Vinnie would touch him again, he thought. Perhaps Vinnie would make a fist and draw it back. Then no one could blame Stanley Levy. Tortora would have to understand that Stanley Levy had had no choice.

A pair of headlights washed halfway across the church and then went out. Stanley put his hand over his own lips as if to dismiss the matter as he pointed. "Please step into the back seat, Vinnie."

Vinnie hesitated. "I'm gonna talk about this some more," he said.

"To business first, you thug. This is a judge coming. Be respectful."

Stanley wondered for the dozenth time about the upbringing Vinnie must have had. His mother must have died in childbirth. If God was merciful, she never lived to have her heart broken. Vinnie wheezed sullenly as he slid from the car and climbed into the back seat. He did not acknowledge Judge Lawrence Bellafonte or look at him.

The judge had been drinking. In the brief glow of

the dome light, Levy saw the damp and florid face and the look of sly yet stupid cunning that seems common to drunks who try to think. He knew at once that the judge would not respond to reason. Just as well, he thought.

Bellafonte barely glanced toward the shadow that slouched behind him. "This is the muscle?" he asked, jerking a thumb at Vinnie.

"My associate," Stanley answered.

He smiled his satisfaction. "Please convey my respects to Mr. Tortora and give him my thanks for his swift assistance in this regard." The old man said the words by rote and slurred some of them.

"Mr. Tortora acknowledges your friendship," Stanley intoned, as if reciting a boring ritual, "and he expresses the hope that you will be guided by his advice."

Bellafonte began to nod and then stopped. What was this about advice?

"Mr. Tortora," Stanley continued, "deeply feels your grief. He reminds you that your son Andrew has been a valued friend of his own son, John. He understands your desire for justice but regrets that he must ask you to be patient. In other words, I think he has different plans for the guy, Baker."

Bellafonte's face darkened. "Baker is mine," he said. "The injury has been done to me."

Stanley shrugged. "This is Mr. Tortora's message."

Bellafonte was silent for a long moment. He turned in his seat to face the blackness outside the window. "Did Mr. Tortora give instructions concerning the daughter of this man?"

Stanley was afraid that he knew what was coming. "All other matters are left to my discretion," he said.

"Then if the man who injured me is to be under the protection of Domenic Tortora, he should at least know of my suffering and my grief."

Levy stifled a yawn. "For starters, judge," he said, scratching his thinning head, "the guy's wife is dead. I think he knows from grief."

"His daughter isn't dead."

"Your kid isn't either."

"My son has no face." Bellafonte's voice tightened and shook. "Baker's daughter has a face."

Stanley Levy shut his eyes and shook his head. When he opened them, he glanced back at Vinnie Cuneo and touched a finger to his temple. Vinnie sat up straight and locked his eyes on the back of the judge's head.

"Judge Bellafonte," Stanley asked quietly, "what is it that you are asking of us?"

"Justice," he said, spraying spittle with the word.

"You want us to carve up the kid's face?"

"I want justice."

Stanley folded his hands on his lap and smiled. "That nice little girl?" he asked. "Who never bothered anybody? You want us to turn out her lights like that would be an even payment for whatever happened to that little fucker of yours?"

The older man stiffened and shook as if shocked by a bolt of current. He spun fully to face Levy, his expression twisted between disbelief and fury. "You . . . you little kike," he blurted as his right hand flew up and his palm slashed down toward Stanley's cheek. He saw the blur of Levy's hand rising up to block it and he saw an object in the hand, but he ignored it. His own hand stopped short of its mark against something that was not flesh. He could not see in the dark. It was a small object, the pressure against his palm told him. What he felt was no bigger than a coin. But it stung him. It pricked at his palm and it burned the back of his hand, and now the prickling was turning into a deep ache that rolled across his wrist and sent currents of pain up his forearm. He tried to pull his hand away, but a bolt shot to his shoulder. His mind turned from Stanley Levy and the insult and tried to focus through the darkness on what was hurting him, gripping his hand, paralyzing it, forcing it down and away from Levy's face and pressing it flat against the dashboard.

Stanley reached for the dome light and turned it on. He wanted the judge to see. He also wanted to see if the judge was making a mess.

Bellafonte blinked his eyes in disbelief. He saw his

own convulsing hand pinned like a bug to the padded dashboard. He saw single drops of blood as they fell away, and he saw the rest as it coursed over his wrist and began soaking his white cuff. And he saw the ice pick that was doing this. "This way you're behaving," Stanley asked softly. "What would your mother say about behaving this way?"

In the back seat, Vinnie tensed. There he goes with his mother shit again. He felt a chill. It was the only time he was afraid of Stanley Levy.

"I asked you a question." Levy's eyes bored into the judge, who could only stare in return, barely able to believe that this was happening. "Tell me," Stanley persisted. "Tell me what your mother would say if she knew you wanted to hurt some little girl or that you were going to smack a small person like me. Tell me if she would like you using words like *kike.* She wouldn't like that, would she? She'd tell you to say you're sorry."

Bellafonte was almost sober now. But he was half in shock. "You did this," he whispered, "to me?" This last part was louder. He drew in a breath and Stanley knew that the next sound would be a scream. He nodded to Cuneo and pointed to the judge's neck. Cuneo punched him there and the scream became a squawk.

"Are you going to tell me you're sorry?" Levy asked him.

His eyes glazed, Bellafonte scanned the outside darkness for help. Forgetting his hand, he tugged at it, and the pain made him shriek. "You're insane," he gasped finally. "Tortora will . . ."

Stanley brushed aside the irrelevancy. "Your mother's passed on, hasn't she?" he asked gently. "That's too bad. I would have asked my mother to go see her and they would have talked. That would have been good. It would have been a way for you and me to understand each other better."

Only a part of the judge's mind heard Stanley's words. The rest was on his quivering hand and what was being done to him. This outrage. This incomprehensible assault upon his person . . . upon the person of Justice

Lawrence Bellafonte. First Baker had laid hands upon him and now this . . . thing. But he must humor him. He must humor this little maniac until he could get away from him. He would get to a phone and he would tell Domenic Tortora what the crazy Jew had done. No, he thought. He would not call Tortora. Not yet. First, he would call another number. And after the daughter screamed like his son screamed, then he would call Tortora. Tortora would understand. And then someday this man too would scream.

Bellafonte's eyes betrayed him. Stanley knew that this man would never be reasonable. Better he should be with his mother.

Tina had been dreaming.

They weren't bad dreams, exactly. It was more that they were confusing. A whole bunch of little bits and pieces with good parts and not so good parts all mixed together. Most of it was about her father. He was in the building someplace. She knew that. And he was talking to Dr. Bruggerman about her leg and about reconstruction and stainless steel screws and therapy and cosmetic surgery. Part of it, the heel, would always be numb. She didn't mind that so much as long as it wasn't tingly. Tingly is much worse than numb. And her father seemed to feel okay about what Dr. Bruggerman was saying except he thought the doctor was a little bit afraid of him. And at the same time, like through another ear, she could hear things being said about her father that weren't so good. Tina knew that she was remembering the radio, mostly. The radio was talking about what her father had done to that man until the nurse came in and pretended to want to talk about her daughter who Tina kind of knew at junior high, but what she really wanted to do was turn off the radio.

The really confusing stuff, she thought, was not from one ear or the other but from someplace in between. It wasn't like thinking and it wasn't like remembering. It was more like seeing and hearing. For instance, she knew that a man was talking about her father and the man was with that judge she didn't like. Then all of a sudden, the man was talking about her. Like he liked her. But then the man talking became an old woman talking and then switched back again. It was all dumb like that. Except she didn't have to be afraid of that judge. She didn't have to be afraid of anything. Because whenever she started to feel afraid, or to really start to miss Mom, all of a sudden there'd be her new grandpa smiling at her and spinning that little blue thing that made her feel yummy sleepy. She could almost see it. Ooops! Daddy's coming.

Tina rubbed her eyes awake. She pressed the button that elevated the top of her bed and made her hospital smock as neat as she could. She'd be glad to get rid of it as soon as Daddy got here with her own stuff. Tina straightened her hair with her fingers, then squeezed a bit of toothpaste into her mouth and swished it around with water. She sat back and watched the door.

"Hi, Daddy," she called before she even saw him.

She got him to smile after a while. He'd come in smiling, of course, but it was the kind of smile you put on right outside the door instead of just letting it happen. She told him the joke about the world's greatest pass receiver who was walking past this building and everyone recognized him and yelled for him to catch this baby who was hanging from a top-floor window. And he was afraid to try but everyone told him he had to, being the world's greatest pass receiver and all, and how he finally ran and caught the baby and everybody cheered and he was all happy and he did a little dance holding the baby up above his head and then he spiked it. Her dad laughed out loud. It was really kind of a gross story, but it was funny.

Then after a while they watched *M*A*S*H*, and he was laughing because Klinger had a nightgown that looked just like the one he brought for her. He brought three. He got all embarrassed when she took off the hospital gown right in front of him and he kept his head turned. For pete's sake. He also brought more underwear and her own shampoo and toothbrush. He brought some flowers that he picked from the yard and put them on the windowsill with the flowers her class sent and the ones from Mrs. Carey and the plant from Mrs. Willis with the little rabbit family in it. And he brought her schoolbooks and her C. S. Lewis stories, lots of writing paper, and her scrapbook. From her wall, there was her cat poster, her Miss Piggy poster, and especially her autographed picture of Tanner Burke and the other one with Tanner handing her her trophy. He didn't bring any pictures of himself or Mom. He said he couldn't find them, she thought, but he probably just left them behind so they wouldn't make me cry. They wouldn't. Not now. It was nice to have Tanner Burke, though.

"Daddy?" He was on the bed with her, one arm around her shoulder. Tina looked up at his face. "Daddy, will they try to put you in jail?"

He squeezed her. "It'll work out, honey."

"You think they'll try, don't you?"

He didn't answer, but she felt a thump inside him. They would try. She knew that. And she knew that he would hurt them if they tried. Tina knew that too but she didn't know how. And she knew that he wouldn't want to hurt them. He just would. It would be much better if they didn't try. If they couldn't try.

"You could go away," she said.

"No." He squeezed her again.

"Just until I'm better. I really think you should go someplace and fix it up for when I can come. Even if it takes a long time." Tina's own words surprised her when they came. Most of her hated that idea. Most of her didn't even want him to go away until morning. But a part, the part in the in between, thought that going away was the best and the smartest and even the happiest idea of all. She thought of the blue spinning thing.

Baker heard sirens halfway home. They snapped him out of his thoughts. He'd been dwelling on his own sorrows and on the lonely and frightening maze that was his future. Other people had their troubles, the sirens reminded him. Sirens at night always meant misery for somebody.

He turned off the Post Road. A police car passed him, going his way.

Baker's right eye began to water.

He turned left across the tracks and onto Summit Road. Now he could see the flashing glow of strobe lights blinking like fireflies across the night sky. They were on his street. He knew they were at his house. Baker coasted past Spruce Street. There were four police cars that he could see and several others that were unmarked. An ambulance had just arrived. In the brief flash of a photographer's bulb, he thought he saw a man sitting in a chair in the middle of his lawn.

He turned right onto the next street and parked the car. Then he walked to a dark connecting street at the end of which stood his house. Sam Willis's driveway was on his right. Staying to the shadows, he ducked into it. He could see Sam and Peg on his front lawn talking to two policemen. Peg seemed to be shivering, although the night was not cold. Baker saw her say some words to the police, both of whom nodded, and she moved away toward her front door. Now Baker saw the sitting man again. He seemed to be praying. His palms were pressed together as if they'd been clamped and his face was bent skyward. Baker could see only his throat and the line of his chin. It occurred to him that no neck could bend like that. He knew he was looking at a corpse.

Baker heard kitchen sounds. He backed away from the edge of the Willis house and turned the corner, quickly mounting the two concrete steps to Peg Willis's kitchen door. She jumped at his tap but turned and opened the door without first looking through the curtains.

"Jared?" Backing away, she forced a smile. But Baker had already seen the fear. "Jared, where have you been?"

"At the hospital," he answered. "Peg, what's going on over there?"

Now he saw surprise, then doubt, then a new rush of fear. She glanced toward both doors but did not move. "Jared," she said, keeping her voice level, "I think you better go talk to the police."

"Damn it, Peg ..." He moved toward her but a hand shot to her mouth. "Hey," he asked, "what are you going to do? Scream? What's the matter with you, Peg?"

"What's the matter with ... Jared, did you kill that man or didn't you?" Peg Willis was about to cry.

Baker waved both hands in a gesture of exasperation. "What man? Who the hell are you talking about?"

"That judge. The kid's father." She waved a hand in the general direction of his front yard.

"Bellafonte? The old man?" Baker wanted to run to a front window and look again. But he knew it was true. And he knew that Peg Willis would run from him if he gave her the room. Wait a minute. Peg. Peg couldn't possibly believe that he would ... "Peg." His voice, he knew, was almost pleading. "Peg, I've been in the hospital since fifteen minutes ago. And the hospital was the last place I saw that judge."

"Tell the police, Jared." Peg Willis wiped her eyes and folded her arms tightly across her chest. She could not look at him. "Please go out now and tell the police."

He wanted to hold her. He wanted to take her by the arms and make her look into his eyes and tell him why she was so afraid. Instead he asked, "Can you really believe that I would murder an old man and then sit him on my lawn, for Christ's sake?"

"Someone saw you, Jared." She looked at the floor.

"Someone ... Who saw what?" he stammered.

"I don't know who. The police got an anonymous call." The tears came freely now. "Oh, Jared, what happened to Sarah and Tina has made you sick, that's all. Anybody would have snapped under such a ..."

His hands did take her arms and she squealed. "Don't touch me, Jared!"

Baker backed off and could only stare. She was terrified of him, but he saw more than that. He saw the agony of a woman with whom he'd laughed and at whose table he'd eaten fighting against the belief that he could be some sort of maniac and losing that fight. She was so sorry, her eyes told him. But much more, she wanted him away from her.

Baker backed out the door.

He would go to the police. He would tell them he could not have done this. He was at the hospital. Ask Tina. Ask Dr. Bruggerman. The duty nurse too. And the one who came in with Tina's pill. How could two people have seen him?

Baker realized that he was walking away from his house. Away from the police. He walked faster.

And that crazy judge. He wasn't there when I left. I'd remember. I remember everything that happened. I took a shower first. Then I got a shopping bag and started gathering Tina's things. And I looked for the pictures and couldn't find any, even the ones I knew were up on Sara's dresser, but I saw all her things there and started to cry and just lay down on the bed for a few minutes until the dreams woke me up. The dreams. The judge was in the dreams.

Baker reached his car.

The judge and someone else, and the judge was hating and then the judge got hit and couldn't move. Who else was there? My God, not me. It couldn't have been me. It was a dream.

The car turned around, and once again it passed the end of his street. He saw policemen running to the Willis house.

He could straighten it out, he thought. But not now. Not when everything was so confused and so many people were afraid. Peg Willis. The doctor. The nurse. Damn it! Who do they think I am, the Wolfman? Who did I ever hurt except that kid?

Baker climbed onto the thruway. A sob rose in his throat.

"Tina?" he whispered.

And she whispered back that it was all right.

Baker knew that he must be insane.

At Exit 3, he looked off into the dark hills to his

right where the hospital was. He sped past. Tears streamed down his cheeks and he knew he was crazy. Sane people didn't hear voices. Sane people didn't see things happening that they couldn't possibly know. Sane people didn't climb into cars and run and have a part of them crying like this and have another part that was . . . happy. Excited.

There was a toll gate ahead. Baker swung into the automatic lane and reached for the change in his pocket. He rubbed the wetness from one eye with the back of his hand and fed in the coins. He felt the keys in his hand. Sonnenberg's keys. A car behind him honked and he moved through the raised gate.

He must be crazy, he thought again, and once more wiped the moisture from his left eye.

His right eye wasn't tearing.

His right eye was shining.

5

Tanner Burke pushed open the door of her small suite on the Plaza's fifteenth floor and took several steps across the gold carpet of the sitting room. She turned to see Baker still in the corridor. He stood shuffling uncomfortably as he had while she reclaimed her key from the message desk. The prim little night manager had arched an eyebrow at her dishevelment and then at the rather furtive man whose jacket she was wearing. Then, as now, Tanner was afraid he would bolt. He seemed to be sniffing the air and listening. She didn't know whether he reminded her more of a skittish animal or of a timid teenager at the end of his first date.

"It's all right to come in, Harry," she said.

He looked away. "It's late, Tanner. I really have to go."

She shook her head. "And that's another thing," she said. "I refuse to call you Harry. You don't look like a Harold and you're not a Harold. I'll call you Peter. That name is at least possible for you." One hand went to her hip. "Now, Peter, will you come in here please?"

Baker had to smile. And he had to admire her. In fact, he realized, this was his first good look at her. She was smaller than he remembered. It must have been the ski clothes and thick-soled boots. But she was lovelier, if anything, even with the purplish swelling on her cheek and the bits of dried leaf in her hair that the night man had noticed. He'd like to have stayed. But no, he thought. Baker shrugged apologetically and shook his head.

First there was confusion in her eyes and then what looked like hurt. Tiredly, she brought both hands to the sides of her face and took a breath.

"This might sound a bit conceited," she said, her voice starting to catch, "but do you hang around actresses so much that it's old stuff when one invites you into her hotel room?"

"Nope." Baker tried to lighten the moment. "Skiers are old stuff, maybe. But not actresses."

Tanner blinked but didn't smile. "Maybe you're one of those people who think any actress has to be promiscuous."

"No, really." Baker took a step toward her. Damn! "Tanner, it's really nothing like that at all."

"Well, I'm not."

"Tanner . . ."

"Except tonight. Doggone it, Peter, tonight I'm not going to be alone. You can't just walk away after what's happened to me. If you do, I swear I'm going to get on that phone and call the first man I know who's awake and get him up here no matter what I have to do to keep him here."

"You could call a woman friend to stay . . ."

"Dumb!" Her chin began to quiver.

"I'm sorry. I suppose that was stupid." Baker said it, but he wasn't sure why. He would have thought that the last thing she'd want was a man near her or touching her. Baker didn't like that thought either.

"I can call room service." Her face brightened a shade. "You offered me a drink before, Peter. You can stay at least that long," she said in a small fading voice. Baker knew that she was still very much afraid and that her control was an actress's control. It was only his presence and, in no small part, the mystery of him that kept her mind from focusing back on the knives, the terror, the screams. Baker listened for a warning from Abel. None came. The other one was silent too. The only voice

he heard was his own. It reminded him that the hour was
late and that he needed a quiet place to rest and to stay.
It said he wanted very much to stay. With her.

His expression must have told her that. She moved
quickly toward him as he crossed the threshold and
closed the door behind him. Tanner Burke stopped
inches away, her hands raised toward his shoulders but
not touching him.

"I . . . I don't want to make you uncomfortable," she
said, swallowing back a hot feeling that welled in her
throat. "Just so you're . . ."

"Close." He nodded. "I know the feeling."

In Greenwich, forty miles north, Tina Baker sat bolt upright in the dark of her bedroom. It had come again.

She looked at the illuminated clock by her bedside.
Almost one in the morning. An hour since the last feeling
came. But this time was different. Not scary like before.
No knives and wet leaves and yelling. This one was all
warm and neat. Exciting neat. Like when you see your
best friend after a long time and she's just as laughing
glad to see you. Daddy? Daddy's with a friend of mine?

No, that isn't right. It's a grownup. It's somebody
pretty and it's okay for Daddy to be with her because he
knows her and I know her and . . . The television! Tina
felt something about the television. What? Well, turn it
on, dummy.

She slid her legs from beneath the light blanket and
dropped her good leg to the floor. With both hands gripping the bedpost, she pulled herself upright and then
held on, biting her lip, waiting for the blood to sear
through her other foot. She counted ten seconds and
then pressed the injured foot against the carpet. Tina
walked the five paces to the dresser on which the television sat. It was working, she thought. The more she tried
to keep the foot from knowing that it hurt her, the less it
seemed to try.

The set snapped on, washing the room in an instant
blue light. Tina had no idea what she was looking for. A

Kojak rerun? That was on Channel 5. Channel 4. Hurry. She clicked the changer one stop. Clairol Nice 'n' Easy. The end of a Clairol commercial. She waited. The commercial faded and there was Johnny Carson saying goodnight to a couch full of guests. Was it one of the guests? No. She didn't even know them. The commercial. It was something about the commercial . . . she thought.

One by one, she scanned the other channels just in case. There was nothing. Just movies. Tina reached for the remote control unit, which she kept on the set itself. She refused to use it from her bed. The set and the room went black.

She retraced her five paces. Daddy? I couldn't find it. Was it the Clairol commercial?

Tina sank deeply into her bed, her blanket hugged up against her chin. That was a good one, she smiled. That was a really good one.

A long crosstown block from the Plaza, where Sixth Avenue dissolved into a northbound road that snaked through Central Park, a near-frantic Michael Biaggi struggled to collect his thoughts. That he'd lost Baker and the girl was the least of his problems. Anyone could lose a tail in Central Park. Baker would turn up. Sooner or later, he'd turn up at the St. Moritz.

But how would he explain the rest of it? How would he explain Baker finding that one particular punk in the whole goddamned city of New York? And if Baker meant to find the kid, why was he so damned surprised when the kid said his name? How do you explain that? And how would he explain just lying there watching it happen when he could have stopped it? Tortora would cut his heart out if he knew. But what was he supposed to do? Shoot Baker? Then Duncan Peck would have had his ass.

The answer, he thought, is don't explain. Don't explain because you didn't even know. Let Harrigan figure out what the kid was doing in there. Let Harrigan find his name in the wallet. You never looked. Harrigan will know you were just as surprised as he. Christ, he thought miserably, how did you ever get into shit this deep.

Biaggi peered onto Central Park South from behind the high stone pillars that marked the roadway entrance. The blue Oldsmobile was still there. He could see Harrigan's arm on the . . . Biaggi stepped back. A uniformed policeman had stopped on the sidewalk and was looking over Harrigan's car. Now he was approaching Harrigan, shining a light on him. Good, he thought. It'll give Harrigan something else to think about besides trying to read my mind every time I blink twice.

The policeman bent low to read the card Connor Harrigan held in the flashlight's beam. Even at a distance, Biaggi could see the anger and frustration in the older man's face. But the policeman seemed satisfied. He straightened, touched his cap, and continued toward Fifth Avenue at an easy pace. Biaggi waited until the foot cop had passed the Park Lane and was halfway to the Plaza fountain, then dashed across the street and slid into the passenger seat next to Connor Harrigan. Harrigan was still fuming at his luck.

"What's the big deal?" asked the young man in the gray raincoat. Biaggi wiped a mixture of rain and sweat from his face. "You flashed a card, right? All the cop knows is that a fed is working his precinct."

Harrigan sucked noisily on his pipe. "If that cop has any career smarts, he will now call his sergeant who will call his captain. In fifteen minutes, they'll be down here putting a glass to us in case we're close to a bust they can get a piece of. What if one gets lucky and spots Jared Baker?"

"On a fugitive want from Connecticut?" Biaggi began to relax. "That's a hell of a long shot."

"So were the '69 Mets," grumped Harrigan. "Anyway, what about this girl Baker found? Wherever she is, Baker figures to be with her."

"If she ever got out of the park. That maniac might have left her all carved up someplace just like the other two."

"Baker's no maniac," Harrigan said quietly.

"You didn't see him work."

Harrigan chose not to correct him.

"I mean," Biaggi went on, "one minute he looks like Joe Normal out for an evening stroll, and the next he's taking those two bums like they were Girl Scouts. And he's methodical, you know? Like he's trained for years. Like he knows he can do whatever he wants and they can't do shit back to him. Even when he had a knife hanging out of his hip."

"He's had no training." Harrigan frowned at the thought of Baker being wounded. How bad? Bad enough to make him hole up? Don't hole up, Baker. Stay on track. Keep moving so old Uncle Connor can see who you flush.

"Like hell, with due respect."

"What?" Harrigan had stopped listening.

"Training," Biaggi said. "Down at the Farm, I graduated second place in unarmed combat and first in silent killing. But I have to tell you, I don't think I could have taken Baker without an ax."

Harrigan stretched and yawned. "I know Baker from the minute he was born," he said. "He grew up in a box right here in the apple. He went to school, played some sports, got a job, got married, and bought his own box up in the burbs. For a living, he pushes laundry soap. For kicks, he draws pictures and sails around on a little boat. For real excitement, he skis down hills. That's it. Never in any service. Never any training. Not the kind you mean."

Harrigan cracked the window and relit his pipe, gazing thoughtfully through the smoke that spread across the windshield. "Back to the girl. On the radio, you said she looked familiar."

"I didn't get that good a look. Middle, late twenties. Dark hair. Very sharp, and I think I've seen her more than once. Not on the job, though. I'd remember."

"An actress or a model?"

"Maybe."

"Would it help if you heard a name?"

"I don't know. Yeah. Maybe."

Harrigan chose not to comment on the clarity of Biaggi's reply. He reached for the radiophone and punched out a number. "Listen, Katy, this is Connor. Call up somebody, wake up somebody, who works for an outfit called the Celebrity Register. I'm looking for what youngish, brunette, good-looking actress is in town. She's probably staying in the East Fifties or Sixties, but give me everybody. Also, I had to flash my ID for a street cop from the Sixth Precinct. I told him we're staking out a hotel where some bad paper's been showing up. If anyone checks, you confirm that and tell them it's strictly little league, okay? . . . We'll be here, darlin'."

"I thought Kate was inside the hotel." Biaggi tried to make his question sound casual. He didn't like giving wrong information to Duncan Peck.

"Baker got his own girl." Harrigan shrugged. "I sent Mulgrew back to Central."

Biaggi patted his raincoat and took a breath. "Oh," he said, "speaking of ID, I took the watches and wallets off those two that Baker chopped up."

"What did you do that for?" Harrigan looked at him.

Biaggi blinked. "Mostly to dirty things up so it looks like something else."

"You got good instincts." But Harrigan saw an odd light in Biaggi's eyes. "What's the other part? The part that's left over when you say 'mostly'?"

"I got curious. Those two weren't street bums or junkies. Good clothes, good watches." He fished out the wallets and held them in his hand, the watchbands hanging from one finger. "You want a look?"

Harrigan shook his head. "Toss them over the first bridge we cross."

"Even the cash? I mean, there's got to be money in these."

"You saying you want to keep it?"

"No, but it's wasteful. Maybe the poor box, even, down at St. Patrick's."

"St. Patrick hasn't seen any poor people since he opened on Fifth Avenue. Deep-six it."

Biaggi fumbled with the one that had blood on it

and riffled to the credit cards and papers of the one called Sumo. "The fat one is Warren H. Bagnold of Seventy-three Cedar Lane in Bronxville, New York. See, I told you. And here's a membership card for the Westchester Restaurant Group Dining Club. That's money up around there, right?"

"The Westchester Restaurant Group is also Mob." There was a quiet hum in the back of Harrigan's head like the buzz of a shorting wire.

Biaggi was relaxing again. "Warren doesn't know from Mobs. He just eats. Except he's going to eat through a tube for a while if he makes it at all. This one's from the guy called Jace." The other billfold was an ostrich-hide from Dunhill. Biaggi's hand trembled slightly. He slipped it open. "This one's also Bronxville. John C. Tortor . . ." He allowed the name to die on his lips.

Harrigan jerked, disbelieving, then slid the wallet from Biaggi's fingers. Involuntarily, Biaggi wiped his hands against his raincoat.

"Holy sweet Jesus," Harrigan whispered. The wire was beginning to smoke. With his thumb, he folded back the plastic files of photographs and credit cards. Most of the cards were in the name of John C. Tortora. J. C. . . . That's the Jace, he guessed. Other cards, however, were courtesy cards. A special parking permit issued by the local police and an accounting number for an Italian-American social club bore the name of Domenic Tortora. Harrigan folded the wallet shut and placed it lightly on the dash.

"Domenic Tortora *is* the Westchester Restaurant Group, Michael, among many other things," he said quietly. "And that was his little boy you left out there."

"What do you mean, I left—" Biaggi caught himself. Damnit! He was almost sure Harrigan was laying bait. Maybe not. Harrigan seemed bothered by more than who the kid was.

"This is beginning to stink, Michael. This is too goddamned much of a coincidence."

"What coincidence?" Biaggi affected indifference.

"What you got here is two punks who get their kicks prowling Central Park at night because cops don't go in there and sometimes stupid civilians do. They see a girl and they figure they'll rip off a piece of ass. Except the way it works out, one local Mob loses one trainee who's probably a psycho anyway. The punk has to be related to somebody, right? Why not Tortora?"

"Relax, Michael." Harrigan's bright and ambitious special assistant was suddenly talking nonsense.

"And what was I supposed to do out there? Give the little bastard mouth-to-mouth in case his old man had connections?"

"Michael," Harrigan said calmly, "let us pass over your Christian duty for the moment. This very evening, I pointed out two of Tortora's known thugs wandering about the Warwick Hotel. Then, when Domenic Tortora's only son is revealed to be the victim of our very own Jared Baker, you act like there could be no possible connection."

"It could still be . . ." Biaggi thought better of it.

"And the other lad in Connecticut. The one Baker maimed to start off this whole business. Do you recall who the father of that one was?"

"Yeah." He nodded. "Some hack judge from the Stamford Superior Court."

"Not some hack judge, Michael. Tortora's hack judge. The man whose murder caused Baker to take flight. Curious, isn't it?"

Biaggi opened his mouth to comment, but Connor Harrigan waved him into silence. He needed a minute to back up. What did he know? He knew that, murder warrant or not, there was hardly anyone who believed that Baker had killed the old judge. Yet the warrant is kept alive. Why? To remind Baker that he's a fugitive? To keep him from coming back? There's a thought.

Then there are Tortora's friends. Mobsters. They had been looking for Baker for a year and a half. Not looking hard, especially. Not even as hard as they'd look for someone who stiffed one of Tortora's loan sharks. But looking. The interest in Baker was there, all right, but it certainly didn't have the smell of a contract. More like keeping tabs on him. How about it, Baker? Why is it important that one dog or another keeps nipping at your heels? Why, before tonight, would Tortora even care? To avenge some batty old judge? Hardly. If anything, Bellafonte was becoming an embarrassment to him. Which, incidentally, makes Tortora a prime suspect in his murder. But if that's so, why doesn't Tortora just close the circle by putting an end to the fugitive Jared Baker? Do you know, Baker? You don't, do you? So why would you tempt fate so outrageously by grinding up Tortora's son? The answer, I think, is that you wouldn't. You don't know who that was, do you, Baker?

And speaking of nipping dogs, the word is that old Duncan Peck has been busy strengthening his bench of late. Telling people who owe him one that he might need a favor soon. Dropping hints that his old friend Connor Harrigan might be selling out or losing his grip or both. What's he afraid of, Baker? What is it he thinks I'm getting too close to? The fact is, between you and me, that I don't know much of anything. Just pieces. I know that Sonnenberg is salting spooks all over the country, but I don't know why. I don't know what Tortora's interest is. I don't even know what Duncan Peck's interest is beyond what he told me. Only that there's much more. With Duncan Peck, there's always much more. But I don't have to know all these things, Baker, because what I do know is you. I'm getting to know you better every day.

"Connor?" Biaggi rolled down the window to clear out some smoke.

"Yeah?"

"So what do we do? Do we toss this stuff or not?"

"We don't toss it. We . . ." Harrigan looked past Biaggi's worried face toward the dark, wet treeline. He listened. "You hear anything?"

"Yelling." Biaggi bit his lip. "Yeah, screaming. I think Warren's discovered his suppository."

"Sounds that way."

"Well? Do we do anything?"

Harrigan considered for a moment. "Yeah," he said.

"Go into the St. Moritz and call nine-eleven from the lobby. Tell the cop who answers that you're a guest there and you hear screaming from Central Park, like somebody's getting killed. You got change? You don't want the desk clerk remembering that you—"

"I know, I know." Biaggi produced a quarter from his pocket and reached for the door latch. "What about the wallets?"

"Let me think about that," he said, reaming out his pipe. "Let me think about a lot of things."

Biaggi hesitated, just for a beat, his eyes on the billfolds. There was fear in his expression and Harrigan saw it.

Her breath was coming soft and deep. Baker reached for her glass before it could slip from her fingers.

Tanner had changed her clothes. The torn and soiled garments from the park lay in a wastebasket. She wore instead a full-length robe of Oriental silk. It was green with muted gold embroidery and it buttoned almost to her chin. She'd wanted to shower. She'd wanted to scrub and soak for hours to wipe away even the memory of those two men touching, but this other man would be gone if she had. The robe was enough for now. It was clean and warm. And the white wine from room service was making her even warmer.

From a long way off, she heard the man . . . What did she decide to call him? Peter. Peter was whispering to her. Now his hands were on her shoulders and he was steering her gently through her bedroom door. She let her body fall across the deep quilt, all but one hand, which held fast to the hem of Peter's jacket. Stay, she asked him in her mind. She was too deeply tired to find the words that might make him stay close to her. Her fingers tightened on his jacket.

After a long moment, Baker eased himself onto the three feet she'd left for him at the edge of the bed. He smiled, and lightly ran his fingers over her back and shoulders until her sleep was sound.

Now Baker sat against two pillows in a darkened room, fully dressed but for his shoes. Feeling her warmth rising toward him, he reached across her body and folded the quilt over her. She twitched and was still.

Baker felt strangely at peace. Almost happy. The men outside seemed far away. It seemed as though there were more than before. There was a policeman. There was something about him. He thought of asking Charley, but he quickly put that thought aside. He did not want Charley here. Anyway, the men outside would keep. Until morning.

Tomorrow he would ask Charley why that one in the park seemed to know him. And how Tanner Burke just happened to turn up here. These questions bothered him, but they too could wait. For now he was warm and safe. And he wasn't lonely.

Baker yawned and looked down at the softly snoring shape beneath the quilt and shook his head in a kind of amused wonder. It seemed so unreal. A fantasy. Every man's fantasy. Rescue the beautiful lady and she takes you gratefully to her bed. Sort of.

He made a face. He wondered how much Everyman would envy Jared Baker tonight if they also had to be Jared Baker tomorrow. Not many, he thought. Most might wish they could be like Abel from time to time. Sometimes even like Charley. But not like Jared Baker. Being Jared Baker was just too damned empty.

Tanner's body twitched and tightened. He could hear her fingernails scraping against the sheets. She was dreaming, he knew. And it was an action dream. A tense dream. Baker hoped it was not about the park and wondered whether he should wake her. Maybe stir her just enough that she could switch to another channel. He saw one hand rise and push from beneath the quilt. It was a motion of fending off. Better give her a nudge. He placed one hand on her shoulder and shook it gently. It seemed to work. The fending hand relaxed, then reached back and rested along his hip. Baker wanted to move it but he waited. It was too close to the puncture wound from Sumo's knife, the wound he deserved for interfering with

Abel. The cut had closed, but it was not quite healed and was still tender to the touch. He had not been Abel long enough for it to heal.

Her fingers stiffened and her body followed, as if she knew suddenly that the body she was touching was not her own. Baker seized the hand too late. Her nails dug deep, tearing at the soft scab. She spun upright and lashed wildly at his face. Her lungs sucked in air.

"Tanner, it's all right." Baker struggled to keep his voice even. It didn't help. She was not yet awake, and Baker's voice was muffled by her own gasps and by the squeaking and knocking of the bed. She didn't know him yet. He brushed aside her biting fingers and grabbed her by the forearm. She drew in a new breath that he knew would come out a scream.

"Tanner!" He slapped her.

The blow, reluctant and with little force, had an effect of less than a second. Again her free hand lunged at him and again another intake of breath. He seized her by the neck and threw her down on the pillow, knowing that he was Jace or Sumo in her mind and detesting the picture that must have been there. His body dropped across her heaving chest, and his hand clamped over her mouth as her fingernails tore at his scalp and neck. The nail of one thumb found the soft flesh above his collarbone and it hurt him. Abel sprung into his mind and he fought to send him away, lest the pain make him slip and say Abel's name. He lay there enduring it. Think of Charley. Charley would be better. Charley would accept the hurt and he wouldn't hurt her back. Baker winced and shook Charley away too. Charley would make her sick.

"Oh, my God!" she cried suddenly, going rigid. The clawing hand relaxed and flew to his cheek. "Peter . . . Oh, my God, I thought . . ."

"It's all right." He tried to keep the pain from his voice. "Give yourself a minute. It was just a dream." He eased her hand away and reached for the light on the nightstand.

"Oh, dear Lord!" She sat upright when she saw the row of bleeding welts that curved across his neck. The tears welled again. "Here," she said, tugging at the arm that supported him. "Roll over onto your stomach. Let me see what I have to put on those."

"I'd better get up," he said, resisting her. "There's . . . Don't get upset, but there's an old cut on my hip that opened up. I'll get blood on your quilt."

Startled, Tanner pushed aside the quilt and saw the smear of blood between his fingers. She looked stricken.

"You didn't do it. It's a few days old. I knocked the scab off, that's all."

"Let me get something." She sprang from the bed and half-ran to the bathroom.

Baker watched her. He raised himself on both elbows and watched her reflection in the mirrored bathroom door as she rummaged through a leather kit. He knew that he was staring. Her body, what he could see of it beneath the robe, was smoothly muscled. An athlete's body. But there was more to Tanner Burke than that, he thought. She had a way of carrying her head high even while looking down. Graceful. Strong without being mannish. Like a dancer. Baker's eyes fell upon a breast that was partly bared. Buttons, those little looping kind, must have torn away as she struggled. He tried to look away but could not. And as he watched her, his admiration began to slide into an ache of longing. God, she was lovely. And so very nice. Oh, Baker, how do you know what she's like? You want her to be nice. You want her to like you a little. Then what? Baker shrugged, and his mouth relaxed into a tiny smile. It was only Baker talking to Baker. Sometimes he had to stop and think to be sure. But what's the matter with wanting her to be like me? And not just a little. It doesn't mean I'll do anything stupid. Charley? What does she think about all this? What does she think about me?

"Charley?"

"nothing."

"How can she be thinking nothing? Look at her."

"nothing about you. she doesn't care about you."

"Charley, why did you say that? Anyone can see that she's feeling something. Even if it's only pity or fear or

maybe gratitude. Why would you say she doesn't care about me?"

Tanner's image ripped from the mirror as she appeared in the bathroom doorway. A dampened towel was in one hand and her travel kit in the other. She drew up, startled, at the sight of Baker's face now curiously slack and flaccid. Glazed eyes that seemed to be looking through her . . . She blinked and it was gone. There was only the gentle face she knew, shaking jerkily as one would clear away a daydream.

"Take off your pants," she said, tugging at his pocket. "I'll run some cold water on the blood so it doesn't set. The shirt too."

When Baker hesitated, she set her kit on the bed and reached for the buttons of his shirt. He closed his hand over hers and looked at her. Her hand tensed.

"Peter, I don't think . . . ," she stammered. "Tonight . . . all that's happened . . . I just can't . . ."

Baker pushed to his feet, embarrassed. "I didn't mean anything like that." He blanched. "I just meant I could do it myself." He walked to the bathroom, stripping his shirt as he went, leaving Tanner Burke furious with herself for misunderstanding his touch, for making him say that he didn't want her.

Baker was at the sink. The lighter stains of his shirt washed out quickly. Next, he removed his trousers and, fingering the knife cut he didn't want Tanner to see, held the bloodstain beneath the running tap. The thinned blood flowed as if a vein had opened. But it went away. From the cloth and from his fingers, it mixed with the swirling water and rushed to the drain. Baker turned his head and shut his eyes. It was not the blood. It was the drain. Sometimes looking at a drain could make the iron door dissolve. Think of something else, Baker. Think of Tanner Burke. Think of how she could be here. Think of how, of all the people that might have been in the park, Abel led you to Tanner Burke. How could he have found her? She couldn't have been thinking your name. She doesn't know you. So, it was the other one. The one, Jace, who spoke your name. That's how Abel found him.

But why? And still, why would Tanner Burke have been there? Abel? What's going on, Abel? And why is Charley lying to me all of a . . .

"Peter?" She was standing at his side, her fingers buttoning the Oriental robe. If anything, the act made her more alluring as the green silk tightened like a sheath over her body. "Peter, I'm sorry." She let her eyes say the rest. "Come on." She took his arm. "Let me clean you up a little."

Soon it was Baker who drowsed under a light cool touch. Tanner had cleaned the wound that was just below his hip joint, and she soothed it with a layer of zinc oxide. This she covered with a fold of gauze bandage. Turning to the scratch marks, she softened them first with a hot, moist towel and then touched a styptic pencil to the places where the skin had been broken. The ridge of welts had already reduced, and those nerve endings too were drifting off to sleep.

"Peter?" She whispered the name she had chosen for him.

"Ummmm?"

"Isn't there anything you can tell me about yourself?"

Baker opened one eye. "You'd have trouble understanding, Tanner. We're both better off if you don't know much."

"Would you be in danger if I knew more?"

"I think so. Yes."

"Well, how about just personal things? You're not married, are you?"

". . . No."

"You hesitated just then."

"I'm not married, I promise."

"Divorced?"

"No."

"Never met the right girl?"

He rolled over and looked at her. "I did. She was killed."

"I'm very sorry."

"I've gotten over it."

"And whoever killed her, they're after you now? Or are you after them?"

"No, Tanner." He turned to sit up. "It's nothing like that. There isn't any connection between that and anything else." It was not quite a lie. Sarah's death had everything to do with what he'd become. But it was no more than the first link in a chain whose pieces seemed to form a circle going nowhere.

"But you loved her?"

"Yes, very much."

"Is that why you were reluctant to stay with me? You thought I just wanted a body?" Baker put his fingers to her lips.

"She's dead and gone, Tanner. One thing has nothing to do with the other."

Tanner Burke was silent for several moments, not thinking exactly, rather waiting for her emotions to settle and separate. The park was settling fastest. It seemed so distant. But this man ... There was something familiar about him. Like they'd met, although she knew they hadn't. It was more as though they shared the same friend. An odd thought, she knew. No reason for it. And also, from someplace very far away, she felt another presence. A terrible presence. For a moment there, in the bathroom, she almost knew what it was. But then another man was listening to her ... watching her ... a man she didn't know ... but he was familiar too. Peter? No, it wasn't Peter ... or Harold or whoever.

"Peter." She touched him. "After you ... leave in the morning, will I ever see you again?"

"I don't know. I hope so."

"Do you feel anything for me?"

"Tanner ..." The question thrilled Baker, but he could not show it.

"I'm sorry. Forget I asked you that."

"I do feel something. You're a very special woman."

"How?" she said, fishing.

"You're very accomplished, for one thing."

She seemed disappointed by the answer. "You mean because I'm an actress? Peter, that doesn't make me special. I was just a skier who was asked to be in a commercial for ski clothes. That led to more commercials and then a small TV part and then some bigger parts. But what I am, still, is a woman and I'm still a skier too. A good one. If anyone's going to think I'm special, it ought to be for that."

Baker let out a sigh. "I wish you'd try to get over being hung up on that actress business."

"I just didn't want it to matter. I want to see you again."

"It matters, Tanner," he said kindly. "If you were a waitress or a doctor or a plain girl skier, I know I'd try to see you. I'd try hard. But like it or not, you're famous. You attract attention."

"Which you can't afford." She dropped her eyes to his chest. Baker did not answer. "What you did," she asked, "was it so terrible?"

"It was like tonight in some ways. I hurt someone. I didn't want any part of it, but it happened."

She raised her eyes to his face and reached out to brush aside a curl that blocked part of it. It was a good face. Eyes that were kind and honest, with tiny lines of humor at their edges. She lifted off his aviator glasses. There was no enlargement when she did that. Glass, she realized. Plain tinted glass. It had no purpose other than to mute the vivid gray-green of his eyes. She studied the eyes. There was a scar near one and another near his chin. One was old, perhaps from boyhood. How hard it was to imagine this ghostlike man as a boy. The other scar was fresh. Perhaps from that other night he spoke of.

"I've been trying not to ask you about that," she said. "About the park, I mean. Partly, I guess I just don't want to think about it. But there's more. I'm looking at a very gentle and sensitive man. What I see doesn't fit at all with the way you hurt those two."

"That wasn't a time for being gentle. This is." Baker could see that if the answer didn't satisfy her, the last part pleased her. For the moment. But tomorrow would be different. Tomorrow, she'd look in the New York tabloids for news of the two men and she'd know what Abel had done to them. The stories would use words like *maim* and *impale* and *disfigure*. The words describing him would be *maniac* or *beast* or *animal*. It's not that she'd feel pity for those two. Not with the memory of what they tried to do to her. What she'd feel would be shock and disgust. And she would be afraid of him. No, he would not try to see her.

"Will you promise that I'll see you again?"

Her question startled him. "I'll try," he lied. "I'll look for a way."

She looked deeply into him for a sign that he meant it. That he would really try. She saw, she thought, that he wanted to see her. But she knew he wouldn't try.

"Then I'll find you, damnit." Tanner rose abruptly and stepped away from his reaching hand. She took three quick steps to the chair where his jacket was draped and snatched the American Airlines envelope from his pocket. She opened it with a flip of her thumb.

She sagged. "Philip A. Metzger," she read. "That's not your right name either, is it?"

"No, it isn't."

"Los Angeles!" She brightened. "This is a return connection to Los Angeles. My God, we're neighbors."

"Tanner, that ticket means I'd planned to end up in Los Angeles. It doesn't mean I still will. Certainly not on the date you just memorized."

"Shit!" Tanner Burke threw down the ticket. "How can you not trust me?" she flared. "How can you think I'll do anything to harm you after tonight?"

Baker rose slowly to his feet, glancing toward the trousers that hung on the bathroom door, drying. "Tanner, I'd better let you get some sleep."

Tanner Burke stepped toward him and pressed a hand flat against his chest. "You're not going anywhere," she said quietly, "and I want an answer."

"For Pete's sake, Tanner." Baker threw up his arms. "Think what you're asking. You're asking me to bet at least my freedom on the emotions of a badly shaken up woman who's known me all of four hours. You're already just a little bit afraid of me and by tomorrow night you might despise me."

"Dumb again. To say nothing of sexist. What's 'woman' got to do with it?"

He shook his head helplessly.

"And, whatever your name is, I've known you a lot longer than four hours. I don't know how long, or how I know, but you do, don't you?"

Again, Baker was startled. He could only shake his head and hope that the confusion on his face would persuade her that she must be wrong. Abel kicked. Be careful, the kick meant. Get out of here. You don't need her, Baker.

"And I'll never despise you," she said, touching him. "I'm not afraid of you either."

Baker didn't answer. She saw the tear in his right eye and thought it meant sorrow. "I care about you, Peter," she said. And I care about you, Baker thought. And God, I'd like to stay. But you just don't know what it could cost you.

"Will you promise," she asked, "that you'll call me? You'll know how I feel if you call me."

"Yes," he answered. "Yes, I'll know." Charley would know.

"You'll call?"

Baker nodded. She picked up the ticket envelope once more and groped for a pen in the desk.

"Write your number backward," he said. "Add any two digits to the beginning and the end."

She studied him for a moment, then wrote her private number as he specified. "You really have to be so careful? In everything you do?"

"For just a while," Baker lied. "Now get some sleep, Tanner." He stepped toward the open bathroom door and lifted his still-damp trousers.

"Peter?" she called.

Baker turned.

"Please stay."

"It's better if I . . ."

"Please stay." Her fingers loosed the buttons at her throat. Then they moved slowly to those beneath.

"You don't have to do that, Tanner."

"I want you to stay." Her voice caught. Baker crossed to her and took her shoulders gently.

"We'll both just get some sleep," he whispered.

The buzz of the Oldsmobile's radiophone shook Connor Harrigan from his train of thought. He heard sirens now too. And the klaxon of an ambulance. The shrieks from the park had weakened and stopped. Harrigan slid the microphone from its hook. "Yes, darlin'," he said.

"Mr. Harrigan," came Kate Mulgrew's voice, "did you say that uniformed policeman was from the Sixth Precinct?"

"That's what his collar said."

"You're not in the Sixth. That's way down around Greenwich Village. And there isn't any foot patrol either on Central Park South this late."

"Any chance he's on loan from the Sixth?"

"Not unless you have a parade or a rock concert going on up there, Mr. Harrigan. He shouldn't be there— Can you hold, Mr. Harrigan? There's another call."

Harrigan sighed and eased his seat into a reclining position.

"Ah, Baker," he said aloud, "it gets curiouser and curiouser, doesn't it? We now have a cop who's not a cop. That's on top of a Baker who is not a Baker, two muggers who are not muggers, and an oddly nervous Michael Biaggi who is . . . I don't know what Michael is. That Michael serves two masters has never been in serious doubt. Not if I know tidy old Duncan Peck. But could there possibly be more than two? And how many phone calls could the lad be making right this minute?"

"Mr. Harrigan?"

"I'm alone, by the way, Katy darlin'."

"Hi, Connor." Her voice smiled. "That was your man Dugan over at the Warwick. There's no sign of Baker, but he says the two hoods who were prowling around the place have been joined by a third. They seem to be holding a strategy meeting. Dugan says the new shooter is Stanley Levy."

"Stanley's not a shooter. He's an ice pick, Katy."

"Whatever. Do we assume he's after Mr. Baker?"

"Yes, Katy. I'm afraid we must. Let me have just a moment, darlin'."

Connor Harrigan laid the telephone mike across his leg and squinted through the film of moisture on his window. "Mr. Baker," he said softly to the night, "did I mention that it was getting curiouser? Yes, of course I did. The field keeps getting bigger. We now have Mr. Stanley Levy, who is smaller, older, and balder than yours truly and who commands a handsome retainer for the employment of his ice pick and his tenaciousness. Likes to leave calling cards. Such as the one that pinned the hands of old Rent-a-judge Bellafonte. Mr. Levy's presence at this particular starting gate has at least two meanings. First, he knows you're here, which raises other obvious and vexing questions such as how he knows. Second, we must assume that Mr. Tortora's interest in you has definitely been enkindled anew. It should positively blossom when he discovers how disagreeable you were toward his little boy."

Harrigan brought the phone back to his ear. "Katy, is there anyone there who can relieve you?"

"Janet's here. She's working the darkroom."

"How would you like to be a Sixth Avenue hooker for a few hours?"

"I'm getting just a bit long in the tooth for that sort of thing, Connor. But if it's dark enough, a dollar is a dollar."

"Sorry, Katy. No actual partying, unless of course you should come upon a fine-looking Irishman sitting in an Oldsmobile." He smiled. "Otherwise, what I want you to do is patrol Sixth Avenue from the Warwick to the park. If Levy moves in this direction, I want to know that. Bring a transceiver."

"Sure, Connor. Anything else?"

"Now that you ask . . ." Harrigan pulled a Kleenex

from the visor and wiped the brown dampness from the inside of the windshield. "If you see an opportunity, Katy, and you can do it neatly, I'd like you to kill Mr. Levy and leave him in a doorway."

"I'll bring something quiet."

"Be well, Katy love."

Harrigan put the phone on its hook. "Remember what Thoreau said, Mr. Baker? He said, 'Simplify. Always simplify.' "

She lay pressed against him. Her head and one arm upon his chest. Neither had moved since the light switched off. Neither slept. She was not afraid while they were touching. She felt warm and safe and cared about, and the night stayed far away. Now and then she felt him shudder and each time sink more deeply into the quilted bed. It was as if a hurt was being slowly drained away. She was glad. Someday, she thought, they'd make love. They would. Away from here and on a different night. And they'd be able to see tomorrow. And next week.

"Peter?"

"Yes, lovely lady."

"Do you ski?"

"Not in your league, but yes."

"Suppose everything else were to work out. Would you go skiing with me someday?"

"How does Sun Valley sound?" he asked dreamily. "Or maybe Klosters. I hear there are parts of the Swiss Alps where you can ski for twenty miles." She answered with a purring sound.

"But how about you, Peter? What are your special things?"

"Oh, I like to sail," he said. "Especially racing one designs, but I haven't in a while. I play some racquetball to stay in shape, and otherwise the things I like are pretty simple. Walking in the snow, tailgating at football games, and I . . ." He almost said "paint." That would have been too close. He knew that he shouldn't have mentioned sailing either. "How about yourself?"

"I have a boat," she answered brightly. "It's a little J-24 that I bought from an actor who moved East. He taught me to sail kind of. Not enough to race. She's my get-away-and-be-quiet machine, even if all I do is sleep on her and listen to the wind. Her name is *Lady Liz.*"

"Liz?"

"It's my first name. Elizabeth Tanner Burke. My parents call me that. And most of the kids I grew up with in Boulder."

"Liz," he repeated, nodding. "It suits you. Tanner isn't quite as soft. But I guess Tanner is a better name for an actress."

"There's that, I guess." She yawned. "But I used Tanner on ski race rosters since I was five. Tanner's my mother's maiden name. Beth Tanner. She was a pretty hot downhiller and I wanted to keep up a tradition." She squeezed him. "Say 'Liz' again."

"Liz. Liz Burke." Baker, too, listened to the sound.

"I like the way you say it." She lifted her head to see the blur of his face. "What about yours?" she asked. "Can you tell me at least your real first name? Just the name other people call you?"

She tried not to let it hurt her that he hesitated. "Can that really worry you? I mean, if I knew your name was Jack or Tom, I'd have at least that much of a real person to remember when I think about you. How could telling me your first name hurt you?"

"It's just that it's an unusual name."

"Throckmorton? Abercrombie? Margaret?"

The name formed on his lips and the warning came. Just a tiny spark of pain behind his eye. But the anger was his own when he realized that Abel had been there all this time. What if he had made love to her? Damn it. Would Abel have shared in that? Abel kicked again.

No, he thought. Abel wouldn't care. All he'd think about is me not getting too close. You can go to hell, Abel.

"Did you say something?"

"Jared," he answered. "Liz, my name is Jared."

"Jared," she repeated. "It's a good name for you, Jared," she said again. And soon she was asleep.

But not Baker. There were too many new and happy thoughts. Awake, he could choose his dreams. He could play a long ski run on the ceiling and he could see Liz Burke ahead, waiting for him to catch up, and she had Tina with her. My God, they look like sisters. Liz must have been teaching Tina. Teaching the leg to work again better than ever.

And now he saw a beach. He felt Liz Baker's . . . Liz Burke's hand in his and a warm August surf brushing over bare feet. And then a boat. He was at the helm, and he saw Liz on the foredeck dropping the genoa as the boat coasted to an anchorage. It was a cove. A place to take a swim and then pour wine and grill steaks over the stern. They'd watch the sun go down. Baker's eyes grew heavy. In no more than a blink, the boat was different. Bigger. Oh, damn, he thought. Now he was on Sonnenberg's boat and Liz was gone and where was Sonnenberg? He's here somewhere. Sonnenberg's always here. Listening. Watching. Recording. For a week and then another week. Every day. That's enough, Doctor. I want to get off this boat.

"They'll kill you or imprison you, Jared. Be patient. I hope to have news for you soon. Glorious news."

"I want to see Tina. I'm going to find a way to see Tina."

"Come to my home, Jared. We'll leave the boat and you'll stay at my home. It's not far. I have a surprise for you there, Jared. And you can call Tina. There's a way that you can talk to her from my home."

Baker rubbed his eyes and opened them. Liz? Where was Liz? He tried to sit up so he could turn on the light and look for her, but a weight pressed him back. She was still there. She'd been so close against him that it was hard to tell where her body ended and his began. She was there. For now. But so, in his way, was Sonnenberg.

For now.

6

It was only a month since he'd found Baker. But such a month. What was Ben Meister's expression? The mother lode. Yes. Well, we'll know in the morning, won't we. In the morning, Mr. Baker, you may take one giant step. May I, Doctor? Yes, you may, Baker. And once we both find out what you're made of, we'll try one giant leap.

Sonnenberg grinned and shivered. The very prospect was making him giddy. Composure, Marcus, he chided himself. Calm yourself. If Mrs. Kreskie sees you excited, she'll be at your door with a bowl of chicken soup, folding down your bed.

Marcus Sonnenberg listened at the door of his bedroom on the second floor. He heard the sound of a television program coming from Baker's room. There were no other noises. Then, satisfied that Mrs. Kreskie had stopped dawdling over the silver service and had either taken herself to bed or gone prowling in the night, he bolted his door from the inside and limped to the larger of two bookcases. There, from a hollowed volume of *The Oxford Book of English Verse,* he chose one of the four entubed Monte Cristo cigars he kept hidden there. He had long since come to terms with the destruction of the book for such a purpose. Shelley, Oscar Wilde, and certainly Kipling would understand completely. John Milton and Alexander Pope, however, and Mrs. Kreskie, who was easily their peer at fussbudgetry, would doubtless visit great scorn upon him for pursuing this secret vice at all, let alone compounding the act with literary vandalism. Odors in the odes, so to speak.

Sonnenberg dragged his stiffened leg to a window that overlooked the darkened twelfth fairway of the Westchester Country Club. Sniffing the cigar at its length and testing its moisture content with gentle pressure from his fingertips, the bearded man eased himself into a bentwood rocker positioned there. He lit his prize slowly with a wooden match and readied himself for an hour of peaceful contemplation.

As the smoke drifted through the open window, his eyes fell upon the small parabolic microphone that sat on a collapsed tripod near the sill. Sonnenberg enjoyed, during idle moments, listening to the chitchat of passing golfers. It was often amusing and sometimes instructive. Sonnenberg like to know his neighbors.

All asleep now, though, he thought. And no one on the golf course except land turtles laying eggs and raccoons eating them. His random thoughts began to focus, for no reason that he knew, on a small but odd event of a fortnight earlier. He'd been listening at his window, headphones over his ears, and peering through a cloud of good Havana toward the twosome on the twelfth tee. A loud *thunk* caused him to blink. The sound came through his feet. A simultaneous "Oh, shit!" came through the headphone from a hundred and seventy yards away and another voice said, "The hell with it, Dunny. Take another one."

Dunny's tee shot, probably attempted with an ill-advised driver, had cleared Sonnenberg's high stockade fence and caromed off the house itself. The doctor silently congratulated himself for opting against aluminum siding, even though the economics were sound enough when compared to the triennial five thousand dollars he paid to Puzo and his two Sicilians. But there were other considerations. One could literally envelop an aluminum-clad home with unseen listening devices. And, as Dunny's errant shot had demonstrated, to protect any investment in siding would have required the education of the entire membership of that silly club as to the physical laws that apply to successfully negotiating a short par four with a dogleg to the right. A three iron at most would likely have stayed in bounds. It would have left the ball in position for a reasonable second shot. And a law requiring the use of a three iron would spare him these seasonal mortar attacks on the roof and walls of his house.

A golf cart purred to a stop outside the stockade fence. Only its surrey top was visible to Sonnenberg. He depressed the platter-shaped microphone and sat back to listen.

The erring golfer had just read aloud a sign on Sonnenberg's fence that said, BEWARE. ATTACK CAT ON PREMISES, and had discovered a small pail of balls that hung from a peg beneath it.

"The sign's just a nice way of saying keep out," said the other man. "If you come through here tomorrow, your ball with be in the bucket."

"I suppose he's had trouble with people climbing the fence," the one called Dunny wondered. Sonnenberg recalled that he was a tall man, over sixty, with a boardroom look about him even dressed in Izods.

"Nope," his partner told him. "No one ever does. Even if you got to the top without breaking your neck, there's a jungle of high rhododendrons on the other side. On top of that, the whole house is electronically rigged like nothing you ever saw. It has electric eyes, pressure plates, silent alarms, klaxons, and hidden cameras. He's even got recorded screams and gunshots that'll scare the hell out of you if you happen to break the wrong beam."

"What is he, a nut?"

"If he is, he's a pleasant enough nut," Dunny's partner answered. Sonnenberg knew this one now. Blair Palmer. Across the street and two houses up. A broker specializing in arbitrage. Two daughters and one son. The son had had a minor homosexual encounter in New York the year before and almost went insane when his erstwhile companion learned his address and began calling him at home demanding "loans." Sonnenberg had played

the tapes for Mrs. Kreskie, who quietly put a lasting stop
to that.

"That's old Doc Sonnenberg," Blair Palmer continued. "He invents all that stuff. Lives there alone except
for a mute housekeeper and some technicians that come
and go."

"How well do you know him?" Dunny asked.

Sonnenberg arched one eyebrow. An odd question
for a golfer newly burdened with a two-stroke penalty
and facing an even more vexing shot to the green.

"Not that well. He throws a party for the neighbors
once a year and that's about it." Palmer glanced back toward the tee and the waiting golfers, who were becoming
restive. "Listen," he urged Dunny, "you better take a
drop right here and then try to lay up short with a seven
iron."

Sonnenberg listened to the soft *wock* of the shot being made and watched the ball soar to Blair Palmer's ap-
plause. It faded past a tall elm and bounded confidently
toward the twelfth green. Sonnenberg's other eyebrow
went up. Very deftly done for a man whose previous shot
was mishit so heroically. He listened to the fading voices
of the two men as the cart pressed a path into the
Karastan fairway and wished he'd had a better look at the
one called Dunny. The thought nipped at Sonnenberg for
the next two weeks.

Probably nothing to it, Sonnenberg decided now.
He reached absently toward the dials of a small black
console that sat on a Parsons table to his left. Still,
Sonnenberg wished that he'd thought to tune in to the
Palmer house that same evening to see what might be
said about Blair Palmer's golf partner. Probably nothing,
though. For the second time in as many weeks,
Sonnenberg dismissed the man called Dunny from his
conscious thought.

He rested one finger on the console's power switch.
What to do? Do I spend another evening listening to
Baker's tapes or do I visit the neighbors for a change.
There's not much more to be learned about Baker. Not
without stirring the soup, and we'll try that tomorrow.

For now, how about listening in to the Dickersons first. They're entertaining, I understand, if the word applies in their case. Allison Dickerson could discourse with equal ignorance on the subjects of Szechuan cookery, post-impressionist art, the care of African violets, and the devotion of her husband, of which he had not a whit. Allison Dickerson. Sounds like Higgledy-Piggledy. I must write a piece of doggerel someday about Allison Dickerson. Perhaps I just did. Higgledy-Piggledy Allison Dickerson, egregiously boring and tiresome twit. Higgledy-Piggledy, Allison Dickerson, who reads *Reader's Digest* for wisdom and wit. What else rhymes? Grit. Warm spit. Split? Now there's a notion. What if I could draw from Allison Dickerson what is there in Baker? What is the counterpoint to a boring woman? An aggressively boring woman? A violently boring woman? A woman who'll tear your head off if you wince at the taste of her Peking duck? Steady, Marcus. And sorry, Jared Baker. I'm just a bit flighty this evening. I hope you'd understand this electronic eavesdropping. A harmless entertainment. One that sometimes has a salutary effect, however, as in the case of young David Palmer. Above all, I simply like to know what's being said of me from house to house. I like to know that I've succeeded in being reclusive without seeming more than a touch eccentric or unduly mysterious. An inventor of electronic exotica is expected to follow a different buzzer, as it were.

Sonnenberg flipped on the switch.

Even if rarely seen, Sonnenberg was a popular neighbor. Somehow, he always managed to know of anniversaries and graduations and other happy events in the lives of the people nearby. A bottle of Mouton Rothschild, for which he was known to have a passion, would appear at their doorsteps with a gracious note that began: "I seem to recall . . ." At Christmastime, each of the local policemen had come to expect a boxed gallon of Chivas Regal and their superiors received some portion of a case of wine. Sonnenberg hoped sincerely that this division did not smack of condescension. There was only so much of the better vintages to be found, and experience, in any case, had shown him that the Scotch would be perceived as the greater gift by the men in uniform. This he accepted reluctantly, convinced that this particular blend of Scotch was genetically undistinguished, pretentious to the point of fraud, and dreadfully overpriced. One neighbor, who was in advertising, had once remarked that if there were neither a Christmas nor a Harlem, there would be no Chivas Regal. The insight delighted Sonnenberg and impressed him with his neighbor's wit. He made a mental note to listen in on more of that man's conversations. But be that as it may, the effect of his holiday remembrances was that his house was regularly patrolled and checked, particularly during his frequent absences.

This too pleased the neighbors. All forms of protection that embraced the Sonnenberg home also embraced their own. Most, in fact, boasted possession of one or more of his security devices, often experimental, and installed by one of the technicians, who often stayed at Sonnenberg's house for weeks, sometimes months, on end. There was never a charge for the service, save the unwitting cost in the coin of privacy as each became a channel on Sonnenberg's console.

Once a year, the neighbors and a handful of local business people would receive a glitteringly formal invitation to cocktails at the Sonnenberg home. It was the party Blair Palmer had mentioned to his friend Dunny. The invitation always came during the holiday season, a time when good will was pandemic and when the baser forms of curiosity were at their lowest ebb. A gift box containing a delicate tree ornament from Tiffany's would invariably accompany the invitation. Some of the neighbors had collected nine of them.

Sonnenberg was a superb and elegant host. He would appear at the door, leaning on his cane with one hand, holding a champagne glass aloft in the other, and he would greet each of his guests, enthusiastically pronouncing each of their names and bowing slightly in the

European manner. If a guest brought a small gift, as did most, he would profess a childlike delight at being remembered. Such a wonderful season, he would say. Such wonderful friends and neighbors. Such a wonderful country.

Although the act of walking was obviously painful for him, Sonnenberg would insist on taking the curious on a tour of his house. Even veteran guests usually followed with equal interest. There was always something new.

The tour presented a portrait of the man. Inside the hall closet, where furs and topcoats would be hung, Sonnenberg first had to push aside a tangle of fishing rods and other gear that had an oft-used look about it. An old wicker creel and a dented tackle box sat conspicuously on the shelf. Polite questions about how they were biting resulted in an immediate visit to Sonnenberg's den, where he would point to a mounted bluefish or sea bass of awesome dimension. Underneath and on top of the mantel, which framed an antique Franklin stove, were two mounted photographs. In one, Sonnenberg posed proudly beside a seven-foot Mako shark on a Montauk weighing dock. In the other, he stood beside a boy of perhaps thirteen whom he identified as his favorite grandson and sometime fishing companion who was now attending school in Switzerland. In truth, Sonnenberg had no notion of the boy's identity.

Passing the mantelpiece, the guests would confront a floor-to-ceiling collection of Sonnenberg's books. They were arranged in groups, the largest being two dozen or more volumes dealing with pre-Columbian art. A single volume lay open on the same shelf, a tasseled bookmark holding flat a color plate that showed an ancient Mayan bird carved in gleaming obsidian. Its beak and the tips of its feathers were of hammered gold so finely blended that they seemed to grow from the stone itself. Photograph courtesy of Dr. Marcus Sonnenberg, read the acknowledgment below the text. The priceless artifact itself sat unpretentiously on a lower shelf, as if it claimed no greater worth than the half-dozen other carvings displayed above and below it.

Another cluster of books dealt with fishing, including a first edition of Walton in a presentation case. A third contained a considerable collection dealing with antique furniture and reproductions. More color plates. The designs of Thomas Chippendale, Duncan Phyfe, George Hepplewhite, and Thomas Sheraton. Inevitably, a guest would show interest in the subject, and Sonnenberg would call attention to the Hepplewhite bookstand that supported the massive Sonnenberg family Bible. He would delight in confessing that the bookstand was not a Hepplewhite at all but the product, time-worn dents and wormholes included, of his basement workshop. A marvelous hobby, he would say. Superb therapy when the mind wearies of circuits and transistors and when the fingers itch to create form rather than function. There is profit enough in alarm systems but precious little humanity. His visitors would answer with rueful smiles and then follow him from the room, usually pausing before a large sepia photograph of several dozen smiling men in combat uniform posing on a brace of Sherman tanks. Someone always stopped and asked about it.

"It was taken just after my outfit entered Aachen," he would say, and a mist of nostalgia would cloud his eyes. "I'd buried that photograph in my attic for years. There was a time when it saddened me because I neither looked nor felt like that adventurous young man anymore. But, remembering all the other grand young men whose bodies were broken or who died in that conflict, I came to look upon it rather as a celebration of life. As that, and as a reminder that chance survivors such as myself ought to see an obligation to justify that survival . . . Goodness, that was pompous of me, wasn't it?"

All would rush to disagree.

"Which one are you, Doctor?" one would ask, his or her fingertips tracing lightly over the montage of faces.

"The one with the beret." He'd point. "The tank commander's arm is around my shoulder. I joined the

Third Army as a scout after I was liberated from a camp near Neufchâteau."

All would nod. "Can't mistake those eyes." It was usually a woman who said that. That and, "You've become much more handsome. Distinguished. The beard makes you look like one of those 1914 archdukes of the Hohenzollerns." This last was once pronounced by Audrey Thronhill, a pretentious boob whose sum knowledge of significant events was drawn from the pages of *Town & Country*.

Nevertheless, Sonnenberg would blush and wave off all compliments. "Come," he'd say abruptly. "Perhaps you'd like to see where the mad inventor works. Or would that be boring of me?"

More disagreement.

So Sonnenberg would lead the small group through his expensively understated living room, past an obviously original Duncan Phyfe sofa, under a probably original Winslow Homer, and by a possibly original Henderson butler's table. They could no longer be sure, having seen evidence of his skill at reproduction. They would line up behind him as he stiffly negotiated the narrow basement steps. As he descended, he'd explain that among the reasons he looked forward to this little entertainment was that it forced upon him the incentive of cleaning up his workshop once a year. Then he would wait while someone complimented him on its tidiness.

It was actually two distinct workshops. His lathe and bandsaw and router table were at one end. A canister vacuum stood at attention, as did a rank of wood chisels that hung from a pegboard. At the other end was a well-lit work area whose centerpiece was a large, flat drafting table. Several pages of dog-eared specification sheets were tacked to one corner and a thick file of catalogues lay close at hand. No tools were in evidence, save several spools of insulated wire and a single transformer. Against one wall stood a high oak cabinet painted white, with separate glass doors enclosing each shelf. Behind the glass was a random jumble of electrical parts, printed circuits, testers, and exotic-looking modules, all in some stage of construction or disassembly. Sonnenberg had memorized their names and functions.

Here the tour would end. Sonnenberg would answer perfunctory questions about his most current project, being understandably vague, or he would commiserate with that inevitable guest who thought to remark ruefully on the unhappy need for such devices of protection. But Sonnenberg's mind, by then, was on the white cabinet and on the unsuspected door behind it. The door, which led to a tiny room where Sonnenberg's real work was done, opened onto a world without props or façades or false trails, a room in which Sonnenberg's world was real and thrilling. Of all the living, only Mrs. Kreskie had seen it.

Sonnenberg would force himself back to his entertainment. Go, Marcus. Go complete your work with these people. Disarm them. Enlist them. They are your insulation. If you are real to them, it follows that you must be real in fact. Study and record them as they sip your wine and munch Mrs Kreskie's rumaki. Bottle them against the day when their behavioral clones will spring into existence in some distant city. Let them, meanwhile, wander about, discovering Marcus Sonnenberg, as long as one of them doesn't take it into his head to wander out among the rhododendrons with a spade in his hand. The result would certainly be high drama but hardly worth the consequent inconvenience. Someday, though. Someday the house would change hands, and the new owner would decide that the manicured fairways of the Westchester Country Club were too much of an environmental asset to be blocked from view, and he'd tear down the fence and rip up the bug-ridden old rhododendrons by their roots. "Hey, Marge, look at this. There's some kind of animal under here. Maybe two or three animals. Wait a minute . . . these aren't . . . Holy Christ . . . these are skeletons here . . . No, damn it, I mean people skeletons. Holy Christ . . ."

Then it would be only a matter of a day or so before they found the room downstairs. They'd bring in a trencher that would break its teeth against the reinforced concrete of the room's ceiling. Or else it would slice through the vent that led to the inside wall of the well. Sonnenberg winced at the probable fate of the marigolds and geraniums in the trencher's path and hoped that the event would occur in winter, when only sleeping tubers would be disturbed. On the other hand, marigolds mean contempt in the language of flowers and geraniums mean deceit. How very apt. There was a certain poetry to the vision of these two flowers hurling a last, defiant insult at their murderer.

As for the room downstairs, Sonnenberg knew that how he'd managed to excavate it would become one of the enduring mysteries of the case. Actually, he didn't build it. Luther Dowling the elder built it and he's dead, so he isn't telling. Luther Dowling the younger is alive enough except that he isn't Luther Dowling anymore, so he won't tell either. The room, in fact, was the feature of the house that had most attracted him when he bought it from young Luther nine years earlier. A century before that, it had been a root cellar, then a coal bin until the house was converted to oil, and finally a bomb shelter built by batty old Mr. Dowling in 1954 without benefit of a building permit. Contractors of the time, who competed to construct these Eisenhower Specials, often disguised what they were doing at the request of the client, who frequently preferred that the shelter's existence remain a secret. If the Russian bombers ever actually came, it wouldn't do to have fear-maddened and less provident neighbors hammering at the door, begging to share the measured rations of food and water as nearby New York City boiled into the stratosphere.

The room measured eight feet wide and nearly ten feet deep. At one end was a louvered metal door resembling the grate of a furnace. An air conditioner jutted from the wall beneath it. The door led to a concrete tube, twenty-eight inches in diameter, that was both an air shaft and an escape tunnel leading to the inside wall of the well. The well had long been filled to a level six feet below its lip, which was covered with a latticed grating that served as a base for potted plants.

The room itself offered only the barest amenities. A studio couch, a small kneehole desk, and a Morris chair. It didn't seem that old Luther had made provision for his son. The built-ins included a large water tank, hermetically sealed, and an attached washstand that folded into the wall. Farther along the wall was a group of horizontal steel cabinets, each with its own combination lock. The lowest one contained a month's supply of assorted dehydrated dinners. The middle one, which was lined with asbestos, held a Coleman gas stove with a reserve supply of Sterno, and a rain slicker, clothing, a fire extinguisher, and miscellaneous hardware. The third was all Sonnenberg. It held his files, his notebooks, and his journals. A separate case held dozens of tape cassettes labeled with coded names and dates plus a battery-powered player. Sonnenberg had added only two significant refinements to the room. The first was an air conditioner that, like the electric lights, tapped into the power line outside and ran unmetered. The second was a thermite charge that would explode among his files if the air conditioner was not first turned on or if it was set at any combination other than Low Cool–Exhaust.

On the opposite wall, he'd replaced Luther Dowling's gun rack with a large map of North America. More than forty colored pins dotted its surface from Saskatoon in the north to Cuernavaca in the south and to the island of St. Croix in the east. Each pin was a person—or an identity, to be precise—that had not existed before Sonnenberg.

Sonnenberg needed no map to know where they were. The map was an indulgence and he recognized it as such. It was fun to play with and to contemplate. Much more tangible in its way than booby-trapped records entombed in steel. He could look at a pin and imagine, with no small degree of accuracy, what that man or woman would be doing at that hour. He knew each of them intimately. He knew their occupations, their hobbies, their favorite foods, and their styles of dress. Sonnenberg had shaped and polished all of them. Most, or certainly many, had nearly forgotten whom and what they had been before. Backsliding was rare because few could go home again, anyway. The need for discipline was rarer still. Excellent subjects, on the whole.

And such accomplishments. Sonnenberg beamed. Darrel Finney, from a Utica policeman marked for assassination to a successful sculptor in Tucson barely a year after he picked up his first chisel. Melanie Laver, from a Boston murderess—manslaughteress, actually—to a newspaper columnist in Christiansted. Probably hadn't written so much as a postcard since she was a girl in summer camp. Or Milo Barney, the vacationing investigative reporter from Chicago who spotted Melanie, began tracking her transformation, knew a good thing when he saw one, and converted, eventually resurfacing running a ski shop in Killington, Vermont. A man whose prior interest in snow began and ended with snow tires. And then we have our born-again intellectuals, Luther Dowling the younger among the first. Brought up by an emasculating zealot of a father who was obsessed by the prospect of Armageddon and his exclusive survival thereof, the son was left with little sense of self and seeing even less practical value in being Luther Dowling the younger. That condition ended when Luther the elder was found beaten to death with a copy of the Old Testament. Young Luther is Philip Poindexter now, an admired curator in a museum where his focus is on the preservation of beauty rather than its vaporization. William Berner's transformation is even more impressive. Captain William Berner, the near-cretinous gook killer from Vietnam who metamorphosed into a gentle Smithsonian scholar. The list goes on. All loyal, all eager, all useful. Forty-three precisely. Forty-four with Baker. And that's if you only count him as one. Ah, Baker, how many of you are there? And which one will I find first?

Sonnenberg's cigar had gone out. It was cold. He blinked and shook his head to clear away the memory of Christmas entertainments past and of his map of pins two floors below. He switched off his console. The Dickerson house was quiet and only static came through the speaker. Marcus, he thought, you've been woolgathering.

It's a sign of a mind not at peace. Next thing you know, you'll be talking to yourself. And like Baker, getting answers.

Sonnenberg giggled.

Baker, Baker, Baker! Just think of it. A small army of Bakers. An elite force of men and women who could be anything they wished or needed to be. Without effort. Without fear. Without guilt. A legion of will-o'-the-wisps. A strike force at the leading edge of a new society. Men who can touch the tiller a few points this way and that and then fade away until the course must be corrected anew. And you, Baker, could be at the legion's head. The men and women you lead will be policemen when the need is for police, surgeons when the need is to cut away what is putrefying, seekers of learning when the power lies in knowledge, and seekers of truth when strength lies in understanding.

Sonnenberg studied the cigar, considering idly whether the stub was worth saving for another day. He'd lost his taste for it. Sonnenberg leaned forward toward the window and shook out the saucer of ashes. The cigar followed, dropping among the rhododendrons. Mrs. Kreskie never went there.

Ah, Baker, he thought, pushing to his feet, what wouldn't a Hitler have given for a specimen like you. Or an Allen Dulles, not to compare the two. Or a Duncan Peck, to split them down the middle . . .

Oh, my heavens. Dunny. No wonder that episode kept tugging at me. My uncharacteristically erratic golfer was Duncan Peck, wasn't he? Of course he was. He's lost weight. It's that jogging foolishness. How long has it been? At least twenty years. One of his people must have spotted Ben Meister's picture after all. How much could he know? That Baker is here? Possibly. What Baker is? That I may have found a Chimera? Also possible. Oh, Duncan, I'm going to have to pay much closer attention to you, I'm afraid. I do hope you're not about to do something melodramatic. That would be terribly, terribly inconvenient. No. No, you won't, will you, Duncan? You like things tidy. You'll snoop for a while first. Or you'll prevail upon a good friend to snoop for you. It's a wonder where you keep finding foolish friends.

Well, he thought, clapping his hands together, we're just going to have to move along, aren't we. Put the fleet to sea, so to speak.

Sleep soundly, Mr. Baker. Tomorrow we begin in earnest.

7

"Tell me what you see there."

Sonnenberg rapped on the thick manila folder that he'd just placed on the butler's table in front of Baker, then returned stiffly to his couch.

Baker looked up. He saw without interest that a photograph of himself was clipped to the cover. It was a confident face. At least not a beaten face. He was sure he didn't look like that today. He hadn't even bothered to shave.

"Tell me what you see," Sonnenberg repeated.

Sonnenberg's manner, in contrast to Baker's, was almost gleeful. Like a grandfather on Christmas morning presenting a gift that was certain to be prized.

The folder itself was three inches thick. Baker looked away from the photograph. "That's all me?" he asked, incurious.

"More than you can imagine." Sonnenberg smiled. He didn't want to rush this part. He reached for a carved silver samovar and gestured with it toward Baker's cup. Baker waved it off. He'd almost rather have had a drink. Sonnenberg shrugged. Too slowly, he filled his own cup, then carefully stirred in some heated cream and, from an enamel box, a few grains of chicory. This he tasted, then took from another bowl containing honey. Only when Baker began to fidget did he reach into the folder and slide out a second photograph of Baker's face.

"Now tell me what you see," Sonnenberg waggled one finger toward the twin black and white prints as he sipped from a Lenox cup.

"Stills." Baker shrugged. "Head-and-shoulder shots of me." He recognized the second one as a picture cropped from a larger one with Sarah and Tina in it. He had planned to do a portrait. It annoyed him that their bodies had been airbrushed away.

"Are they identical?" Sonnenberg cocked his head.

"They're copies." Baker shrugged again.

"Look more carefully."

Baker touched the prints with his fingertips and slid them up and down against each other as if comparing the ballistic markings of two bullets.

"They're identical," he said finally, "except that the one on the right is reversed."

"Correct. A mirror image. And incidentally, it's convenient that you've had very few taken. It's even more convenient that you winced as your police photograph was taken. You'll be recognizable only to dentists and proctologists. You're sure you wouldn't like some of Mrs. Kreskie's Turkish coffee?"

"Yes. Yes." Sonnenberg clapped his hands lightly. "Get on with it, you say. In fact, it does become more interesting about now."

He drew out a third version of the same photograph. It was identical to those already on the table except that it was cut neatly in half. A curving line had been precisely scissored down the middle of Baker's face. He placed the two halves before Baker but left them several inches apart.

"Now tell me what you see."

"I see that you're playing games. Why don't you just tell me what—"

"Indulge me, Jared. Please."

"It's a picture of me cut in half." Baker sat back, waiting.

"Ah, but it isn't. Not exactly." Sonnenberg reached across and pushed the two halves together. "Compare that to the other copies of the same photograph."

Baker leaned forward and stared, more than a bit startled, at the face glaring back at him. It was a hard face. The lines of the mouth were tight and cruel. The eyes were slightly hooded and they seemed to lock on his, holding his, like the eyes of a puff adder would paralyze a bird. The face and head seemed larger than the others, although Baker knew the dimensions had to be the same. And the face was ... intimidating. Baker had always thought of himself as a nice man. Perhaps even nice-looking. There was nothing nice about the man in front of him.

"How did you do this?" he asked, his eyes still fixed upon the face.

"Simplicity itself," replied Sonnenberg. "But first a question. If you didn't know that man, what would be your impression of him?"

"He's tough. A mean son of a bitch. I'd stay away from him."

"Not the sort you'd have over for Sunday brunch. More than that, you're saying you'd hate to have that man as an enemy."

"Yes." Baker nodded thoughtfully. "I know you're pump-priming, but you're right. And I know that this is only a doctored photograph, but it's ..."

"Frightening? No ... I'm sure that's not the right word."

"It's a terrific word." Baker looked up. "That face even scares me. And it is me."

"But what if that man were your very good friend?"

"He doesn't look like anybody's friend."

"You're quite wrong." Sonnenberg smiled. "He's very much your friend. Absolutely reliable. Unequivocally on your side. He would defend you to the death. Moreover, he's a friend who would be perfectly comfortable in any situation that you might find alarming. Or unpleasant. Or menacing. A perfectly compatible friend. He shares your values, your standards, your sense of what is right. He probably even shares your fears and inhibitions, but his threshold for those emotions is much higher than yours. He is largely unencumbered by them.

On the flip side, his threshold for love and compassion, even mercy, is probably much lower."

Baker picked up the right half of the photograph, fingered it, and held it up to the light.

"I think I see what you've done," he said, returning that half to its mate. "You took the right half of my face, made a mirror image of it, then put two right halves together to form one whole face."

"Exactly. Don't you think the result is rather remarkable?"

"If it means anything. I'm sure you can do this with anyone's face."

"Indeed I could. Behavioral researchers use this trick to demonstrate the hemispheric dominance of the brain. Except it's more than a trick in your case." Sonnenberg patted the folder. "Before we go on, aren't you at all curious about the left side of your personality?"

"Personality?"

"Your face, then."

"Let me guess. The left side will go to the opposite extreme. Timid as opposed to aggressive. Weak instead of strong. Am I getting warm?"

"Only tepid." Sonnenberg gathered up the photographs and slid two new likenesses in front of Baker. On his right was a retouched version of the two right halves, artfully airbrushed into an unmarred portrait. On his left, Sonnenberg had done the same thing with the two left halves of Baker's face.

"My God!" Baker whispered.

"Go ahead. Say it."

"It's like night and day, isn't it?"

"Rats!" Sonnenberg pursed his lips. "I bet myself that you'd say it's like Jekyll and Hyde. You would have been very much mistaken."

"There's a difference?"

"Like night and day." Sonnenberg smiled. "What you're looking at has nothing to do with good and evil. They are simply the opposite poles of your personality."

"There's that word again. The face on the left doesn't look like it has any personality at all."

Baker studied the likeness. He knew he'd guessed wrong. It was not a weak face, he decided, nor was it strong. Bland, perhaps. Or blank. Yes, blank would be much more correct. Like the face of a cow. Yet the other one had the face of a wolf, a feral quality. The eyes and the set of the mouth showed a ferocity that was barely under control. It was a face that seemed to lean forward whereas the other face seemed to pull back. That was an illusion, Baker knew, because the camera's depth of field was the same for each.

"Don't take Charley too lightly, Jared. He might surprise you."

"Charley?"

"It's the name I've given him. An easygoing sort of name. Very apt, don't you think . . . Baker?" Sonnenberg smiled expectantly.

"I'm to conclude that the animal on the right is called Abel?"

Sonnenberg threw back his head and laughed. "Excellent, Mr. Baker. You have yet to disappoint me . . . although our friend Abel may have cause to sulk over your characterization of him." The doctor drew out a copy of Baker's legitimate full-face photograph and placed it on the table between the others.

"Tell me now," he said, rubbing his hands. "With your newly acquired insights, what is your impression of our friend Baker here?"

Baker's mind had wandered. It was that laugh of Sonnenberg's. It had seemed familiar before this, but he couldn't place it until now. It was Franklin Roosevelt. That was the way Roosevelt laughed. There were other Roosevelt mannerisms too, even to the accent, which lately seemed more Brahmin than European. Baker dismissed it as an affectation that had no significance. He found himself wondering, though, what might lie beneath if he peeled away the outer skin of Marcus Sonnenberg. Would he find anything at all?

"I beg your pardon?"

"You are now the centerpiece of an alliance called

Abel Baker Charley. You are a living mean. You, Baker, are the midpoint of two distinct personalities."

"Is that supposed to be a revelation?"

"I would expect so." Sonnenberg was disappointed.

"You're saying my personality is the sum total of its elements. Whose isn't?"

"Yours, perhaps. The assumption that you alone have substance and Abel and Charley had none may border upon arrogance. What if the entity called Jared Baker turned out to be little more than a muddled conglomerate whereas each of these is, in his own way, singularly talented?"

Baker studied Sonnenberg. He knew by now that the doctor was not a man given to pointless theoretical exercises. Baker was more than a bit uncomfortable.

"You're saying you can isolate them, Doctor?"

"I'm saying that I believe I can teach you to isolate them. I believe you can learn to employ either Abel or Charley at will."

"Hypnosis?"

"Suggestion will play a role, yes."

"That's been the reason for all the hypnosis sessions? You've been probing for these two characters while I've been under?"

"Not at all. I've simply been testing your responsiveness to suggestion. You can listen to the tapes if you have any doubts."

Baker hesitated for a few moments before brushing the offer aside. Sonnenberg had, in fact, expressed delight several times at his ability to concentrate his way into deep hypnosis in ever-shorter periods of time. Still, to Baker's mind, the purpose of these sessions had nothing to do with Abels and Charleys.

"I don't mistrust you, Doctor," he said evenly. "But this isn't why I agreed to come with you. I certainly didn't come to be a guinea pig."

Sonnenberg's genial manner faded. He lifted his crippled leg past the butler's table and swung it toward Baker so that his entire body faced the other man.

"You came to me, Jared, because you were a frightened man."

"Not frightened, Doctor. Just a man who wanted peace and freedom. A new start. Your offer was very attractive under the circumstances."

"Let's not play semantic Ping-Pong, Jared. I offered you a new life and a new identity and you required very little persuasion. Only frightened people leap at such an offer. Some seek to outrun failure and disappointment, some to escape their sins, and some, like you, are hunted men. All of you are frightened."

"If you say so."

"I do say so. And be good enough to forgo any macho protestations that Jared Baker is beyond fear. Fear is not the same as cowardice. I do not approach cowards. Fear has value. Managed fear equates with prudence. With the proper training and the correct documents, you could live a rich new life, yet the fear will always be there. You would always be watchful for that unexpected familiar face, or ducking camera lenses that are innocently pointed in your direction, or wonder why some stranger seems to be staring at you."

"I understood all that going in. I also understood that the point of the hypnosis sessions was to learn how to deeply ingrain a new personality so that even I would believe in it. But through it all, I'd still be me. Not some freak."

Sonnenberg made a visible effort to soften. He paused, nodding and smiling, as he lifted his cup and saucer and slowly sipped. Let out more line, Marcus, he thought. Go slowly.

"You'll still be you, Jared," he said. "You'll still be your daughter's father. She, for one, will see no difference."

"What does my daughter . . ." Baker stopped himself. He knew that Sonnenberg was trying to switch him onto another track and it was working. Sonnenberg understood the images that still filled his mind at the mention of his wife or daughter. The street outside his home. Sarah dead there. So broken and torn she can only be dead. Tina screaming, crawling toward her mother. Why is she crawling? Her foot. It just bumps along behind her, leaving a wash of blood. And the Frisbee, circling. The one with the motorcycle. The one who speeds by here and gives you a finger if you ... He's yelling at them. He's yelling at Sarah for being dead ... The Frisbee still rolling ...

"Jared." Sonnenberg reached for his arm and squeezed. "Jared, I can stop that too."

"What?" Baker asked dully.

"I can stop those pictures from coming back. You don't have to live in that world anymore."

"Tina has to." His voice was distant.

"Only until the foot is repaired and healed, Baker," Sonnenberg whispered. "Only until the limp is gone. She cannot be with you while she limps."

"It's hard to wait. I ought to be with her while she's hurting."

"You'd be waiting anyway. But you'd be waiting in prison if not in a prison morgue. This way is much better for her. She knows you are well and that you're free. This way you're a hero to her, not a convict in a cage or a corpse."

"I want to call her more often," said Baker, looking away. "I ought to talk to her every day."

"You know you can't do that."

"I know you said I can't, but I don't know why. You told me I'm safe as long as I limit the call to forty seconds and call at random hours."

"Comparatively safe," Sonnenberg corrected. "Each call that you place is a challenge to the authorities. It announces that you're near, at least in spirit, that the tie to your daughter is strong, and that you may attempt to see her. Each call breathes new vitality into the hunt, challenges the hunter to new effort. This is doubly foolish in your case because the authorities never had much stomach for it anyway. But even that is not the critical problem. Your daughter, God bless her, is a distraction. You must learn to ration your thoughts of her if you are to accomplish your ultimate goal of being together."

"That's my goal, all right." Baker nodded. "I begin to get the feeling, though, that it's not yours especially."

"Quite possibly true." Sonnenberg's eyebrows went up and his head went back in another Rooseveltian gesture of candor. "I've begun to conclude that my goals were too modest."

"I'm not a plaything, Doctor. I expect to pay you for a service."

Sonnenberg patted Baker's knee. "We'll do all that I promised, Jared," he said slowly. "We'll do it together. If you will go forward with me one step at a time, I assure you that you may draw any line you wish. But I've discovered, you see, that I may be able to give you much more than I promised. Much, much more. I believe I can offer you the ability to deal confidently with any situation that might arise. It could be within your power to choose at will from three uniquely talented entities, selecting the personality that is most suited to any challenge, physical or intellectual, that you may face."

"Who's the third personality?"

"You are, of course."

"Does that mean I can do something the others can't?"

"Not necessarily. Obviously, all three are still you. The three faces of Baker, so to speak. What you are is their control, which is, of course, a singular talent not shared by the famous Eve. Your judgment will be more balanced than that of either except in situations of high stress. But on the whole, you'll be more circumspect. Think of yourself as a football coach who sends in the right player for a particular situation."

"Why me, Doctor?"

"Why not you?"

Baker shook his head. "I think you had this in mind from the very beginning," he said.

"I was hopeful," Sonnenberg admitted. "Now I'm more than hopeful."

"You haven't said why me?"

"The young man who drove the motorcycle, the motorcycle that killed your wife. You attacked him, Baker.

Angrily, clumsily, out of control. You attacked him and you beat him. It was an impassioned act. But it was also an unskilled and awkward act. In brief, your inept assault was quite in character for an ordinary, civilized, domesticated, and atrophic suburbanite."

"But not so inept when he came back again?"

"However"—Sonnenberg raised a hand to stay Baker's interruption—"this fine young product of your community, this privileged and pampered son of a superior court judge, he came back, didn't he? He came back to settle a score with the angry man who beat and shamed him. He cared nothing for the consequences. The death of your wife and the maiming of your daughter were irrelevant to him. He wanted vengeance. He hurled a bottle of flaming gasoline at your house and another at your dog, who stood snarling at him. And then you came out. Your home was burning. The home this man had already twice devastated. Your pet retriever was writhing in the midst of flames. What did you do then, Jared?"

Baker didn't answer.

"You must tell me, Jared. It's time to speak of it."

"I went after him . . ."

"And did what?"

"I hurt him worse than before."

"You say that as if you remember it."

"I do remember it. I just don't remember doing it. It was more like I was watching."

"And what did you see?"

"You know what. I hurt him."

"You destroyed him, Baker. You did it systematically, carefully, dispassionately. You methodically shattered each of the young man's arms at the elbow and shoulder, where the pain would be greatest and the healing slowest. You did this, according to witnesses, without apparent anger. As if you were changing a tire, as one said later. Your golden retriever, your pet, for whom you presumably felt some affection, was in its last moments of agony. Yet this caused you no noticeable anguish. You forced the young man's face . . ."

Baker was seeing it. He was watching the scene from a place near his own right shoulder. He was part of himself, but he was not. Baker remembered looking down as his hands moved and feeling surprise that they were moving. He was not attached. But he remembered wanting them to do what they were doing.

. . . Come on, asshole . . . Come on, the young man sneered. He stood in a crouch, a baseball bat in one hand, the fingers of the other beckoning Baker . . . daring him. It was at that moment that Baker fell back but his body went forward. The young man coiled and struck, first hooking with his fist, then bringing down the bat across Baker's shoulder. Baker thought both blows had landed, but they had not. At least not the baseball bat. His own hand had caught it, and now the other hand was twisting it, breaking it, snapping it in two, so that each hand held a short wooden sword. The hand with the thicker half let go and gripped the young man's arm below the shoulder. It turned him and it lifted him. And now the right hand pointed the wooden sword between his legs and pushed. Baker couldn't see the bat anymore. He saw that the right hand was free. It joined the first hand, gripping the young man's arm below the shoulder. The lower hand was at his elbow, and both hands drew the screaming man's arm like a bow, very slowly, until it snapped, and then still farther, until the grinding of bone against bone could no longer be heard. Then the flapping limb moved up and then backward until the shoulder's joint cracked free. The sounds the young man made were beyond a scream. He shrieked and whooped, falsetto squeals and yips pumping out in a mindless rhythm. Baker remembered wondering that a pair of human lungs could sustain so long a scream. And he remembered wondering at the strength of his own left hand, which now held the full weight of Andrew Bellafonte at arm's length. Bellafonte, half-conscious, was kicking at Baker's legs, but Baker felt nothing. Someone else was screaming too. A woman. A neighbor. And now a man was shouting his name. Baker didn't answer. He wanted to watch.

Another bow was being drawn. Another arm. He

didn't remember how the transfer was made, but the young man was turned and hoisted again and the new screams were half-choked in vomit.

Baker looked away. There was no satisfaction now. Only disgust. He looked to where Macduff lay on his side, the upper two thirds of his body still wreathed in lapping flames and his hind legs moving in small, convulsive kicks. Baker wanted to turn away from that too but he was moving closer. His own body and that of the coughing, mewing Bellafonte were moving closer to the dog, and now the others were screaming again and Bellafonte's face was being . . .

"You forced that young man's face into the pyre that was your dog. Do you recall that, Baker?"

Baker looked past him, saying nothing.

"With your hand, you gripped his hair and you held his face against the flaming head of your dog and you held it there. You held it there until the screams were quiet. You held it there until his face was cooked and until the young man's eyes had turned to grease."

Baker looked pale and ill. Perspiration beaded on his forehead, and his eyes flashed angrily at Sonnenberg.

"I know," the doctor said gently. "That was cruel of me. But you must begin to see the question that it raised. Was that the behavior of an ordinary, civilized suburbanite, no matter how great the provocation?"

"You're saying it was Abel." Baker's voice was flat and dulled.

"Was it Jared Baker?"

"No."

"It was Abel. He's always been there, sometimes not very far beneath the surface. On that occasion, Abel broke through. You let him through. He seemed out of control, but I don't think he was. He certainly didn't go back by himself. You put him back. I'm convinced that you can control him. You can control him by a simple act of will."

Baker glanced at him doubtfully. But Sonnenberg was right on at least one point. Baker had never tried to stop it. It ended when Baker wanted it to end. And then this other one was gone.

"Do not fear him, Jared. Abel is your friend. He did only what Jared Baker would have wished to do but for the constraints of his upbringing."

"And you chose me because you knew? You knew that Abel, and I suppose Charley, are both in here someplace?"

"They are there in everyone. Anyone can do what I did with those photographs. It works with any face at all. What makes you unique is that your Abel has come out. He is therefore close at hand. Yes, I knew. That is why I sent Ben Meister to you. I would have gone to any length, Jared, to keep you from harm. I confess that I do not regret your fugitive status. The murder of Judge Bellafonte was a blessing to me in that it narrowed your options. On that matter, by the way, I'll attend to the housekeeping later. For now, though, it remained only for me to determine whether you were a half-decent subject for hypnotic regression. If it developed that you were not, I would have had you painting houses in Wichita or some such place and sending me a monthly fee for maintaining you in your fugitive identity."

"You said 'hypnotic regression,'" Baker said slowly. "Doesn't that mean going backward into other lives?"

"Did I say regression?" Sonnenberg blinked twice. "I meant suggestion, of course."

Baker didn't believe him. He knew that Sonnenberg was holding something back. It had to do with . . . painting? Being a house painter in Wichita? What was that he'd promised during the first day? "You said I could paint. That I could be an artist."

Sonnenberg drew in a long breath. "I'm becoming very impressed with you, Jared Baker."

"Was that what you were thinking?"

"I was rather saving it until later. Not to muddy the water, you understand."

"How could I be a painter?" he asked. "Regression is part of it?"

Sonnenberg threw his arms wide in a gesture of

frankness. "Regression, I'll tell you, is almost all of it. The technique, incidentally, has developed well beyond the random popping up of Bridey Murphy types from past lives. Quite exciting things are being done, pioneered particularly by the Russians. For example, Jared Baker the artist of modest ability might be regressed under hypnosis to another life in which it is suggested that he was van Gogh or Degas or Delacroix. Under deep hypnosis, you would be one of those men. You would recall much that you've ever known about the period in which they lived. Your imagination would provide much more. You would then be brought forward to approximately your normal conscious state, although you'd be left in a light trance, which would be no impediment whatsoever. Within that light trance, you would never consciously believe that you were actually Edgar Degas, for example, but you would develop a very strong psychological affinity for his techniques, his tastes, and for those aspects of his personality you find attractive. The result would be a much faster development of your own ability. You could learn to write sonnets by the same method. Or study medicine or architecture or Keynesian economics, even if you've had no aptitude whatever for those subjects in the past."

"Or law?"

Sonnenberg smiled. "Benjamin Meister is a legitimate attorney. Among other things. But yes, even law. The technique is well established and, yes, I've used it myself. It's a dandy."

"Not theoretical?"

"No."

"How theoretical is this multiple personality business?"

"Hillman out at Cal Tech has dipped a toe into it. He was the first to discover an independent consciousness in an otherwise entranced subject. I'm not sure he knows what he's got."

"Or he's afraid of it."

"He's never found a Jared Baker."

Baker slowly returned the smile. His expression

showed that the hook was taken. Not deeply. Not irrevocably. The barb still hadn't entered flesh. But the hook was in and more line would be played out. The business about Degas and the rest seemed to have helped after all.

"One step at a time, Dr. Sonnenberg?"

"One step at a time. Jared Abel Baker Charley."

8

It was a month later in a different place.

Connor Harrigan had not yet heard the name of Jared Baker. Or that of Marcus Sonnenberg. His mind then was on black thoughts of Duncan Peck and on what he would do if Peck insisted on running one more god-damned yard.

The older man was smirking. He gave Harrigan an encouraging slap on the rump and pointed to the Rochambeau Bridge, still two miles distant. Harrigan's eyes widened in outraged disbelief.

"What are you? Crazy?" he gasped, but kept on. He swept his arms wide to take in the several dozen runners who cruised without effort along the paths of East Potomac Park. "All you people are crazy," he wheezed. "Lunchtime. The only one you get all day and half the government is out here running their asses off."

Duncan Peck waved him forward but said nothing, only smiled his satisfaction. He was fifteen years older than Connor Harrigan and thirty pounds lighter. And it was a point of pride with him that he could run five miles without once parting his lips for air.

Harrigan answered with a digital gesture indicating noncompliance. "Bullshit." He spat, using the last of his air to expel the word. He staggered to a halt, stepping off the hot asphalt track that felt as if it were melting through his sneakers. Peck turned, jogging in place for several beats until it became clear that Connor Harrigan would run no more except at gunpoint. Harrigan collapsed on the grass under the shade of a Japanese cherry tree.

"You know who you look like right now?" Peck asked. "You look just like Tony Galento after Joe Louis clubbed him into a sitting position. Have you ever seen that photograph? Galento, leaning on one arm, his great belly heaving, his face spent and beaten . . ."

Harrigan looked up through eyes hooded with fatigue and malice. He didn't bother to reply.

"Look at me," Peck boasted, standing over him. "Not even out of breath. You can get yourself into this sort of shape, you know. All you have to do is work at it."

Harrigan spat again. "You think I didn't work to get like I am?" He grabbed the four inches of flesh that hung over the cord of his borrowed sweatpants. "There's a bloody fortune in Roquefort and martinis there. Be respectful."

Peck rolled his eyes in despair. "You were almost there," he told Harrigan. "You were right on the edge of getting your second wind. You would have felt a certain rush of pride and strength . . ."

"What I was about to do was die. Not that you'd give a shit because you could still jog alongside the ambulance. And I'd never find out why you have me out here playing chicken with a coronary."

Peck feigned wounded innocence. "Why must there be a reason for two friends to . . ."

Harrigan curled his mouth and raised one eyebrow. Peck had to smile. Two more joggers ran by. Connor Harrigan looked past Duncan Peck's legs at all the other runners, noting the number of men and a few women who were running in pairs. Or in groups of three. And the number of conversations that seemed to be going on through lips that were kept close together and from faces that did not turn sideways. But the faces were animated. It was possible to know the intensity of a discussion even at a distance.

"I can remember when people used to get a sandwich and a beer at lunchtime," he observed. "Or if they had to talk quiet, they'd take a walk or sit in a parked car. These days they go jogging. How many of these guys do you figure are meeting off the record right now?"

"A few, I suppose. But they're not conspiratorial meetings, necessarily. It's healthy and it's private, that's all."

"Plus which, a jogging track is a bitch to eavesdrop. But of course that never occurred to you."

"Ah, Harrigan," Peck sighed, affecting a weary sadness, "would that I could refresh your cynical soul."

"Right!" One lip curled up. "When do I find out what's on your mind?"

"Walk with me."

"What for? You think the cherry tree's wired?"

"An individual will come running by here in a few minutes. He's like clockwork. He'll be wearing a Notre Dame jersey with its sleeves cut off. I want you to take a good look at him."

Duncan Peck offered a hand to the reluctant Connor Harrigan and pulled him to his feet. Peck moved closer. Reaching into a zippered pocket of his windbreaker, he drew out a plastic envelope containing several papers along with a supply of blister pads and ammonia capsules. It amused Harrigan that Peck tried to conceal the latter with his hand. Peck avoided his eyes as he handed him a small color photograph of a man in uniform.

"You're looking at Captain William Berner. West Point, 1965. Two Vietnam tours between 1966 and 1973. Some combat. Mostly Special Operations. His fitness report mentions that he's exceptionally discreet. Do you know what that means?"

"Yeah. He kills people when the army tells him to and he never brings it up again."

"Very good. Over the next three years he sat around hoping for a nice new war. None came, and Berner resigned his commission. On the day his separation came through, he drove out of Fort Ord and went straightaway to a VA hospital in San Diego, where he slipped a cyanide pill to a sergeant named Dengler. Dengler had been

Berner's driver until he got his arms and part of his face blown off. Dengler's wife, who visited him rarely, finally filed for divorce, citing irreconcilable differences. It seems he never hugged her anymore. Dengler, as you might imagine, was despondent and had to be held under restraint to keep him from ending his own life. In any event, Berner killed Dengler, no doubt at Dengler's request, and then drove to Reno, where he killed Dengler's wife, no doubt against her wishes. The killings were in all the West Coast and hometown papers. Berner vanished."

Peck took the photograph from Harrigan and returned it to the plastic envelope. He was zipping his pocket shut when, without warning, Harrigan lurched and stumbled against him, clutching his chest. Harrigan sucked air grotesquely as rising blood enflamed his face and pounded at his temples.

"Connor?" Duncan Peck shouted. "Connor, what's happening?"

Harrigan shook his head but appeared unable to speak.

"Here," another voice said. "Get him on the grass." It was a heavily mustached man in his late thirties. His hair, dripping sweat, was almost the color of copper. And he wore a Notre Dame jersey with the sleeves cut off.

"It's okay . . ." Harrigan protested. "It's all right."

Notre Dame eased him to a sitting position and placed his fingers lightly against Harrigan's throat. "Pulse is quieting down," he said. "Are you in pain anywhere?"

"No . . . no. Everything just went bright for a second and I got dizzy is all. I'm okay. I'm just embarrassed as hell."

"You're not okay," Peck answered angrily. "Do you know what those symptoms are? They're warning signs of a stroke. You can't keep yourself in such rotten shape and . . ."

"Your friend's right." Notre Dame's voice was gentler. "Running is something you have to ease in to. And you really should see a doctor."

Harrigan was breathing normally, and the redness of

his face had drained away. "This afternoon," he said, looking at Notre Dame. "I'll get a checkup this afternoon."

Notre Dame smiled and tapped him on the shoulder as he rose to his feet. "Just start slow, okay? If you work at it, you can be passing me by next summer." Notre Dame waved and glided into an easy lope toward the Jefferson Memorial.

Duncan Peck watched him go, then turned and looked into Harrigan's eyes.

"Are you able to walk, Connor? Perhaps I should call for a ride."

"Will you stop? I'm fine." There was now no sign of his recent distress.

"But you're . . ."

"Listen. You wanted me to look close at Notre Dame? I looked close at Notre Dame."

"You . . . ? You son of a bitch. That was an act?" Now Peck reddened as he shoved abruptly to his feet.

"You're sputtering." Harrigan clucked. "And you're getting all flushed. Those are warning signs that you're getting all pissed off and you're going to have a worse stroke than I did."

"Well, it's just lovely that you got a good look at him." Peck's voice was dripping. "But our friend also had a very nice look at you."

"And I'll tell you something else," Harrigan said, ignoring the last. "He's as big a pain in the ass as you are. Did you hear all that about how terrific running would be if I work at it? You guys all sound like you read one book in your whole life and that was *The Complete Book of Running*. In a few days, I might decide to be out here again doing this shit. And your Captain Berner there is going to be pulling up alongside me asking me what the doctor said, telling me what he forgot to say, and then he's going to tell me where to buy the right kind of shoes."

Peck stared at him, appraisingly at first, then trying not to smile. "That was very neatly done, Connor."

"I work at it."

"You're satisfied that was Berner?"

"Under the sweaty mustache? No question. His hair is that color because he went swimming in chlorinated water too soon after dying it. He's got an old scar high on his cheek that's not old and it's not a scar. Someone tattooed it on using bleach. He's wearing colored contact lenses and his face is shorter, probably from dental work, to give him more of an overbite and a new profile."

"Connor," said Peck, applauding on his fingertips, "you really are quite extraordinary."

"I'm a treasure. What name's he using now and who turned him into Notre Dame? I assume he's got all new paper."

"It gets a lot more interesting than fake documents. His name, these days, is Roger Hershey. He works for the Smithsonian as an archivist in the anthropology section. Been there two years. Before that, he was a field archaeologist for six years, mostly in Mexico and the Southwest. His specialty is the pre-Columbian era. Graduated from Notre Dame in 1965. Master's from Arizona State, and he's working toward a doctorate between field trips. Never been in the service."

"That's good paper. Someone went to a lot of trouble."

"You have no idea." Duncan Peck paused and scanned the area in a three-hundred-and-sixty-degree sweep, then beckoned Harrigan to walk with him.

"About four months ago, Berner was spotted. Right here on this track. He was seen by a major who was in town on temporary duty with the Joint Chiefs." Peck pointed across the river toward the distant tan mass of the Pentagon.

"This major," Peck continued, "was sure that Berner was Berner until he talked with him for a while. Then he realized that the two men, Berner and Hershey, were about as different as a lion and a lamb. Berner, for example, was always rather stiff. A loner. He had a few fierce loyalties, viz. Sergeant Dengler, but few if any friends and almost no outside interests. He wasn't what you'd consider rousing company. Hershey, on the other hand, is cultured, friendly, soft-spoken, kind, as you've seen, and an enthusiastic hobbyist whose interests range from fishing to carpentry, to say nothing of pre-Columbian art. This is all one man, Connor. One man with two entirely different personalities. More remarkable, Hershey has a depth of knowledge in a number of fields that Berner cared nothing about only thirty months ago. That's roughly when he disappeared."

"And Hershey's been at the Smith how long? Two years?"

Peck nodded vigorously. "Which leaves him with six months to complete a ten-year course study." He held up his hand to stay further questions.

"Back to the major," Peck continued. "Try as he might, the major simply could not get over the resemblance. He was loath to mention it to anyone official because he didn't want to discomfit his new jogging buddy. But he did mention it to a friend in his apartment building who happens to work for the IRS. Just for the fun of it, and not really expecting to find anything, the IRS man punched out both names on a cross-check computer. It turns out that both men do exist and that Roger Hershey's background is legitimate."

"Except Hershey isn't Hershey." Harrigan nodded. "Next he checked the handwriting, right?"

"Very good. Berner's handwriting and Hershey's were basically the same. There were some differences, believed at first to be an attempt at disguise. But on further study, Hershey's writing now had all the loops and sweeps that one associates with an extroverted personality. In brief, he's not acting. His personality has been radically altered in an impossibly short time."

"Lobotomy?"

"No brain surgery did that. A lobotomy wouldn't turn a military slug into an engaging intellectual. If anything, the reverse would be true."

Harrigan shrugged. "So anyway, how did you get into this?"

"The IRS man used some imagination. He chose not to go to his superiors when he smelled a possible rat, and he knew better than to go to the FBI. He felt that Hershey's cover was so thorough that he must have been set up by the Relocation Section at Treasury."

"What Relocation Section?" Harrigan asked innocently.

"Behave yourself, Connor."

"What behave? I'm not supposed to know anything about a—"

"You're not but you do. What's more, our friend at the IRS had another friend who knew. Happily, he went to that friend and the friend came to me. I looked into it personally. He's not one of ours, of course, but his cover is, if anything, better than the best we've done. His personnel file over at General Services is a thing of beauty. University transcripts, letters of recommendation including one from the associate curator of the Metropolitan Museum of Art in New York, birth and baptismal certificates, a driver's license—most of which seem to be genuine Roger Hershey. He had press clippings from more than three years ago that seem absolutely authentic and of course are not. It's Berner in the photographs and Hershey in the text. What would you conclude from all this, Conner?"

Harrigan produced an empty pipe and sucked on it for several yards. "Someone planted him. He's not doing a solo. Someone good. If Relocation didn't do it, and I gather no one over at Justice planted him, who did? And why would they use the Smithsonian for his hole? What's he going to do there? Steal Orville Wright's blueprints? And anyway, where's the real Roger Hershey?"

"Excellent, Connor. There was indeed a real Roger Hershey. Four years ago he had a six-month life expectancy. Leukemia. Hershey left a note saying that he was going to try to die usefully and privately. He's certainly dead now."

"What about the new Roger. You tried wiring the guy, right?"

"Yes, we tapped his phone and the three pay phones closest to his home and office. Nothing for several weeks except a lot of purring between Berner-Hershey and a female researcher over at the National Gallery. That's probably a dead end. At one point, however, he received a long-distance call. An apparent wrong number. But then he promptly began making calls himself to three different numbers around the country, each time asking for a particular person, and each time being told that he too had dialed a wrong number. The numbers he called, by the way, were all public phones. This process has been repeated several times since then, sometimes to the same numbers. Any observations, Connor?"

"Wrong numbers to pay phones." Harrigan shrugged. "That code's older than I am. What you got is probable cause to suspect a conspiracy. Do I get to hear the rest of this in one shot or do I have to get stroked some more first?"

"Patience, Connor." The older man raised a staying hand.

But Harrigan was beginning to feel uneasy. He knew Peck was about to tell him that one or two other clones had popped up. Peck would do it his own way because he was into sequential logic and tidy patterns. He probably also knew who was pulling the strings. That meant he was about to ask good old Connor Harrigan to dig around the guy and find out what he was up to. But so far, it didn't sound like any of the Treasury Department's business. Which meant Peck was going to ask him to do this on the side. Which meant unofficial. Which meant it was his ass if he stepped on the wrong toes.

He wasn't worried about the FBI so much. Hershey wasn't their plant because they tended to be much more slipshod about placing people. Not so much that they were incompetent. They just didn't seem to give a good goddamn about most of the hide-and-seekers in the Witness Protection Program. Who could? Bums, mostly. Hoods who testified about mob activities to save their own asses, political activist informants, communists, Klansmen . . . shit! If you took all the FBI informants off the KKK and Communist Party rosters, they'd lose half their membership.

Anyway, the FBI wasn't Berner's connection. Then

who? The CIA, maybe. Not all that likely, considering the Dengler killings, but possible. They would have worked with him in Nam, and if they liked his style they would have tagged him for future use. There! That's a connection with the Relocation Service. Relocation was set up to provide deep cover for defectors and for CIA operatives who either had prices on their heads or who committed a major crime in the course of their jobs. Treasury took it over in the late forties because Treasury had access to the IRS, which could create a whole taxpaying past for the new guy. Treasury also had the Documents Section, of course, and a staff of engravers who could doctor any piece of paper in the world. Plus which, the guy who set it up was a genius. What was his name? Ivor something. Sounds like blunt. Blount? It doesn't matter. He's dead. But the bastard was good. He could hide one person or a whole bureaucracy. Maybe fifteen other people in Washington know that Relocation is anything more than an administrative section that finds apartments and moves furniture for transferred Treasury personnel. Anyway, back to Roger Hershey and his phone calls . . .

"So let's hear it." He tapped Duncan Peck on the arm. "Hershey called his wrong numbers and your tap told you which numbers. Who was on the other end?"

"That's one step ahead, Connor."

Harrigan's eyes rolled skyward.

"First I must tell you I already had his wrong number list, although I couldn't be sure until he actually made the calls." Peck waited for Harrigan to be either curious or impressed. He showed neither reaction and Peck continued.

"Our people visited Hershey's apartment during one of his Saturday five-mile runs. They examined and photographed virtually every item there, including the contents of his wallet. We found nothing enlightening until I came upon one of those cards on which you list credit card numbers in the event of loss or theft. Hershey's list, however, contained not credit card numbers but coded telephone numbers. The code consisted of fourteen digits. The two on either end were random numbers. The middle ten were the area code and the number written backward."

"How the hell would you know that just looking at it?"

"I'd seen the device before. No connection with this matter. The real giveaway was the fact that he carried such a list in his wallet at all."

Where it would be lost or stolen, thought Harrigan, right along with the credit cards. Dumb! So we know Hershey's not perfect. "Okay, you had a bunch of numbers. I keep asking who owned them."

"Five were public telephones. A sixth was the home phone of his sponsor at the Metropolitan, a man named Poindexter. A seventh was a private residence in New York's Westchester County, but we'll come back to that. Of the five public phones, four were outdoors in busy locations. A difficult surveillance problem with my limited staff. The fifth, however, was inside a tavern in Dayton, Ohio. We concentrated on that number for want of a better choice. The man I sent established another wiretap and took some routine photographs of the tavern, its owner, and a few of the regular patrons. The owner, by the way, is a very pleasant black fellow named Howard Twilley. Would you like to hear about him?"

"I'm breathless." Peck's delivery could be exhausting. But it was getting interesting.

"Four years ago, Howard moved from Waycross, Georgia, to Dayton. He quickly found a job in a tavern that had, incidentally, an all-white factory worker clientele. Over time, he purchased the tavern from its absentee owner. An attorney named Benjamin Meister."

"Meister? It rings a bell."

"He's been in the papers. A Bronx grocer who decided late in life he'd rather be Melvin Belli. Passed the bar exams of several states within a year. Some with record grades. No established office or practice, however."

"Sounds like he and Hershey played for the same coach."

"But back to Howard. Howard Twilley lives in an apartment above the bar and keeps much to himself. His only hobbies seem to be the hermetic pursuits of wood-working and fishing. Vanishes for days at a time in quest of brook trout."

"Duncan." Harrigan made a time-out signal with his hands. His lips moved as he groped for yet another way to ask Peck to stop the bullshit and get on with it. "Listen," he said finally, "you're waiting for me to notice that both Hershey and Twilley are into carpentry and fishing. I notice. Sooner or later, you're going to tell me that Twilley isn't Twilley either. Why can't it be right now?"

"You're no fun, Connor."

"Come on," he insisted, ignoring the other man's pout. "You connected Notre Dame with this black guy who runs a redneck bloody knuckle in Ohio. Notre Dame is a very nice and very talented guy who used to be a shit. Howard Twilley, you told me now, is also a very nice guy. You're about to tell me that there's something freaky about him too and probably that he used to be an even bigger shit."

"He's Benjamin Coffey." Duncan Peck dropped the other shoe with a thud.

Harrigan gaped. He stopped on the running track and stared after Duncan Peck. "Jesus!" was all he could manage.

"Bad Ben," Peck repeated. His expression betrayed his satisfaction at Harrigan's loss for words.

"You're sure?" Harrigan asked.

"As sure as I can be from a photograph and a voice print. I couldn't very well run a fingerprint check or the FBI would be all over this."

Harrigan took a long breath and whistled. He could see the old headlines in his mind. Ben Coffey. Bad Ben. Black activist. Sometime Panther. Their minister of defense. Long history of juvenile crime and random violence. Then straightened out, after a fashion, under Cleaver's tutelage. One subsequent bust on a drug charge and another on weapons. Both possibly rigged.

Broke out of the Alameda County Jail, killing a guard in the process. Went underground, what . . . five years ago?

"Interested, Connor?"

"What's different besides nice? What's his talent?"

"An alert question, Connor." Peck smiled approvingly. "All I have in reply is rumor. Folklore has it that he's an almost hypnotically persuasive man. It's been useful in calming truculent patrons. One story has him convincing a gun-toter that he was holding a live rat instead of a weapon. Probably apocryphal. But by all accounts a remarkable man. Possibly a troubled man."

Harrigan waited while Peck did an isometric while walking. Peck was given to dramatic pauses and Harrigan had learned to indulge him.

"Twilley placed a call last month to the suburban New York number I mentioned earlier. Mamaroneck, actually. Would you like to hear the transcript, Connor? I know it by heart."

Harrigan nodded.

" 'Doc?' Than a hesitant, 'Is this . . . ?' 'It's George.' 'Please hang up at once.' 'I've had it, Doc. Four years. I want to use it.' 'I'll contact you.' 'Soon, Doc.' Click. Click."

"That's it?"

"That's rather a lot," Peck countered. "Right there you have your probable conspiracy. We don't know what the 'it' is that Twilley wants to use, but I'm inclined to guess it has something to do with his talent."

"What about 'Doc'? Who's he?"

"The phone is unlisted. But it belongs to a Dr. Marcus Sonnenberg of Mamaroneck, New York."

Harrigan glanced curiously at Peck. Peck's eyes had done something when he said that name. A switch opened in his brain and that impression was filed there. He stopped at a stone bench and began thoughtfully adjusting his laces.

"A medical doctor?" he asked.

"I don't know." Another distant look. A spark of coloration. "If he is, he doesn't practice. IRS says he's an inventor. Quite successful. Lives well and under extremely tight personal security, which may or may not relate to the fact that his business involves security devices. I've taken a look at the home myself and I now have it under daytime surveillance. Michael Biaggi's up there. You know him, Connor?"

"Young, bright, ambitious. Yeah, I know him. He get anything?"

"On Sonnenberg, nothing. It's apparently quite difficult to get close to the house or to spend much time in the vicinity without being questioned by the police. However . . ." Another dramatic pause. Harrigan sighed and looked at his watch, but the sarcasm did nothing to quicken Peck's delivery. "However . . . the mysterious Dr. Sonnenberg has a house guest. On two occasions, that house guest has slipped from the house and made his way to a public phone a quarter-mile away. He makes his call and returns immediately. The man leaves the Sonnenberg home at no other time and for no other reason." Peck paused and waited.

"So?"

"So, doesn't that suggest anything to you?"

"Hey." Harrigan threw up his hands. "What am I, your straight man? The guy walks to a phone because he doesn't want to call from the house. He doesn't call from the house because the call is private. That would end that except you got more, don't you. Biaggi would have taken the guy's picture during the first phone call. Or he'd lift the guy's prints off the receiver, in which case you'd have a positive ID within twenty-four hours. You know who the guy is but you're taking your time telling me. You're doing that because you want to get me interested. You want me interested because you're going to ask me to do something illegal, unofficial, or at least outside your jurisdiction. Then I'm going to ask you 'Why should I?' and you're going to say 'Trust me.' I'm going to say 'In a pig's ass,' and then you're going to lay a lot of shit on me about how I'm the only person in the Fed who you can trust to do this right because I operate as a free safety and don't have to play politics. You might even wave the flag. But what it's going to come down to is, you want to be the only guy in Treasury who knows what's going on. You want that so much, you're going to make almost any deal I ask for. How'm I doing?"

"A shocking display of cynicism."

"Duncan . . ."

Peck raised a silencing hand until two runners, both women in their late twenties, passed by. One stopped, bending over to pull up a sweatsock, then continued on without glancing at the two men.

"The house guest's name is Jared Baker." Peck dropped his voice by several shades. "An unremarkable man, at least compared to Berner and Coffey. There are, however, at least two key similarities. Mr. Baker committed an act of extraordinary brutality against a young man who caused the death of his wife and crippled his daughter. It was the daughter, incidentally, whom Baker left Sonnenberg's house to call. In any case, Baker was arrested, bailed out by none other than Benjamin Meister, and then fled upon the murder of the young man's father, who was bent on vengeance. Baker may or may not have done the deed. I rather think not."

"How come?"

"The killing of the father was too unlike the maiming of the son, although both were uncharacteristic of Baker. And the killing of the father, a judge named Bellafonte, had the look of a frame. My hunch is that Meister, or Sonnenberg, wanted Baker in a fugitive's role. If Baker was tried and imprisoned, there seems to be some doubt that he'd have survived his incarceration. The judge had considerable political clout. There's also some vague connection with organized crime in there somewhere, as if Baker didn't have enough reason to run already."

Harrigan made a face. "Bellafonte!" he repeated. "Every dago with an uncle claims some connection with organized crime. Most of it's bullshit. What's the second similarity?"

"That he vanished, obviously," Peck answered. "Just as Berner, Coffey, and Lord knows who else vanished. And that all three are connected with the mysterious Dr.

Sonnenberg. At the moment, by the way, only you and I know that."

"What about Biaggi and whoever identified Baker's picture?"

"Biaggi knows little or nothing about Baker. Identification does, obviously, but they don't connect him with Sonnenberg."

"One last question. Why don't you just feed all this to the FBI?"

"Because the FBI, assuming they don't muck the whole thing up, will only want to know what Sonnenberg is doing and why, and whether he's violated any federal law. Clearly, he's part of a conspiracy, but conspiracy is difficult to prove. They might get him on three counts of abetting a fugitive ... *if* I were to tell them about the Berner and Coffey connections, but even that is hard to prove. Their investigation would accomplish little more than driving Sonnenberg underground. I want to know more than what he's doing, Connor. Even more than why. I want to know how he's doing it."

Connor Harrigan's mind seemed to have wandered. His head had turned toward the Jefferson Memorial. Peck followed his eyes. Harrigan, Peck saw, was looking not at Thomas Jefferson but at the distant swaying rumps of the two women who had passed them. Duncan Peck reddened.

"This is important, Connor."

Harrigan raised one finger, smiled, and walked a few feet closer to the receding women as if for a better look. With his back to Duncan Peck and without moving his head, he looked down at the spot where the one runner had paused. He saw it. A button microphone lying low in the grass. Harrigan turned and retraced his steps back to the irritated Duncan Peck.

"Let's walk again. I'm beginning to feel healthy."

"Connor—"

"Where were we?" Harrigan interrupted, guiding Peck away from the microphone. "Oh, yeah. You're saying that you want to go to school on this Sonnenberg guy.

I thought your people were already the best around at burying people."

"Connor, have you been listening at all carefully?"

"Yeah," Harrigan answered quietly. "I'll even summarize it for you." He walked with Peck for a few more yards as if gathering his thoughts. "Try this on. Berner goes down and Hershey comes up. But as a different person. Professional gook-shooter becomes Mr. Nice Guy and bookworm.

"Coffey goes down and Twilley comes up. Angry black activist becomes friendly saloonkeeper beloved by honky rednecks, maybe even makes like the Shadow and clouds men's minds.

"Now Baker goes down and you want to see what comes up. But you already know that Baker has done something entirely uncharacteristic. And you tell me what you want to know is how. Not why, as in 'I'm a responsible federal official and I want to know if a law's being broken,' but how. And you want to know so badly that you're willing to risk an obstruction of justice rap for not blowing the whistle on Baker and those other guys.

"Here's what you didn't say. You want to know how so maybe you can do it yourself. But not just to hide people, because your job is bigger than that, isn't it, Duncan? You don't just hide people. You train people. You want to see if you can put people in the field who can do head tricks like turning guns into rats or becoming legitimate experts in archaeology overnight.

"Next comes this Relocation Section that no one's supposed to know about. If it exists, which it does, it's expensive as hell. But it's not funded out of Treasury's budget, is it? Treasury has to account for what it spends. Which means you're funded by someone who doesn't have to account to the GAO. Which probably means the CIA, because you've been working with them anyway on most of the people you stash. If it is the CIA, you figure they'll pay up the ass if you can train spooks who can go into the field doing what Berner and Coffey can do."

Peck walked in silence for another hundred feet. "Harrigan," he said at last, "you did well not to seek a career in the diplomatic service."

"No disrespect, Duncan. I wanted you to know I'm not stupid."

"You've been showing me that for years. You're certainly not a stupid man."

"Neither are you, Duncan," he responded. "Neither are you."

"I detect a certain pregnancy in that compliment."

"You told me what I had to know." Harrigan looked directly into Duncan Peck's eyes. "You didn't tell me all of it. I want you to know I know that."

"Meaning?"

"I'll play straight with you until or unless I find out that you're suckering me. From then on, it's hardball."

Duncan Peck stared back, appraising Harrigan. His eyes didn't waver.

"What I hoped for, Connor," he said at last, "was your friendship, your trust, and your loyalty. Perhaps we should drop the matter here."

Harrigan appeared to be considering it. Backing off. But it was more that he was considering how great a distance to keep between himself and Duncan Peck. He knew that Peck trusted him. Respected him, anyway. But only for what he could do. The friendship and loyalty part was almost true. Peck liked him. Peck would like him even while he was pulling the trigger if he happened to open the wrong door somewhere. Like finding out what's really between him and Sonnenberg. There was something. It was on his face.

On the other hand, maybe life's too short for this kind of shit. What do you think, Connor? Do you go have a beer and forget it? If you do, do you then hope that nobody figures you're already smarter than they can afford? Yea, though I walk through the valley of the shadow of death, he thought, remembering some career advice he'd heard years before, I shall fear no evil ... as long as I know where the bodies are buried. And as long as I know who's listening in the grass.

It could be anyone. But why do I think it's Sonnenberg?

"What you hoped for, Duncan," Harrigan reminded him gently, "was to get me interested. I'm interested."

9

Sonnenberg set the little blue spiral in motion and left it on the desk facing Baker. He said nothing about it. Sonnenberg simply talked on about an experience he'd had as a child in Switzerland. It had no apparent point. Just a nice story. And only mildly interesting.

Soon, Baker felt his mind drifting. He thought of Tina, which was in no way unusual. But he thought of Sonnenberg being with her. Tina and Sonnenberg and this dumb blue toy. Tina would look at the toy and she would feel better. Better about her mother. Better about the trouble her father was in. Better . . . even glad, about him running away.

Baker pushed aside the thought. Tina was not involved with Sonnenberg. He wouldn't be either. Except for the money Sonnenberg was providing for Tina. And to Jane Carey for taking care of Tina.

"Relax, Jared," Sonnenberg whispered. "Watch the hypnodisk and let your body and mind relax."

He could not.

Letting it teach him to draw and paint was one thing. Letting the hypnodisk carry him backward into some dreamy past where he could think and feel like Eugène Delacroix. Where he could almost see the rooms in which Delacroix lived, smell the air that reeked of open sewers, feel the vitality and dramatic power of the man. That astonished Baker, but it did not frighten him.

What astonished him was that Sonnenberg had been right. He could paint like Delacroix. Only a little, perhaps, but still far more than Baker would have dreamed possible. He did a portrait, upon waking, of Frédéric Chopin. He had no idea why he chose that subject, but it was good. For Jared Baker. Better than Jared Baker. It captured the anguish of Chopin's genius, his rebelliousness, his strength. And then Sonnenberg showed him a plate of the original. Baker hadn't even remembered it. When had he seen it? In a museum, perhaps? In a textbook? He didn't know. But there it was and he had done it. Something close to it, anyway. Who, Sonnenberg asked, would you like to be tomorrow? An American this time? Winslow Homer, perhaps, who shared your love of small boats under sail. Or Caleb Bingham. Choose your teacher, Jared. They are all within you.

"Relax, Jared. Please."

He could be those people, perhaps because they were dead and gone. And then he could be Jared Baker again. He could come back. But this new thing that Sonnenberg wanted to try . . . He couldn't relax. What if he's there? What if Sonnenberg is actually right?

Sonnenberg switched off the hypnodisk. He had been saying something. Baker cleared his head to listen.

" . . . how insensitive of me. What if he really comes out, you say? How do you know you can stuff him back?"

Baker sat straighter and answered Sonnenberg with a nod.

"Of course you're concerned, Jared. You're concerned that this frightening entity in your photograph will pop loose like a genie from a bottle. You're afraid that some Frankenstein will leave you imprisoned in his place while he wreaks havoc among the villagers and strangles little girls for their daisies."

"Something like that crossed my mind, yes."

"Ah, but he can't," enthused Sonnenberg. "You, Jared, are Abel. This procedure is simply designed to help you bring him to the surface. Suggestive response is essential because your conscious mind isn't even entirely sure that he's there. But once he's been brought up, once we get acquainted and we satisfy ourselves that he's housebroken, hypnosis will no longer be necessary. If I'm right, you'll be able to bring him out at will by using a response word and to send him back just as readily."

"Response word?"

"A verbal trigger," Sonnenberg answered. "It's learned under hypnosis, and using it enables the subject to move readily from one state of consciousness to another. A hypnotist might tell his subject to awake on the count of three, for example, or to fall into a trance when he says goodnight."

"Or shoot a president when he sees the queen of hearts?"

Sonnenberg smiled indulgently. "No Manchurian Candidates here, Baker. Only you and what is already within you. Hypnosis cannot alter a personality. Personalities are altered by chemical imbalances and sometimes by trauma. A physical cause in either event.

"The normal brain is a sort of factory that produces those chemicals in the right combinations and in the right quantities to keep imbalances from happening. No amount of suggestion can turn those spigots on and off. What hypnosis does is enable you to pass through barriers that are learned or artificial and that needn't be there. For example, one of the classic clinical demonstrations involves asking an entranced subject to recite the alphabet backward just as rapidly as he does it forward. Obviously, the subject has all the required information for reciting the alphabet backward, but his conscious mind blocks him from efficiently rearranging that data. Theoretically, you're also capable of reciting every fact you've ever committed to memory long enough for that information to pass from your temporal lobe into permanent storage. Your Chopin portrait ought to be all the proof you need of that." Sonnenberg waved his hands, signifying that they were getting off the track.

"Enough pedantry." He patted Baker's knee. "We were speaking of response words. In this case, it will be simplest to use names. If you want Abel, say his name. If you want him gone, say Baker's name. And so on. Could

anything be simpler?" Sonnenberg watched Baker's face
for a long moment, then rose stiffly and walked to a small
wet bar concealed behind a panel near his desk.

Baker was less than reassured. For all that
Sonnenberg seemed to know his subject, for all the actor
that Sonnenberg was, he could not seem to resist that last
little locking of the eyes after a pronouncement to see if
Baker was buying it. Baker didn't as yet. Not quite. But
more and more, he found himself wanting to believe that
what Sonnenberg proposed was possible. That he could
be whomever and whatever he needed to be at his discretion. And that he could come back. That he could be
stronger than Abel. There was the question. Baker had
already seen what just a shadow of Abel, a leashed and
fettered Abel, was capable of doing.

"Here you are, Jared." Unasked, Sonnenberg had
mixed a rum and tonic and placed it in Baker's hand.
Baker sipped it absently, then made a face. Sonnenberg
had added bitters.

And Sonnenberg's wrong, he thought, about not really believing he's there. He's there, all right. He's right
down there in that little blue tunnel. He's as tough and
as strong as you've ever wanted to be. And you know
something else, don't you, Jared.

"Jared? Excuse me, please."

You know that you want him. You want to be Abel.
You can think of a dozen times in your life . . . when if
you could have been Abel for just five minutes . . . times
when you despised yourself for being so damned civilized. No, not civilized. The word is scared, Jared. Times
when you'd like to have busted someone's teeth but you
didn't because you thought too much about the consequences. Or afraid of being humiliated. Or afraid, period.

John Wayne wouldn't worry about consequences.
He'd have just belted the guy. There's a thought. Maybe
Abel could be tamed just a little into a John Wayne type.
They're probably a lot alike. John Wayne never breaks a
knuckle when he pops someone. Or spits out a tooth.
John and Abel both seem to heal fast. There's that hand

I hurt. And the burns . . . On the other hand, John Wayne never sticks anyone's face in a fire, does he?

"Baker." Sonnenberg tapped Baker's arm with the end of his cane.

"I'm sorry, Doctor . . ."

"Jared, I must take a rather personal call. Might I ask that you excuse me for just a few minutes?"

Baker looked at him blankly. No phone had rung. Only the . . . A desk lamp had turned on by itself. Gadgets! Baker smiled that he understood. He pushed to his feet, experiencing a flash of vertigo, and reached for the door latch when the dizziness passed. He wanted a few minutes to himself anyway. Baker closed the door behind him and wandered toward Mrs. Kreskie's kitchen.

From the tap over the stainless steel sink, he ran a tumbler of water and sipped it slowly. There was an odd aftertaste to Sonnenberg's rum. But bitters or not, it did seem to be clearing his head. Wiping away a few troubles. A few worries. Helping him admit a thing or two to himself. Admitting, for openers, that he did want to be Abel. Sometimes. That there are times when it would be nice to stand outside your own body and watch someone else being afraid. Like that biker when he came back the second time.

Funny. He'd never thought about that before. Outside his own body. But yes, Baker, that's right, isn't it. That's where you were. While you were watching from there, all the fear and hate and misery were gone. Strange. And looking back, it didn't seem that Abel especially hated that biker either. It doesn't seem that Abel was bothered by any emotion at all. He must be very basic. Elemental. Like an attack dog. Abel sees an enemy, Abel attacks. Abel sees a threat, Abel removes it. You have to wonder whether Abel would be capable of feeling loneliness, or of missing Sarah, or of feeling the hurt of not being able to see and hold Tina. Probably not. Not my attack dog.

If Abel is like that, then what is Charley? Nice? Easygoing? Sonnenberg agrees he's probably bland. And Sonnenberg probably knows. He knows a hell of a lot more than he's willing to let on. On the other hand, almost everybody is bland or easygoing compared to Abel. Everybody, period, if you don't count Dracula.

Wow! Getting giddy. Could have done without that dumb rum. Rum dumb. Rum, dum dum dumb.

Abel? Are you down there? I'm afraid, old buddy, that you're going to have to wait a bit longer. Our friend Sonnenberg is dying to meet you, but he's going to have to wait too. This is your captain speaking. Able-bodied Abel is to remain below until further orders. We're going to break this act slowly. What we're going to do, Sonnenberg or no Sonnenberg, is start with good old Charley. And to tell you the God's honest truth, Abel, I'm so relieved I just might kiss him when I see him. Nothing personal. It's just that Charley seems a tiny bit more likely to remember who's the skipper.

That's right, isn't it, Charley? Charley? Where are you? Probably in a hammock somewhere. You're wearing a grubby old hat with fishing lures stuck through it and you're asleep with a six-pack lying across your little potbelly. Or you're in some dark corner wearing an eyeshade and working on your stamp collection. No . . . bugs. I bet you collect bugs. Boring little crawlies that no one else cares diddly-squat about.

How'm I doing? Am I getting warm? If only . . . if only I could get a look at you first. I think I know where you are. You're right on the other side of that little blue tunnel, aren't you. If I turned on Dr. Marcus Sonnenberg's magic whirling hypnosis machine and I watched it really closely and I followed the swirl right into the tunnel, I bet I'd find you right on the other side. I don't even need the machine, I bet. All I have to do . . . is turn on the cold water like this and watch it spinning and circling down the drain. Down where you are. Come on, Charley. Come out, come out, wherever you are.

"Come on, Charley."

"Jared?"

Sonnenberg stood framed in the kitchen doorway. His expression was thoughtful and distant.

"*Coriolis,*" Baker answered.

"I beg your . . ." Sonnenberg shook off the distraction. "Jared, something pressing has come up. We'll have to end our session early."

"That's the Coriolis effect." Baker was staring at the clockwise motion of the water as it raced into the drainpipe of the sink.

"Coriolis . . . Oh, the water. Yes. Jared, I'm afraid I must—"

"It's not the same in the southern hemisphere. I know that from someplace. Down there the water swirls the other way. Pitchers should know about that."

"Pitchers?"

"Baseball pitchers. A curve ball won't break the same way when you go way south."

Sonnenberg had to strain to hear him. Baker's voice was curiously soft and his back remained turned to the doctor. The running tap muffled it further.

"Jared, why don't you make yourself at home with some of my texts or relax perhaps with a television program. I'm afraid I'm going to have to leave."

"Teach him a lesson."

"What did you say, Jared?" Sonnenberg took a step forward.

"Snoopy Dunny. Teach him a lesson. Ben Coffey. Stanley. Ben Meister snooped on snoopy Dunny. Teach him a lesson."

"Jared, how did you— Were you eavesdropping at my door?"

"No." Baker turned to face him. *"I heard you now."*

Sonnenberg recoiled as if he'd been struck. His cane clattered to the tile floor and he had to grip the doorway for support. Baker's face had changed. It was a more innocent face. Like that of a child. The natural lines had softened and the eyes were . . . more than innocent. They were almost blank. Somehow a paler green than before. Even his skin seemed to have less color. But most stunning of all, and impossibly, Baker's lips were closed against each other. When he spoke the words "I heard you now," the words were as muted as those spoken against the running water. But they did not come from Baker's throat. Baker's lips had never moved.

"Charley?" Sonnenberg gasped. "Are you Charley?"

"Charley." Baker nodded.

"Charley, are you able to talk? To form words?"

"I don't know." Charley's voice was childlike. And he answered with an air of utter unconcern. Sonnenberg was enthralled.

"Where . . . where is Jared?"

"Baker."

"Very well, where is Baker?"

"On the other side of the drain."

"The drain? do you mean in the sink?"

"Down the tunnel. The blue tunnel. Except it's not blue here."

Sonnenberg began to understand. The Coriolis effect. The effect of the earth's motion on draining water. Swirling water. Swirling hypnodisks. Whether accidentally or by design, Baker had created his own hypnodisk and gone looking for Charley. Sonnenberg's brain was flying. It raced through all the relevant volumes he'd ever read like a random access computer, searching out those bits and pieces of data that seemed to match what was happening here. There were so few. The Russians. The Russians had found something like this. Bor . . . Borodin. Mikhail Borodin. The Borodin arc. Where the telepathic voice seems to be coming not from within the brain but from a point in space someplace between observer and subject. But the Russians reported no accompanying physical change. But of course they wouldn't report it. Not if they thought they had a Chimera.

No, Marcus, never mind the Russians. You have your own physical change. Charley seems absolutely slack. And why should he be telepathic at all? Could the personality be hemispheric? Is it possible that he doesn't speak because there's no speech center where he lives? Of course, it's possible. Mrs. Kreskie doesn't speak either, and now we know why, don't we. Oh, Baker. Baker, are you watching this? Are you understanding it?

"This blue tunnel. It leads inside you to Baker, doesn't it, Charley."

"No."

"But you said he was on the other side."

Charley stared.

"Charley, is Baker far away?"

"Baker is behind me. Touching."

"Touching? Can Baker hear me now?"

"I don't know."

"Do you know what Baker is doing?"

"Baker's drunk."

"Drunk? From a single rum and tonic?"

"From the rum and what you put in the rum. You put reserpine in the rum." Charley's tone was that of a disinterested child idly playing with his toes. There was no accusation in it.

Even so, Sonnenberg felt his chin begin to quiver. Whether it was from fear or excitement, he didn't know. Whatever the emotion, he knew it was clouding his mind and interfering with . . . so many questions . . . so much to learn, to observe. His thoughts were vaulting and crisscrossing, leaping across doctrine and conventional knowledge. Leaping across the continent. To Cal Tech. Could the people at Cal Tech have come this far? Or were they still creeping cautiously along for fear of losing their precious grants? Simulated genetic regression would still be little more than theory had not Marcus Sonnenberg plunged full tilt through the crack in the door that they opened. And Captain William Berner wouldn't have known an archaeological dig from a foxhole or a shard from a grenade fragment, let alone have become a cultured and respected anthropologist. An infusion of live brain tissue didn't hurt either. Another Cal Tech baby step. Hillman would never have dared try it with human subjects. Not with all those people watching. Even if the watchdogs slept, disposing of the leftovers would have been much too delicate a problem for them. As it was, our own leftovers played absolute hob with the acid level of the rhododendrons outside.

Don't be derailed, Marcus. Concentrate. Could Cal

Tech have found a Charley? Surely they must have tried. Even illicitly. They know that the independent consciousness exists. It's there in everyone. Could they have found it? No. Hillman would have told me. Or does it require a stupid accident such as this. A reserpine-tranquilized subject happening to look into a draining sink that resembles a hypnodisk. The happy combination of slightly diminished capacity, a recent hypnodisk experience, and a desire to find out what's at the other end of Charley's blue tunnel.

"Charley," he asked slowly, "does Baker know about the reserpine?"

"Baker is drunk."

"Yes, but will he know when he's sober? When he comes back?"

"I don't know," Charley answered in a singsong.

"Would you be able to tell him? If you wanted to?"

"I don't know."

"If you wanted to tell him something . . . If, for example, he was in danger, how would you tell him?"

"I don't know. Baker knows. Baker knows what I know if he thinks about it."

Sonnenberg wasn't sure he understood. Did that mean that Charley had no independent consciousness when he was back inside or no independent memory?

"That was not very clear, Charley. Can you explain that part?"

"No."

"Charley . . . By the way, is your name Charley, actually?"

"Yes."

"How do you know that's your name?"

"You said so. Baker said so."

"Did you hear us saying it?"

"No. Baker knows it."

"And you, just now, thought about what Baker knows? About your name, I mean?"

"Yes."

"Charley, who is Dunny?"

"Bad man. Hits golf balls. Found Sonnenberg."

"And yet he's holding back. Do you know why, Charley?"

"No."

"No." Sonnenberg waggled his hands distractedly. "Of course you don't." Charley didn't know Duncan Peck. Nor did Baker. So Charley would have no way of knowing what was on Duncan Peck's mind. But Baker knew Ben Meister. What, therefore, would Charley know of him?

"Charley, who is Ben Meister?"

"That." Charley pointed a limp finger toward Sonnenberg's arm.

Sonnenberg understood. "My right arm?"

"Yes."

"What does my right arm do?"

"He goes places for you and does things. He fixed Baker to be not in jail."

"And Stanley. You mentioned someone named Stanley."

"Stanley fixed the judge to be dead so that Baker . . ." Charley's voice trailed off. His eyes narrowed briefly and then, as if further concentration were not worth the effort, they relaxed again and went blank.

Sonnenberg had, in his head, visualized the slamming of a great iron gate. He imagined carpenters there, nailing boards over the gates, and plasterers with trowels of wet cement. Sonnenberg focused hard upon that confusion and through it conjured up new pictures of the men who were Ben Coffey and Benjamin Meister and of the man he knew as Stanley Levy. Very new pictures. Pictures as different from the real men as his imagination could concoct.

"Charley, besides being my right arm, who is Ben Meister? And who is Ben Coffey?"

"Santa's little helper and the tooth fairy."

Sonnenberg's mouth fell open. There it was. Without any doubt. That was the nonsense he was thinking. Clearly, Baker or Charley had not been listening when Meister told him of the meeting between Peck and this Connor Harrigan. They were not listening at his door.

They were listening to his mind. At least Charley was. Just as he was listening now to Charley's mind.

"*Tooth fairy.*" Charley seemed to brighten as Sonnenberg lost his concentration. "*Black tooth fairy. George Twilley fairy. Muzzles and leashes and Sonnenberg don't let tooth fairy go and shoot shoot shoot—*"

"That's enough, Charley!" barked Sonnenberg.

Charley snapped his head to one side and held it there. The knuckle of one fist rose slowly to his open mouth. Astonishing, thought Sonnenberg. He's acting like a scolded dog. Or a small child. One who's been shouted at but who doesn't understand what he did wrong.

"Charley." Sonnenberg felt the beginnings of a hunch. "What you said about the black tooth fairy, what does that mean?"

"*I don't know.*"

Sonnenberg raised the iron gate and in front of it began to create new facts. His brain darted from detail to irrelevant detail, trying to avoid concentrating overlong on a single truth. He was painting a mental portrait for Charley.

"Are you sure you don't know?" he asked finally.

"*I know. Stanley was bad because he ate too much porridge. He turned into butter so I can't think of him anymore. Meister and Coffey are sad because the cupboard is bare and they don't have any Rye Thins or Camembert for Goldilocks, so the bear drank Coffey and I can't think about him anymore either.*"

Sonnenberg smiled. Let's see Baker make any sense out of that mess. "Say the alphabet backward, Charley."

"*Z, Y, X, W, V, U, T, R, S—*"

"That's enough." Sonnenberg raised a hand. "How about every second letter going backward from Q?"

"*Q, O, M, K, I, G—*"

"That's enough." Sonnenberg picked up a box of crackers that had been left on the counter and handed it to Charley. He pointed to a section of the package.

"Read that, Charley," he ordered. He counted off fifteen seconds and then took back the box. "Did you read it, Charley?"

"*Yes.*"

"What did it say?"

"*Ingredients enriched flour niacin iron thiamine mononitrate riboflavin lard and or coconut oil and partially hydrogenated soybean oil rye flour sugar—*"

"That will do. Thank you, Charley." Sonnenberg was beaming. He'd been right. Charley was almost pure concentration. Effortless concentration. And undiscriminating, left to himself. The man, if this marshmallow could be called a man, was indeed a living sponge. As for Charley's inability to speak, this entity was clearly a creature of the left hemisphere of Baker's brain, or some passive droning segment of it. As for the telepathic ability, Sonnenberg was mystified. How did it work? Would it work with anyone else? And wasn't it just as remarkable that Sonnenberg could receive as it was that Charley could send? But most remarkable of all was the revelation that Charley could be controlled. Managed. That he would accept false information and very likely act on it. Or would he. That business about Goldilocks and Stanley Butter didn't suggest much in the way of a functional intellect.

"Charley, are you able to . . ." Sonnenberg paused, looking up at the ceiling as he gathered his thoughts.

"*He's Abel.*"

"No. Are you able to understand . . ." Sonnenberg's eyes fell back upon Charley, and once again what he saw hit him like a blow to the stomach. There was no Charley. Charley was gone. And in his place was the man Sonnenberg knew from the airbrushed photograph he'd shown Baker. It was not supposed to happen.

"How . . . how do you do, Abel?" he stammered, struggling to regain his composure. This should not be happening this way. Not from Charley to Abel. "I'm very pleased to—"

"*Shut up, Sonnenberg.*" The man who was Abel was not looking at him. He was staring into space as if trying to focus. His body rocked backward, and he grabbed the countertop with both hands to steady himself. Now he turned his face toward Sonnenberg. The doctor took a step away.

"But how did . . ." Sonnenberg felt a trembling in his knees. It was a cruel face. And powerful. The whole body seemed a coil of animal strength, but the animal could not yet seem to get his bearings. He was drugged, Sonnenberg realized. Or drunk. He looked like every mean but ineffectual drunk Sonnenberg had ever seen. But Charley wasn't drunk. And Baker could have been no more than mellowed. A few milligrams of tranquilizer and perhaps two ounces of spirits. Baker! Where was Baker! "Where is Jared Baker?" he asked the reeling man who gripped Mrs. Kreskie's counter.

"I'm a message from him." Abel's lips drew back over his teeth and his hooded eyes pinioned Sonnenberg. *"No drugs, Sonnenberg. That's his message. The message from me is, if you do it again, I'm going to break both your legs."*

10

Kate Mulgrew was the first to die.

She died on Sixth Avenue, at night, when the first light was still more than two hours to the east. Janet's voice quivered over the radiophone of the blue Oldsmobile.

"Mr. Harrigan?" The pain was evident even in those two words.

"What happened, Janet?" he asked softly.

"Katy . . . Katy's dead. Your man Mr. Dugan at the Warwick . . . He found her in a car . . . Oh, Mr. Harrigan."

Harrigan chewed his lip. "Finish your report, Janet."

"She was sitting in the back of a parked car with her face against the window. Like she was watching people walk by. Just staring. At first Mr. Dugan thought she was . . ."

"I know, Janet. I know, darlin'." Harrigan kept his voice even. "Janet, you must tell me what Mr. Dugan said and what he did."

"He said he opened the door and she almost fell out, but he caught her and he laid her down on the back seat, but he knew she was dead. He said to tell you there was a little puncture wound under her chin. And there was a pen stuck in her mouth like the way you hold your pipe."

"What sort of pen?"

"Mr. Dugan said to tell you it was an ordinary ball-

178

point pen. Why would anyone . . ." Janet's voice made a hiccupping sound and she swallowed hard to regain control. Harrigan reminded himself that she was new. Less than a year. She had not seen death before. Not this kind of death. In addition to the puncture wound that had popped through Katy's palate and into her brain, Stanley Levy had left a message. Katy had almost surely taken a pen gun when she went out. Levy was announcing that he had it now, along with at least one unspent cartridge of cyanide crystals. But why? Who was the message for? What could Stanley Levy know of Connor Harrigan?

"Go on, Janet," he hushed. "What about Mr. Dugan?"

"He asked if he could leave his post to bring her in." Good girl, thought Harrigan. She was managing to hold a level. "He said he could boost the car she's in."

"Yes, Janet. Tell him to do that before it gets light. Then tell him to join me here. Do you have anything else for me, darlin'?"

"No sir . . . Yes. A woman from the Celebrity Register called. I had to give her a Washington number so she could verify. Then she called again and said there were three women who answered your description. Marlo Dunne, an opera singer, she's staying at the Regency. Tanner Burke is at the Plaza until Sunday. Then there's an English actress named Gwen Leamas who's staying down at the Helmsley Palace."

"Thank you, Janet. You've done very well." Harrigan could have kicked himself for not anticipating the verification call. If Katy had been there, she would have given a Washington number that routed back to her own call director. She would have answered the call herself in a southern accent or some such. Well, spilt milk. But the call was now logged. And coming in the dead of night, it might just arouse Duncan Peck's curiosity before Harrigan wanted it aroused.

As for the names, thought Harrigan, assuming Baker's new friend was one of them, Tanner Burke is the way to bet. Gwen Leamas's hotel is just too far from the park. The Regency was closer, but Marlo Dunne probably wouldn't be familiar to Biaggi. Biaggi wouldn't know opera from root canal. Tanner Burke, however, was all over the magazine racks and on the TV screen. You're elected, Tanner Burke. At least you're worth a peek. But first, one or two changes in the lineup might be useful. And Janet needs to be succored if she is to keep a clear head for the next few hours.

"Janet," he said at last into the mike, his voice bereaved, "Katy would be proud of you for holding up so well. I know that. She and I were quite close."

"I know, Mr. Harrigan. I mean . . . I heard."

"Yes Janet," he whispered, "very close indeed. But she would expect us both to put aside our grief until we can honor her memory in a proper way. Are you able to do that, Janet?"

"Yes sir." Janet made an effort to sound strong.

"After you call Mr. Dugan, please contact Michael Biaggi. He is now somewhere on Fifty-eighth Street, watching the back entrance of the St. Moritz. Tell him about Tanner Burke and ask him to move down the street a bit so that he can watch the rear entrance of the Plaza."

"The Plaza. Yes sir."

"Now Janet." Harrigan dropped his voice even further. "Be sure you mention Tanner Burke and the Plaza to absolutely no one but Mr. Biaggi. Is that clear?"

"Yes sir."

"Good girl, Janet."

Harrigan closed his eyes after cradling his microphone and sat very still for several minutes. Oh, Michael, he thought. A thousand Hail Marys. A thousand Hail Marys is what I'll say if I have grievously wronged you in my heart. But if I have not, and if another living soul now shows an interest in Tanner Burke, then Mary herself and all the blessed saints will not save you.

He blinked to clear a hotness that he felt inside his eyelids and looked out into the fading night. And you, Stanley Levy, he thought. Truth be told, Stanley, I did send Katy to do you in. Truth be told, you had an equal right. But life isn't fair, is it, Stanley. You're going to answer, Stanley, for the death of Katherine Mulgrew because someone must if I am to find peace. And when you do answer, you'll wish to God that your life was all I took.

Baker had given up trying to sleep. It would not come. Twice, he'd felt his body become heavy and warm to the point of drifting off, but each time his thoughts would fall upon the softly breathing body next to him. He thought of what it might be like to wake up with her each day. To linger in bed on a chill winter morning. To feel the joy and the fire and the thrill of— Damn! He felt himself begin to stiffen.

Annoyed, and fearful that she might reach to touch him in her sleep and discover his condition, he rose quietly from the bed.

There was a hot plate in the bathroom for making tea and instant coffee. As silently as he could manage, Baker produced a steaming cup and walked with it to the window fifteen floors above the expanse of Central Park. He stood watching and thinking. And listening.

Just west of the zoo he could see the strobing blue lights of police cars. Three of them. And the red and amber of a single ambulance. There was something about the blue strobes of a police car at night. They're like a scream, he thought. He remembered the way those lights lashed across his house the last time he saw it. Baker shook away the image.

The red lights moved. They were dipping through the trees as they crossed from left to right. The ambulance was leaving the park by the Sixty-fifth Street exit. Right through the zoo. In his mind Baker could almost see the animals sniffing after the blood scent that the ambulance trailed behind it.

Blood.

Baker didn't remember much about the one called Jace. Only the snap of bones. And those puncture marks. Absently, he touched the pocket that held the felt-tipped pen Abel had used. It struck him that Abel had never toyed with anyone like that before. He'd never gone out of his way to mark anyone. Usually, it was the way it had been with Sumo. Baker winced. He saw in dim memory the way Sumo had jerked and danced as the knife pushed through his organs. The way his body had arched into an obscenely stiff and prolonged tremor as if it had touched a third rail. The way he shook even after he fainted. That one would almost certainly die. And Abel killed him. Why? Why these two?

Baker frowned and cocked his head. Someone else had died, he thought. A woman. What woman? The only woman he knew here was sleeping safely behind him. Was there another woman?... Tina?

His stomach twisted. "Tina?"

In Greenwich, Tina awoke suddenly from a dream. A dumb dream. She was in this cave, just napping there, and her father rushed in all excited to find out if she was all right, and she said sure. And then he just let out a breath and went out again. Dumb dream. She turned over and closed her eyes.

Baker relaxed. It wasn't Tina. Who was it, Charley? He pressed close to the glass to look down at the deadened street. He couldn't see the sidewalk. Who's there, Charley? Who's moving around down there?

Never mind. He really didn't want to know. Time enough to deal with it when daylight came and there would be crowds of people rushing to work. People in too much of a hurry to notice a man who didn't look quite right. To notice Abel.

For now, Baker felt safe from those who were moving around on the street. Taking positions. And if he was safe, so were they. From Abel. "Count your blessings," he whispered aloud.

He raised the cup to his lips and sipped. A thin haze of steam coated the window as he did so, blurring the reflection of his face. The image he saw glowed red from the dim light of the digital clock near Tanner's bed. For an instant, he thought he saw Abel's face looking back at him. Slowly, he raised his left hand and covered that side of his face so that only the right half showed. The image of the right half glared back.

"Go back to sleep, Abel." Baker wiped away the haze and stepped away from it. Then he drew a chair toward the window and sat listening again.

Connor Harrigan had folded a blanket from his trunk into six thicknesses and placed it on the pavement outside the stone wall of the park. The place he chose was in deep shadow. From one coat pocket, he drew a quart-size thermos of tea and from the other a small binocular of the type used by birdwatchers. These he laid beside his transceiver and he eased to a sitting position.

At that spot, the wall of Central Park South turned north, perhaps thirty yards short of Fifth Avenue. There was a sign there, a green metal legend of the park, that further obscured his position. From it, he could not see the blue Oldsmobile where Tom Dugan now manned the radiophone. But he could see the main entrance to the Plaza and the fountain entrance as well.

It was not quite dawn. The streetlamps still gave more light than the morning sky, and the streets were largely empty. Anyone passing, he thought, would see him as a sleeping bum if they noticed him at all. Harrigan realized idly that the horse-drawn hansom cabs that normally would have blocked his view were gone. He wondered where. Where does one keep a horse in New York? Certainly not at the Plaza. And only a single taxi sat at the Plaza's hack stand, its driver dozing. No doorman could be seen. Up the street, he could hear the grind of a garbage truck.

Harrigan focused his field glasses and studied the cab driver's profile for a few moments before deciding that he was legitimate. None but a trained actor could have simulated the heavy-lidded boredom of a taxi driver during the first hours of a four-to-noon shift.

Nor did Harrigan expect much of a disguise on the part of the visitor he was waiting for. But a visitor there would be. He or she was somewhere near. Probably arguing with a superior. Arguing that it would be better to wait until full morning. Until the breakfast crowd or at least the joggers began moving through the lobby. And the superior would be arguing back. No, he would say. We have to know if he's in there with her. We don't even know if she's the one. Go there and ask the night clerk. One hundred dollars, and all he has to do is tell you whether she's there with a man. Say it's not her you want. It's him. Say you just want to slap a subpoena on the terrible man for not paying child support on the four little girls he abandoned, the dirty dog. Gets them every time.

But that, Harrigan thought, is assuming Tanner Burke is the lady in question. And assuming, even then, that Mr. Baker is still with her. But if she isn't, and he isn't, then the appearance of a visitor would tell one tale at least. It would tell that you, Michael Biaggi, you little bastard, are a man of flexible loyalties. It might tell that you're on a second payroll, possibly even a third.

He was on his second cup of tea when the visitor came. Harrigan grunted in disgust as he once again raised the binoculars. He'd been hoping for Stanley Levy. The appearance of a Stanley Levy would have been definitive. It would have explained Michael's odd nervousness upon learning that the lad whose destruction he did nothing to prevent was the son of Domenic Tortora. It would have meant that Michael had somehow found his way onto Tortora's payroll. The appearance, on the other hand, of a government type would mean that Michael had made a quiet call in that direction. Grounds there for a reprimand, to be sure, but perhaps not the fatal reprimand that a Tortora connection would require. And it would mean that old friend Duncan Peck does indeed have an interest that is something more than academic.

But it was not Stanley Levy, nor was it one of the trenchcoat types. It was a man who would need no tale of neglected children to pry loose information from a desk clerk. The man climbing the green-carpeted steps was the tall, uniformed policeman from the faraway Sixth Precinct.

Stanley Levy too was in the park. A mile from Harrigan's station, Levy shivered on a bench he'd just wiped clean with one of the handkerchiefs he carried. Vinnie Cuneo loitered a few feet away at the curb of the Eighty-fifth Street roadway, spitting through his teeth as he watched for the headlights that would turn into the park from Fifth Avenue.

Domenic Tortora's summons had come an hour earlier. Stanley had answered it reluctantly. He'd been very close to Baker. And he'd sensed an increase in activity along the block of hotels that bordered Central Park on the south. Perhaps Baker was about to make a move, or place a call he shouldn't place, or take one of his walks again. If he did, Stanley would have been near. And ready. Had not the summons come. Had he not been forced to wait here with this ignorant lump of shit, watching him expel his excess saliva.

The rising sun had almost touched the horizon. The softly lit sky reflected now off the huge glass expanse of the new American Wing of the Metropolitan Museum of Art. It sent a dim veil of light across the place where Stanley waited, exposing him. Uneasily, he looked at his hands. It had been almost two hours since he last washed them. Levy fished a dew-dampened cloth from his pocket and began working it between his fingers.

"Boss is comin'," Cuneo muttered.

The headlights of a dark Mercedes swept across the museum as the car turned into the park. The thug waved and gestured in what he presumed to be a posture of vigilance. Levy remained seated.

The car's high beams locked on the larger man's body and homed on it, stopping only inches from his legs. It sat there idling, its tinted windows closed, as if waiting for Vinnie Cuneo to conclude that it was time to take another post. Time to wait where he could watch the park entrance. Vinnie nodded that the message had penetrated and lumbered quickly in that direction. The door at last fell open, inviting Stanley.

"Good morning, Stanley," came the curiously gentle voice from inside the car. Tortora was in the driver's seat.

"Good morning to you, Mr. Tortora." Stanley rose to his feet and eased his body into the sedan's front seat, closing the door behind him. He did not extend his hand. Tortora, he knew, would understand that. Tortora's own hands remained folded on his lap and his face was almost swallowed by the collar of an oversized coat that was too warm for this time of year. He sat sunken into the farthest corner of the soft leather seat, his features gaunt in the blue glow of the dashboard lights. He seemed very small, much smaller than Stanley knew him to be. A white silk scarf that covered most of his lower jaw gave him all the more a look of frailty. And his cheeks and eyes had a powdery cast to them, the somehow hollow look of a man wasted by illness or blanched by too little sunlight.

Stanley Levy had never seen Tortora in the light of day. He was, Stanley knew, only three years past sixty, but he managed to look twenty years older. Levy knew what his mother would say. She'd say all it took was some cod liver oil every day starting sixty years ago and he wouldn't look like he had one foot in the grave, and besides, he shouldn't be driving his fancy-shmancy car in the damp air instead of being home watching out for his health, which is the most important thing along with a good upbringing. But Stanley had a feeling that cod liver oil wouldn't have helped the way Tortora looked. Maybe years ago it might have, but he was past that. What it really was was the genes. Tortora must have had genes like from hanging judges and witch burners and those monks from the Spanish Inquisition. In picture books with old-time drawings, these guys always looked like Tortora, especially with that white scarf around his face. But that's appearances, Stanley reminded himself. You can't go by appearances. Style is what counts. Next to health and upbringing, style is the most important thing.

Stanley's admiration for Tortora was as total as his

loyalty toward him. He could not remember a time it had
been otherwise. Sometimes he could not recall a time
before Tortora at all. He regarded Tortora as a "serious
man," a high compliment in Stanley's mind. A contem-
plative man not given to rashness. To Tortora, violence
was a tactic sometimes unavoidable and always regretta-
ble. It was to be employed only when the gentler forms
of persuasion had failed. Tortora was a conciliator. And
that was good, Stanley thought. But he never stepped
over the line into appeasement and that was even better,
and it made him easy to respect because you knew no
matter how slow he moved, he'd always get the other
guy. The other hoods knew that. That's why they left
Tortora alone and never tried much to move in on him.
It's respect that does that, he thought. And style.

Tortora, for all his apparent esteem within Greater
New York's extralegal community, was an almost delicate
man. A bookish man. Dickens was one of his favorites.
And Trollope and Jane Austen. But especially Arthur
Conan Doyle. Domenic Tortora could recite whole pas-
sages from *The Adventures of Sherlock Holmes* without
missing a single nuance of dialogue. He knew when a
semicolon required a lowered voice and when a pause
suggested an arching eyebrow. The escapades of Holmes
and Watson were a minor passion that Tortora delighted
in sharing with Stanley Levy. Levy remembered a time
long ago when Tortora quoted from *The Hound of the
Baskervilles* and he, Stanley, astonished him by replying
with the answering line from the text. Stanley couldn't
remember when he'd read it, but he knew he must have.
And then Tortora found out somehow that Stanley had
once been a member of the Baker Street Irregulars. At
least that's what Tortora said. Stanley couldn't remember.

Anyway, it didn't matter now. Now there were much
darker thoughts on Tortora's mind. He seemed lost in
deep thought. Perhaps two minutes had gone by since
his greeting before he spoke again to Stanley Levy.

"You know about my son, Stanley?"

Levy shook his head slowly. He knew almost nothing of John Tortora except that he was an embarrassment

to his father. A freak, speaking of genetics. One of those bad jokes that God plays on some men in the same way that big athletes seem to have nothing but daughters and business big shots always seem to have sons who are faigeleh.

"I've come from Mount Sinai Hospital," Tortora said quietly. "My son has been beaten. His face . . . has been devastated. His jaw, his teeth, his nose. There is one cheek so shattered . . . so pushed in . . . that it will never again come fully to the surface. There are blue holes near his eyes that will always mark him. And his arm . . . There is no bone left in one of them. Only splinters of bone like a board that has been crushed."

"Who did this thing, Mr. Tortora?" Stanley's voice was gentle.

Tortora did not answer. Rather, he sat slowly shaking his head in the manner of a man who knew the answer but could not bring himself to accept it.

"A friend was with my son," he said finally. "His injuries are even more terrible. It's the boy Warren. Perhaps you've seen him with John."

"Fat kid." Levy nodded. "Eats fettuccine by the bucket."

"No longer," the older man answered. "Warren is dying. I saw it in him. He has the look of a man who is afraid to live."

"I'm very sorry, Mr. Tortora." Stanley cared less for Warren, if that were possible, than he did for John. What was significant, however, was not that these two nudniks were hurt, but that a son of Domenic Tortora had been attacked.

"Mr. Tortora," he asked again, "do you know the people who did this?"

"Jared Baker did this." His voice was hard and flat. "Your man, Jared Baker, got away from you and destroyed my son."

Levy held his breath and watched the old man carefully. "Your man." What's that supposed to mean? Does it mean he was somehow to be blamed for the harm that had come to John Tortora? Levy slipped his fingers over the shaved handle of the ice pick he wore at his wrist and flicked his eyes back toward Vinnie Cuneo's post. He would not have used the ice pick on Tortora. Not even if it meant his life. But he would use it on Vinnie if Tortora waved for him. Then he would go away for a while until Tortora could get over being upset.

Tortora sensed his unease. He smiled sadly and reached to pat Stanley's sleeve.

"I am not deranged by this tragedy, Stanley. You would be the far greater loss. My son, as you know well, is a swine."

"He's a kid," Stanley protested, relieved. "Kids grow up. You could still be proud of him someday."

"Your sympathy and good will are noted, Stanley. We may now forgo all ritual condolence. The boy was a despicable child and a worse adult. My . . . stature, if you will, only served to make him a bully in the bargain."

Stanley shrugged and sat back in his corner. He drew a dry handkerchief from his pocket and used it to wipe away the film of nervousness that had formed on his palms. Although he was mildly surprised by Tortora's assessment of his son, it surprised him not at all that the boy had turned out badly. It's what happens, he thought. It's what happens when a kid grows up without a mother. The kid's mother got tuberculosis or something just as bad, he remembered hearing, just after the baby was born. Ended up in a grave out in Tucson, God rest her. And God only knows what he, Stanley Levy, would have turned into if he hadn't had a mother who looked after him and taught him things like only a mother can show you. Refined things. And how to be nice. And about going to the library and reading books and going to the museums on Sunday. Boys need that kind of teaching just as much as girls. And now look at Baker's kid. It was an especially terrible thing, her losing her mother, because now she has to grow up with one leg all mashed and ugly and she won't have a mother to talk to her about how she's got other things she can feel good about. You watch what happens. Baker's kid was going to get all screwed up too. Who's going to teach her different? Her father?

Even if he doesn't die too, which now the smart money has to say he will, he's already all fucked up.

"So what happened? Did John and his pal try to show off by taking Baker for you?"

"They did not seek out Baker. I'm convinced of that."

"You talked to the kid?"

"To the extent that John was lucid. It seems that they knew Jared Baker was in town and that a dénouement might be at hand. John, you'll recall, was a sometime friend of young Andrew Bellafonte, who suffered a similar fate at Baker's hand. He and Warren decided they'd come to town and watch the excitement."

Stanley frowned. "How did they know about Baker?"

Tortora gestured toward the rear window with his head.

"Cuneo?" Stanley asked.

"Your associate was apparently in the habit of telling them campfire stories dealing with his own thuggery. John's own pathetic standards were such that he was impressed. Most recently, he took to regaling them with tales of Jared Baker and of an imminent clash of titans, specifically Baker and Cuneo. The idiot even showed them Baker's picture."

"And they found Baker. But you said they didn't seek him out."

"They didn't. They might have, but something distracted them." Tortora grimaced. Stanley saw that whatever was coming was especially distasteful to him. "It seems that an opportunity for forcible rape presented itself in the person of a visiting actress named Tanner Burke. They seized her when her evening stroll took her too near the park entrance for her own safety. They tormented her, I'm sure, just as John liked to torment birds and cats as a boy."

"Except then Baker shows up," Stanley offered.

Tortora didn't answer. He sat back, waiting. It became clear to Stanley that he was expected to draw some penetrating conclusion.

"Am I supposed to call this?" he asked.

"If you have a thought, I'd like to hear it."

"You say Baker and the kids really didn't know each other?"

"Baker knew nothing of John's presence in New York and probably not even of his existence."

Levy turned up his hands. "That only leaves two ways," he answered. "One, Baker just happened to be taking a walk himself and he heard the action where Domenic Tortora's son just happened to drag this new bird he found. You don't like that answer because it's a million-to-one shot. Two, Baker knew the girl and it's her he was tailing. It's still long odds that the son of a man who's been on his ass shows up out of nowhere, but at least you've got a reason for Baker to be there. Those odds I'd make maybe a half-million to one. If you have to bet, the way to go is, Baker knew the girl."

"How much of your own money would you bet?"

"Not a dime."

"Where does that leave us?"

"It leaves us that you were wrong about Baker not knowing the kids would be there. He was looking for them. Girl or no girl, he was going to dust them in order to get at you. Look how Baker marked him. It sounds like he took his time. Maybe Baker wanted to leave you something to look at for the next twenty years. If this is true, you still want to find out how he found them, because the way you talk, the kids were in the park on impulse. What that leaves is that they were set up. If so, the finger would point to Cuneo, except he couldn't set up a pup tent."

Tortora nodded. "I'll expect you to do something about him, by the way."

Levy returned the nod. "Or that Fed, what's his name . . . Harrigan. Maybe Harrigan put Baker on to—"

"Impossible."

"Which leaves us right back where we started."

"No," Tortora corrected, "it leads us to choose a direction. There can be no action without an assumption. And the assumption I choose is that Baker knew my son was in the park, that Baker hurt him in order to provoke me."

"So," shrugged Stanley Levy, not bothering to point out the obvious flaws in the theory, "what action do you have in mind?"

Tortora was deep in thought for several moments. "I want Baker's daughter. Please take Vinnie Cuneo to the house in Greenwich where she now lives with a woman named Jane Carey. Do not harm Mrs. Carey, but take custody of the daughter. Can you manage that without undue violence, Stanley?"

Uh-oh, he thought. "But what if one of Harrigan's people is watching the place?"

"Incapacitate him if you must," Tortora sighed, "but I want the girl. Is there a place where you might hold her in comfort, Stanley?"

"My mother's place, over by Yorkville."

Tortora studied Stanley, looking deep into his eyes. There was a brooding hesitation that Stanley noticed.

"My mother can read to her," Stanley offered. Although he sensed Tortora's reluctance, he did not understand it. "She can do the kid some good. If you're worried the kid will finger my mother, I can keep her eyes covered."

Tortora nodded slowly. "It will only be until this evening, Stanley. Please have the girl on this spot promptly at nine o'clock tonight."

"You got it." Stanley Levy relaxed. "Then what happens?"

Tortora wiped some haze from the window and pointed toward the American Wing of the museum. "We'll wait in there, Stanley. Mr. Baker will doubtless want to pay us a visit."

"So will about six museum guards and their dogs."

"I'll attend to that, Stanley. And to my personal security as well." Tortora met Stanley's curious stare. In truth, the arrangements would not be difficult, but he would not take time now to explain. "Speaking of intrusions, however, this man Harrigan is likely to be a nuisance. Can something be done about him?"

"I'll handle it."

"Who, by the way, was the woman you killed earlier this morning?"

Levy made a face. How the hell did he know about that already? "I'm not sure. Could have been Harrigan's. Could also have been a vice cop out to set up a solicitation bust. It could even have been a straight conventioneer rip because she was about to shpritz me with this tear gas shooter here." He produced a metal cylinder resembling a pocket flashlight. "Anyway, I left a message for whoever it was."

"Could you not have otherwise neutralized her, Stanley?"

Levy shrugged and turned his index fingers toward his chest, inviting Tortora to consider his physique. He knew how Tortora felt about killing. Tortora didn't even like to use the word. "I'm just not built for any John Wayne stuff," he said respectfully. "I mean, I can probably handle Baker's daughter as long as she only has one leg working good, but anyone else, I can't fool around."

"Connor Harrigan will be more difficult, Stanley. Try not to do anything irreversible, but you must on no account endanger yourself. Connor Harrigan is to his trade what you are to yours. Be respectful, Stanley, or it is you who will be handled."

"I'll be respectful, Mr. Tortora." Stanley placed his hand upon the door latch and awaited Tortora's dismissal. When the nod came, he hesitated. "Where can I reach you if something happens?"

"I'll be considering Dr. Sonnenberg's role in tonight's events. And his point of view," he added.

Confusion clouded Stanley's face, but he remembered something far away and nodded. Still he hesitated. "This direction you picked. Do you mind me asking why you went for the long odds?"

"Remember your Sherlock Holmes, Stanley," Tortora replied, his hand moving to the ignition key. "If you've read of the man and not just the man's stories, you'll know that he made an observation that I've often found useful. He said, 'It is an old maxim of mine that whenever you have excluded the impossible, whatever remains, however improbable, must be the truth.' "

From the curb, Stanley Levy watched Tortora's taillights melt into the blackness of the park.

"That's wrong," he whispered distantly. "That was in a story also. *The Sign of Four* is what it was in."

Stanley had no idea how he knew that. It was enough that he knew it.

The Plaza's night manager was a prissy little man with the suitably prissy name of Wilton Pinchot. Sixty years earlier, he would have been dressed in black tie, a pencil mustache across a rigid upper lip, and hair gleaming with pomade. Now he wore a Dacron blazer and regimental tie, but still surviving were the brisk, flitting hand movements, the smile that employed only the mouth, and the hint of cologne dabbed at the hairline of his neck.

Mr. Pinchot had already been discomfited once that night by the appearance of a uniformed policeman in the Plaza lobby. The general manager, Mr. Bouvier, would certainly remind the police commissioner that the Plaza was neither a school crossing nor Madison Square Garden. An appalling gaucherie. Still worse, potential embarrassment to the Plaza now took another quantum leap with the appearance of this unshaven dreadful who looked for all the world as if he'd been sleeping in the park. What he was asking was impossible. Quite in violation of the sanctity of the Plaza guest rooms.

"Have you looked carefully at my credentials, Mr. Pinchot?" asked Harrigan patiently. He pulled an ID from its plastic sleeve and placed it face up on the desk. "Now." He took a weary breath. "Way down there at the bottom you see a phone number. It's there to be used by people like yourself who reject the evidence of their senses. And the act of calling that number, don't you see, occasionally keeps officious little men from being cited for impeding a federal investigation."

Pinchot read the name on Harrigan's card. "Mr. Fenton." He drew himself up. "When a guest books accommodations with us, he or she has every right to expect confidentiality—" The desk man stopped when Connor Harrigan held up his hand.

"Ah, but I have no interest in Miss Burke, don't you see!" Harrigan leaned closer to Wilton Pinchot, who tried not to back away or grimace but failed on both counts. "My sole interest is in the safety of the fellow I believe to be with her. The lad has a certain task to perform. The task is in the interest of your government, Mr. Pinchot, and he is not to be compromised. Not by you, sir, and not by me. And definitely not by an inquisitive street cop who had no business strolling through such a grand establishment as this."

The last part seemed to hit a nerve, and the night man softened by several degrees. He tilted forward, hands behind him. "However, Mr. Fenton, the policeman never asked about a man. You did. Nor did the policeman even ask for Miss Burke's room number, which naturally I would never—"

"Naturally," Harrigan whispered. "What was it the fellow asked, Mr. Pinchot?"

"I can assure you that the policeman was no threat to anyone who might or might not have been with Miss—"

"Mr. Pinchot, what was it he asked?"

"For an autograph." The night man straightened and offered his best don't-you-feel-silly-now look to Connor Harrigan.

"An autograph, you say?"

"Actually, he was quite shy about it. He said he'd been trying to muster his courage for hours even though it was really for his niece. He simply left a sheet of his notepaper and requested that I ask Miss Burke to write 'To Sandra' and sign it."

Harrigan's eyes drifted past Pinchot toward a digital message console set into the marble wall behind him. Several room numbers blinked in red. "And upon accepting his notepaper, Mr. Pinchot, you then pushed one of those little red lights, didn't you!"

Pinchot answered with a tolerant smile. "I'm hardly

an amateur, Mr. Fenton. Naturally, I waited until the policeman was gone."

"Naturally." Harrigan nodded. "And where did he go, by the way?"

"I haven't the foggiest. He walked past the Palm Court toward Fifth Avenue. Toward his beat, I rather assume."

Harrigan picked up his identification card and returned it to its case. He rested both elbows on the night manager's desk.

"Now, Mr. Pinchot darlin'. I want you to listen carefully. Miss Burke's room number which you don't want to share with me is very probably 1502. It's a suite facing the park. And your bashful policeman didn't leave right away, either. He would have come back one more time, perhaps to thank you again, or to ask for a match, or to tell you when he'd return for his autograph, and how pleased little Sandra was going to be. How do you suppose I know all these things, Mr. Pinchot?"

"I'm sure I have no idea . . ." A flush was rising from Wilton's collar and his lips clamped into a thin line.

"You're beginning to get it, aren't you, Mr. Pinchot? In all that great bloody rank of numbers behind you, only six are lit up at this hour of the morning. Only one of those is among your suites facing front, and I'm guessing that it belongs to Miss Tanner Burke and the lad she's sheltering this night. But the policeman didn't have to guess, did he, Mr. Pinchot? And that's because there were only five little lights burning when he walked away but there were six when he came back to say good night."

Harrigan waited while it penetrated. The night man's eyes darted about the lobby, bouncing several times off his telephone before coming to rest on it. Harrigan followed his line of sight.

"And now you're going to make it worse, aren't you, lad!"

"I don't . . . What shall I . . ." Perspiration showed across Pinchot's waxen forehead.

"It's possible, mind you, that the policeman was indeed innocent enough. If he was, there the matter will rest and there's no need for your employer to know of your lapse. What I'm going to do, Mr. Pinchot, is take a ride up to the fifteenth floor and find a quiet place to puff awhile upon my pipe. I'm going to do that until I hear wake-up calls jingling in the rooms around me and until I hear showers running. By the time I hear those sounds, the occasion for any possible mischief will have passed. I too will then pass from your life, Mr. Pinchot, may it be long and happy. Do you approve of that course, Mr. Pinchot?"

"Yes . . . certainly. As long as you don't . . ."

Harrigan pursed his lips.

"Thank you, Mr. Fenton. That will be fine."

In Dayton, Ohio, Howard Twilley's phone call came two hours after closing. He listened, smiled broadly, and replaced the receiver without speaking. A short time later, showered, shaved, and dressed in a dark business suit, the owner of the Riverview Grill locked its front door for the last time.

In the trunk of his car, he stacked a large duffel, a briefcase, and a leather two-suiter. This last had been packed for a year. The car and the duffel, which contained his fishing and camping gear, would be abandoned in the long-term parking lot of the Greater Cincinnati Airport. It would be a week before his absence seemed unusual, weeks more before the car would be found.

The airport would be his first stop, and there Howard Twilley would cease to exist. His next stop would be Denver. There, he would acquire a suitable weapon before going on. He would be Ben Coffey again.

Marcus Sonnenberg eased the telephone onto its cradle, a look of tired satisfaction on his face. Pushing himself erect, he limped to his bookcase, where he plucked a new Monte Cristo from his *Oxford Book of English Verse*. He lit it ceremonially, watching the fine smoke as it sought out his draperies. The faint morning light made it shine like a silver mist.

On any other day he would have smoked by an open window, lest the lingering scent betray him to Mrs. Kreskie. But she would not be back for many hours. Perhaps not at all. In any case, he thought, perhaps she would understand his indulgence on this occasion. Yes, she would certainly understand.

His thoughts turned to Jared Baker.

"Understanding," he said aloud but softly. "There indeed is the rub. How much do you understand, Jared, and how well do I understand you?"

He thought of the several weeks that had passed during which Baker had failed to acknowledge his messages, saying only that he needed time to think.

"What has your period of insubordinate meditation taught you, Jared? To be shortsighted? To be selfish? Is it possible you've chosen to reject a gift for which half of humankind would trade all that they possess?

"You're about to tell me, aren't you, Jared. Oh, I know that you're in the city. A little bird told me. The little bird also told me that you were out hunting tonight and that you're now ensconced with some tramp and that soon you will come to see me.

"Those two in the park, Baker. How did you find them? Our friend Mr. Tortora will want to know that too. He also has a little bird. And the words whispered by his little bird have left him ill at ease. You have now twice struck down a firstborn within the reaches of his brotherhood.

"The first of these he more or less regarded as your due. In compensation for your dead wife, that is. Oh, you were to be assaulted if possible. You were to be punished in the name of fraternal duty. Not the strongest stimulus for a pragmatist like Tortora but an obligation nonetheless. One in his position must keep up appearances. And from my point of view, of course, such attacks upon your person constituted excellent field training."

Sonnenberg sat back and rubbed his eyes, taking a few moments to organize his thoughts.

"Be that as it may, my brooding friend," he continued, "we now have what is called a situation. I leap to the conclusion that you have come East to resign your office, to scoop up your daughter who will doubtless cast off her crutches at the sight of you, and then fade with her into the setting sun to live happily ever after.

"You arrive in New York and your presence is immediately known. You become aware that it's known by a brace or two of thugs who are, you must have assumed, in the employ of Domenic Tortora. It ought to have struck you that, assuming they are indeed Tortora's people, his attention to you now shows a vigor that was not evident before. You would then assume that he intends you immediate harm.

"In the meanwhile, you are also being observed by an agent or agents from the federal bureaucracy. Agents whose activities seem to transcend the usual constraints of a government discipline. Your Mr. Harrigan seems to have an almost clinical interest in you. Mr. Harrigan is a man of considerable reputation in the investigative arts. His attention, in turn, suggests that he has become aware of at least some of your capabilities and now seeks to learn how you intend to apply them. And why. Meaning, ergo, that his ultimate interest is in me. But on whose behalf is he interested? Does a man like Connor Harrigan really forge blindly ahead on the word of an inveterate manipulator like Duncan Peck? I think not.

"And what of old Duncan? How long has it been since we eavesdropped on Duncan's recruitment jog with Mr. Harrigan? More than a year? At that time, Duncan, Connor Harrigan gave every clue that he would not be fully controllable, didn't he. I'll wager that he's been less than meticulous in reporting to you. No doubt, therefore, you'd be able to sympathize with my own frustrations concerning Jared Baker. And now you're about to purge yourself of these frustrations, aren't you? The same little bird told me that too. You're about to do something untidy.

"But we were wondering about Mr. Harrigan, speaking of untidiness. I've been forced to conclude, Duncan, that Mr. Harrigan's interest is not all on your behalf. On whose, then? His own? The notion cannot be dismissed."

Sonnenberg paused to relight his cigar, which had gone out. But he'd lost his taste for it. He considered saving what remained or casting it out among the rhododendrons. No need, he thought. They are amply fertilized by the likes of Roger Hershey the First, and the game is too far afoot to worry about Mrs. Kreskie's displeasure. He left the butt on the edge of his table lamp.

"So let us summarize. Back to you, Jared Baker. If your intent is to make off with your daughter under the delusion that your union will make you whole and happy again, I have every confidence that your immediate pursuers will be hard-pressed to stop you. I rather expect that your plan is to stop them, isn't it, Jared. Thrice now you've been recognized in other cities by hoodlums who made the mistake of taking you at face value. Hoodlums who'd obviously been equipped with a Wanted poster of some sort in the event you passed through their fiefdoms. Hoodlums intent on bashing you about rather than ending your life. You may correctly assume that this bashing was prescribed by Mr. Tortora partly as an appeasement to the friends of the late rent-a-judge. It had another purpose, but I'm not going to tell you that yet. In any case, the ease with which you chastised those Tortora chain-wielders in Dayton and elsewhere has apparently caused you to move up in class. *Voilà*, Stanley Levy. And you, being a person who dislikes such nagging annoyances, you likely intended to remove these annoyances at their source. Meaning Tortora. Oh, Jared, won't that be something to see! And oh, what a surprise I have for you!

"Be that as it may ... You, Jared, are also an intelligent and perceptive man. I say this to remind myself that I should not underestimate you no matter how naive your plan seems at this moment. I rest assured that you have prepared an escape route and a safe harbor someplace where you'll not be easily found. After all, I blush to point out, look who taught you.

"Unlike any other fugitive in the world, you needn't even live with paranoia. You needn't worry about constantly looking over your shoulder. You have Charley. If anyone should become curious, Charley will know it, and you will take whatever action you think necessary.

"But alas, Baker, where there is Charley there is also Abel. You can try and keep Abel locked away, but he'll always be there waiting. Someone, sometime, will push you too far. Another bully in some redneck bar. Another mugger. A short-tempered truck driver. A robber with a weapon. A pack of teenage toughs abusing someone you care for. Will you really keep Abel in check, Baker? I think not. But if you insist that you will, what makes you think that Abel won't find a way out on his own. Abel, after all, is not some evil spirit, some demon that can be exorcised. He's not the insane and homicidal twin whom the frightened family keeps chained in a basement room. He's you, Baker. He's the primate within you. The hunter. The predator. He's the rage you controlled all your life.

"He won't let you keep him down, Baker. Don't you see what he's done? That was Tortora's son in the park, Baker. Do you even realize that yet? Abel knew it. I have yet to learn how, but of this much I'm certain. Abel knew. And he hopes now that they'll come, Baker. This time they'll come killing. They'll all come killing.

"Baker?" Sonnenberg said in a louder voice as he rose and stretched before reaching for the phone again. "I think Abel is smiling, Baker."

Harrigan paused at the door of Tanner Burke's suite and listened. He heard nothing. The creak of a chair, perhaps, but he could not be sure. An odd wave of anger came over him as he stood there. It had no cause that he knew. And it receded as he left the door and walked toward the emergency stairwell.

Carefully, he checked the fire stairs for two floors in each direction. All was quiet. Harrigan returned to the fifteenth-floor landing, where he sought a comfortable place to wait. The stairs were of cold concrete, softened only by several coats of gray paint. He eased onto the second step, then squirmed sideways to relieve the pressure of his service revolver against his kidney. He wished he'd thought to visit the men's room before leaving the lobby. That last cup of tea would be asserting itself before long.

A door opened several floors below him, followed by the soft padding of sneakered feet running steadily down the remaining stairs. He checked his watch. Not ten after six and there go the joggers, thought Harrigan. God save us all. What will be the next perversion of civilized behavior that captivates popular fancy.

Harrigan had jogged only twice in his adult life. The first time was that once with Duncan Peck and then once more with Notre Dame. Nice fellow, incidentally. Multiple murderers don't come much friendlier. Anyway, it was only twice. And both times in the line of duty. Harrigan was sure that God would forgive him as long as he swore never to acknowledge either event at a cocktail party.

Duncan Peck.

You tried to sucker me, you old bastard, didn't you! You made me run with you until just short of the point where I'd vomit all over your Nikes, and then in my weakened state you plied me with selected truths. You left out the big truths. And the biggest of those is that you're very much afraid of this Dr. Sonnenberg, aren't you! Oh, Duncan. We're going to see who'll sucker whom, now won't we!

Harrigan's brain exploded with light.

The image it held Duncan Peck's face shattered like a crystal bowl, and through the pieces Connor Harrigan could see the concrete landing rushing up at him. His arms flew across his face and his elbows painfully broke his fall. Goddamn, he thought. His mind still worked, but his body would not follow. Was he shot? his brain asked.

Hands were on him now. A knee dug deeply into his back, arching it, and a pulling hand had gripped his forehead. Another hand appeared and the arm behind it tried to tighten across his throat. With a burst of effort, Harrigan jammed his palm across the forearm before it could close against his windpipe. It helped, but little. God, he was so weak. Or was the man that strong. Baker? Is it you, Baker?

Another door opening somewhere. Noises. Grunts. More weight across his back. Now less weight. The man is rising. Still holding on but rising. Something is pulling him up.

A slipping, clawing hand twisted Harrigan's head to one side. He could see two men. Part of them. And another shape at the landing door. The choking arm, he could see, was dressed in blue. Oh, Harrigan, damn you for a careless ass. It's that false cop who's killing you.

The uniformed man let go. Harrigan felt him scraping to his feet and then he saw him spin away, slamming against the fire hose that hung in folds on the landing wall. Harrigan rolled to his knees, gulping air and pushing at his eyes to make them focus. Baker! The man helping him was Jared Baker. And the girl, her eyes wide with fright, stood at the door behind him.

Baker, he saw, was struggling desperately. His face flamed red and his arteries bulged at his temples. One arm was locked around the policeman's head while the other clawed at his gun hand. What gun is that? Harrigan wondered. An odd-looking thing. An air pistol, he realized.

The air pistol, if that's what it was, shook loose and clattered to the floor. The policeman grasped at his service gun, but it was pressed hard against the wall. Enraged, he drove his fist savagely into Baker's stomach. And again. The blows made Baker gag, but still he held fast, his eyes washed with tears and turning toward Harrigan. They seemed to be begging for help.

Harrigan, his legs not yet steady, lurched toward the two men. A third blow, low against Baker's groin, broke his hold at last, and Baker half-collapsed against the wall. His hands flew to his eyes and forehead as if the pain was there and not where the blows had landed. Harrigan heard him cursing someone.

The freed policeman spun toward Harrigan, whipping a stiffened hand toward the older man's throat.

Harrigan slapped it past him and turned the man, aiming
three fast, chopping blows to his kidney. A wild elbow
crashed against Harrigan's ear and staggered him. Before
he could recover, the policeman had cleared his revolver
and lined his sights against Harrigan's chest. Baker
lunged for the gun, but the policeman knocked him aside
with a backhanded slap. The gun hand began an arc toward Baker's head but hesitated. Only for the smallest
amount, but enough. For then another foot flew against
the policeman's face. A woman's foot. It struck again and
a third time. Now Baker seized the gun and through his
pain fought to bend it backward over the blue-coated
wrist. The policeman tried to twist away and stumbled.
Off balance. And then Harrigan had him. Now it was
Harrigan's arm that snaked over the policeman's neck
while his right hand gripped the big man's jaw.

The policeman knew at once what was happening to
him. He'd done it twice himself. Once very slowly to a
woman in Montréal while her boyfriend watched and
screamed. He thought of her and tried to scream himself.
It would not come. Desperately, he threw both legs forward, hoping that his descending weight would break the
older man's hold. It was a mistake. Harrigan's grip had
become a noose, and the man had thrown himself
through an open trap. Baker could see the horror in the
policeman's eyes even as his neck snapped with the
sound of wet wood. His body trembled, sagged, and
died. And with a final wrench, Connor Harrigan destroyed his brain.

Tanner Burke moaned and gripped the doorway.
Baker reached her before she could faint. The act kept
him from fainting.

Silence.

Several moments passed before anyone spoke.
Harrigan, exhausted, had sunk quietly to the step, where
he sat massaging his neck, twice glancing curiously at the
man who was Jared Baker. At the monster who just
fought like a schoolboy. Tanner Burke's eyes had hardly
left the dead man's face.

"He's not a real policeman, miss," Harrigan whispered hoarsely. He said that although he was not truly certain.

Tanner Burke swallowed. "Who are you?" she managed.

"Ah, yes." The bald man grunted, shifting his weight to free his leather case He saw an odd, faraway look come over Baker's face and then it was gone.

"Mr. Baker, Miss Burke." He nodded, pulling a card from its plastic sleeve. "My name is Lawrence Fenton. You're wondering, of course—"

"Good morning, Mr. Harrigan," Baker said wearily.

11

To the extent that anything at all could unnerve Connor Harrigan, it startled him that Baker knew his name. Knowing his face was another matter. The face he'd allowed Baker to see, just once or twice, he thought, as he'd done with Notre Dame. A bit of eye contact and a few words exchanged. Sometimes risky, perhaps, but a way of getting the feel of a man. And, in Baker's case, a way of knowing whether the quarry had knowledge of the hunter.

But when first they had seen each other months before, Harrigan could recall no light of recognition in Baker's eyes. No uneasiness. On the contrary, he remembered only a glazed and distant look. A momentary mental flabbiness. Eyes barely in focus. Except . . . when that other change had come over Baker. When Baker was hard and the eyes were those of a snake . . .

Forget that, he thought. The point was that Baker knew both his face and his name. And the knowledge was hardly recent, judging by Baker's manner. That notion offended and embarrassed Harrigan. It meant that those months of professional unobserved surveillance were not so unobserved and professional after all. It seemed to mean that Baker had been indifferent to his presence, which offended him most of all.

Steady, Connor, he thought. No prima donnas here. Do not let the insult cause you to trip over a bloated professional ego. Instead, think! Think of what it means so that you can proceed unencumbered by wounded pride.

Did it mean that Baker knew of your presence from the beginning? From the day of jog number one, when you spotted that little bug in the grass of Potomac Park? Not likely, he thought, even if the bug was Sonnenberg's, which he had to assume it was. Could Baker have known all the time that Connor Harrigan's glass was trained on Sonnenberg's house while he slipped in and out to make those telephone calls to his daughter? Of course not. There was at least one answer right there. He'd never have called his daughter if he'd known he was being watched and recorded. Which meant in turn that Sonnenberg, given that the jogger's bug was his, had never shared what he learned with Baker.

On the other hand, Harrigan thought, allowing his mind to graze a bit, Baker did not share much about his daughter with Sonnenberg. The phone calls told him that even before he knew what was said. The foolish, chancy phone calls to an invalid Tina Baker. Harrigan supposed that he knew from the first days of his surveillance that young Tina would be the glue that would hold the pieces together in the end. In spite of Sonnenberg, apparently. Each time Sonnenberg and his housekeeper drove off on an errand, there would be Baker, an uncharacteristic hat pulled down over his face, strolling down to the Mobil station to call his daughter. Peck had been right about that. And it was stupid. The Mobil station phone booth was an easy wire. Not like the house, which was a god-damned electronic supermarket full of responders that would blow your ear out if you tried to listen. Baker could have called from the house but he didn't. It had to be that Sonnenberg had told him not to call. Sonnenberg would have had his own phones wired to make sure, and Baker must have known that.

On the day of the final call from the Mobil station, the one that said, "Tina, honey, I have to take a trip," Harrigan had taken over Biaggi's shift. Biaggi had come down with the flu, which was just as well because Michael, Harrigan flattered himself, would likely have missed Baker when he moved. Harrigan damned near missed him himself.

A splattered van had passed through Sonnenberg's electric gate. PUZO PAINTS—FREE ESTIMATES was stenciled on the side. One man emerged, no doubt a Puzo, and entered the house with a canvas tarp over one shoulder and a canvas sack full of paint cans hanging from the other. Harrigan logged the visit and waited.

Two hours later, Puzo emerged carrying the same materials and freshly stained with green paint. He climbed behind the wheel of the van and ground the gears twice before figuring out which one was reverse. So, Harrigan recalled, the astute observer concludes either that Puzo needs to be retrained every time he climbs into his own van or that the guy in the painter's suit isn't Puzo. Good morning, Jared Baker.

Harrigan followed the van with some difficulty. Baker had not spotted him, he was sure, yet he drove as if he was being tailed. He was using evasive techniques that Harrigan recognized. Chalk one up for Peck's conspiracy theory. The guy had been trained.

The van stopped eventually on a side street off Tremont Avenue in the Bronx. Baker locked the car carefully, then walked around the corner, where he entered a Minute Man dry cleaner and walked to the back of the store after a brief chat with the proprietor. Playing a hunch that the van had already served its purpose and gambling that Baker would leave by another door, Harrigan searched for and found a rear alley once used by trucks delivering coal. Baker rewarded his choice, not twenty minutes later, by appearing large as life in a fresh business suit and climbing into a silver Pinto that had clearly been left for him.

Excited now, Harrigan ran to his car. The cooperative Mr. Puzo might not have meant much by himself, but now he had someone else, a cooperative dry cleaner at the very least, who had gone to considerable trouble to stash a car and perhaps some luggage for a fugitive from a very shaky murder warrant. Why was Baker worth it? Harrigan wanted to know. Beating a stretch in jail might have been of consuming importance to Baker, but it simply should not have been that big a deal to anyone else. It didn't seem worth all this. But obviously it was. To Sonnenberg, at least. And to Sonnenberg's increasingly impressive network.

He nearly lost Baker at La Guardia Airport. The car turned out to be an Avis rental, later shown to have been rented by someone who did not exist but who had papers to show that he did. Baker paid cash for an American Airlines flight to Atlanta and, as boarding was announced, he eased himself toward the adjacent gate, where he calmly stepped aboard a plane bound for Indianapolis, with stops at Pittsburgh and Dayton. Harrigan realized too late what had happened. Gambling again, and remembering Duncan Peck's briefing, Harrigan booked himself aboard the next available flight to Dayton. Once there, he rented a car and drove it first to the nearest Goodwill Industries donation bin, where he helped himself to a frayed windbreaker and a pair of dried-out brown shoes. Next, with the help of his Avis map, Harrigan made his way out Germantown Road and to the Riverview Grill, which stood near the main gate of the Dayton Tire and Rubber Company. The sign on the door read: HOWARD TWILLEY—OWNER/MANAGER. At seven that evening, the new relief bartender showed up for work. Harrigan had guessed right again.

It was a new Jared Baker, a coarser version. This one wore a cheap plaid shirt, open at the neck and showing a white T-shirt underneath. His hair had been slicked with Brylcreme, then flattened and combed straight back. He chewed gum with his mouth hanging open and did his best to affect the dull-eyed boredom of a blue-collar bartender. His name, Harrigan learned, was Jimmy Flood.

Harrigan had parked quietly at one end of the L-shaped bar. Behind him, a Space Invaders game blinked colored rows of descending alien craft. A black man stood washing glasses at the end near the door. Harrigan recognized him at once. Baker was closer, in the center. It was Baker who'd served the beer that

Harrigan was nursing. It was then that the glaze came over Baker's eyes. As he took Harrigan's dollar bill. It wasn't much. Just a momentary pause as if a dim memory had kicked at him from within. On a hunch, and for reasons he'd only understand months later, Harrigan forced his thoughts away from Baker and onto the country & western ballad that wailed from the jukebox. Baker relaxed visibly. Harrigan slid from his stool, his instincts telling him to give Baker room, and took a seat at the idle electronic game. A tool and die maker named Eddie Kuntz held up a quarter questioningly at Harrigan. Harrigan nodded and gestured toward the opponent's seat opposite. Harrigan had lost his fourth straight game when Albert Doviak pushed noisily through the front door.

"Oh, Christ!" muttered Eddie Kuntz, glancing up briefly.

Harrigan followed his eyes. The huge man who entered stood smiling and breathing heavily as he scanned the faces at the tables. He wore only a soiled T-shirt against the chill night, yet his face, arms, and shaven head gleamed with sweat. Harrigan saw a splatter of blood on the T-shirt and more on the knuckles of the man's right hand. Several in the room exchanged looks and dropped their heads.

"Trouble?" Harrigan asked.

"Probably. Doviak's lookin' playful tonight." Kuntz kept his attention on the screen.

"Who's Doviak?" The question came casually.

Kuntz raised both eyebrows. "You're not from around here?"

"Akron," Harrigan answered. "Goodyear plant."

Eddie Kuntz shrugged in acknowledgment. "Doviak's not so bad usually, but he's in training. He's gonna be lookin' for a couple of tuneup fights tonight."

"Tuneups for what?"

"Tough Man competition starts tomorrow night." Kuntz fished for another quarter.

"Tough Man competition? What's that?"

Kuntz looked up. "You kidding?"

Harrigan returned a shrug. "In Akron, competition is bowling leagues."

"Tough Man"—Eddie leaned forward—"is this thing where they have all the toughest guys in town enter this tournament and beat the shit out of each other in the ring down at the auditorium. Winner gets ten grand. Doviak lost in the finals last year, but the next night he took on the winner, big nigger named Floyd, for a side bet. Without no rules, he butted Floyd's face in and left him on top of some garbage cans."

Harrigan flicked a look toward Howard Twilley, who he was sure had overheard. He thought he saw a faint smile on the black barkeeper's face. Twilley stepped around Baker, who now seemed distinctly nervous, gently squeezing his shoulder as he passed. Baker nodded and tried a weak smile of his own.

"Good evening, Albert." The black man grinned broadly at Doviak. The bigger man still stood blocking the doorway with the look of a restless bouncer.

"Good evening yourself, dark person," Albert boomed pleasantly. Two black patrons looked up. The younger one reached for the neck of a Budweiser bottle and eased it to his lap. Two more men made a space for Doviak at the end of the bar.

Twilley drew a beer and poured a shot from a Seagram's bottle. He placed them before the vacant stool. "This is on the house, Albert," he said. Then the smile faded. "It's one for the road."

Albert laughed. He looked to each side as if making sure his good humor was noted. He laughed again, louder this time, as he straddled the stool and brought his face closer to Twilley's.

"Don't do that, Howard," he said more quietly. "Don't buy me no drinks and tell me to walk."

Harrigan nudged his playing partner. "I think Albert has found his tuneup."

"No." Eddie Kuntz shook his head. "He won't fight Twilley. Twilley's got his number. You know how some guys have another guy's number no matter who's the meanest? Doviak tried his shit the first night after Twilley bought this place, and Twilley made him back down just by lookin' at him and talkin'. I seen Twilley do it other times too. To Doviak and to some of the other boomers that come in here. Twilley has their number."

Harrigan nodded, believing for the first time the story Duncan Peck had told him. He heard Twilley's voice again.

"It's for your own good, Albert," he was saying. "If you came in looking for a workout, you're going to find more than you can handle." Twilley's thumb waved over his shoulder. "My man, Jimmy Flood. He's going to go the distance this year."

Startled, Harrigan's eyes lashed back toward Jared Baker. Baker trembled. Harrigan saw it. Baker knew what was coming and he was afraid.

"Who the hell is Jimmy Flood?" Doviak peered past the barkeeper.

"My new relief man," Twilley answered nonchalantly.

The big man's scowl softened into a grin as he appraised Jared Baker. At an inch over six feet and a hundred eighty-five pounds, Baker was still a full three inches shorter and sixty pounds lighter than Albert Doviak. Smaller and softer. And Albert too could see he was nervous.

"You're shitting me, aren't you?" Doviak asked.

"Fifty dollars."

"Fifty on what?"

"Fifty says he can take you tonight, next week, or next month, and he can put you down in sixty seconds."

The bigger man hesitated. "This is fist-fightin', Twilley. None of that karate crap."

"Flood wouldn't know karate if it fell on him. He's just cat quick and he's strong."

Doviak craned his head for another look at the relief bartender. He could see nothing that concerned him. Still, he was uncertain. "You're saying he can put me down inside a minute. Does that mean rasslin' and rollin' or does that mean I stay down and he don't?"

"It means you don't get up until he's back in here tending bar."

The room was quiet but for a throaty Tanya Tucker number.

"Got his number," Eddie Kuntz whispered. "Maybe Twilley's man got Doviak's number too." He raised his head. "I'll take some of that," he called. "I'm holdin' thirty dollars I'll put on the new guy."

Another man, older, leaped at it. "I'll cover Eddie's dough and I got another twenty on Al." The bar erupted into an auction.

"You said fifty dollars?" Doviak asked.

"More if you like."

"What's in it for him?"

"He needs a tuneup too."

One more time, Doviak studied the man called Jimmy Flood. Baker felt the stare but would not meet Doviak's eyes. Instead, he drifted closer toward the kitchen door and turned his back on Doviak.

"Make it a hundred," Albert said, rising. "I'll be in the parking lot."

The others, except Harrigan, watched him go. Harrigan's attention was locked on Jared Baker and on a shudder that moved in ripples across his back. And then Harrigan realized that what he saw was more than trembling. He did not know what it was. Only that it was more.

At last Baker reached behind him and pulled at the strings of his white apron. Lifting it above his head, he turned, first facing the door and the dwindling crowd of men now jamming through it, then looking squarely into the eyes of Connor Harrigan.

Harrigan's last breath jammed in his chest as he saw Baker's face. Then Baker turned away, easily lifting the heavy, hinged gate of the bar and flowing, it seemed, toward the door of the Riverview Grill.

Harrigan was thunderstruck. Transfixed, he sat in the almost abandoned bar waiting for the strength that had drained from his legs. The man who'd looked at him, the man now gone outside, the explosive and violent man who'd been so visibly frightened only moments before was, by God and to hell with everybody else, no longer Jared Baker. And the man he became knew Connor Harrigan. He knew him!

Recovering, Harrigan braced to rise from his chair and follow the excited sounds outside. A clink of glass told him he was not alone. Twilley stood half-hidden behind the cash register, calmly wiping the varnished surface of the bar. Harrigan sat back, studying this man who had once been Ben Coffey. The man who had Doviak's number and who turned guns into rats. He watched as Twilley worked his way toward Harrigan's end of the bar. There was more than calm in his expression, Harrigan thought. There was satisfaction. Howard Twilley had just accomplished something. Something had been set up and made to happen. Harrigan remembered the comforting hand on the shoulder of a lost and worried Jared Baker. And Harrigan knew. He knew in a flash of intuition what was happening here tonight. It was a testing ground. A training arena. A match with a ranking contender. And here was his promoter, his corner man, wiping a bar with no shadow of concern about the outcome of a blood brawl fifty feet away.

He saw something else as well. Just a flicker, really, when the satisfaction on Twilley's face faded for a moment. It was so out of place and out of context that he would have missed it had it not been for his memory of the call to Sonnenberg that Peck had intercepted: "I've had it, Doc. I want to use it. Soon, Doc. I mean it."

What Harrigan saw, he was convinced, was a profound and crushing loneliness in the soul of Howard Twilley.

Outside, a sudden silence fell, and the shadow passed from Twilley's face. He turned in Harrigan's direction to watch the second hand of a Coors Beer clock that hung on the wall behind the game table. Twilley nodded to himself and snapped his fingers. He looked like a horse trainer clocking a furlong sprint. That was it, Harrigan realized. Jared Baker wasn't here to hide any more than he'd been hiding in the Sonnenberg compound these past four months. Nor had he been schooled there just to beat up bullies in midwestern shot-and-a-beer joints. By whatever means and for whatever reason, this new Jared Baker had been created by Marcus Sonnenberg. Jared Baker now and Benjamin Coffey before him. And the good Lord knows how many others.

Harrigan felt a draft and turned toward the opening door. It was Baker. The real Baker. Alone, he stepped inside, shutting the door against the murmur of stunned and shaken voices behind him.

"How did you do?" Twilley asked, his voice more caring than curious.

Baker hesitated. "Someone said twenty-eight seconds."

"How bad?"

"I . . . was able to hold him back," Baker answered. "If I hadn't, Doviak might have been . . ."

Twilley raised a hand to silence him, gesturing toward Connor Harrigan with his head. Who the hell is "him"? Harrigan wondered.

"Congratulations, champ." Harrigan waved and forced a smile. He stepped fully into the light toward Baker, wondering as he did so what Albert must be looking like.

"Thank you . . ." Baker faltered.

"I'd like to shake your hand," Harrigan said, the tension he felt beginning to drain. "Also, good luck in the tournament."

Baker took the extended hand and gripped it weakly. There was a shyness, an embarrassment, on Baker's face. But there was no recognition. This Jared Baker did not know Connor Harrigan. This Jared Baker didn't know him from Adam.

Harrigan stayed for the first three elimination rounds of the Tough Man Tournament. Baker won his first fight with just three quick blows of his left hand. Some insisted it was a single punch. Without a replay, it was hard to tell. When his opponent, a red-haired trucker named

Doyle, collapsed against the lower rope, the opening bell was still echoing in Harrigan's ears.

In Baker's second and third fights he went the full three rounds. He seemed to be holding back, taking some punches, slipping others, but never reacting to the other man's blows or to the crowd or the referee. He seemed to see nothing, feel nothing, except the presence of the other fighter. At the sound of the bell, he would lock his eyes upon those of his opponent. Seconds later, Harrigan saw, the other man would seem terrified. But Baker would bide his time. Near the end of each third and final round, Twilley would call Baker's name and Baker would strike. His blows, which avoided the face and head, were astonishingly precise and quick. Almost surgical in their artistry. A jab would be answered with a blur of an uppercut against the muscle on the underside of the jabbing arm. The truncheoned arm would collapse, useless. The opponent's right arm would rise in defense, and again its soft tissue would be crushed. A third blow at the base of the ribcage would leave the man gasping and helpless as the bell sounded. Baker, it was clear, could destroy any of these hardhats at will. It was terrible to watch. By the second fight, the crowd did not cheer Baker. A few booed nervously.

The man in the ring was not Baker. Of that, Harrigan was certain. The man in the ring was the man who knew him in Twilley's bar a few days before. Yet Baker was there. It was Baker, or Jimmy Flood, who was introduced to the crowd, and Baker who received the referee's instructions. It was a tense and nervous Baker, a reluctant Baker, who dropped his eyes when his first opponent tried to glare him down with a Sonny Liston scowl. The second made no such attempt. The third dropped his own eyes. And it was Baker in the corner between rounds. It was, at least, until Twilley wiped his face at the start of a round and again at the conclusion. Harrigan knew, by that time, what must have been happening under the oversize yellow bath towel Twilley used. He'd almost seen it in the bar but for Baker's back being turned. Harrigan knew. But he could not yet bring himself to believe it.

On the night of the semifinal round, after cracking the ribs and collarbone of a sandlot football player at least twenty years younger, Baker took a long shower and waited for the crowd to leave the arena. A television crew had already begun laying cables for the taping of the final round. Harrigan waited in the shadows of the parking lot.

When Baker emerged, Twilley trailing well behind him, Harrigan thought he saw a curious lightness in his step. An air of relief, perhaps, although odd with the next night's final still to be faced. Harrigan began to hear the familiar buzz in his head. But before he could make sense of it, the sound of running feet swept the warning aside. Two men were running. They came from another set of shadows, and they ran not at Harrigan but at Baker, a length of heavy chain in each one's hands. Harrigan crouched and reached toward his pistol but froze in that position. For there was Twilley, hanging back, arms folded, as the two burly men advanced upon Baker. Harrigan tried to see what was happening, but his view was obscured by a scattering of cars. He could hear, however. He heard moans and grunts and the rake of steel chain against pavement, and by the time he found a better vantage, there was Baker walking quickly away. His tutor walked with him, smiling.

Harrigan could not know why the attack on Baker took place. Or who the men with chains might have been. He could only listen to his instincts. The two men, he supposed, might have been friends of Albert Doviak or of Baker's other three victims. But somehow he doubted it, given Howard Twilley's role as an amused spectator. Another test, perhaps? It seemed hardly needed. Perhaps to keep him on edge? Harrigan thought. To keep him what else? Vigilant? Moving? Moving is what his instincts answered. And then he remembered the television cables and was sure. Baker would never let himself be taped. He would have to disappear before the final round.

The disappearance was faster than even Harrigan expected. Twilley drove Baker directly from the parking lot to the Cincinnati airport. By the time Baker left Twilley's car, he was dressed once again as a traveling executive. Harrigan followed Baker onto a United L-1011 bound for Los Angeles, spending the entire four-hour flight in the first-class lounge, where he could stay out of Baker's sight.

Late the following morning, Harrigan followed Baker through three changes of cabs until he arrived at the rental office of Marina Del Rey. There he used a cashier's check to lease a houseboat, which he chose from among the six thousand tightly packed pleasure craft moored there. Interesting, Harrigan thought. A man pursued could leap endlessly from boat to boat as if they were tenement roofs. And access to Baker's section was restricted by an electric gate activated by a coded plastic card. Harrigan booked a room overlooking the marina and settled in.

Baker was Peter Binford there. A freelance film researcher, if anyone asked. The houseboat never left its slip, although Baker would occasionally rent a Soling or a Hobie for a singlehanded sail. On shore, much of his time was spent in libraries. Harrigan would watch from a distance as a curiously flaccid and torpid Baker would leaf through as many as forty volumes in a day or a year's worth of microfilmed files and newspaper pages.

Only Harrigan knew he was there. For several months on and off, ignoring increasingly anxious queries from Duncan Peck, who was ignorant of the whereabouts of either man, Harrigan watched. He watched until he began to notice subtle changes in Baker's behavior when he was near. He had the odd feeling that Baker seemed to know, sometimes quite abruptly, that Harrigan was close. Harrigan discovered one day, accidentally, that if he backed away to the proper distance, Baker would relax. It was his feeling, although he could not say why, that Baker's comfort had more to do with range than with distance. There was a point at which Baker could feel his presence, he thought, or someone's presence, and a point at which he could not. Harrigan learned to recognize that point through a curiously unmotivated anger he would feel when he crossed it. Harrigan understood that least of all.

He began watching from greater distances. He watched and followed as Baker began to fly off every week or so to a different part of the country. Four times, Harrigan managed to follow him to a particular town before he lost him. During three of those visits, someone in that town disappeared. In the other, the office of a corrupt city commissioner was wrecked and two burly staff members critically injured by an unidentified berserk who walked in off the street. It might have been coincidence. Harrigan thought not.

Then there was Las Vegas. Harrigan tracked him there twice, although Baker might have stopped there as many as six other times en route back to Los Angeles. That many days were unaccounted for. There were at least two differences, Harrigan thought, about the Las Vegas visits. The first was that Harrigan detected a certain furtiveness about Baker in Las Vegas that was not present elsewhere. It was as if Baker was somewhere he was not supposed to be or doing something he was not sanctioned to do. The second was that Baker amused himself in Vegas. He gambled.

Perhaps *amuse* was not the right word, Harrigan reflected. There was a clear seriousness of purpose to the man. Nor, come to think of it, was *gambling* the right word. For Baker did not gamble. He simply won.

He won at twenty-one and he won at baccarat. He would play for an hour at most, until he won significantly or until a crowd began to gather, then he would move on to another casino. And it was the limp and distant Baker, the Baker of the library, who played these games, but the ordinary, average Baker who walked from resort to resort. Average! More than once the word struck Harrigan as particularly apt, but the source of the impression remained just out of reach.

In any case, Baker won. He would play silently, communicating only with nods to the dealer, and just as silently pocket his winnings and move on. Then, during the second visit to Las Vegas that Harrigan observed and at Baker's sixth casino of the evening, two men approached him and steered him firmly toward an office marked Security. Harrigan knew at once what had happened. Baker had been spotted not as a fugitive but as a card counter, a professional player of any game in which cards already played could be memorized. Harrigan knew the procedure once a suspected counter was spotted. He would be photographed by the security staff of any casino, then banned, and his photograph would be distributed among all the major gaming houses. Won't this be interesting! thought Harrigan.

Halfway to the office, Baker the limp and silent gambler became the erect and speaking Baker whom Harrigan knew best. It was, in fact, a protesting Baker. Twice he held back, shaking off the hands that guided him as he attempted to persuade the men that the floor manager had been wrong. They were not having it. One man advanced to open the door while the other pressed his palm against Baker's back and pushed. Harrigan saw Baker's body stiffen and coil as the door closed upon him. All that was missing was the large yellow towel and Howard Twilley.

Harrigan didn't bother to try listening at the door. He knew what was happening there. And he knew that there would be no photographing Jared Baker. Besides, he fully expected Baker to reappear in a matter of minutes, which he did, a look of weary resignation on his face. He left at once for the bus station.

From that day forward, Baker became something of a homebody. He settled in on his houseboat, and for almost two months more he barely budged except to walk to a pay phone every few days. All the calls were to his daughter. Harrigan had no means of tapping all the pay phones near the marina office, but the phone of the Carey house had been tapped for nearly a year. After each call, Harrigan would dial a number, and the conversation just recorded would be played back to him. They were harmless, caring calls that gave away nothing. But

Harrigan began to notice a pattern of long interludes of silence on the tapes. Occasionally, Tina would respond to a silence as if words had just been spoken. Troubled, Harrigan began observing Baker's calls through a powerful telescope, fearful that Sonnenberg might have provided some exotic scrambler that deflected Baker's voice when he chose not to be heard. There was no such device. Baker's mouth did not move during the periods that matched the recorded silences. Nothing at all happened except that his body seemed to sag during those moments.

Then suddenly, soon after the longest of the silences was followed by a happy squeal on his daughter's end, Baker moved. He abandoned his houseboat and went to New York. He flew via four different connections and under four different names and then proceeded to two different hotels. The last, as Harold Mailander. A klutzy name, mused Harrigan, for such a slippery son of a bitch.

"But why are you here, Baker?" he'd asked during the plane ride that beat Baker's flight by half a day. And again as he stared through prisms of rainwater on the windshield of the blue Oldsmobile. Could it simply be to visit your daughter? Or to be reprogrammed by the mysterious Dr. Sonnenberg? Or to make someone else disappear? Or, more precisely, to make your little girl disappear! In that case, Mr. Baker, if that's it, and I'm growing goddamned sure that it is, I'm afraid I'll have to take some action. Because if you get away with her, we'll never see you again, will we, Mr. Baker?

There, said Harrigan to himself. That much is reasonably straightforward. Not what you'd call buttoned up, but straightforward. I spend these many months getting to understand you, watching you develop your talent, watching you run recruitment errands for your Dr. Sonnenberg, and then, I think, watching you begin to regret that talent. I have an overpowering intuition that you were about to become a dropout twice removed, funded, apparently, by the casino establishment of Las

Vegas, Nevada. I suspect, incidentally, assuming
Sonnenberg taught you to forage for funds in that manner, that Las Vegas is at least one source of his own considerable ·income. Yes, Baker, this business gets more
straightforward all the time.

Until tonight, that is. Tonight, Baker, something very
peculiar happens. Let's consider it together. Baker takes
an idiotic stroll through the park. Baker comes upon two
young pigs who are about to ravage a covergirl type.
Baker goes Wolfman again and rips the bejaysus out of
them. Except one of them isn't just any pig. He's
Domenic Tortora's pig. I know you weren't tailing him
because I was tailing you. No way, therefore, for you to
know that those particular bums would go looking for action in this park on this particular night. And even if you
did know, how would you find them? Young John and his
mesomorph friend certainly didn't leave a map showing
where they hoped to waylay a screen goddess if one
should happen by.

What does that leave? It leaves coincidence. Or it
leaves that Baker knew where he'd find them. Coincidence leads nowhere of interest. We'll ignore it. So if you
knew, Baker, and we skip over the question of how you
knew, the next question becomes why. Why would a man
who goes so far out of his way to lay low do something
that is sure to bring Tortora and everyone Tortora can
buy right down on his ass? It doesn't make sense, Baker.
It probably makes no more sense to our friends
Sonnenberg and Tortora, or even Duncan Peck, all of
whom are no doubt going through this same exercise
about now. The difference is that I've got you, Baker. Or
do you have me? We're about to find out, aren't we, lad?

12

Connor Harrigan knelt at the edge of the bathtub in Tanner Burke's suite, grunting as he worked his fingers over the dead man's pockets and the lining of his uniform. Behind him, Baker stood quietly, apparently indifferent to Harrigan's work. Now and then he would stare thoughtfully at his own image in the washstand mirror.

The more Harrigan searched, the more certain he was that he had not executed a New York City police officer. The man's second weapon, a gas pistol equipped with either killing or tranquilizing darts, tended to argue in that direction, but the possibility remained, however dim, that he was a legitimate cop moonlighting as a contract killer. Possible, but not at all likely, he thought. The man carried nothing. Not a label. Not a scrap of paper except the blank sheets of his notebook. Only a single coin.

He was not likely to be an associate of Stanley Levy, who worked alone except for accompanying muscle, or any other criminal hireling. Contract killers rarely, if ever, bother to strip themselves of traceable documents and never of cash. Too much of an inconvenience for a useless theatric that would cause only a modest delay in their identification. Nor would the ordinary hoodlum worry much about protecting his patron's anonymity once he himself was cold meat. Even religious killers seemed unwilling to pass anonymously to their reward these days.

What about Sonnenberg? Could he be another of Sonnenberg's spooks? Probably not. Sonnenberg, in his arrogance, would have laid a masterful trail of false paper before he'd do anything so banal as a stripping of documents. The coin, Connor. Why a coin? Coins are for telephones. You were going to call someone, weren't you, you rascal.

Suddenly, very suddenly, Harrigan felt a change inside him. It was a curious surging. An emotion. An anger. And then it passed. He waited for a moment, thinking it might return, but it did not. There was only the sensation of Baker behind him. Baker was moving.

A glance over his shoulder told him that it was not danger that he felt. Baker made no move toward him. The tall man's eyes were upon the policeman's black notebook, which lay on the tile floor.

Harrigan pushed to his feet. He threw a towel across the dead man's face and closed the heavy shower curtain. A drawer slammed shut in the other room and some wooden hangers clattered across a closet rod. Tanner Burke was dressing. The sound seemed to disrupt whatever it was that disturbed Jared Baker. His face softened. Baker glanced once in the direction from which the sound had come and then toward the bathtub, and his eyes saddened. Harrigan could almost read his mind. What was she feeling? he was wondering. What could she be thinking, knowing that she'd just held doors open so that the first corpse she'd likely ever seen could be carried in and dumped in her bathtub? Harrigan knew because he wondered those things himself. And what of you, Baker? he thought. Harrigan turned to study him, idly picking up the policeman's notebook as he did so.

The two men had barely spoken. Harrigan's response to Baker's return of his greeting was only to take a weary breath and to reach for the feet of the dead policeman, indicating the heavier end as Baker's portion. "His eyes" was all that Tanner Burke had whispered, and Jared Baker bent to close them. Jared Baker the family

man. Jared Baker the suburbanite from green and tran-
quil Connecticut. For most of his life, his bigger problems included whether his lawn had enough lime on it
and what to do when the shit backed up from the septic
tank. Now it's a year and a half later, and he can stand
around a bathroom daydreaming after almost getting
shot, after meeting a guy who's been dogging him for
months, and after carrying two hundred pounds of dead
beef through a hotel corridor with a movie star, for
Christ's sake, trotting ahead of him. What does it take,
Baker? What does it take for you to say fuck this, I can't
handle it, and then give the job to your friend I saw in
Dayton? I want to see that, Baker. I want to see you do
it right up close and then I want to know how.

"Does the woman know what you are?" Harrigan
asked quietly.

Baker straightened. "The woman? If you mean Ms.
Burke, the answer is no."

"God save us." Harrigan blinked. "A feminist Frankenstein."

Baker ignored the remark. His eyes fell upon the
notebook turning in Harrigan's hands.

"If she doesn't know, she must damn well be curious
after seeing you do your tricks in the park."

"She didn't see that." Baker kept his voice low. "Not
clearly, anyway. She didn't even know my last name until
she heard you say it. Ms. Burke is not a part of this,
Harrigan."

Harrigan jerked his thumb toward the shower curtain. "Can I assume that's why you sent in your scrub
team against our friend in there? If it is, your consider-
ation for the lady's sensitivities could have gotten all goddamned three of us killed. In fact, Mr. Baker, it seems
that she's a hell of a lot handier in a brawl than you are."

A smile tugged at Baker's mouth and he looked
away. The thought seemed to please him. Harrigan made
a disgusted face. So much, he thought, for provoking
Baker by impugning his virility. The pain in the ass is
proud of her. She dances in with those dumb little kicks
that she probably learned from some picture she did,

kicks that wouldn't have knocked a zit off the cop except they surprised him, and he's proud of her. He lets her do the fighting while all the time he could tear the guy in half, but instead he holds on for dear life like he learned to do in the fourth grade and . . . Ohhh, Baker . . . stupid me.

"She's going to know, Baker. She's going to read the papers this afternoon."

Baker turned away. Toward the mirror. Slowly, hesitantly, he reached for the hot water tap and turned it on. Next, he reached for a hotel towel, which he held under the running water for several moments before bringing it to his face. Harrigan tensed. He lowered his hand and placed it over the gas pistol, which lay on the tub's edge. With one finger, he quietly worked back the bolt so that part of the chambered dart could be seen. It was yellow. A tranquilizer dart. Three cc's were enough for a water buffalo, and there would be more in the pistol's butt. Harrigan eased off the safety.

But it wasn't happening. What he'd seen happen behind a towel in a Dayton, Ohio, boxing ring wasn't happening. No swelling sensation. No cooling of muscles. If anything, Baker seemed to be softening.

"*Charley?*"

No answer.

"*I feel her, Charley. I feel her thinking my name. What is she thinking about me, Charley?*"

"*scared.*"

"Scared of me?"

"*scared. telephone.*"

"She's afraid of the telephone?"

"*afraid to call. afraid to not call. abel says don't let her call.*"

"Never mind what Abel says."

"*now she thinks don't call police. don't get baker in trouble.*"

"Never mind that either. Charley, what's in that notebook? Why do I keep wanting to look at that black notebook?"

"telephone number. i saw a phone number there and you didn't."

"Whose number, Charley? Why is it important?"

"ask abel."

"Tell me, Charley."

"abel says don't tell you. abel says send him out now. there are more bad people outside. abel says don't tell you who because you don't send him anymore when i tell you. abel says you should have called him on the stairs before. abel says that's why i told you those men were there. i told you so you could send him and you didn't."

"Charley, damn you . . ."

"Jared?" Tanner Burke's fingers reached from the doorway and touched his arm. Harrigan saw the towel fall away from his face and he saw the face harden again. All but the eyes. The eyes took on a smitten look as they absorbed the lovely young woman who'd entered. She had changed into a brown tweed jacket, slacks, and a yellow turtle neck that made her natural coloring seem all the more healthy and clean. Tanner wore no jewelry save the simple gold studs in her ears and a single topaz ring. She was dressed to go out. Harrigan relaxed his grip on the gas pistol and smoothly tucked the weapon under his coat.

"Jared," she said quietly, not looking at the older man, "are you going to tell me?"

Baker half-turned and reached out a hand. She took it tenderly and held it in both of hers.

Oh, Jesus, thought Harrigan. And now we have the bride of Frankenstein. We don't have enough trouble already. What's worse is, if he gets away from me, he's going to try to tell her. He won't show her, but he'll tell her. And he probably hasn't sense enough to tell her a decent lie.

"Jared," she said, her voice firmer now, "I sat in there staring at the phone. I came this close to calling the police and telling them that one of their officers is in my—"

"He's not a policeman." Baker shook his head. "There's nothing in his pockets except a coin and a phone numb—" Baker caught himself too late. Out of the corner of his eye he could see the wave of astonishment that crossed Connor Harrigan's face. By the time he turned fully, the notebook was in Harrigan's hand again and Harrigan was riffling through it a second time. And then he saw it. The light was right and he saw it, not in the notebook but written in ink across the spine of the black vinyl cover. There were ten digits. And they were written backward.

Baker watched as the astonishment faded and a small satisfied smile began to take its place.

"I think we'd all better have a chat," said the older man.

"Here's the thing," said Connor Harrigan, squeezing a tea bag over his cup. He was speaking to Tanner Burke. "I wish with all my heart that you were not involved. I wish it even more than Mr. Baker—"

"Could I ask who you are first?" Tanner interrupted.

Harrigan wiped his fingers on a Kleenex and reached for his small cowhide case, which he opened and passed to her. "The name is Connor Harrigan. The card you're reading says that I'm with the Department of the Treasury. I am, but loosely. There are other cards in that case saying that I'm a lot of different people doing a lot of different things. Those are false. The absolute truth is that I am indeed Connor Harrigan and that I am in the permanent employ of the General Accounting Office of the United States Government."

Tanner looked blankly at him. Baker seemed to be barely listening.

"Disappointed, aren't you?" Harrigan smiled pleasantly. "You wanted James Bond or at least Gordon Liddy."

"What I wanted," she said evenly, "was to be told who you are and what your interest is in Jared Baker."

Harrigan shrugged and gestured toward Baker, inviting Tanner to ask his confirmation. Ask the man, he thought. Let's both find out what Baker knows.

Baker met his eyes and held them. Harrigan thought he saw a twinkle, as if Baker was letting him know that he understood the game. Baker turned to face Tanner Burke.

"It's true as far as it goes," he said. "Harrigan's an investigator. He can investigate any department he pleases if the use of federal funds is involved. His base is the GAO because no one can fire him if he steps on the wrong toes in the course of any of the special jobs he takes on."

"And you're a special job?"

Baker shook his head. "It's not really me they're after. Harrigan's investigating a man who trained me to live under an assumed identity. He's trained others too. There's nothing illegal about that unless the fictitious identities are used to defraud. There's no fraud in this case, but there's the matter of aiding and abetting a fugitive. You might be guilty of that too if you knew that I'm wanted by the police. Of course, you don't know that because I've never told you."

Tanner seemed confused. Harrigan had given no sign that he was interested in arresting Baker. Baker understood.

"Harrigan doesn't care that I'm wanted. All he wants to know is what the man who trained me is up to. In fact, he's not really up to much of anything except helping people start their lives over. Most pay him a fee. As it happens, however, the government has at least two relocation agencies of its own. Those people get paranoid when they learn that someone else has set up shop in competition with them or that they might be losing a numbered taxpayer here and there. As for me, I'm not up to much of anything either. All I want from this day on is to have some kind of life where I'm free and where I'm left alone."

Tanner nodded her sympathy and her understanding. She looked accusingly at Harrigan, who slapped his thighs and returned a look of pained exasperation.

"Is it possible you believe all that pap?" he asked, leaning forward in his chair.

"I believe in Jared, yes." She reddened.

"For Christ's sake, young lady," Harrigan blustered, "you have a stiff in your bathtub wearing a phony police suit. You very possibly have another stiff or two in the park who were made that way by Clark Kent over here. You know that, and yet you rush to believe your new boyfriend when he says all that's going on here is a little bureaucratic curiosity?"

"My new boyfr——" Tanner blushed angrily. "Jared didn't kill that man in there. You did, and you didn't even have to. And you have a wallet full of fake papers, speaking of phonies. And now you of all people want me to believe that what Jared says is a lie."

"My turn," Harrigan snapped. He could see the anger in Baker's eyes as well. Get mad, Baker. Get goddamned mad. "Like he just said about me, it's true as far as it goes. What he didn't say is that none of these fictitious identities is some ordinary slob looking for a second chance someplace. And Baker here, if I have to point it out, is the least ordinary of the bunch."

"That's enough, Harrigan." Baker's voice was low and quiet.

"You think you're protecting her?" Harrigan spun on him. "She's up to her neck right now. She's been made, Baker. She's been made by me, by Washington, which in this case is not the same thing, and very likely by Domenic Tortora. Is it possible you don't know that yet? Whoever paid that cop knew to send him to this room."

Baker seemed confused by the Washington and Tortora references, but he recovered quickly. He gestured toward the bathroom door. "You and your friends can get rid of the body, Harrigan. I'll handle anyone else I have to. But I'm not going to let you involve her."

Harrigan took a long, slow breath. When he spoke, his voice was almost gentle. "Baker, how are you going to stop me?"

"I think you know," Baker whispered. His right eye twitched. He could feel the pressure building.

"No, I don't know." Harrigan raised both eyebrows. "Could you mean that you'll use physical force?"

"Don't do this, Harrigan."

"I mean," the smaller man continued, "you might like to think you can bully a fat old fellow like myself, but the fact is you don't have the heart for it. You certainly don't have the skills. I think I might just slap you around a bit for even suggesting such a thing."

Baker was horrified. With a shock, he realized what Harrigan was trying to do. The first tear fell from his right eye, squeezed out by the pounding behind it.

"Ah." Connor Harrigan raised one finger, as if struck by a revelation. "I know. It's not going to be you all by yourself, is it, Baker? You're going to bring a friend. You're going to call out the man who was in the park, aren't you? The man I myself saw in Dayton. Well now, that's different. There's a man who might intimidate poor old Connor."

"What's this?" Tanner Burke asked uneasily.

"Show her, Baker." Harrigan slapped him.

"Harrigan, don't do this." Baker rose slowly to his feet, the fingertips of his right hand pressing against his temple. The pounding had become a stomping. From within the darkness of his brain a foot was slamming against the steel door that Baker had built there. The upper bolt half-turned under the impact. The bolt's housing began to bend, and stress lines showed white upon the metal. Another surge of pain. Now Baker saw dust trickling down from the hinges where they were set in cement. And Baker saw himself. He saw his own shoulder braced against the door from the outside, holding it, pressing Abel back.

"*Abel, get back, damnit. He's bluffing.*"

"Jared? Jared, what's wrong?"

She was going toward him. He could see through a wet haze that she was reaching for his face and holding it. Her eyes were wide. Stunned. Afraid. Someone's shouting. Harrigan. He's yelling something about those two in the park.

"Jared!" Her voice was almost a scream.

"*Stop it, Abel. I can't hear ... What? What's Harrigan saying about the park? Names? What names?*

The two with knives! ... I don't know their names. How would I know? ... Abel! Stop! Come on, Baker. Hold on! You're starting to get lighter. You're drifting ..."

Tanner was shaking him, pressing him backward toward a chair.

"Tanner, don't. That'll make him mad."

Her hand was cool against the back of his neck. It slowed the drifting. But then he saw Harrigan's face appear near hers, and Abel lunged again.

Harrigan's face was afraid for the first time. He must have seen it. Harrigan looks like he wants to run, but he's staying there. Come back, Baker, he's saying. And he's still asking about those names. *"Charley? What's he talking about? Abel, shut up. Let him answer."* Hold on, Harrigan yells. I'm going to help you, lad. Hold him back. Tanner's face doesn't know why he's yelling that. Arm stings. Harrigan did something to my arm. It stings. Tanner knows it stings. She's looking at the place where my arm hurts and trying to pull out a little silver thing that Harrigan put there ... and Harrigan's pushing her away.

Baker felt the drift stopping. He was just floating now. Sinking. He could feel his body losing buoyancy. Easing downward into an almost liquid warmth. And she watched him, calling him as he floated, but her voice was getting farther and farther away. She's crying. And now there's just her voice, and now even that's gone. There's nothing. Just the long blue tunnel. Swirling slowly, going down. Slow and easy. Oh, Tanner! Liz! You saw it.

Baker fainted.

On the street below, Tom Dugan had left the blue Oldsmobile and was standing in the shadow of a small service alley near the Essex House. It was full daylight, although the streets and sidewalks remained nearly empty. Except for one white van. It had already passed twice, too slowly. If it passed again, he wanted room to move.

Ten minutes went by and he could see it. Only its

front end was visible as it waited out a Sixth Avenue light before turning east again in his direction. He thought he heard a car door slam up there. His service pistol was already in his hand.

The light changed and the blinking van continued its turn. MIDTOWN OFFICE SUPPLIES, it read. It approached the Oldsmobile slowly, but this time it did not pass. Dugan crouched. Abruptly, a rear door swung open, and Dugan heard two feet slap against the damp pavement. A parked truck blocked his vision. Dugan waited.

"Boom!" A voice came from the van.

Dugan steadied his weapon.

"I surrender," came the voice. A white handkerchief waved above the door.

"Who's that?" Dugan called. "That you, Biaggi?"

Smiling, hands raised, Michael Biaggi stepped away from the van and showed himself over the parked truck's hood. "What do you think this is, *Gunsmoke*? Come on, We got relieved."

Dugan hesitated. "Why have you been cruising in that thing?"

"Dropping off our relief, dummy. Let's go. Harrigan's already down at the Federal Building. Leave your keys in the Olds."

Tom Dugan was still unsure. There was always something funny about Biaggi. He wasn't sure Connor Harrigan liked him that much either. "What the hell's going on?" he asked. "And who relieves Connor Harrigan's people?"

"Right at the top. Come on. Mr. Harrigan wants to see the look on your face when you hear about our new job."

Dugan held back for another beat before he holstered his Colt. "The keys are in it," he said and stepped quickly toward the open van. Biaggi followed and closed the double doors behind them.

There was only one seat inside in addition to the two in front. Biaggi's topcoat sat on the rearmost. Dugan passed it by.

"Who's driving?" Dugan asked.

"Say hello to Ed Burleson. He's Special Operations."

Dugan climbed into the front passenger seat and strapped himself in. He turned to extend a hand to the man next to him. "Special Operations?" he asked. "No offense, but I didn't think Connor Harrigan ever worked with . . ."

The man's grip was crushing. Dugan's brain lingered on that message, not wanting to accept the next. Something thin and almost invisible had winked down across his face and kissed against his collarbone before it slid against his throat and tightened. He felt his tongue leap forward and then his eyes. He argued with his brain. This could not happen. That was Mike Biaggi back there. Even Biaggi wouldn't . . .

Tom Dugan was the third to die. An hour earlier, Warren Bagnold had convulsed once more and then was still.

The tunnel was slowing. Stopping. The blue spirals faded into gray shadow and there was nothing again. Not even memory. There, he floated for a while and he was happy. The place was warm and dark and no thoughts came to him. But the peace didn't last. Soon, too soon, he was rising again. He did not want to come back. But then he saw that her face was there waiting. And it was different. Not frightened now. Curious, and caring, and growing bigger as he drew close. She was saying something. ". . . eerie." It sounds like "eerie."

". . . hear me? Jared? Can you hear me?"

". . . eer . . . me. Liz . . . Yes . . ." He pushed through all but the last wisps of fog like a diver breaking the surface. One hand went to his arm. There was a soreness. A small lump below his shoulder. Both arms felt so very heavy.

"What happened?" he asked, his voice thick and distant.

Harrigan moved into focus, the yellow tranquilizer dart rolling between his outstretched fingers. "You were right on the edge, lad. It seemed wisest that you rest for a while."

"How long . . . Did I do anything?"

"You just slept," Tanner Burke answered. "You even smiled once. You called me Liz." She looked down at the hand she was holding and then again into his eyes. "Jared," she whispered, "Mr. Harrigan told me about you."

Baker looked away. "He told you what about me?"

"Most of what I know," Harrigan answered, "about Jared Baker, anyway. How it began, what happened to your family, and about this thing you do. She knew what you'd done in the park, Jared. She was trying to believe it was a dream."

"Why?" he asked hoarsely. "Why didn't you leave it that way?"

"Because like I keep telling you, she's involved. And there are people who'll be nervous about what she might know. We can keep her from harm, Baker, if we help each other. And believe it or not, I'd even like to help you."

"I don't need you, Harrigan," he said quietly, pulling himself to an upright position on the couch.

"You haven't heard my offer."

"If you want to deal, we'll deal about Tanner. I don't need your help for the rest of it."

"My offer is this," Harrigan said patiently. "I will not ask you to betray any person who is in hiding. Nor will you be asked to testify against anyone at all. Moreover, I will help you to be with your daughter anyplace of your choosing in the Western Hemisphere. That's what you get lad. Freedom, peace, and protection for Jared and Christina Baker."

Harrigan felt something from Tanner Burke when he said the last. He glanced at the back of her head and then at Baker. "You can build any life you like, Jared lad."

Baker felt it too. He didn't look at her. Whatever future he had, he could not let himself imagine that it might include her. This was not a time for fantasies. And even if it were more than a dream, even if they both shared the dream, it was impossible. But that dream was what that bastard Harrigan was trying to sell. As for Tina, though, I will be with her. With or without you, Harrigan. Around you or over you.

"I said I don't need you, Harrigan."

Tanner Burke sat beside him, her hand still on his. "Jared, listen to him," she urged softly. "At least hear him out. It doesn't hurt to ask what he wants from you."

Baker looked up at Harrigan and waited.

"Knowledge," Connor Harrigan answered. "Knowledge and friendship."

"Which means?"

"I want to understand you," he said. "I want to know how you are possible. I want to know why you exist and why the others exist. I want to know what you can do now and what you might do. I want to know why there are people who fear you, and especially why they fear Sonnenberg."

"And after you have your evidence?"

"I said knowledge, Baker. Evidence and knowledge are not the same. Evidence is slower."

Baker waited again.

"I mentioned friendship," Harrigan added. "Friends stay in touch. Now and then they do each other favors."

Baker nodded. It was about what he expected. "You're not stupid, Harrigan," he said. "I think you know I have a place to go and it's not likely to be that houseboat. You haven't told me why I need you."

Tanner Burke touched his thigh. "Do you care what I think?"

"Yes." More than you could know.

"You might need someone who understands the people who want to hurt you. Someone like Harrigan. You're just not like them, Jared."

"I can handle anyone I have to, Liz." He tried to say it in a way that did not sound brutal.

"Except for that thing inside you."

Baker heard the loathing in her voice when she said

that word. He'd expected it. But he'd hoped he'd never hear it.

"That isn't true," he said with a trace of sadness. "He came out when we were in the park because I called him out. I wanted to help you and so did he, even if our reasons were different. When he was finished, I sent him back. I'm not crazy, Tanner. And this is not some sickness. This 'thing' is simply a part of me that I've learned to use. Even you have a . . ." He chose not to finish the thought.

Harrigan looked up from the pipe he was packing. "I'm afraid it was him who was using you, lad. Do you remember just before I stuck you? When this friend of yours was trying to get out?"

"He wouldn't have."

"All the same, at that moment do you remember me asking you a question about the park? About the two men there?"

"I think so." Baker blinked.

"Try to remember. I asked you several times."

"I remember. You kept asking me their names. I have no idea what their names were."

Tanner Burke looked from Harrigan to Baker and back again. There was confusion in the tilt of her head. She recalled no such question. Certainly not a repeated question.

"You're sure now?" Harrigan pressed. "You don't remember their names?"

"They called each other nicknames. One was Jace or maybe Chase. The big one was called Sumo. Why does this matter?"

"It matters because the one called Jace or Chase happens to be the only son of one Domenic Tortora."

Baker's eyes flashed. Tanner felt his shoulder muscles go taut.

"I take it you know the name."

"That's not possible." Baker seemed thunderstruck. "I didn't even know he had a son."

"It's not only possible, it's a fact. You've attacked and severely injured the son of a man who's been dogging you since you jumped bail. You found him at night, in the middle of a very large park, within two hours of your arrival in one of the biggest cities in the world. Food for thought, isn't it? And what do you suppose Mr. Tortora is thinking?"

"You're both thinking I must have known he was there. I didn't. And that either means a hell of a coincidence or I was set up."

"My view exactly. Would you like to know who set you up?"

Baker waited.

"It was your violent friend."

"He'd never do that. He'd never hurt me."

"He didn't hurt you. He hurt them. All he did was get you to deliver him there. All he had to do was get you to stroll through the area where the young scamp had laid hold of his victim." Harrigan apologized to Tanner with a bow of his head.

"You're wrong, Harrigan." Baker pushed up from the couch and began to pace. "He wouldn't have known a thing like that was happening."

"He would if he could read their minds."

Baker stiffened. "He can't do that."

"Charley?" Baker called the name silently.

"For true, Mr. Baker?" Harrigan asked.

"It's the truth, Harrigan. Depend on it. *CHARLEY!"*

"Then who can read minds, Mr. Baker?" Harrigan struggled not to show his excitement. "Someone can read minds. Someone is telepathic. If it isn't the violent one, who is it?"

"No one is telepathic," he lied. Baker stood drumming his fingers on the mantel of a false fireplace. A small mirror hung above it between two sconces. He moved toward the mirror.

"But it keeps happening, doesn't it, Baker? Let me count the ways. In California, you knew if I got too close. It now appears that you've known my name for some time as well. You knew that I was out there on the landing. Maybe you even knew about the guy in the cop suit before he jumped me. Next, you knew he was a fake and that his pockets were empty when I'm the one who searched him with my back to you. I think you even know who sent him."

Baker didn't answer.

"The guy had a number he was supposed to call after he iced maybe all three of us. You kept looking at his pad. But you weren't sure it was there until after I spotted it. You knew when I knew, Baker. You read my mind."

"It isn't true." Baker turned, looking not at Harrigan but at Tanner. "I'm a man," he told her, "not some freak. Sometimes I know what people are thinking or feeling but just in little flashes. I'm like you, Liz. You do it too. Just tonight, you knew the name I gave you was wrong. There were other little things you sensed about me. I don't want you thinking I can get into your head or into anyone else's head who doesn't want me there."

Harrigan raised a hand before she could speak. "I've mentioned several ways, Baker. The next one is a peach. It has to do with the names of those two in the park. Have we established that you recall that question?"

"I remember," he said absently, turning back to face the mirror.

Harrigan faced Tanner Burke. "And what of you, miss? Do you remember me asking that question?"

"Before you stuck him with that thing? No, I don't remember. I don't think you did ask."

"Mr. Baker." Harrigan clapped his hands together. "Why do you suppose Miss Burke can't recall a question that you and I know was asked right in front of her?"

Baker stared at the mirror.

"It's because I asked that question only in my mind, Mr. Baker."

From across the room, Baker could almost feel the chill that went through Tanner. He kept his back to her, his eyes locked upon his image in the mirror.

"How, Charley? How did you know they'd be in the park?"

No answer.

"Talk to me, Charley. Talk to me or I'll say your name out loud right here."

"you won't."

"Answer, Charley. If you don't, I'll let them ask you. You'll be all alone with them and they'll make you tell, Charley."

"i didn't do anything."

"You told Abel those two were in the park. Why, Charley? Why did Abel want to hurt them?"

"they were like the first one."

"First one? You mean the one who killed Sarah?"

"yes. they even knew the first one."

Baker put aside his surprise. *"So they wanted to get even with me. Is that it, Charley? You heard them thinking bad thoughts about me and you told Abel?"*

"no. they weren't thinking about baker then. only about tanner burke and vinnie cuneo and tortora."

Baker whispered Vinnie Cuneo's name aloud questioningly. The name meant nothing to him. Harrigan heard the name and stiffened, not at the mention of a minor hoodlum but at the realization that a conversation was taking place in Baker's head. From his chair he could see half of the image facing Baker in the mirror. Its gilded fruitwood frame dissected Baker's face. The half that showed was slack and dull. It did not reflect the tension evident across Baker's shoulders.

"Charley, if they weren't thinking about me, how did you know they were there?"

"they were thinking tortora. that tortora might be mad at them for doing bad things to tanner burke. they would tell vinnie cuneo because he would laugh and say it was good, but they would not tell tortora because tortora wouldn't laugh."

"But how could you hear that, Charley? You know when people are thinking my name. You know when they're thinking Sonnenberg's name. But that's all you learned to do. You don't know when they're thinking other names. Do you know a new trick, Charley? Did Abel teach you another trick?"

"no."

"What names can you hear, Charley?"

"baker and sonnenberg just like now. sometimes tina. that man. he's thinking baker and sonnenberg now. that lady. she's thinking baker. baker and cooper shaw."

"Cooper Shaw?" he murmured. "That's a new name, Charley. Who's Cooper Shaw?"

Tanner Burke's head snapped up at the sound of the name. She opened her mouth to speak, but Connor Harrigan slashed an open hand through the air, silencing her.

"most times he's her boyfriend out where she lives. sometimes she lived with him and slept with him and everything. she did things in bed with other men too. things like she didn't even want to do with baker. she's thinking how she liked cooper shaw better than you. she's thinking—"

"Shut up, Charley!" Baker was livid. "What goddamned business is that of— and why, goddamn it, are you saying it?"

"abel said to."

"Well, fuck Abel," Baker fairly screamed in his head. "And anyway, Abel didn't hear her thinking. You did. And you also made up part of that, didn't you, Charley? I know damned well that at a time like this, Tanner Burke is not sitting around comparing the men in her life."

Charley did not answer.

"Last warning, Charley. You're coming out."

"i made up the last part. abel said to."

"Why, Charley?"

"because she wants to be your friend and help you. because harrigan wants you to be his friend and help him. but abel says you don't need friends. abel says you only need charley to know things for you and you only need abel to keep people from hurting you. abel says that way we don't need friends. abel says they don't even like you. they want to hurt you."

"Charley, you just said they want to be my friends."

"abel says that was wrong. they don't like you. they don't want you to be free. the man wants you to be his

*friend for years and years just to tell him things and to do
things for him. the woman doesn't want you to need us.
she wants you to need her so you won't be free. she wants
you to have tina so you won't be free too."*

Tanner Burke was fuming. She was feeling her third
or fourth flash of anger since Baker revived, but this was
the first time that she understood. It's true, she thought.
It's true that Baker can reach inside my head and he has
no right. Even if it was just to read a fleeting thought
about a sometime lover and what a simple little boy he
now seems compared to Jared Baker.

She felt Harrigan watching her and she glared back
at him. Now, damn it, Harrigan's trying to read my mind.
Isn't anyone in this town normal? Every time she got a
little mad in the past half-hour, she'd look up, and
Harrigan would be watching her. It was as if he knew the
anger was there, but he couldn't have because it came
out of nowhere. Nothing happened to cause it. There
would just be a tiny crowding feeling inside her head
and she would feel her blood rising toward it. Next, there
would be a new feeling. A sort of sucking feeling, like a
tissue being drawn from its box, and then the anger
would leave. She would have ignored these feelings or
dismissed them as a product of fatigue except that
Harrigan seemed to feel them too. He had the same little
startled expression whenever she felt her own tissue being pulled away.

Harrigan reached his hand over and gave her a
touch meant to be comforting. Then he bit his pipe and
returned his attention to Jared Baker. His own crowding
feeling, he was almost sure, was Baker probing him. As
much as possible, he made an effort to keep his brain on
idle. As for the anger, Harrigan was less certain about
that. When it first passed, earlier, he thought it might
have been a sense of indignation, a resentment of this violation to his inner self. But he knew that it had to be
more. He'd felt it, of course, during the months of his
surveillance and long before he'd had any notion of Baker's probing his mind. Yes, this was much more. There
was something almost primal about the anger he felt.

There had been a moment earlier, and another just now, when he wanted to hurt Baker. It was a flash compulsion that surged from deep within his brain and receded just as quickly. He leaned closer to Tanner Burke.

"Keep your mind off him for a moment if you can," he whispered. "Did you just get a feeling that you wanted to hurt someone?"

"Yes. It was like—"

Baker flung a look over his shoulder that silenced Tanner. He stepped closer to the wall mirror, his face now only inches away. Harrigan saw that Baker was more than angry. His fists were opening and closing, and the muscles of his back were already knotted. He knew that he was watching a man at war with himself. Harrigan folded his arms and settled back. Barely moving, he worked the bolt of the gas pistol at his belt and slid a new dart into place. That was in case Baker lost.

"Charley, what was that about my daughter?"

There was no answer.

"Charley, if either of you try to cut Tina out of my life, so help me, I'll ... Charley, answer me."

"abel says don't. i'm going to sleep now."

"Abel can't help you if I bring you all the way out, Charley."

"you won't."

"Charley!"

"abel says you won't. you're afraid it will make her not like you."

"You just watch me, you little bastard," he whispered.

Harrigan and Tanner heard him. She leaned forward in her chair as if to stand and move toward Baker. Harrigan pressed her forearm. Wait, he mouthed.

"He's going to explode again."

"I don't think so. Don't stop him."

Baker turned to face Harrigan. The slackness that Harrigan thought he had seen was gone. In its place, beneath the anger, was the look of a man betrayed. Baker's eyes softened as they fell on Tanner and his head shook just a fraction, as if in apology. Harrigan put more pressure on her arm.

"I'm going to the bathroom," Baker said.

"Yes," Harrigan answered.

"I'd like you to not bother me for a while. You'll know when to come in."

"Jared!" Tanner pulled free of Connor Harrigan. "You're not thinking of doing anything . . ."

"He's fine," Harrigan answered softly. "He'd simply like to go to the bathroom."

Baker hesitated for a moment, holding Harrigan's gaze. Go on, lad, thought Harrigan. Have your private meeting of the minds and see if you can sort out who's going to be in charge. And perhaps you'll come back with an answer or two.

Baker walked to the bathroom door and closed it behind him.

Tanner jumped at the sound of the lock being turned. "What is it?" she asked. "What's happening to him?"

"I don't know, to be honest." Harrigan glanced up at the sound of the bathroom tap running. He had at least begun to understand the man who had just left the room. What might now emerge from that bathroom was another matter entirely. If it turned out to be the beastie, Harrigan would very probably have to kill him. He raised a hand, interrupting as Tanner was about to speak. "Miss Burke," he said, "I'm going to have to ask you to trust me."

"What are you going to ask?"

"I'd like you to leave at once and not look back. I promise that I'll take care of Baker and that I'll do all I can to keep you from being involved further."

"I won't do that," she answered.

"You can't help. You can only distract. You can end up losing your hide and costing me mine as well."

"I've already helped, and that includes your hide. Anyway, Jared could have been killed in the park last night, but he didn't walk away from me."

"That wasn't the same, Miss Burke." Harrigan shook his head. "The two in the park didn't have a chance in the world against Baker. The man isn't who you think he is."

"You mean this other-personality business. Well, there's a real Jared Baker who's a good and decent man and . . ." Harrigan raised a hand again and Tanner pushed it aside. "And stop shutting me up, damn it. If you think I believe for one moment that Jared Baker is some sort of monster, I have to tell you that I know him a hell of a lot better than you do, no matter how long you've been watching him."

"You know him so well that you'd bet all you have on him? It's a wasteful risk, Miss Burke. He doesn't need you."

"I'll leave when he tells me that."

"Is that a promise?"

"No."

Harrigan sighed and he rose to his feet, moving closer to the bathroom door. He listened. There was nothing. Only the hushed sound of water from an aerated faucet. He returned to Tanner's chair and eased himself onto one knee beside it.

"It's like this is a railroad train," he said, "and this is the only stop. You must get off here or stay until the end. I must tell you that the likelihood of a happy end is almost nonexistent."

"You're patronizing me, Mr. Harrigan."

"No, I'm trying in my clumsy way to find the argument that would make you leave a situation you're not equipped to help."

"I've already helped, Mr. Harrigan," she said stubbornly.

"So we're talking in circles?"

"And we're wasting time," she answered. "I'm willing to trust you, Mr. Harrigan, because you seem to know what you're doing. I'll help you as long as I can believe that."

Harrigan let out a long, defeated breath. I know what I'm doing, is it? There's not a damned bit of it that makes any sense. Not Sonnenberg's intentions, not Tortora's involvement, and least of all the anxiety of Duncan Peck. All that's clear is that I have Jared Baker and that now everyone involved will be forced into action of some sort. Including Jared Baker.

But how much to tell Tanner Burke? She can hardly claim a need to know. Oh, to hell with that, he thought. It's her life as well that might end without a decent breakfast. She might even have a useful thought to offer. But where to start?

"Let's find out together just how well I know what I'm doing, Miss Burke." He frowned. "Shall we begin with Dr. Sonnenberg?"

Tanner Burke nodded attentively.

"He's the fellow at the core of all this, you know. Sonnenberg created your friend Baker. In fact, he created several others who are just as remarkable in their own way. I even have some notion of how Sonnenberg does it because I've been reading his mail for the past nine months. He's forever receiving research papers from Cal Tech and one or two other institutions involved in the study of behavioral modification. It wouldn't surprise me if he's planted one of his people out there.

"The material ranges from hypnosis to psychosurgery to brain cell transfusions, much of it very advanced stuff that's never been tried on humans. Except, it seems, by Sonnenberg. If we're to believe Jared Baker, what he's doing with it is scientifically risky but not necessarily sinister. Putting the best face on it, he might, like many scientists, be doing it simply because it can be done. His subjects may indeed be no more than men and women who want to start new lives. If that sounds farfetched, you heard Baker say that there are at least two federal agencies whose function is to create new identities for people who are in mortal danger otherwise. Beyond that are the entrepreneurs, mostly private detectives and lawyers, who make a business out of showing people how to get lost. Each year there are literally thousands of takers. It gets so I can hardly look at a moving van anymore without wondering who the new people really are.

"As for Sonnenberg, I have no clear idea of what he's up to. He may not be a Boris Karloff type out to rule the world, but he's not the pussycat Baker thinks he is either. There's a possibility that Sonnenberg murdered a man named Roger Hershey in order for a new Roger Hershey to replace him. I also suspect, without evidence, that Sonnenberg may be behind the murder of the judge who Baker's accused of killing. The manner of Judge Bellafonte's death points to Tortora's man, Levy, but the motive points to Sonnenberg. He needed Baker to need him."

"And Sonnenberg sent that man to murder us, didn't he?" she asked, her head turning toward the bathroom door. Tanner squinted as if she'd heard a distant sound.

Harrigan blinked. "May I ask why you think he did?"

"I saw the phone number written backward on his pad. Jared writes phone numbers that way too. The same man must have taught them both." Tanner hesitated. "At least, I thought so a minute ago."

Connor Harrigan sucked deeply on his pipe. The buzz inside his head had started again. She was wrong, of course. He'd known at a glance that that coded number rang in a bedroom in Alexandria, Virginia. Duncan Peck had ordered that cop to kill him, and possibly Tanner Burke, and then use the dart gun on Jared Baker until they could cart him off to a test tube someplace. But what else did she say? She said the same man must have taught them both. That was wrong. But the buzzing sound told him there was something else there.

"It wasn't Sonnenberg," he told her. "It was the number of a man in Washington, a very powerful and devious man, who's afraid of what I might know and who seems to be especially afraid of Sonnenberg. And you can be sure, incidentally, that the dead man has at least one partner waiting downstairs to hear that it's safe to come and haul our carcasses out of here. That's why I wanted you to leave." What the hell is it? he wondered. Something about teaching them both.

"I'm glad," she said. "I'm glad it wasn't Sonnenberg."

A curious sentiment, thought Harrigan.

"And I don't believe Dr. Sonnenberg is a criminal," she added. "Or that he's hatching any grand conspiracy either."

"Could I ask how it's possible to doubt it?"

"Just a feeling." She squinted again and turned her eyes toward the bathroom.

"Feminine intuition, I take it."

Tanner Burke straightened. "Would you try to be less of an ass on the subject of my sex, Mr. Harrigan?" She tried to say it without sharpness. And Connor Harrigan tried not to flush.

"What sort of intuition then?" he asked.

"Try *perception*, Mr. Harrigan. Or *judgment*. Believe it or not, I am capable of offering a useful thought. I've even been to college and managed to graduate without ever being a cheerleader or a prom queen. I've sat through lectures on history and political science without ever once doing my nails, reading *Modern Screen*, or offering to screw the professor in return for a passing grade."

"I'm deservedly abashed, Miss Burke." He sighed. "I take it that your education has prepared you for an insight that applies to Dr. Sonnenberg."

There was still an edge of sarcasm to his tone. Tanner chewed her lip, wondering whether to bother.

"With respect"—Harrigan dipped his head—"I would indeed like to hear your thought." It appeared to have struck him for the first time that this piece of Hollywood fluff might have substance. Tanner saw that in him, resenting him no less for it. But she relented.

"I had a professor," she said slowly, "who used to say that the answer, when found, would be simple."

"Meaning that Sonnenberg is simply a benevolent eccentric?"

"Meaning that there are more conspiracies in the minds of people like you than there are in the intentions of the people you investigate. In the history I've read, best-laid plans never work anyway. Murphy's Law. Even Hitler made things up as he went along and got caught up in his own momentum. I think Dr. Sonnenberg is doing the same thing."

A faraway look came over her, the same squinting concentration he'd seen twice in the past several minutes. She'd also played back a thought he'd had, almost verbatim. Harrigan leaned forward, interested now, where only moments before he would have dismissed her opinion as simplistic prattle.

"Without trying to reason it out, Miss Burke," he said carefully, "are you able to tell me why you think this way?"

She glanced toward the door. Involuntarily, he thought.

"Because I trust Jared," she answered, speaking very slowly now, "and because I think Jared would know if Sonnenberg was ... dangerous. And ... you're right. You're right about the same man teaching them both." A look of surprise crossed her face. She had no idea why she'd said that. Tanner turned once more toward the bathroom door. "And ... my God. I know Tina Baker. She's written to me. And once I gave her a trophy for ..."

Harrigan stared disbelievingly. Stupefied. The buzz in his head had become a siren. He barely heard the part about Tina.

"What ... what man?" he stammered.

"The man who taught Jared was the same man who taught ..." She closed her eyes. "It wasn't the policeman. He taught a man named ... Duncan?" Tanner brought her hands to her face.

Harrigan slammed a hand against his thigh. Tanner saw an expression, half astonishment and half fury, on his face.

"Oh, sweet Jesus, what a boob I've been!" Harrigan raged at himself. The answer had been there almost from the beginning. From the day Peck had told him about the coded numbers in Roger Hershey's wallet. A code Peck recognized because he'd learned it himself from a man who was now dead. The genius, Harrigan remembered, who could make whole departments disappear. The man could field operatives so immersed in deep cover that they might not recognize their mothers on the street. A tinkerer with minds and memories. A behaviorist. An eccentric.

And now Harrigan retrieved from his memory those odd and fearful little reactions whenever Sonnenberg's name was mentioned. God in heaven, was it possible? Ivor! That was his name. Ivor Blount! Now what did Harrigan remember about him? That he was a genius? He'd said that. Eccentric? Yes. Foreign. Swiss, he thought. And unstable. At least that was the rumor. But who said it? Who was closest to him? Damn! It was Duncan, all right, wasn't it? It was Duncan who talked of his unhappy visits with Ivor Blount at, let's see, St. Elizabeths in D.C. And it was Duncan who told sadly of Ivor Blount's tragic death.

Harrigan was pacing now, driving one fist against the other as he stalked the room. You're an ass for fair, Harrigan. The lady was right about that. Peck had given you just enough to get you interested and held back just enough to get you suspicious. He played you like a fiddle. He knew that your interest would cause you to seek out Baker and that your suspicion would cause you to work alone. He knew that in the end, whatever the outcome, there would only be Connor Harrigan to silence.

"Mr. Harrigan!" Tanner called.

Only old Connor, he thought, and whoever worked for him. Merciful God, poor young Thomas Dugan was alone on the street.

"Mr. Harrigan!" Tanner Burke called sharply. She was close to tears.

Connor shook himself, realizing for the first time that he had crossed the room and was methodically tearing apart a bouquet of flowers. A crushed carnation bled in his hand.

"Was Baker right, Miss Burke, when he said that you too sometimes get into people's minds?"

"I don't know." Her voice was anguished. "I don't

know why I said all those things. I just started thinking them."

"Do you begin to sense that I've not been entirely in control of events?" Harrigan drew his pistol and checked the breech.

"I think we're all in a lot of trouble."

"In fact, my own vanity may have killed us. I realized that while you were having your chat with Baker just now."

Tanner looked at him uncomprehendingly at first. Then she turned and moved toward the bathroom door.

"Where are you going?" he snapped.

"I'm going to get Jared out of this town and hide him until you can do your job, Harrigan."

"Baker can hide himself very nicely, believe me. Except he won't go without his daughter."

"Then we'll get her."

"Does that 'we' include you?"

"I'll get her myself if I have to. We know each other."

Harrigan allowed himself a smile.

"Why are you smirking?"

"It's admiration." He grinned. "You're a classy lady. Except you're getting damned near as spooky as Jared Baker. I'll ask you about that Tina Baker business later." Harrigan pried the long gas pistol from his belt and hefted both weapons in his hands.

"What are you doing with those?" she asked, backing away.

"This one puts people to sleep," he answered, "and this one cripples or kills. It's good you should see them. You have to know that I might use either and that people may die. You must also make up your mind that you'll do exactly what I say. Starting in ten seconds."

"What's going to happen?" she asked uneasily.

"I'm going to interview whatever's in that bathroom. And I intend to live through the experience."

He had no more than leaned toward the door when a sudden shriek echoed from the tiles inside. Even Harrigan flinched at the sound. It came again. A shrill, terrified "NOOO!" that washed over the room. Then a long desperate wail that sounded like Baker's name.

"Stay behind me."

The howls came louder as Harrigan, both weapons leveled, took three long steps and smashed his shoe against the lock.

On the sidewalk, near the entrance to the New York Athletic Club, stood a clubbish-looking man of about thirty-five. One arm embraced a bulky golf bag that had Bancroft emblazoned on the side. He wore a three-piece business suit. A Georgetown class ring was on his hand.

A few car lengths away, a Buick with tinted windows had just crunched to the curb. He pretended to ignore it. From a device on his belt, three musical notes sounded. He turned to see the Buick's trunk yawn slowly open. The man waved toward the car as if in sudden recognition, then lifted the golf bag and carried it to the trunk. A rear door swung open on the sidewalk side, an invitation. He ducked inside and closed the door behind him.

"Good morning, sir," he greeted the gray-haired man in the rear seat. "I hope you had a nice flight."

"A disingenuous salutation, Edward," Duncan Peck replied, "from a man who roused me from the comfort of my bed just three hours ago."

"I'm sorry, sir."

Peck patted his knee. "Just grousing, Edward. This Harrigan business has me upset. Has that been attended to, by the way?"

"I don't know, sir. Hackett should have taken him out two hours ago and then put Baker to sleep. But there's been no sign of either since that time."

"You sent one man after both Connor Harrigan and Jared Baker?"

"He was dressed as a uniformed policeman, sir. He should have been able to get close. And Hackett's very good at what he does."

"Harrigan, however, is superb. And Baker is barely human. Your man is dead, Edward."

That possibility had been troubling Burleson. He regretted equipping Hackett with Duncan Peck's phone number during his briefing. That was before Peck's decision to join them. Although an alternate contact was standard procedure, he chose not to mention it to Duncan Peck. Peck might think it untidy. Besides, Peck was correct. The man was almost certainly dead.

"Yes sir. That occurred to me. I now have four people covering the hotel, including Harrigan's man Biaggi. One of my operatives replaced Tom Dugan in Harrigan's car. I felt it necessary to sacrifice Dugan, sir. Michael Biaggi accepted the mission."

Peck nodded his approval. "I'm sure you regret the Dugan matter as much as I do, Edward. One can't blame a man for loyalty to his superior. Dugan may have had no idea that Harrigan had turned. As for Biaggi, I'm afraid he can't be trusted much beyond today."

"I'll see that housekeeping takes care of it, sir." Ed Burleson hesitated, chewing his lip. "It really is too bad about Connor Harrigan, sir. I understand you two have been very close."

Duncan Peck closed his eyes. "We go back many years," he said sadly. "Looking back, Connor has always been something of a tilter at windmills. But a traitor? A conspirator? If any man had said so in my presence, I'd have knocked him down."

"I guess the evidence is pretty strong, sir?"

"And very sensitive, Edward. I can well imagine you'd like to see it before carrying out so harsh an order. You're not a man to do this sort of thing casually."

"An order from you is enough, sir."

"You're a good man, Edward."

"Thank you, sir."

"Give them another hour to get clear of the hotel or at least get clear of the actress. If they haven't appeared by then, you and your men will have to go in. Baker will have to be taken and the actress will have to vanish. You will be neat, won't you?"

"Yes sir."

"How is my golf bag equipped?"

"Good sticks. They're Haig Ultras with aluminum shafts. The putter is a mallet type that might be a bit heavy for your touch. I'd suggest a shorter takeaway. In the shoe compartment, there's an Uzi with two extra thirty-round clips and a transceiver. There's also a sixty-power telescope in the umbrella sheath."

"Excellent, Edward. I'll expect to see you and your men in the parking lot of the Westchester Country Club no later than noon. If you need to reach me, I'll be playing the front nine with a member named Blair Palmer. I assume you'll have completed this assignment successfully before the main event begins?"

"Yes sir. Count on it, Mr. Peck."

"You're a very good man, Edward."

"*BAYKERR!*" The scream seemed to surround Connor Harrigan. "*BAYYYKERRR!*"

"Sweet Mother of Christ!" he gasped.

Tanner Burke pushed against his shoulder from behind. "Oh, my God!" she cried. "Jared!"

"*BAYYYKKERRRR!*"

He was on the floor, his back pushed against the tile wall behind the toilet tank. One leg pumped against the floor in a useless attempt to shove his body farther from the figures at the door. The shower curtain was pulled as far as it would reach across his chest. He held a fist-sized clump of it tightly against his mouth. His eyes were wide but not in focus.

"Stay back, miss." Harrigan holstered his automatic and shifted the dart pistol to his right hand.

"But that's not even him yelling. Look at him. It's coming from ... It's ... it's just not him."

"Just take it easy, lad." Harrigan lowered the dart pistol slowly. Baker appeared not to notice. "It's just old Connor Harrigan. No one's going to hurt you, lad." I don't fucking believe this, he thought. Baker looked like someone had let out half his air.

"Jared, what's happened to you?" Tanner wasn't sure

whether she felt pity or disgust. "Did Harrigan do something to you?"

The figure on the floor cocked an ear, seeming to listen to a distant sound. Then he shut his eyes and answered her with three crisp shakes of his head.

"Is it me you're afraid of?" Tanner asked. Her voice was several tones too loud, as one would talk to the deaf or blind or feeble-minded.

He paused and cocked his head once more. His head shook once.

"Then who is it, lad? Who's frightening you?" Harrigan kept his voice slow and soft.

"Baker."

"Holy Jesus!" Harrigan backed up a step and reached a hand toward the space between them where the voice seemed to float. "Holy good Jesus Christ!" His voice rose. "There are *three* of him."

"You said . . ." Tanner Burke swallowed and folded her arms tightly across her chest. "You said you were afraid of Baker . . . Does that mean you're not Baker?"

"Charley."

"You're Charley and you're afraid of Baker?"

"Tell him to come."

"If he can come, why doesn't he?"

"Because I wouldn't tell."

Harrigan took a breath and let it out. Soundlessly, and without moving his lips, he formed the question: Charley. You're the one who can read minds. Isn't that right?

"No."

"Yes you are," he said aloud.

"Uh-uh-uhhh!" Charley answered in a singsong.

"Charley, you just did. You just read my mind." Perspiring now, Harrigan moved a step closer.

"Noooo."

"Then what did you do?"

"I listened."

"Does that mean you can hear me whether I speak or not?"

The question seemed to confuse Charley. *"It's the same,"* he answered finally.

"And because you listen, you know things that Baker doesn't know?"

"Yes."

"Like what, Charley?"

"Stanley turned into butter and the tooth fairy is sad because the cupboard is bare and Sonnenberg won't let him shoot Goldilocks."

"What?"

"And I know Z, Y, X, W, V, U . . ."

Harrigan turned to Tanner Burke. "I don't suppose you can make any sense out of that."

Tanner wrung her hands. "Ask him . . ." She stopped. "I don't know where to start. I want to ask him why all this is happening. There are so many pieces. I mean, I thought last night was just one of those things that happen in New York and I was lucky that Jared was there. But now I find out I know Jared's daughter. I feel like he told me that, but I know he didn't. And I find out that Jared knows about Cooper Shaw and that those two in the park knew Jared and that he—a part of him—knew them."

"Ask him." Harrigan shrugged. "Ask him about Cooper Shaw." He knew it wasn't the most pressing question they could ask, but he was curious himself. Anyway, it might get the ball rolling.

Tanner hesitated. She was blushing deeply. "Charley, what about Cooper Shaw? Who is he?"

Charley pointed a bent finger. *"He was laying down with . . ."* Charley flinched. His face jerked as if he'd been slapped. He seemed to sulk for several seconds and then said, *"That doesn't make the ball roll."*

Harrigan's eyes widened. "Apparently we're expected to ask more penetrating questions," he said.

"Ask him about the park. Ask him about the two men."

Harrigan nodded. "Did Jared know Jace and Sumo . . . that John Tortora and Warren Bagnold would be in the park?"

"*Not Jared. Baker.*"

"Baker? We have to call him Baker? All right, Charley. Did Baker know they'd be in the park?"

"*No.*"

"Then how did he find them?"

"*I knew. I heard them.*"

"What did you hear, Charley? Were they talking about Baker?"

"*No. Mostly her. I heard her too before that. She was thinking about Baker.*"

Tanner shook her head. "That's not true. I swear I never heard of Jared Baker before."

Harrigan nodded that he believed her. "There must be a faster way to do this," he said, easing himself to the tile floor. He splayed out his legs in a posture approximating Charley's and affected a pleasant grin. Charley returned it. "Charley, my friend, you're saying that you knew all three were in the park but Baker did not. How did you know?"

"*I heard them while Baker took a walk.*"

"Do you mean you can hear anyone at all from any distance?"

"*No. Only from where they could yell loud.*"

"What does that mean, Charley? Does it mean you can hear from a block or two away, for example?"

"*Yes.*"

"You can hear anything being said or thought by anyone within two blocks of you?"

"*No.*"

Harrigan shook his head and glanced up at Tanner. "This isn't faster after all. I don't know how much time we have, but apparently we have to pump questions at him until we hit the right ones."

"I think he's saying that he can only hear certain people. Charley," she asked, still with a distasteful curl at her mouth, "who is it that you can hear within this yelling distance?"

"*I can hear when they're talking about me or Baker or Abel or Sonnenberg. Sometimes Tina.*"

"My gosh, that's right." Tanner clapped her hands.

"I remember now, thinking about Tina Baker. It was just for a minute. Tina's written to me off and on for about three years, and I thought of her when I was daydreaming about when I used to ski Stratton Mountain here. I knew Tina was recovering from an accident, but I never knew the rest of it. I had an impulse to call or visit while I was here, but I couldn't remember the town. That's all of it."

Harrigan waited her out. It was interesting enough, but he was more interested in who else Charley could hear.

"Charley, who is Abel?" he asked.

"He's the one who's always mad."

Abel, Baker, and Charley! Jesus! "Abel is the one who hurts people and he's a part of Jared Baker?"

"Yes."

"The two in the park. You heard them talking about Baker?"

"No."

"Who were they talking about?"

"Sonnenberg."

"They know Sonnenberg?"

"Yes."

"What were they saying about Sonnenberg?"

"That he'd be mad if he found out about them grabbing Hollywood but that Vinnie Cuneo would think it was funny. They would tell Vinnie Cuneo all about it the next time he bragged about what he does with girls he knows who make suck-and-fuck movies. When the camera stops, he ties them up and—"

"That's enough, Charley," Tanner snapped. Charley's fist flew to his mouth.

"Thank you, Charley." Harrigan smiled. He shook his head as if to clear it and cocked an eye up at Tanner Burke. She was just as stunned. Her eyes were still wide open, fixed upon the flabby mass that was Charley. Hugging herself, she lowered her body to the bathroom floor. "This is really happening, isn't it?" she asked weakly.

Harrigan felt for his pipe. "I don't think we both went insane at precisely the same moment."

"Well, what do you make out of all this?"

"Oh, we've only just tapped the keg. Offhand, I'd say that your friend Jared Baker knows perfectly well what's going on. I think he wants some more information, or wants us to have it, and he's going to leave old Charley out here until we dig it out of him."

"What kind of information?"

"For starters, how the one called Abel set him up. He apparently did. It's clear that Baker doesn't know everything these two know unless they tell him."

"Can Jared hear all this, do you think?"

"Who knows?" Harrigan shrugged. "I have an idea that he and Abel might be having a showdown while we're out here entertaining Charley. Which reminds me . . . Charley, I gather you can't call Abel yourself. Can I assume he stays where he is and behaves unless Baker calls him?"

"Most times."

The hair on Harrigan's neck went up. "Most times," he repeated. "Charley, could this be one of those times when Abel might decide to join us?"

"No. Just when Baker's drunk."

Harrigan whistled, relieved. "I must drink a toast to Baker's temperance very soon. Who is this Cooper Shaw, by the way? I gather you're acquainted."

She looked at her hands for a long moment and then toward Charley, half-expecting that he'd be waiting eagerly for her reply. His face was blank, staring into space. She turned toward Harrigan, avoiding his eyes. Harrigan thought she might cry.

"Is it something you don't want Baker to hear?" he asked gently.

"It's not . . ." She stopped. "I just don't want him to think . . ."

Harrigan understood. "Baker's no kid, Miss Burke. He doesn't think you sprang into existence an hour before you met him. People do foolish things during their lives. Baker, no doubt, has been as foolish as any of us."

Tanner appreciated Harrigan's kindness. But it was nothing like that. No black secret from the past. Just a boyfriend and lover, the latest of . . . She shook away the number before it could form. The latest of not very many, she thought. Anyway, none of that was the point. The point was that she'd remembered lying in bed with a snoring actor named Cooper Shaw on the morning of the last day that she'd ever be with him. She lay there thinking about her life and what parts of it were worth keeping and whether she'd ever find a man worth holding on to. And as she remembered that morning she thought about Jared. And Baker saw what she remembered. Or Charley did. And Charley told him. Charley would always tell him, wouldn't he?

"Miss Burke." Harrigan touched her. "We have to get on with this."

"Let's talk about somebody else," she said.

He nodded. "Charley," he asked, "how is John Tortora involved with Marcus Sonnenberg?"

Charley did not answer. He stared blankly past Harrigan's head.

"Can you tell me that, Charley? I want to know what the connection is between the Tortora family and Dr. Sonnenberg."

Charley blinked, but there was still no reply.

"I'm not sure he can give opinions," Tanner whispered. "Maybe he's like an idiot savant. Maybe he can give information but can't deal with an abstraction."

"Good thinking, but where to start? He says that Baker didn't know John and Warren and they weren't worried about him. They were worried about Sonnenberg finding out what they did to you. It's obvious that John and Warren must have been exposed to Sonnenberg, but it's a difficult association to imagine. He's too cultivated a man. The connection must be between Sonnenberg and John Tortora's father."

"Charley, Sonnenberg and Domenic Tortora know each other, don't they?"

"*Yes.*"

"Jackpot! Are they friends, Charley?"

"*No.*"

"Do they work together?"

Charley blinked again and hesitated. *"No."*

"But they do know each other. What sort of things do they talk about? Do you know that?"

Charley smiled with the look of a child who was being teased by grownups saying silly things. *"They don't talk."* He giggled.

Harrigan made a face at Tanner. "Apparently I've just asked a very foolish question. They're not friends and they don't talk, but they know each other. So, Sonnenberg and Tortora are enemies, right, Charley?"

"No."

"It can't be both ways, Charley. If Sonnenberg is Baker's friend, and if Tortora is trying to hurt Baker, Sonnenberg and Tortora must be enemies, right, Charley?"

"Noop noop noop." He grinned.

"Then," Harrigan barked, "what the hell does it mean?"

Charley's head snapped up at Harrigan's angry tone and both fists now pressed against his cheeks. He reddened suddenly like a scolded infant, and his finger jabbed out toward Harrigan.

"They'll hurt you," the voice shouted.

"Who will? Tortora and Sonnenberg?"

"Edward."

"Edward who?"

"Edward who sent Hackett." Charley's finger tilted toward the dead man in the bathtub.

"Wait a minute." Harrigan stiffened. "Who's Hackett? The stiff?"

"Yes."

"And someone named Edward sent him?"

"Edward sent him. Edward is going to hurt you and Tanner and make Baker sleep. The other man is going to hurt Sonnenberg, and they know you hurt Hackett and they'll hurt you worse."

"What other man?"

"I don't know. The white-haired man."

"How can you know Edward's name and Hackett's name and not the other man's name?"

"They didn't say it yet."

"Jesus Christ," Harrigan sputtered. "It must be going on right now. Charley, are they talking now? This minute?"

"Yup."

"Within a block or two? Yelling distance?"

Charley blinked.

"Did they say any other name?"

"Tom Dugan. They sacrificed him. Biaggi. Biaggi helped them. Haig. Haig has aluminum."

"Who is the white-haired man, Charley?" Harrigan's voice was like flowing ice. He knew the answer. He wanted it said aloud. He wanted Tanner Burke to hear it.

"He's sir. He's . . . Mis . . . ter . . . Peckkkk." The ball of sound seemed to stretch thin this time and then dissolve into a distant echo. Charley went rigid. There was a stiffening surge to his body, much like the effect of water slowly winding through a coiled garden hose. One hand reached for the edge of the bathtub. By the time it touched, there was a purpose and tone to the movement where there would have been only a half-slap before. In the time that Harrigan glanced toward the reaching hand and then returned his attention to Charley's face, the eyes had become keen and focused. Harrigan let his own hand fall across the dart pistol on his lap.

"You can relax, Harrigan." The voice was clear and strong. Jared Baker pushed slowly to his feet.

"Jared!" Tanner half-shouted.

Baker met her eyes and looked away. "Not very attractive, is it?" he muttered.

"Attractive? Jared, never mind that, for Pete's sake. Are you all right?"

"I'm better. Thank you." Baker seemed relieved. If she felt disgust, she didn't show it. "Listen, Tanner," he said uncomfortably, "about Charley listening in to your private thoughts, there's something you should understand."

"Can we save all that?" Harrigan waved impatiently. "Baker, do you know what's happened here?"

"I know," he answered, his eyes still on Tanner. "I

heard you outside before the door was kicked in. You said you'd pick up my daughter. Did you mean that?"

"We talk first," Harrigan said.

Tanner ignored him. "I meant it. I'll get her myself if I have to."

"I have no right to ask you to do that." This was a new Jared Baker, Harrigan realized. Much more controlled. Not the confused and troubled man who locked the bathroom door a short while before.

"I have a right to give something back to you," she answered. "And anyway, Tina is my friend."

"What you're going to have is the right to get your ass shot off," Harrigan spat out. "My turn to read minds. Baker's thinking maybe he shouldn't try for his daughter himself because he's going to be drawing shooters everyplace he goes. He figures if he can draw them off someplace else, Miss Burke can waltz in and take Tina bye-bye. Forget it, Baker. If I figured that's why you're here, so did the shooters. That place will be covered like a rug if it isn't already."

"Can you get Tanner in and out?"

"I imagine," he answered. "What'll it buy me?"

"Information."

"Shit!" Harrigan shot back. "What are you going to tell me? That Duncan Peck is downstairs ready to blow us all away? I knew he'd be around sooner or later when I saw his number on Hackett's pad. Edward figures to be Ed Burleson out of Special Operations. Peck also figures to be moving in on your pal Sonnenberg this morning. I know why better than you do. And most of all, I know you can't count on Abel the terrible anymore. He's not going to let you retire him."

"He'll behave," Baker answered. "We reached an understanding."

"Bullshit!"

Baker ignored the response. And Harrigan softened almost at once. He could see by Baker's expression that it was more than wishful thinking. Maybe they did make a deal.

"What do you want, Harrigan, for delivering Tina?"

"Your enduring friendship," Harrigan answered. "No vanishing acts. Go wherever you want but stay in touch. On my end, I guarantee no one else will know where you are. Believe that part, Baker. Because you're going to be my life insurance."

"What you get is one day at a time. Get my daughter, meet me afterward, and we'll talk about tomorrow. That's if you do your job right and no one even looks cross-eyed at anyone I care about."

Harrigan saw Tanner Burke brighten a shade at the last part. One way or another, he thought, he'd keep in touch. The dealing's not over. "I'll deliver," he said simply.

"Don't get overconfident, Harrigan. This might be your kind of business, but I have to tell you, you're all alone."

"Yeah!" His eyes went cold. "I got the feeling from Charley that I just lost my bench."

"Someone's laying for you down in your car. Can you handle him?"

"I'll handle him. Where do we meet you?"

"The ape house at the zoo. I'm going to call and let Tina know you're coming."

"No dice. That house probably has more wires than Western Union by now."

"No one will hear me but Tina. Anyway, both she and the woman caring for her know I'm coming sometime today. This is just to tell her about you."

Harrigan's face darkened. He hadn't forgotten about those silent phone calls. But it hadn't fully sunk in that the daughter could do head tricks too. Now it's Frankenstein's daughter, he thought disgustedly.

"It's past seven o'clock now," Harrigan said. "Figure we'll get back to Central Park near noon. You going to be in the neighborhood?"

"By then, yes. I'll be nearby."

"Doing what?"

"Listening. Keeping things simple."

Harrigan understood. "Speaking of simple"—he pointed to the bathtub—"ordinarily I could make a phone call and get old Hackett hauled out of here in a laundry cart. Right now, no one can connect him with Miss Burke except the night manager, and all he saw was a uniform. I think we take the uniform with us and stash him a couple of floors down on the fire stairs."

Tanner shivered. "Naked?"

"You want modesty or you want to stay off the front pages?"

"He's right," Baker told her, wincing at Harrigan's gracelessness. "If it helps, keep in mind that his job was killing people and that he liked doing it."

Knowing that helped Baker even more. Even Abel didn't kill like that. And it helped him understand Sonnenberg's view of a world he didn't much like living in. Baker didn't have much use for it either.

"You'll need a suitcase." Tanner straightened. "I'll see what's in the other room."

Harrigan waited until she closed the door behind her before he reached for the knot of the dead man's tie.

"What is he, Baker? Freelance or one of ours?"

"One of yours, Harrigan. Your government isn't mine."

"Treasury? CIA? What?" Harrigan unlaced Hackett's shoes.

"I don't know. All I heard was 'animal house' from the street. And while he was creeping down the stairs I heard how glad he was that he got to kill Connor Harrigan. He wanted to make it last if he could. Your people are a class act, Harrigan."

"CIA." Harrigan nodded, tossing the trousers in a heap. "Animal house is a nickname. The CIA is divided into Intelligence Services and Special Operations. Staffers and field agents. The field agents in Special Operations are called the animals. They're not all like this, Baker. Don't get down on the Fed because there are guys like Hackett and Burleson. Burleson would have killed Hackett anyway if he found out the guy wrote down Peck's number. And I'm going to have Burleson's ass."

"You talk like this will be easy."

"I got a hell of a partner."

"You haven't paid for that yet."

Harrigan tossed the jacket to Baker, who folded it and added it to the pile. "When the actress and I move, we can use some blocking. That what you had in mind?"

"I'll cover you. I'll leave fifteen minutes ahead of you."

"Now you're talking like it's easy. These guys won't be patsies."

"Neither am I, Harrigan. Not anymore."

"Yeah!" Harrigan nodded. But you're not a prick either, he thought. Sooner or later you're going to stop to worry about who deserves to get hurt and who doesn't. And that's going to get you killed. That, or your two friends inside you are going to pick the wrong time to stop playing ball. And what's left wouldn't last ten minutes. "These guys inside you," he said. "You're sure you're back in the driver's seat?"

"There isn't any they, Harrigan. They're me. Just like yours are you."

"What the hell does that mean?"

"You have your own Abel and Charley."

"Like hell I do." Harrigan stood up, bunching Hackett's blue shirt into a ball. He stared expectantly at Baker.

"Forget it."

"You prove it."

Baker took a long breath and let it sigh out slowly. Tell him, he thought. Tell him you heard all the Frankenstein and Wolfman wisecracks and tell him he doesn't have a goddamned thing to be smug about. Tell this man who thinks you're a freak what's sitting inside him and everyone else right now. "I was standing at the mirror before. You remember?"

"Out in the other room? Yeah. You were talking to yourself and going into some kind of trance."

"And it made you angry, didn't it? Do you remember being very angry, Harrigan? You felt something like it in Dayton and again in California."

"I remember." He shrugged. "Tanner Burke felt it

too. You were trying to read my head is what I figured and it pissed me off."

"I can't read minds, Harrigan. I told you that."

"So?"

"But Charley can. Would you like to know how?"

Harrigan threw the blue shirt to the floor. "Come on, Goddamnit. No games."

Baker smiled. "You felt a sucking feeling. What that was, Harrigan, was my Charley probing your Charley. Forming him. Pulling him together and then letting him go. Your Charley's all there, Harrigan. He's only in pieces now, but he's there. He's everything you ever feared or despised about yourself, Harrigan. He's a fat and frightened little man."

"Bullshit!" Harrigan reddened. "It's your guy who was a piece of suet. I didn't feel like that. What I felt like was tearing your head off."

"Do you begin to get the picture, Harrigan?"

Harrigan's lips moved but no sound came. The color began to drain from his face.

"When your Charley is pulled together, Harrigan, what does that leave? Wanting to tear my head off should have told you something."

13

At the elevator bank in the lobby of the Plaza, another athletic club type named Carter Merrick paced distractedly. Now and again he would dip his fingertips into the unzippered leather briefcase he carried, brushing them over the two pistol butts hidden between its folds. His eyes, wherever he paced, did not stray far from the elevator dials above him.

At his back, forty feet toward the Central Park entrance, Doug Peterson closed the other end of the trap. Merrick checked his watch. Thirty minutes. If Harrigan or Baker were not down by then, they would go in. In force. But Merrick hoped they'd come. You don't get your ticket punched, he knew, by being one of a crowd. But being the one to take Connor Harrigan, and this Baker character, that's promotion city. That's a month's leave in France or the Greek Islands, with Duncan Peck picking up the tab. And he had the best chance of anyone. Harrigan didn't know him. Harrigan and Baker and maybe the girl would walk right past him into a crossfire, and Harrigan would be down before he knew what hit him. Merrick and Peterson had practiced the move ten times already on guests descending from other floors.

He turned away from the dials, none of which was within four floors of fifteen, long enough to scan the lobby once more for potential interference. It was mostly empty now. Just enough people to make the scene seem normal. A woman, fortyish and expensively dressed, sat with an open purse on her lap and a mirror in her hand, probing an eye with a piece of Kleenex. Lazy rich, he decided, noting the carefully done hair that probably covered a tuck scar and the tan that was the work of several seasons. And probably a screamer if anything more violent than a fallen soufflé happened in her sheltered little life. Merrick mentally prepared himself for the scream. And for the contents of her purse being scattered all over the floor. They would distract Harrigan or Baker, but they would not distract him. Carter Merrick would be ready.

There was one other man, a tourist in a safari jacket, who stood at the desk of the fruity little clerk, trying to decipher a Manhattan street map. The clerk was drumming his fingers and making a face at the tourist's outfit. Neither would be a problem, Merrick decided. He returned his attention to the elevator dials.

On the twelfth-floor landing of the fire stairs, Harrigan paused and raised a hand. He nodded to Baker, who was grunting under the weight of Hackett's body, and pointed silently toward the corner nearest the fire door.

Jared Baker eased to one knee and allowed the corpse, now dressed only in Harrigan's worn raincoat and a pair of socks, to slide from his shoulder. Harrigan crouched and began arranging the body.

"What are you doing?" Baker asked, rubbing his burning shoulders. He tried not to look at the dead man's face.

"Confusion to mine enemies," Connor Harrigan grunted. He tidied the folds of his raincoat, which he'd donated less out of concern for Tanner's emotions than in the hope that the assassin might pass for an hour or two longer as a sleeping drunk. Or better yet a sleeping pervert, which would cause him to be shunned all the more. Now he drew up Hackett's knees and folded his arms across them, forming a nest that would hide his swollen face. Baker was relieved that this was done. Hackett's eyes had begun to open and the skin beneath them had blackened. The tip of his tongue was visible through lips that were covered with a crust of dried foam. The sight was making Baker sick. And he didn't much like Harrigan for being so comfortable with the broken remains of a man who had been alive only hours before.

Harrigan, satisfied with the effect he had created, now began patting his pockets in search of items he might leave with the dead man to confuse matters further. Meaningless little clues that would lead nowhere. An empty airline ticket envelope, perhaps. Or a matchbook from a California motel. Ah, but that would be inconsiderate, he decided. No way to treat the lads of the local precinct who'd be assigned to identify the body of the mysterious Plaza flasher. Simplify, Connor. Always simplify. He drew a fiber-tipped pen from his pocket, and on the back of Hackett's hand he carefully printed the unlisted phone number of Mr. Duncan Peck. Pleased with himself, smiling, he rose to his feet. The smile faded when he saw the look of disgust on the face of Jared Baker.

"This troubles you?" he asked.

Baker told Harrigan with a look that he'd asked a thoroughly stupid question. "I have to get going" was all he said.

"You do get used to it, lad," Harrigan said softly. "You live with it or you fold, as with any other sorrow."

"You're more than used to it, Harrigan," Baker answered wearily. "You enjoy it. You make a game out of it." He gestured toward Hackett's hand. "Living the way you do isn't worth the effort."

Harrigan reddened. His eyes and teeth flashed, and it seemed for a moment that he might bring the back of his hand across Baker's face. But he only shook his head and turned away to make a last adjustment to Hackett's position.

"Notice," he said, standing erect to face the taller man, "notice how I restrain myself from telling you what a smug son of a bitch you are. Not being in the happy circumstance of being able to blame some inner beastie for any unpleasant behavior on my part, notice how I rise above the insult. I won't even tell you that my little game, as you put it, was as much to draw the dogs away from Tanner Burke as it was to cause discomfort for Duncan Peck. I don't tell you these things because my attention is now focused on the business of surviving the day and not on the task of preserving my humanity at the cost of my life. You can go to hell, Baker. You can go to hell and take your two friends with you, which I suspect is what you have in mind if the beastie will not behave. But for all our sakes, go to hell tomorrow, not today. Today you'd better damn well find your own way to live with it." Harrigan brushed past Baker and walked up the three flights of stairs. Baker followed.

Baker hesitated at the door of Tanner's room, then touched Harrigan's shoulder and motioned him down the carpeted hall toward the elevator alcove. Baker pressed the down button.

"You'll watch out for them, Harrigan?" Baker's voice was subdued.

"I said I would. You look out for you. You're sure you can draw Peck's people off without getting shot?"

Baker nodded. "Give me twenty minutes or so. I'll stay around until I know you and Tanner are clear. Is your car still downstairs?"

"It should be. A blue Oldsmobile just west of the Park Lane Hotel. Bend the windshield wipers forward if it's safe to use." The elevator hummed to a stop and the doors slid open. Harrigan placed a hand against them. "You're going to see Sonnenberg, I take it. It must be damned important to you if you're trusting both your daughter and Tanner Burke to a soulless bastard like myself."

Baker lowered his head and stared at his shoes. "I'm sorry about that," he said. "What you said about learning to live with it . . . I haven't found the way yet."

"And you think Sonnenberg might have some ideas? He won't let you go, Baker. He didn't go to all this trouble just to shake hands and wish you godspeed."

"I'm not going to give him a choice."

Harrigan stared at Baker appraisingly, his hand still on the rubber, reluctant to see Baker leave with so much unanswered. What could Baker say to Sonnenberg? Threaten him? With what? There was only violence or exposure. Sonnenberg didn't seem a man easily frightened. As for exposure, even assuming Baker knew what there was to expose, Sonnenberg would simply go underground. Well, he thought, one thing at a time. Let's see if Jared Baker can even reach the street before we start planning the rest of his day.

"Peck figures to have men in the lobby," he told Baker. "They'll be watching for fifteen to light up. You might have more of an edge if you start from another floor."

Baker did not respond except that his eyes glazed over ever so briefly. Harrigan saw that and shrugged. Baker knew damn well who was where. "The stairs are clean?" Harrigan asked.

"At the moment." Baker tapped Harrigan's staying hand and stepped into the car. "But keep Tanner behind you when you use them."

Even as the elevator doors closed on Jared Baker, Harrigan thought he could see his body begin to stiffen.

Carter Merrick watched the indicator as it stopped on fifteen and stayed there. Too long, he thought. It could have been a bellhop loading someone's luggage. Maybe. Or maybe Baker and Harrigan trying to haul Hackett out in a trunk. Whatever. The indicator began to move. Merrick glanced back at Peterson and cocked his head toward the flashing light. Peterson nodded and unbuttoned his jacket.

The elevator stopped at eight. Someone getting on, Merrick hoped. Not Baker or Harrigan getting off. No, they wouldn't get off on eight. If you'd walk eight flights, you'd walk fifteen. And if they did, they'd have to come out in the lobby anyway. Merrick had already jammed the downstairs fire doors. Nor could they ride to the lower level as long as Merrick kept the down buttons lit up.

The red lights were moving again. Get ready. Look relaxed. Look bored. Damn! The screamer with the purse was on her feet and standing too close behind him. And the jerk with the street map was moving into Peterson's line of fire. Merrick shifted his position and the woman moved with him. The indicator light passed three. The hell with it. He'd knock her on her ass if he had to. Merrick dropped his eyes to the elevator threshold and kept them there.

The doors opened abruptly, almost making him jump. Two sets of legs. Don't look up yet, Merrick. Don't look at their faces. Let them go past you. First man's middle-aged. Skinny. Gray hair. Not Harrigan. No woman on the car. The gray-haired man was already stepping by him. Now the second man. No, he's not moving. Merrick raised his eyes, indifferently he hoped, toward the man who hung back. Younger. Taller. Yes. Yes, it's Baker—

Merrick's mouth fell open. The face he saw was the face in Burleson's photographs except—Jesus! He clawed at the pistol in his open briefcase, stepping backward at the same time. But he hit something. The woman, damn her, was in his way. More than that, she was resisting him, leaning into him. Her hand, oh goddamn it, was reaching under his arm and covering his gun butt.

Merrick never saw the hand that snaked to his throat. He saw only the face. The green wolf eyes behind tinted glasses and the terrible grin beneath them. He felt his body floating toward the face as his cheeks and temples swelled, and he felt his shoe tips stuttering across the carpet. Oh God, the barred glass doors were sliding closed behind him. Merrick wanted to scream but could not. He could only kick and twist and slap against the arm that was holding him, hanging him, a full foot off the floor. The face grinned wider at his efforts. The breath coming from its mouth blew at him in short, panting bursts, and the temples pulsated from a heartbeat that was impossibly fast. The face faded behind a burst of light and Merrick remembered nothing more.

In the lobby, the tanned woman turned as if bewildered at the sound of Merrick's partner running toward her from the revolving door. She saw shock on Peterson's face, but she saw also that her own face meant nothing to him. She saw him hesitate, as if unsure of what he'd seen, and then she saw him back away, slowly at first, then at a run toward the doors facing Central Park. Melanie Laver relaxed. She allowed a small automatic to fall from her fingers and closed her Gucci purse over it. The indicator light read *L* for lower level. Melanie nodded almost imperceptibly to the tourist in the safari jacket. Roger Hershey folded his street map, shouldered his rucksack, and headed calmly toward the revolving door. Melanie took the next elevator down.

She found Merrick easily. Melanie followed the trail of his briefcase and an odd-looking pistol toward a passageway leading to a Trader Vic's restaurant. Inside the passageway, near the fire door Merrick had jammed earlier, he had simply been thrown aside. The agent was alive, convulsing, his face in the spilled contents of a cigarette urn. The fire door was partly open, torn from its lower hinge and hanging at a slant. Sonnenberg was quite right, Melanie decided. One cannot expect this one to pick up after himself.

Setting her purse on the floor, Melanie Laver grasped the semiconscious agent by his lapels and dragged him to the stairway inside the fire door. There, she stripped him of his identification, his keys, and his handcuffs, manacling him with the latter to a cast iron radiator. Eyeing his kneecap, she hefted the dart pistol by its barrel, considering whether to disable the agent further. No need, she decided. He would not be useful for several days. Surely not by tonight. After that it would make no difference. Instead, she stripped away his necktie and gagged him.

Next, Melanie returned to her purse and to the

overturned urn, which she straightened as best she
could, leaving Merrick's weapons and the contents of his
pockets in the hollow base. Then, pausing to examine a
nail she'd broken on Merrick's lapel, she made her way
to the nearest exit that Jared Baker could have taken.

"Who was the woman, Charley?" Baker was on Fifty-
eighth Street, walking slowly toward the rear entrance of
the Park Lane, a few doors west of the Plaza.
   "a friend."
   "What friend? I have no friends here."
   *"i don't know. she said something. she said abel
makes messes and doesn't clean up. abel says never mind
that. able says bring him out and leave him out until
we're away from here. abel says you wait too long and
we'll all die, even when you don't want us to all die."*
   "Does Abel remember my promise?"
   *"abel remembers. i remember. you'll let them kill us
all if abel doesn't let you be you and if you can't have tina.
abel says he will be good, but you shouldn't get us killed
not on purpose and—"* Charley stopped as if he'd been
interrupted. Baker couldn't hear, but he felt Charley's
surprise at what was being said. Charley giggled. *"abel
says please,"* Charley told him. Charley giggled again like
a schoolchild at a classmate's humiliation. *"please please
please."*
   Baker nodded to himself. Abel was right, he knew,
about him taking too long. He'd held Abel right on the
edge and sent him back when the man got on at the
eighth floor. The man kept glancing at him. He almost
wasn't ready when the doors opened to the lobby. If the
woman hadn't blocked Peck's man . . .
   "Abel." Baker paused by a glass-framed poster near
the marquee of the Park Lane. *"Abel, if I let you out, you
must walk very slowly. Do you understand that, Abel?"*
   "slowly. yes."
   *"You must not look at the people you pass. Your eyes
will frighten them. You must look down all the time and
you must keep your hand across your mouth. If someone*

is in your path, you must walk around him, Abel. If someone bumps into you, you must say 'Sorry' and slowly walk away. You cannot bump them back or grab their throats or do anything but walk away slowly. If there is a chair or a table in your way, you cannot kick it aside or step on it. You must walk around things and people. Do you understand that, Abel?"

"slowly, look down, don't grab, don't kick. yes. call me, baker. please."

Baker waited for one cruising cab to pass and then stepped into the doorway of a clam bar, where he pretended to study the luncheon menu. Two businessmen left the Park Lane and proceeded at a half-trot toward Fifth Avenue. Baker listened. Whatever their thoughts were, they were not of him. But farther in that direction he could hear the one named Biaggi, thinking Baker's name and cursing the woman who would not stop asking him for the way to the Empire State Building. The woman again. And through the doors of the Park Lane and on the side facing Central Park, he could hear the one called Burleson. Baker drew his tinted glasses from his pocket and fixed them securely over his ears.

"Abel," he said aloud. *"Come out now, Abel."*

Scotty McGuire was in his twenty-sixth year as a bellman at the Park Lane. He'd been promoted once, back in 1965, for climbing down three elevator shafts to help guests who were stranded because of the blackout that hit Manhattan that October. The promotion didn't last long, not that he cared. Scotty never wanted to be a bell captain anyway. Boring job. Carrying bags in and out of the storeroom all day and never talking to no one except to tell them where's the airport limo. Never alone upstairs with some of the big stars and ballplayers that stayed here. Never a chance to get autographs because they're coming and going too fast and definitely no chance to pass the time of day with them. Scotty had over four hundred autographs in his collection. Maybe fifty on photographs. Some with him in them. Orson Welles wrote practically a speech on his. Hell of a guy.

The guy with the yellow glasses might be someone, he thought at first. Not that he was familiar. Just that there was something different about him. Mostly the way he walks. His eyes down on the carpet like his neck is stuck while the rest of his body moves in a kind of jerky slow motion like what you see with fighters when they're moving through the crowd toward the ring. He could be a fighter. Kind of old for it, but whatever he is, he's a mean-looking son of a bitch.

Scotty decided that the guy wasn't anybody. He had just about dismissed him from his mind when the guy glanced at him with a look that said he thought Scotty McGuire wasn't nothing either. And that right there was pissing McGuire off. Keep moving, buddy. He had an odd thought that the man could hear him. Just keep moving. You try anything in my hotel, I'll bust a chair over your head.

Abel forced his mind from the little man in the red coat who'd been staring at him. The little man did not matter. What mattered was the bigger man who stood just inside the glass doors of the main entrance. No. Two men now. The one called Peterson was coming in. Frightened. Too loud. Burleson quieted him and brought a metal thing to his lips. Wait, Abel. Wait and soon there will be three.

Slowly.

"I hear you, Baker. Slowly."

Abel dropped his hand from his mouth and eased closer, hugging the wall where he could, just on the edge of their line of sight. He saw the one called Burleson snap his fingers toward a man outside and turn his palm down in a calming gesture. Only twenty feet now, Abel thought. Slowly. Wait for the new man to come in. Wait until they all come together and they lean close and talk about Baker.

Biaggi pushed through the door. Abel knew him. The one who slinked through wet grass. The one he could have hurt last night but did not so that Biaggi could tell what he had seen Abel do. But now he had told and now Abel could hurt him. He could hurt them all so that they could not use their darts and guns. He would squeeze their necks with his hands the same way Biaggi squeezed the neck of Harrigan's friend with his wire thing. Abel coiled his body.

"Something I can do for you, buddy?" A hand touched his arm.

"No, please," Abel whispered, his wolf eyes locked on Burleson. He began to move away from the smaller man. McGuire's fingers tapped insolently against his back.

"Don't," Abel hissed. *"Thank you, please."* His right hand reached back against the bellhop's chest and pressed him an arm's length away as he stepped toward Burleson.

"A wise guy, huh?" McGuire stepped inside the outstretched arm and bent it into a hammerlock against the small of Abel's back. It was a powerful arm, he knew at once, and he felt a stutter in it much too fast to be a heartbeat. But the arm did not resist him. The arm ignored him. The man continued to move away, indifferent to McGuire's grip. McGuire dug in a heel.

"This way, buddy," he said quietly. "Security officer wants to talk to you." He tried steering Abel toward a door to his right.

"don't hurt him, abel. do not attract attention."

"I can crush his hand, Baker. He'll be in shock. He won't scream until I'm gone."

"no. there's a room there. the luggage room. take him there and see if there's a way to make him stay there."

Abel saw the door that Baker must have meant. There were suitcases there. And a luggage dolly. It was near the other door that the little man wanted him to enter. Abel turned in that direction, glancing around the lobby. No one had noticed them.

"What if there's nothing to make him stay, Baker? What if there's another man in there?"

"then hit them in their stomachs. nothing more. that will give you time."

"Your way will kill us one day, Baker."

A step away from the security officer's door, Abel rotated the hand that McGuire thought he was holding fast and swung the small man fully around so that he was tucked under Abel's arm. "Hey!" the startled bellhop gasped. Abel squeezed an arm under his rib cage and made him quiet. McGuire tried to make other sounds but he had no air for them. In another stride, Abel was through the luggage room door, snapping the lock as he entered.

They were alone. No one was following. It was a small room without windows. Wire racks filled with luggage covered three walls. On the near end was a table laid out with materials for packing.

"the tape, abel. use the tape."

Abel tore a length of plastic packing tape from its dispenser and pressed it in a single motion against the mouth of Scotty McGuire. Then, snatching the roll, he pressed McGuire face down upon the table and, like a frenzied spider, began wrapping McGuire's chest and arms. McGuire was kicking now, suddenly terrified by the knowledge that a human being could do this to him. Abel seized one kicking leg by its knee and pressed his fingertips at the edges of the floating kneecap, looking all the while into McGuire's eyes. McGuire saw the look and made himself relax, even under the pain of Abel's grip. The man's eyes told him that the kneecap would be torn from its joint if the leg kicked again. Abel quickly wrapped both legs at the knees and ankles, and then, slowing himself at Baker's order, he stepped once more into the lobby.

The men were gone. A young couple stood saying goodbye in the space they'd filled. Abel growled in disgust.

"go to the oldsmobile, abel. now."

"I would have had them all, Baker. They're gone because you let them go."

"the oldsmobile, abel. another of them will be there. you can hurt that one."

"You pick and choose, Baker. You stay away from

fights. You try not to hurt. But all of these men will hurt you. None of them would let you go. You let them go and they come again. It's stupid, Baker."

"the oldsmobile, abel. then you can look for the others."

Baker knew where the others were. They were walking, almost running, toward the Plaza. Their hands were on the butts of guns that fired bullets. Baker listened for the man in the Oldsmobile whom he'd heard earlier. There was nothing. He could still be sitting there, he thought, with a mind gone blank or even napping, although Baker doubted it. If he'd left the car and was watching it, he'd still be thinking Baker. But Baker heard nothing. The man must be far away.

Abel waited inside the glass doors until a cluster of pedestrians passed heading west. He slipped onto the sidewalk and fell behind them, his face down, his hand again covering his mouth. Even so, a woman walking the other way looked at him and shuddered, but she kept on without glancing back. Abel passed Harrigan's Oldsmobile and then two more cars before stepping quickly into the street and doubling back toward the driver's seat. Burleson's man was there. Not in the front seat but in the back, crouched low. The window nearest him was open three inches from the top.

Abel moved quickly. In one stride from the bumper of the Oldsmobile, Abel pulled the cuff of Baker's jacket over the palm of his right hand. In the second stride, he closed that hand over the partly opened window and snapped it inward, his other hand following the spray of glass and clamping across the agent's throat. His body jerked toward Abel and lifted an inch or more, but there was no resistance. The man did not react.

"never mind, abel. he's dead. look near his ear."

Abel saw it now. A small neat hole near the hairline. And there was blood from his nose, its coagulation interrupted by the pressure of Abel's grip. Abel pulled the head toward him for a closer look, then flung the body down so it sprawled across the footwell.

"let's go, abel. i'm coming back out."

Abel stiffened. *"There are others. Burleson. Biaggi. More. Finish them now, Baker, and they're finished always. Finish them and we'll be safe. Tanner Burke too, Baker,"* he added almost desperately. *"Tanner Burke will be safe and you can be happy. And Tina, Baker. Tina will be safe."*

"come off it, abel. charley, where's tanner?"

"coming. safe."

"baker's coming too, abel. i'm going to leave this car for tanner. that's how she will be safe. you and i are going to talk to sonnenberg."

"Oh, Christ!" Harrigan muttered. A city police car squealed to an angled stop outside the Fifty-eighth Street entrance to the Park Lane. Two uniformed policemen, one a sergeant, rushed inside. "Subtle your friend isn't," he said to Tanner Burke. "We're going to stroll through this hotel as quickly as we can. Whatever you see in there, if you manage to look resolutely uninvolved, you'll blend in very nicely with the city's population."

"What if he needs help?"

"He didn't need help with that character in the stairwell. Whatever trouble he might be in, he's probably got the enemy outnumbered. Anyway, what do you feel, lass? Do you feel like he needs help?"

"How would I know?"

"Just tell me what you feel."

"I feel ... I don't think he's there anymore."

"Let's go and see, girl."

She more than thought. She knew. She could not fully trust it yet, but she knew. In the same way she'd sometimes known when a phone would ring. Or what certain people were feeling and doing. But never like this. Back in the stairway where they found the handcuffed man, she felt Jared in parts of what they saw there but not in other parts. Harrigan seemed to feel that too. He'd begun looking around them, almost sniffing the air, before he took her arm and led her through a dark hallway to the Plaza's service entrance. Again on the sidewalk, he seemed to feel that something was not as it should be. But now, entering the lobby of the Park Lane, she knew they were safe. Tanner could almost hear Jared Baker saying so.

They saw the police at the far end of the lobby, a cluster of employees and onlookers gathered around them. A man, much smaller than the two policemen, was being questioned. He gestured crazily as two other men in hotel blazers pulled pieces of shiny brown tape from his bellman's uniform. Harrigan pretended a passing interest as Tanner, affecting an air of offended civility, guided him toward the exit with a dowager waggle of her fingers. Good girl, he thought.

"That man's saying he was tied up with tape," she whispered as they reached the outer lobby.

"By the devil himself. I heard. The cops are trying to decide whether he's been on a toot."

"You think Jared did that?"

"Unless you're betting the devil. Let's keep moving. Baker said he'd clear the street, but keep your eyes open."

Harrigan stepped partway through the doors and held one open while he scanned the sidewalk in both directions. There was no sign of danger. He saw his car, both wipers tilted forward as if the windshield had been cleaned. Again he took Tanner's arm, fishing for his keys as they walked. Shielding her with his body, he opened the door on the sidewalk side, admitting her. She saw him hesitate, again seeming to sniff the air, before he snapped the wipers back in place and crossed to the driver's side. The engine started at once. Harrigan pulled partway from the curb and, satisfied that no other policemen were in sight, swung the wheel hard in an illegal U-turn. Seconds later, they had entered the park through the Sixth Avenue roadway.

"That was too easy." Tanner let out a breath. "How come no one was watching this car?"

"Someone was. Baker took care of him."

"How do you know that?" The Oldsmobile paused at

a red light, allowing two young girls on horseback to cross the road.

"Baker left a signal. The windshield wipers. There's also a stiff on the floor behind you."

Tanner snapped upright and spun in her seat. "Oh God." She groaned. Beyond the shock, an expression close to disappointment crossed her face. Harrigan saw it.

"Baker didn't kill him," he said. "Hang on for just another minute." Harrigan was not at all sure of the truth of what he had said. It was a feeling. And another smell that shouldn't have been there.

A half-mile farther, at the edge of the Sheep Meadow, Harrigan slowed and found a cut in the curb leading to a maintenance shed. There, with only some distant dog walkers in view, he stopped the car and dragged the dead man from the back seat to a clump of evergreens. He was armed, like Hackett, with a dart gun. A government-issue revolver was slung under one arm. Harrigan took both in one hand as he examined the small-caliber entry wound at the man's temple. He was back at the wheel in less than a minute.

"Baker didn't do it," he repeated, this time believing it. "The guy's been shot. I thought I smelled the cordite when I opened the door and then I saw him back there. It didn't seem like the time to mention it. Anyway, he's been bleeding maybe twenty minutes, and Baker couldn't have been five minutes ahead of us, especially if he took time to wrap up the little guy at the Park Lane."

"Who could have done it then? Maybe one of your people."

Harrigan made a face. "I'm fresh out of people, as far as I know. Peck knows who I might call for help as well as I do, and he figures to have intercepts in place. For the time being, my people is just you, me, and Baker. Peck's been thinned out a little, but he still has a small army. There's also Tortora's crowd. According to old Charley, Tortora turns out to be in tight with Sonnenberg, but he doesn't figure to be helping you or me. Anyway, Tortora's people make smaller holes. So there has to be someone else. Jesus! They have more teams fielded in this thing than in the fucking Olympics. Excuse me."

Harrigan made a sharp right turn onto the Eighty-sixth Street crossway. The dead man's weapons, which he'd left on the floormat, slid toward his heels. He picked them up. "The stiff had another dart gun. Peck wants Baker alive all right. He'll take Baker apart inch by inch until he finds out how he was made." Harrigan slid the dart gun under his seat and held the revolver out to Tanner. "You want this, by the way?"

Tanner drew back and shook her head.

"You don't know from guns?"

"I don't like them," she answered. "Not handguns."

He reached to her lap and unclasped the suede purse she held there, dropping the .38 inside. "Think of it as a sledgehammer that makes noise. Keep it. You never know." Tanner snapped the purse shut, if only to get the weapon out of her sight.

A sign near Fifth Avenue pointed to the FDR Drive. It was almost lost in the sun's glare off the American Wing of the Metropolitan.

"Sonnenberg," he said. Harrigan bounced a fist off the steering wheel. "It had to be some of Sonnenberg's spooks back there. But this Tortora connection. I can't get it out of my mind. Back in that room with Charley I even started to get the feeling that Tortora . . ."

"That Tortora what?"

"Never mind. It's too dumb. It's just that I keep getting these feelings."

"Like back when you found that man handcuffed at the stairs? You knew he hadn't done all that. You feel things. Like Jared and sometimes me. You were doing it again when we reached the sidewalk." Tanner said this wanting to hear that perhaps Jared's talent, to say nothing of what she was discovering in herself, was not so weird after all. But Harrigan shook his head.

"That was pure cop," he answered. "At the stairs it was too neat. I've seen Baker work. He leaves things where they fall. Someone cleaned up for him there. A woman, maybe. I thought I smelled skin lotion. Then out on the sidewalk it was just that the back door should have been covered and it wasn't. Someone cleared it. Someone's covering Baker's back."

"And his front."

"You got it. The clock says the shooter had to be someone else. So Baker has at least two friends we don't know about. But don't let it go to your head. If they do turn out to be Sonnenberg's spooks, they're no friends of yours and mine no matter what they do for Baker."

Tanner leaned back in her seat and fell silent. They were on the drive now, the East River off to the right. Signs pointed to the Triborough Bridge and Connecticut beyond it. Connecticut. What a peaceful-sounding name after all this talk about killers and guns. Tina. Christina. Skiing and sailing. Clean things. That's where Jared belonged. He didn't belong with these people. Not even with Mr. Harrigan. Why couldn't they have just left him alone?

Then where would I be? she wondered. More of the same? On the waiting list to be one of Charlie's Angels? Or the latest female sickie on *Dallas*? I wonder if Jared watches those programs. I'd be on and he'd be watching and I'd never even know it. I'd get another fan letter from Christina and I'd answer it, never having a clue why her letters were so special to me. Oh wow, there's something you'll never hear me saying out loud. That a piece of me and a piece of Jared had known each other right along. Through Tina. That the feeling of something being missing was him.

That's not so crazy. They say that people who love each other feel as though they've always loved each other. They say long-lost twins feel that way too. Incomplete. Until they learn they were part of a set and then they understand why they felt that way. Jared? I think I just said that I love you and what are you going to say to that? Something sensible, right?

Like . . . Tanner, we hardly know one another.

Call me Liz.

Liz, it just wouldn't work.

It's already working.

Liz, we haven't even known each other twenty-four hours.

Bull!

Liz, I'm a hunted man.

They'll never find us.

Liz, there's something terrible about me.

No, there isn't, Jared. I started to think so, but I know better now. There are parts of you like parts of me that aren't always so terrific. But your unterrific parts come in a whole lot handier than most people's. And the part that's mostly there is very tender and loving. Anyway, the worst of you is a lot less terrible than men like this Duncan Peck, who kills to get something he wants, or Mr. Harrigan here, who can kill, I don't care why, without feeling sick about it, or like Sonnenberg, who thinks people's lives are his toys. You know what I think, Dr. Sonnenberg? Want to hear a wild guess? I think you play with other people's lives because there isn't any you. I think if someone peeled off your skin there wouldn't be a thing underneath. But Jared's real. And Tina's real. And I'm getting realer all the time. And we're getting the hell away from you, Dr. Sonnenberg.

The last part was almost out loud. Harrigan thought he heard Sonnenberg's name.

"What about Sonnenberg?" he asked.

"Just a feeling about him."

"What feeling?"

"Never mind. It's too dumb."

14

Under the striped awning that covered the patio of Jane Carey's Spruce Street house in Greenwich, Tina Baker slipped off the earphones of a Sony Walkman and let them fall across her shoulders. Just ten minutes, she thought.

Just a ten-minute break until the throbbing stops and she'd do one more repetition of her exercises. She had to keep pushing. No matter how much it hurt, she had to keep telling herself that the pain was only the stretching of unused muscles and of nerve endings growing slowly together in her leg. It was progress. Every day was progress as long as she worked at it. The color had long since returned to her foot and ankle, and the numbness of her toes had changed to a tingling that made a spark now and then like an electric shock. But even that was fading. And the scars weren't so ugly anymore, especially if she kept them tanned. It hardly even hurt as long as she didn't do too much. But she had to push. Soon, maybe even today, her father would be coming. And when he did, she was going to walk good.

Tina had told Mrs. Carey that. That he was coming. She told her the day before yesterday and again this morning. Mrs. Carey was nice and said she hoped so, but she really didn't believe it. Tina even told her this morning about the dreams she'd had. First, her father was telling her to look for a friend of hers who was on television.

She was too late. At least she wasn't sure she saw the
friend her father meant. Then later, when the sky was almost light, there was another dream, of her father standing in a glass box way up in the sky, looking down at her
from far away. The same friend was in that dream too,
even if Tina couldn't see her. The friend was sleeping in
another part of the box. Back away from the window
part. Tina still wasn't sure who the friend was. One name
crossed her mind, but that name was a little bit much to
believe. Anyway, the person she thought it might be
wasn't even a friend. Not like a school friend. Just someone she thought about a lot and liked. But Tina did know
for sure that the friend had something to do with her dad
and with skiing. And that the friend wanted to ski with
her. Skiing is probably why that other name popped into
her mind. But she wasn't going to ski with anybody unless she got off her duff and got herself back into shape.

With that thought setting the pace of her day, Tina
had pushed herself out of bed even earlier than usual.
She chose a Stratton Mountain T-shirt from her drawer,
put on some sneakers and a pair of cut-offs, went out to
the patio, and began doing the aerobics she'd taped from
a morning television program. They were better and lots
more fun than Dr. Bruggerman's therapy program, but
she did it too. She'd do a second set of his resistance exercises after breakfast, which, come to think about it,
should have been ready by now. It must be twenty minutes since she'd smelled the bacon frying. Someone
probably called. Her dad? No. She always knew when he
did.

Well, one more set, Tina decided. Then she'd finish
up breakfast herself and start on a list of chores she'd
made up. Mrs. Carey would argue as usual, but Mrs. Carey had done everything for her long enough. Including
driving her to school and back every day for a full year.
Besides, housework was good for you. A good workout if
you put a stretch in everything you did. Tina put her earphones back in place and switched on the Walkman.
Arms up, kick, stretch, feet together, shimmy down,
shimmy up, spin, kick. The last kick almost reached the

face of the funny little man who was watching her and smiling warmly, his lips moving, though she couldn't hear him.

"Good morning," she said breathlessly, once more slipping off her headset. Tina assumed vaguely that this was why breakfast was late.

"A very lovely morning." The man nodded. "It's very graceful the way you do that. What do you call that kind of dancin'?" He stood in the awning's shadow at the opening of the low brick wall that surrounded most of the patio. He had one of those funny New York accents that she'd only heard on television.

"It . . . They call it aerobic dancing. It's basically disco," she answered. Tina added an uncertain "Hi!"

The man frowned. "Disco," he repeated. "It don't look like disco. Disco is how nice girls get into trouble. They go places where they dance with fags and weirdos, and sooner or later some bum gets them to try white powder, and after that it's better that their mothers never gave them life. What you did doesn't look like that. Maybe it's the grass and the flowers and the vegetables out here that makes it look clean. Your geraniums should be repotted, by the way."

Uh-oh, Tina thought. She glanced toward the patio door, hoping to see Mrs. Carey smiling and saying that this was only some old friend and that he wasn't as strange as he sounded. Jane Carey did not appear. Tina took a half-step backward.

"Um, I'm Christina Baker." She almost held out her hand but thought better of it.

The man smiled again. "I'm Stanley." He announced his name as if she was supposed to recognize it. Tina shook her head uncomprehendingly.

"Stanley," he repeated with more emphasis. "Stanley Levy. Your father's friend. It was me that helped out when that judge was being such a jerk about his kid what ran over your foot. But that's in the past. It's all in the past. Now I'm fixing it so you can go to your father."

Tina brightened for the briefest moment, but she knew this was wrong. Her father would never have sent someone she didn't know to get her. Tina took another step backward.

"You don't know my father," she said quietly. "Anyway, you're not his friend." However she knew that, Tina knew it. She backed closer to the patio door.

"Untrue," Stanley said, a small hurt look crossing his face. "I been his friend a lot of the time. I been yours too. My mother will tell you the same thing when you meet her."

"Your mother?" Tina asked doubtfully.

"Her place is where we're gonna wait until your father comes to this other place, and then we'll meet him there."

"I better talk to Mrs. Carey."

"No time." Stanley shook his head. "I've already been waiting around here since just after it got light to make sure there weren't no cops or bad people who would try to stop you or follow us and catch your father. Also, I already thanked the lady for taking care of you, but she don't need to do that no more."

Tina was becoming frightened. She was getting a terrible feeling. "Mrs. Carey," she called, stepping to the patio door and reaching for the latch. Tina felt the man moving toward her. "Mrs. Carey!" She shouted this time, lunging out of his reach. Her foot protested the sudden movement with a stab of pain so sharp she barely felt the other, smaller pain in the back of her neck. An arm wrapped around her chest and she kicked backward, twisting. Now the pain in her neck was huge, like a hornet bite. She groped at its source with her fingertips, but the man seized her wrist.

"Wait!" Stanley's voice was concerned. "You busted off a needle. Stay quiet a second and I'll pull it out."

In the time it took him to say those words, Tina could feel her body melting. "Daddy?" She called his name but couldn't hear the sound it made. Her knees, one at a time, shivered and went soft. Now, floating in front of her, she could see the syringe in the man's free hand. The other was around her waist. He was holding her awkwardly, trying to support her weight with one arm while the other looked for a place to put the broken instrument. He almost dropped her as his hand shifted to avoid accidentally touching her breasts. "Daddy?" she slurred, angrily this time. "Help me, someone." These words made no sound except a groan. The man was lifting her, holding her, easing her down to the ground. Funny, he seemed so far away. She knew she was touching him, but he didn't seem that close. She could even feel her own hand sliding up his chest and finding the stubble of whiskers at the underside of his chin. But it was as if the hand did not belong to her. Too far away. She couldn't fight him anymore. Too tired. Too far away. But there was another hand. Not hers either. Helping her. Helping her fight him. The hand held the earphones from her Walkman and it was wrapping the wire over his head and under the whiskers that she'd felt and pulling it tight. She didn't have to fight. Someone else was fighting. Someone else was making him stop. She didn't even feel mad at him anymore. Just tired. So tired.

"Hey, Levy."

Stanley heard Vinnie Cuneo's voice at the screen door, but he did not look up. He was not yet sure that he could speak. His hands gently massaging his throat, he sat on the flagstone surface of the patio near the softly breathing body of Tina Baker. He stared in wonder at the smooth skin of her face. It was a sweet face, he thought. A nice face. Delicate. Like the kind of doll you keep on a shelf because it would break too easy if you played with it. Fragile like. Little. Maybe ninety pounds, and if he wanted to, he could pick her up right now and carry her easy. A feather.

"Hey, Levy, we're going to have company."

Fragile except she near killed him. She near choked out his lights wrapping that thing around his neck with one hand while she pulled the busted needle out of her own neck with the other. Cut this out, he thought. It didn't happen that way. It couldn't have happened that way. There were times, he knew, when he couldn't remember things right. Times when he had crazy thoughts that couldn't be the way things were, and this had to be one of those times. Look at her. He touched his fingers to her cheek, brushing back her honey-colored hair, then ran them lightly down her neck and the length of her arm. Fragile. Good muscle tone where there's meat but fragile. Delicate.

"Levy!" Cuneo kicked open the aluminum door and gestured toward Tina's body. "If you want to rip off a piece of chicken, do it later. There's some broad workin' the street ringing doorbells. One of them Avon ladies or somethin'."

Stanley, his face white, lifted his eyes slowly to meet those of Vinnie Cuneo. "You said what, you pig?"

The insult confused Vinnie. His expression said he had no idea of the enormity of his remark concerning Stanley's intentions toward this child. "Hey, what pig?" asked Vinnie, offended. "I'm telling you there's a dame gonna come to the door soon."

You should thank her, thought Stanley. Because of this woman you will live a while longer. "What of the Carey woman, Vinnie? Will she be able to call out?"

"Naw." Vinnie shrugged. "I got her so she's quiet."

"Then why don't we just not answer the door, Vinnie?"

"I think she seen me watchin' her. She keeps lookin' over here."

"She shows a special interest in this house, Vinnie?"

Vinnie didn't answer. His attention had drifted to Tina's torso, which he touched with his eyes. "You wanna look, go look," he said. "I'll keep an eye on jailbait here."

Stanley winced like he'd been slapped. He bit his lip and squeezed his eyes shut against the thought of this animal fondling Baker's sleeping daughter. But he could not shut out the voices that wailed inside his head. Women's voices. The voice of Tina Baker's mother screaming her anguish from the grave. The sobs of Vinnie's own mother telling Stanley that better her son was also in the ground that he should even think such a sin. And Stanley's mother. Even Emma his cousin had such shock

upon her face. Tortora was right like always. It was right
that Stanley should so something about this shlub.

"Show me this woman, Vinnie" was all he said.

Connor Harrigan had reached the Carey garage. It was a
detached building, some thirty feet to the rear of the
house and diagonally across the backyard from the covered patio. He'd made his way slowly and quietly
through the adjoining yard, satisfied that the house was
not under surveillance by anyone. The police, as he suspected, had long since lost interest, and Peck's people
had either not thought to cover the daughter or they'd
decided it was enough that they had Baker trapped at the
Plaza. They would think of it now, he knew. He had to
assume they'd be no more than thirty minutes behind.
No point mentioning that to the girl. She'd be nervous
enough as it was.

There were shuffling sounds coming from a covered
patio, but Harrigan could not see their source. He
checked his watch. Ten minutes. Tanner Burke should be
two or three houses away by now, carrying his clipboard
in her hand and taking a poll for the Junior League.
When she reached the front door of the Carey house, she
would use the brass knocker, not the bell. Harrigan
would move for the rear kitchen door at the sound.

His plan of approach seemed unnecessarily elabo-
rate now. Everything seemed so quiet. But better safe
than sorry. He would explain that to Mrs. Carey as best
he could. She wouldn't like it, of course. She certainly
wouldn't like two strangers waltzing in to claim Baker's
daughter no matter what kind of credentials he showed
her. On the other hand, how could she not trust Tanner
Burke. And anyway, Baker said he'd call first. Eight minutes. Harrigan smelled bacon in the air but could see no
sign of movement in the kitchen. He stepped back farther into the shadows and rested against the fender of
Jane Carey's Volvo. Seven minutes.

The kitchen door opened. A man. Jane Carey was
supposed to live alone. A small man. A low-level buzz

that had been rumbling in the back of Harrigan's head jumped several decibels. Stanley Levy? He could not be entirely sure. Harrigan had only seen photographs of the man, taken at night and from a distance. He was walking casually toward the patio. Harrigan listened. He could not watch without exposing himself fully to anyone who might be near the kitchen window. A name. Stanley. And a girl's voice. Polite. Cautious. Now nervous. Harrigan drew his revolver and braced it between his hands. A struggle. Daddy. More struggling. Harrigan broke into a sweat. Wait, Connor. He won't hurt her. Wait. Wait till he crosses back and you can't miss. Now the bang of an aluminum door and another voice. Stupid voice. Slowly, Connor. That's Levy's muscle. Angry voices. Ah, Connor, Stanley is not happy with the man he calls a pig. Wait, Connor. It's a woman they're talking about. A woman outside. Two minutes. Go, Stanley. Go to the front door and see what it is that vexes your man and take the pig with you. Connor smiled appreciation at the sound of the screen door closing once more. He counted ten more seconds and moved quickly toward the kitchen door, barely pausing at his first sight of Tina Baker, lying still on the patio flagstones.

Tanner was frightened. She'd been half a street away when the first uneasiness struck her. A sand-colored Ford had circled the block twice and now was back a third time. And it was stopping fifty yards beyond the house where Tina Baker lived. Two men. One small. One large. And they were walking toward the front door of the Carey house. How to warn Mr. Harrigan? No, don't warn him. Keep on, he said, whatever happens. Do only what a poll taker would do and nothing more or less. Run, scream, and shout only if the poll taker you're playing would do those things.

Easy for you to say, Tanner thought. Besides, you didn't go to that other house down the street and start hallucinating from the minute you looked at it. You didn't see smoke and fire and hear screaming in your head while all the while you're looking at a nice, harmless, Norman Rockwell sort of house. That was Jared's house, wasn't it? Or did you know? Three minutes. One more house, then the Carey house. Oops! Nobody home. Three newspapers on the front steps. Two and a half minutes. Well, I can't just stand here like a dummy. Here goes nothing.

Tanner retraced her steps down a stone walkway and paused at the edge of Spruce Street. Another car passed, a station wagon driven by a woman in a tennis dress. Tanner stepped behind it and crossed the street, passing the handpainted ducks on Jane Carey's mailbox without pausing. She reached for the doorbell, remembered, then gave four sharp raps on the Florentine knocker. The door opened a bit too quickly. It was the man, the small one who'd walked from the Ford.

"Hi!" he said pleasantly. "I seen you up the street. What do you got, a petition?"

"I'm Betty Harris from the Greenwich Junior League." She forced an eye-contact smile and extended her hand. The small man pretended not to see it and stepped from the doorway onto the brick steps, his attention focused on her clipboard. Tanner swallowed and continued.

"It's not a petition yet," she answered. "We're doing a count of residents who might be willing to accept a small tax assessment for the purpose of repaving the station parking lot and maintaining some shrubs and window boxes."

"Oh yeah? What kind of flowers?" Stanley touched the tip of her clipboard and forced Tanner to make a quarter-turn in his direction. She was groping for an appropriate answer when a hand seized her by the hair. Another hand. Both of Stanley's were now pressed against the small of her back, sweeping her over the threshold before she could more than gasp. The front door slammed behind her. The hand meshed in her hair came loose and the same arm slipped around her throat. She could only feel the second man. But now she could see his other hand and the long, thin knife it was holding close to her face.

"One chance," the smaller man said. "Where's Baker?"

Her eyes, wide and frightened, went from the knife's point to Stanley's face and back again. She shook her head as if she did not understand.

"I got no time." Stanley brought his face closer. "You're Tanner Burke. You were with Jared Baker since last night. One more bad answer, your face gets cut. Where's Baker at?"

"Will I do, Stanley?"

Tanner almost fainted at the sound of Connor Harrigan's voice. She felt herself spun in his direction as Vinnie Cuneo whirled her body between his and the revolver in Harrigan's hand. Stanley moved toward Cuneo's back but froze when Harrigan's sights lined up on his belt buckle.

"Tell the ape to let her go, Stanley. Nicely, if you please." Harrigan's voice was almost cordial. But his eyes were cold and black. Their expression made even Tanner cold.

"You're Harrigan, right?" Stanley's own eyes were wary but not afraid. "I hear good things about you."

"Tell him, Stanley." Harrigan showed his teeth.

Stanley shrugged helplessly. "He won't do it just so I won't get shot. Friends we're not. Shoot me, and for sure he's not going to let her go. Even Vinnie ain't that stupid."

Harrigan raised his sights to Stanley's face. Stanley waved the gun away.

"Better we work out some arrangement here," he suggested. "So far no one got hurt. The kid is asleep is all."

Stanley's coolness was reaching Harrigan, enraging him. "Except the woman, Stanley." Harrigan bit off the words. "You like to hurt women, don't you?"

Where Harrigan expected fear to show on Stanley's face, he saw only confusion.

"What woman?" Stanley asked.

"Two women, Stanley." Harrigan knew he should not talk, but he could not help himself. "A woman last night named Katherine Mulgrew. Katherine Mulgrew, Stanley. Remember it. It's in her name that you'll die this morning."

The hooker, Stanley remembered. He nodded that he understood. "What *two* women?" He was still not afraid. That and the question surprised Harrigan.

"Out there, you little shit." Harrigan jerked a thumb toward the kitchen. "The woman with the busted face."

Tanner felt Vinnie Cuneo's arm tense and tighten around her neck. Twisting her head to relieve the pressure, she saw Stanley Levy's eyes look past her into those of the man holding her. There was disgust in his expression, and she could see it was genuine. Disgust and more than a little madness.

"What did you do, Vinnie?" he asked very quietly. "Did you beat up a woman?"

Cuneo took a step backward toward the door, his eyes still on Harrigan. "Get the door open, Levy." To Harrigan he said, "You even point that gun this way, I cut her. I don't kill her. I just cut her. It's up to you how much is left when I reach the street out there."

"What did you do to the woman, Vinnie?" Stanley repeated, now ignoring Harrigan totally.

"Shut up, Levy." Cuneo's voice was desperate.

Harrigan knew he should shoot. He should place one round in the narrow chest of Stanley Levy and then walk up close and place another through Cuneo's head. It would give rest to the soul of Kate Mulgrew and not least to the soul of Connor Harrigan, who sent her to her death. But he could not bring himself to fire yet. For there he was, murder in his heart, yet paid no heed by Stanley Levy or now by Levy's gorilla, who seemed to fear the little man's words more than he feared Harrigan's gun.

"What did I tell you, Vinnie?" Stanley's voice was controlled, like that of an admonishing parent. "I said lock her in the cellar, a closet maybe, maybe tie her up and put her in a nice chair so she wouldn't get all stiff. So what did you do, Vinnie? You punched her, right?"

"No!"

"You used your fist. Your mother never talked to you about punching women? Maybe she was afraid to. Maybe she was afraid you'd hit her also. Did you slap your mother around, Vinnie? Did she go to her grave knowing she had a son who would punch the saint that bore the pain to give him life?"

"Don't start that shit," Vinnie Cuneo screamed. There was panic in his voice. He shifted his knife to the hand that held Tanner Burke, and with the other he groped for the doorknob. "Don't start that shit about mothers. She was grabbin' for the phone. I belted her because she was grabbin' for the phone."

Harrigan raised his gun to eye level. "Miss Burke," he said calmly, "would you tilt your head a wee bit to the right, please?"

Tanner hesitated, her eyes wide, then snapped her head to one side, exposing Vinnie Cuneo. Cuneo knew what was happening. He tried to follow. But something stopped his head. His eye nearest Stanley winced and quivered shut while the other blinked wide. Even as he squeezed the trigger, Harrigan could see what was holding the face in his line of fire. The ice pick in Stanley's hand was buried deep into Cuneo's right cheek. Now, with a roar that deafened Tanner, Harrigan shot off the left cheek.

Cuneo, and Tanner with him, slammed backward against a blood-sprayed wall. The arm fell away, slashing at the air, and Tanner dropped. On her knees, stunned by the muzzle blast of Harrigan's shot, she turned and screamed at what she saw. Harrigan stepped past her. With his free hand, he seized her roughly by the collar of her jacket and threw her aside to safety while his long barrel swung onto Stanley's chest. Stanley had backed away, his hands raised, the bloodied ice pick dangling harmlessly from his fingertips. At Harrigan's feet, the hoodlum thrashed blindly. Harrigan brought his barrel down hard against his skull and Vinnie Cuneo was still.

Slowly, Stanley Levy let his body slide down the corner of the entrance hall until he was sitting on the floor. The ice pick fell between his feet.

"Can you drive, lass?" Harrigan spoke to Tanner. She was behind him, pulling herself erect with the help of a doorframe. Her shoulders quivered and her face was turned away. Harrigan slammed a palm against the surface of a hall table, shocking her. "Can you drive, damn it?"

Harrigan fixed his sights on Stanley's forehead. "Where is your car, Stanley?" he asked. Stanley tilted his head, indicating a place nearby.

"It's right down the street," Tanner managed.

Harrigan stepped once again to Vinnie Cuneo and patted at his pockets. From one he drew a key ring, which he held up questioningly to Stanley Levy, who nodded.

"Bring their car, girl." He singled out the ignition key and held it toward Tanner Burke. "Bring their car into the back. You'll find young Tina on the patio. She's been drugged. I want you to get her into the back seat of the car and then come back for me. Can you do all that, Miss Burke?"

"Their car?" she asked distantly.

"Their car is closer," he snapped impatiently. "Need I do all this myself, Miss Burke?"

Tanner's eyes flashed angrily and she straightened. Besides the anger, they had a certain loathing in them. Harrigan saw it. But more, he saw that his words had had the effect he'd hoped for. Tanner passed behind Harrigan and stepped over Vinnie Cuneo's legs toward the bloodstained door. Harrigan could see her strength returning as she walked across the lawn. Good girl.

"On your feet, Stanley."

"We should see about the lady. No one said nothing about hurting the lady."

"No," Harrigan snarled. "Just a fourteen-year-old girl, you son of a bitch. Get on your feet."

Stanley's expression remained bland. "No one was going to hurt the girl neither. You want to shoot me, shoot me for something else. No one was going to hurt the little girl."

Connor Harrigan had all the something else he needed. Kate Mulgrew's body was barely cold. He could kill Stanley Levy for a lot of reasons, but that one alone would do. Stanley seemed to know what was on his mind.

"Mulgrew." Stanley remembered the name. "Before, you said you'd kill me for that. You're going to kill me for a hooker? She's better dead than with that kind of shame."

"Never mind that now, Stanley." Harrigan's voice was icy.

"You talk to me about hurting ladies, but you got hookers on your payroll? That's what a pimp is, Harrigan. They never told me you was a pimp."

Harrigan leaned forward as if he were going to drive his shoe into Levy's face, but he stopped himself. Levy saw this and understood. So it wasn't no hooker, he thought. So that was one of Harrigan's people, and she was supposed to sucker him into a doorway and then shpritz him with this here tear gas thing. Stanley stretched the fingers of one of his folded hands and brushed the tips across the cylinder tucked under the strap inside his sleeve. She looked like a hooker, she talked deals like a hooker, she was workin' Sixth Avenue like a hooker instead of being home fixing dinner. What was he supposed to think? Now she turns out to be a make-believe hooker who got sent out by Harrigan here and then got dead. It ain't me you should be mad at, Harrigan. But keep getting mad. We see who kills who.

"Why were you taking the girl, Stanley?" Harrigan kept his voice even with some effort.

Stanley leaned back and drew his knees closer to his chest. Harrigan moved nearer.

"If Tortora wants the girl it's because he wants Baker. Isn't that right, Stanley?"

Again, Stanley didn't answer. Harrigan leaned in and

smashed his revolver against Levy's knee. Levy gasped and hugged it.

"Talk to me, Stanley."

"He wants to ask him." He forced the words through his teeth. "He wants to ask Baker why he done his kid in in the park is all."

"Then why, Stanley." Harrigan moved still closer to watch what happened in Levy's eyes when he asked his next few questions. "Why wouldn't Dr. Sonnenberg ask him that? You do know Dr. Sonnenberg, don't you, Stanley?"

Stanley blinked. "Sonnenberg?" His face had a faraway look in reaction to the name, like those looks that would cross Baker's face now and again. He half-expected Stanley to deny knowing Sonnenberg, but Stanley didn't bother. "Sonnenberg don't care nothin' about that," he answered. "You want to know about Sonnenberg, ask Sonnenberg."

"Why don't I ask them both, Stanley? Why don't I ask them both at the same time?"

The question troubled Levy. He blinked again, this time shaking his head as if confused. He opened his mouth to speak but no words came. Only a gagging sound. Again the head shook, more violently this time. One hand moved up and slapped hard against the side of his face. He stared, wide-eyed, past Connor Harrigan, with the look of a man waiting for a terrible stab of pain to pass.

"Stanley?" Harrigan dropped to a squat, watching closely.

"I'm okay." Stanley swallowed. He held his left hand out, off to one side, as if inviting Harrigan to help him to his feet. Harrigan disdained the hand, but on reflex, his own gun hand swung in that direction. The buzz came. Too late, but it came. He saw his gun hand almost in slow motion as it reached the apogee of its loop and too slowly started its swing back again. He saw Stanley's knees come apart to reveal the silver thing that seemed to be exploding in Stanley's hand. A flash and a clap like a pistol shot had begun from the tips of Stanley's fingers,

and a cloud of smoke was rushing toward his face.
Harrigan's reflexes answered but too slowly. His arm flew
up to cover his face, and he hurled his body backward to
roll with the impact of the bullet he knew was coming.
But there was no impact. Only the cloud of smoke and
Stanley's body rising catlike behind it, his ice pick
scooped off the floor where he'd dropped it, now in his
fist. Harrigan's brain screamed at him for his stupidity,
for not bothering to search a man he had been planning
to shoot the minute he heard Tanner pass in the driveway. And now it was he who was shot except still there
was no bullet. Only the cloud and Stanley's ice pick. Another part of his brain told him why. The smell that had
reached it was not sulfur but almonds and locker rooms.
Oh, damn you, Harrigan. Damn you for an ass. The little
bastard has Katy's cyanide gun. Roll, Harrigan. Roll
while there's still a whisper of life in you and rub your
foolish face against the carpet. Rub, Harrigan. Push . . .

Stanley, his ice pick poised and his eyes on the base
of Harrigan's skull, suddenly staggered in midstride and
fell back, snatching at a window drape. His mouth and
eyes widened once in surprise and then clamped tight
like a swimmer's under water. Gas, he realized. Not tear
gas. The woman's thing had gas gas. Stanley tore away
the drape and stumbled back into the corner where he'd
been sitting. With the balled-up fabric held over his
mouth and nose he watched, fascinated, as Harrigan
writhed, furiously rubbing his face against the carpet's
pile like a dog that had been sprayed by a skunk. And
like a dog, Harrigan was kicking, using his legs to drive
his face and body along the surface. But the kicking was
feeble now, no longer able to find purchase along the
rug. Finally, they only trembled and then were still.

Stanley waited a moment longer to see if Harrigan
moved again. Then, throwing the drapery fully over his
face, he crawled blindly through the arched doorway into
the living room. He stopped only when he struck a coffee
table that he knew was half a room away from the poison
in the hall. A fluttering sound startled him. He tore the
cloth away and spun to face it. It was a bird, he realized.

A parakeet, green and yellow. It had fallen to the floor of an antique brass cage near the archway and it too was staggering, unable to hold its perch, and slapping bits of gravel through the bars with its wings. Stanley stumbled to his feet and snatched up the cage. He ran with it toward the kitchen.

He saw Jane Carey now where Vinnie had left her. But first the bird. Stanley carefully placed the cage inside the stainless steel sink and turned on the tap. He took the small rinsing hose in his hand and, after checking the temperature of the water, loosed a gentle spray upon the stricken bird. Still spraying, he reached across the sink and raised a window. It seemed to help. The bird was quieter now, and more steady. Stronger. He whispered to it reassuringly as he lifted the cage and placed it on the windowsill, where the morning sun could warm it. "Rest now," he said. "I'm gonna help your mama now so she can come take care of you."

A troubled look crossed Stanley's face. What if she couldn't? he wondered. To the bird he made a staying motion with the palms of his hands, then he crossed the kitchen to where Jane Carey lay unconscious. He winced at the sight of her face. One eye flamed red and was swollen shut. Her nose was clearly broken, and a smear of blood covered her mouth and chin. The kitchen phone, torn from the wall, lay beside her. Stanley felt for a pulse at her throat. She moaned at his touch and her eyes flickered. Stanley nodded. Not so bad, he mumbled to himself. A terrible thing, but not so bad it won't get better. It won't seem so bad when she sees how he helped her bird. One more thing, he thought. One more thing he'll do so she won't feel so bad about what Vinnie done to her.

Stanley found two kitchen towels and dampened them in the sink. He used one to dab away the blood on her face and then dropped it in the trash can under the sink. With the other, he covered his mouth and made his way back to the front hall.

Harrigan had not moved. He lay still, his eyes partly open. Cuneo was conscious. Still dazed, but with the pain of his shattered face beginning to push through the anesthetic of shock, he was reeling to his knees, both hands against his cheekbone. His eyes, black with pain and fury, darted from Stanley to Harrigan and then to his knife, which lay open several feet away. Stanley crossed to the knife and picked it up.

"It's your upbringing," he said sadly. "One month with my mother and you wouldn't behave like this no more."

Now there was fear on Vinnie's face. Stanley was holding the knife like a schoolteacher wagging a finger.

"Or my cousin Emma," Stanley continued. "I got this cousin Emma. She could have taught you. Emma, she don't even ever say nothing, and still she could have brought you up better than this. But your mother tried though, didn't she, Vinnie? I bet she tried until it broke her heart and put her in an early grave." Stanley lowered the bobbing knife until it reached a point near Cuneo's breastbone. Vinnie's mind would not let him believe what was about to happen. Instead he roared in rage at Stanley: "Help me!" The words sprayed thickly from Vinnie's mouth. "Shut up about your fuckin' mother and . . ." Vinnie's voice became a squeal as the knife found a space beneath his sternum and pushed slowly upward into his heart. Stanley watched his eyes while he died. There was only surprise. What is it about dying that they always look surprised, he wondered. Even Holmes was always finding dead guys that looked surprised. Stanley was reflecting on this when Tanner Burke pulled the Ford up behind the house.

Stanley glanced once more at Connor Harrigan, then crossed through the living room into the kitchen. Jane Carey was conscious now and trying to rise. Outside he saw Tanner Burke, half-carrying and half-dragging the unconscious body of Tina Baker toward the car door she'd left open. Stanley quickly helped Mrs. Carey into a comfortable chair, chatting apologetically with her about Vinnie's behavior and the mess on her hall carpet. He thought of suggesting how to get it clean. Stanley knew about rug stains from a cat he'd had once. But Mrs. Carey did not look like she would have understood him. Anyway, she probably knew. She kept a nice house. He put his fingers to his lips at the sound of Tanner's footsteps and moved swiftly to the back door, his ice pick again in his hand.

Harrigan could hear everything. He kept his breathing as shallow as the pain in his chest would permit and his eyes unblinking in a death stare, and he listened. He listened to the execution of Vinnie Cuneo and then some soft and unlikely words he thought had to do with carpets. He knew Tanner was coming back and that Stanley was waiting for her inside the door, but he also knew he could not help her. He had nothing left. Harrigan squeezed both fists to test his muscle control. It was no use. He could form the grip, but he could not hold it. He heard the back door open. Tanner's voice. Fear and surprise first, then defiance. Now Stanley's voice. Firm, polite, something about Tina and about driving. Stanley wanted her to drive. Something more about him. Tanner asking where he was, her voice rising. Almost crying. No, love. I'm not dead. It's that I can't help you now. Stanley will finish me for sure if I try, but I don't think he hurts women unless they try to hurt him. Go with him, girl. I'll find you. I'll find you and I'll find that little bastard again. I know where to start now.

He didn't know how much more time had passed. Only that there were no more voices. Perhaps he'd heard the car backing out of the driveway. He wasn't sure. Harrigan squeezed both fists again. This time they held. Slowly he rolled onto his stomach and, one at a time, brought his knees up under him. More time passed before he was upright and able to stand without the help of a wall. He stumbled into the living room toward the chair where Jane Carey sat staring dazedly at him. Damn, he thought. I wish it were myself who put out the lights of the bum who did this to you. Harrigan knelt at her side.

"Tina?" Jane Carey managed through swollen lips.

"I'll find her, lass," Connor told her. "I'll call you when I do."

There was nothing more to do for her. Comfortingly, he touched her uninjured cheek and turned away. He would call the police once away from here. If he could walk the two blocks to his car. He had to concentrate to remember where that was. There was Mrs. Carey's Volvo, of course, much closer and easier. But no. Enough had been done to her. Harrigan retraced his steps toward the front door, pausing to pick up the revolver Stanley hadn't bothered to take away, then staggered like a drunken man onto the lawn and off in the direction of the blue Oldsmobile.

He found the car on a winding street called Oval Terrace. Harrigan started the car with effort and stalled it twice before his feet found the rhythm of the brake and accelerator. Disoriented, he swung the car in a direction that he thought would lead to the main road out, knocking over a mailbox in the process and driving off to the shouts of a woman in blue jeans. Harrigan promptly became lost. There was a road, he knew, a straight one that passed the commuter station and led directly to the Connecticut Turnpike. For ten minutes he wove through the tree-lined streets until he came upon it. Harrigan waited at a stop sign until two incoming cars passed and then a van. He could not see the driver of the van. But the man in the passenger seat was a nervous young man named Michael Biaggi.

"Ah, Michael," he muttered to himself. "And what shame have you brought upon your own dear mother this day?"

Harrigan stopped at the public phone of the first gas station he saw and called the police emergency number. He'd been jogging, he told them, in order to explain his labored breathing. He'd been jogging when he saw a van pull up to the Carey house on Spruce Street. And when the men went in, he'd heard a woman screaming.

15

Baker moved away from the hotel slowly. In the doorway of F. A. O. Schwarz, on Fifth Avenue, he stopped and waited, ignoring Abel's sulking over his refusal to stand and fight. Baker listened. He thought he could hear one voice, two perhaps, but neither of them clearly. But he could hear anger. Blame being placed. Baker nodded, satisfied. The recriminations had to mean that Harrigan and Tanner were safely away. Nor could he feel their presence.

Baker stepped from the doorway into the moving throng on the sidewalk and made his way to a Hertz office near Third Avenue. There, he rented an inconspicuous midsize under the name of Harold Mailander. He returned with the car to Central Park South. The Oldsmobile, he confirmed, was gone. It was quiet now. No voices at all that he could hear. Baker looked for a vacant meter near the St. Moritz and, seeing none, elected to double-park long enough to call Tina from the lobby. He stopped the car and climbed out, but a policeman on the sidewalk looked at him and shook his head. Baker slid back behind the wheel and pulled away. He would find a phone closer to the highway. But soon. Harrigan had been gone for at least forty minutes. He would be approaching the Connecticut line by now.

Baker found a telephone kiosk near the Sixty-second Street entrance to the FDR Drive. He parked, once more illegally, and dialed Jane Carey's number. Busy. Damn. Better move on. He would try it again from the next phone he saw.

By the time he reached the Bruckner Expressway and the first enameled signs for Connecticut, Baker's relief was giving way to worry. He should have listened longer, he thought. He should have asked Charley to listen instead of trying to pick through the street noises and random spoken voices himself. Charley would know what they intended next. Where they would look for him next. Not that he didn't know very well what they'd do. Harrigan was right. They'd cover the house where Tina lived and they'd cover Sonnenberg. No other action made any sense. But first they'd have some housekeeping to do. The one handcuffed in the stairwell would need attention. And Harrigan. Harrigan would have to dispose of the dead man in his car. And Tanner would have to see another body. Baker shook his head sadly. She would think Abel did it, he thought. As if she wasn't disgusted enough by him already, she would think that Abel had killed again.

"*Charley?*"

"*yes.*"

"*Who killed the man in Harrigan's car? Do we know that?*"

Charley didn't answer.

"*Yes or no, Charley.*"

"*whatever you think.*"

"*I'm asking you, Charley.*"

"*you don't need me. you're hearing stuff now. you don't even like me.*"

The answer surprised Baker. He lightened his foot and allowed the car to drift into a slower lane. It had never occurred to him that Charley thought in terms of being liked.

"*I do need you, Charley. Today more than ever.*"

"*you need me just today. you just want to get tina and go away and not have abel and charley anymore. you're going now to find out how to do that and you want*

*me to help even when you don't like me and don't want
me."*

Charley's rebuke softened Baker more than it alarmed
him. It was true that he had treated Charley badly, like an
unwelcome guest, almost from the beginning.

*"It's not true that I don't want you, Charley. You're a
part of me, and that won't change. It's just that I don't
want you to be separate anymore. That's just as hard for
you sometimes as it is for me."*

"you like me?"

"I'm learning to understand you better."

"that's not liking."

*"There are things about myself I don't like either,
Charley. I don't like Baker when I'm stupid or thought-
less. I haven't been very nice to you, Charley, and I'm
sorry."*

"you like me?"

"Yes, Charley. I like you."

"i like tina, you know."

"That's good, Charley."

*"i like her just as much as you. in some ways we're
even better friends than you and her. it's me who talks to
tina. you think it's you using me, but it's me too, sometimes you think about her and she knows it because i tell
her."*

*"I don't understand, Charley. Tina knows about you?
And Abel?"*

*"just me, and only sort of. if she knew for sure, i bet
she'd like me."*

"Come to think of it, she probably would, Charley."
Baker smiled. Lots of kids Tina's age had an imaginary
friend, he thought. At least a doll or stuffed animal they
talked to. Imagine having an honest to gosh friend like
Charley.

"you're sure you like me better now?"

"Yes, Charley. I like you better."

"i'll tell you some stuff then. the soldier did it."

"What soldier did what?"

*"you asked who hurt the man in harrigan's blue car.
the soldier fixed him so he couldn't hurt you."*

"What soldier?"

"sonnenberg's soldier. the one who digs for old things and didn't go to notre dame."

Hershey, Baker realized! Roger Hershey. He'd never met Hershey, but he'd seen his file in Sonnenberg's basement room. Now he understood what had confused him when he was making his way toward the street.

"Charley, there was a woman by the elevator. She saw Abel, but she wasn't afraid of him."

"she was a little afraid. she just wasn't surprised."

"She's one of Sonnenberg's people?"

"melanie."

Melanie Laver. Baker nodded.

"Sonnenberg sent them to help me? How did he even know I was here?"

"harrigan knew. then biaggi knew. then biaggi told everybody. he told peck and he told tortora. tortora knew so sonnenberg knew."

"Biaggi may have told Peck. But he didn't tell anyone else, Charley."

"did too."

"How do you know that?"

"it's what harrigan thought. he thought biaggi had too many masters. and i heard biaggi in the park. he was scared of peck and scared of harrigan if they found out he was also tortora's little bird."

"Why didn't you tell me this before, Charley?"

"you didn't ask me then. you didn't like me then either."

Baker shook his head wearily. It all made sense to him now. At least the parts that mattered. Ahead of him, off the Westchester Avenue exit, he saw the crowned hamburger of a Burger King restaurant. He'd try Tina again from there. Some food in his system wouldn't be a bad idea either. Being Abel twice in twenty-four hours must have melted five pounds off him. Baker turned onto the off ramp.

Tortora and Sonnenberg. Sonnenberg and Peck. Peck and Biaggi. Biaggi and Harrigan. Baker said their names as if he were spitting them out of his system. And

I'm the plaything in the middle. The toy. The subject.
You're manipulating me even now, aren't you, Dr.
Sonnenberg. Come on, Charley. Baker parked the car
under the hum of the highway. Let's all of us get something to eat.

Baker tried Jane Carey's number once more. Still
busy.

"Charley?"

"it's okay. she knows we're coming."

"Is anything wrong, Charley?"

*"i don't think so. i think she's asleep. she said daddy
and then she was asleep with bad dreams."*

"Keep listening, Charley."

Baker ordered two burgers and a large container of
coffee and carried them back to his rented car. He would
finish one here and eat the other as he drove.

Sonnenberg! Baker chewed on the name along with
his sandwich. It's over, Doctor.

Damn you.

It's all been a game, hasn't it? Hare and hounds.
You've been playing with my life and playing with Tina's.
And now you, you and the rest of them, are playing with
Tanner Burke's life as well. The one clean and decent
thing to come into my life in two years and, thanks to
your games, it probably doesn't have a chance. No way.
No way in the world any feelings she might have will
ever settle down into two people just liking each other.
Being comfortable together. Loving each other. She'll
never get the sight of Charley out of her mind. Or her
fear of Abel. I don't even know what she feels for the
poor slob who's left over. Sorry for him, maybe. Maybe a
little mesmerized because he's so different from whatever she's used to. But if that's it, it's not going to last.
It's going to end because I'm not going to be different a
day longer than I have to. And when that day comes, I'm
going to melt down into my own world and let Tanner go
back to hers. And there won't be anything left except a
couple of broken toys.

"baker?"

"Yeah, Charley."

"sonnenberg didn't do that."

"He didn't do what, Charley?"

"it wasn't him who made liz be in the game. it was me. i didn't mean to, but it was me. i told you i listened for tina. soon i could hear when anyone else listened for tina too. liz listened when she walked in the park and i heard."

"Tanner . . . Liz can hear like you can hear?"

"no. not the same. it was just like thinking tina. thinking about how tina wrote letters and maybe liz could visit. abel said don't tell you because you'd get all mixed up and slow. then those men started thinking liz and about hurting her. abel said don't tell you because you should only care if they wanted to hurt you. i hated that but i was scared. but then they said your name too and tortora's name. i told that to abel, and abel said i was making it up so he would go help liz instead of watching out for the men who were following you. but i got real scared and then he believed me. he was even happy. he smiled because now he could fix it so you'd need him always."

"You're not afraid of Abel now, Charley?"

"now he says please."

"Thank you, Charley."

Baker put aside the hamburger wrapping and started the engine. He dropped the car into gear and eased toward the entrance ramp.

He was glad to know what Charley had told him, but he wasn't sure how much difference it made. The long and the short of it was that those two would never have been where they could hurt Tanner Burke if it hadn't been for Sonnenberg and his games. And Sonnenberg wanted Baker on the run and needing Abel just as much as Abel wanted it. he even tolerated Harrigan's snooping around because that was pressure too. Mostly he tolerated Harrigan because where there was Harrigan there was Biaggi, and as long as there was a bought-and-paid-for Biaggi, Sonnenberg would know when Peck was ready to make his move. Games. If Harrigan got too close, there were always Tortora's killers to slap him down. Just like they slapped down that loony judge and left him propped outside my house. Yes, Sonnenberg, you son of a bitch, you did that too, didn't you? You or Tortora, as if it mattered which. You were afraid I wouldn't run unless you could give me a reason that outweighed staying close to Tina.

"uh-huh!"

Listen to Charley, Sonnenberg. There's your first mistake. It never occurred to you that Abel and Charley might have minds of their own. You never figured on Abel enjoying the game so much he'd make sure they never stopped chasing him. And it surely never crossed your mind that Charley might have some capacity for love. That's right, Doctor. He loves Tina . . .

Baker snapped upright. His head jerked toward the southbound lanes on his left. Tanner? A trailer truck roared up and slowly passed him, blocking his sight. Tanner's face, a worried face, had popped into his mind and then was just as suddenly gone. Had she passed on the highway?

"Charley? Did she?"

"i don't know. i was listening for tina."

"Well, listen now, Charley."

Baker waited.

"i don't know. i can't unless she's close."

"What about any of the others, Charley? The ones we got away from at the hotel." Burleson had also popped into his head a short while earlier, when he was listening to the highway's noise.

"no. it's the same with them."

Baker was uneasy. Maybe someone had passed him but probably not, he decided. See? That was the other problem with being so damned special. Random thoughts popped into your head just like they popped into everyone else's head, except that you had to start stewing over what they might mean. Look at right now. You think the face of a person you care about and you start to get upset because the face in your head looks worried. Of course she's worried. Then you think another face who's looking to kill someone you care about and then lock you in a

Washington basement someplace, and you wonder why it makes you nervous. You wonder why it makes you want to gun this car and head right for Spruce Street.

Stick with the plan, Baker. Tina will be fine. Harrigan's good at what he does and Tanner cares. Go to Sonnenberg's, Baker. Get to Sonnenberg and end this once and for all.

Baker cleared his mind as he approached carefully. From the exit ramp at Mamaroneck he drove slowly through the quiet town, turning right at the Mobil station where he used to sneak his calls to Tina. Tina? You are okay, aren't you? I'll call you soon. I'm going to wait and use one of Sonnenberg's magic telephones in case someone still has a wire on this one. Someone waiting for whoever is Sonnenberg's latest toy to have the same bright idea I had.

Now a left turn and another right onto a street whose giant elms formed an archway. He was close now and began listening. Nothing. Not Sonnenberg, not Mrs. Kreskie, nobody. Damn. Don't let them be out after all this.

Baker slowed to a crawl when he reached the mailbox of Blair Palmer's house. He could see Sonnenberg's gate from there. It was open. Funny. Sonnenberg's gate was never open. Baker continued and stopped the car near the Dickerson home, fifty yards beyond Sonnenberg's property line. Damn again. He was sure now that the house was empty.

Well, he thought, he couldn't just stand here in the street waiting for the Dickersons to report a prowler. He wasn't crazy about waltzing through that open gate either. Too little cover.

"*Charley?*"

"*nobody there. something's funny, but nobody's there.*"

"*We'll go see, Charley.*"

* * *

Leaving the car by the Dickersons', he passed through the electric gate, leaving it ajar, and walked directly across a small island of lawn in the middle of the circular driveway. Mounting the stone steps of the front entrance, Baker paused under a large ivy-draped pediment, then tried the door. It was unlocked. There was no alarm. Baker stepped inside and cursed.

Immediately he saw that although the furnishings were largely in place, there were spaces that once held possessions especially valued by Sonnenberg. Crossing quickly to the study, Baker confirmed that the house had been selectively stripped. Sonnenberg's precious obsidian bird and lesser pieces of pre-Columbian art were gone. Yet the fading photo of his army outfit was there and the picture of the boy Sonnenberg identified as his grandson sat on the mantel. Two mounted fish that the doctor presumably prized still hung on the wall. Why, Doctor? Baker wondered. Why only bits and pieces?

The basement! Baker hurried into the kitchen and to the door leading to the cellar stairs. He tried the light switch without effect, then backed away and tried another. No power. A look inside the refrigerator told him that the current had not been off long. A few hours, perhaps. Baker found a flashlight in a kitchen drawer.

In the basement he saw that although most of Sonnenberg's tools remained, a few were gone from their assigned places. Baker swung his beam toward the white glass-doored cabinet that concealed the entrance to Sonnenberg's secret room. The uneven shadows cast by its corners told him that this door too was slightly ajar. Baker swung it open and followed his flashlight inside.

The room was cold. Too cold. Baker felt the chill draft that came from the air conditioner at the far end. Why was it on? And where did its power come from? He scanned the room, starting on his left, and now the beam illuminated Sonnenberg's map and its small pushpins. Underneath was a set of file cabinets. Baker began to walk past them, then stopped and swung the beam back onto the map. It troubled him that Sonnenberg would

leave it behind. And something else bothered Baker. The
pins, the display that Sonnenberg had once showed him
so proudly, seemed all in the wrong places. And two had
small crepe tags on them. One just north of Denver, the
other in Kansas City. Baker had no idea what it might
mean. He reached for a file drawer.

"Have a care, Jared." Sonnenberg's voice made him
jump. Baker spun first toward the air conditioner, then
toward the darkened basement. The voice had seemed to
come from both places.

"The speaker, Jared." Sonnenberg's voice directed
him. "It's near the center light fixture." During that sentence, the voice from the air conditioner switched off,
leaving only the outside voice. A fluorescent light blinked
on in the basement. Baker lowered his flashlight and
squinted past the fixture. His eye found a dark circle,
which he knew must be an amplifier.

"Where are you?" he asked.

"A civil greeting would have been nice, Jared. I'm
hardly your enemy."

Baker was in no mood for conventional niceties.
"We have to talk, Doctor," he said.

"We certainly do, Jared. By the way, please step
from that room. There's a nasty surprise waiting there for
some visitors I expect shortly. The same bunch who pes-
tered you at the Plaza. Lovely place, by the way. Should
be inviolate. Duncan Peck has no concept of sanctuary."

Baker knew that he must be on camera. But he saw
nothing unless it was out of sight behind the light fixture.
He looked down at his feet and rubbed the toe of one
shoe across the indoor-outdoor carpet on the basement
floor.

"Yes, Jared," Sonnenberg told him. "Pressure plates.
There are other cameras facing the exterior of the house
and one in the main hall. Also an abundance of hidden
microphones and speakers. I saw you coming, and I hope
to see you leaving within a very few minutes. You're no
longer safe here, Jared. We'll have a long chat later."

"We'll talk now, Doctor. I want to see you."

"About your retirement plans, no doubt." Sonnenberg's voice had a tone of sadness to it, but the words irritated Baker. He'd wondered often whether he ever had a single thought or plan that was private. And that would include his plan regarding Tina. Sonnenberg would know, of course, that he was taking her. Perhaps even that Tanner and Harrigan were going there. He began to feel uneasy.

"I'm going away, Doctor, and I'm taking my daughter." Baker kept his voice even. "I'd like to do that with your help and your blessing. But either way, I have to do it."

"We'll discuss it, Jared. My blessing, certainly, goes without saying because I am genuinely your friend. I'll ask only that you do not totally renounce that friendship. What sort of help, by the way? I assume you've prepared some safe harbor in the course of your travels and are adequately funded by the blackjack tables of Las Vegas."

"I want to be the way I was," Baker snapped. "Come on, Doctor. Where the hell are you? Do I have to start kicking down doors?"

"We'll talk, Jared." Sonnenberg ignored the last. "We'll talk at length. I fully understand that your gifts are not an unmixed blessing. You are not, I assure you, the only one of my people who's had some difficulty adjusting."

"I'm not one of your people," he barked. "I'm Jared Baker. And this not-unmixed blessing you talk about includes Abel wanting to tear apart every young punk he sees who even gives me a snotty look. It's happened more than the twice you know about, and last night he finally killed someone. I think you know damn well who and I think you know why."

"Jared." Sonnenberg cut him off. "We truly do not have time to discuss this properly. But I'll tell you this. You appear to have decided that I am some Orwellian manipulator who influences your every thought and deed. I'm nothing of the sort. What I am is a human behaviorist and you are a human. Much of your behavior is entirely predictable, Abel's even more so. He's as simple as a reptile, which in his essence he is. As for putting him back where you think he belongs, even if it were possible, what on earth good do you think it would do? He'd still be there, you know. The difference would be that you'd no longer know as clearly where he leaves off and you begin. For heaven's sake, Jared, would you really want to sacrifice the clarity of a distinct Abel, Baker, and Charley in favor of a muddled and frightened Jared Baker? Use them, Jared. Understand them. Discipline them if you must, but do not reject them."

"It won't work," Baker answered stubbornly. He stepped back into the hidden room and sat down on the single Morris chair so Sonnenberg could see he had no intention of leaving. "All this time Charley has been picking and choosing what he wants to tell me. Maybe he's started to come around, but Abel hasn't. Abel's hardly been under control at all until I convinced him that I'd let us both die before I'd let him control me again. That goes for you too, Doctor."

"There, you see?" Sonnenberg replied. "You are learning to control him."

"Only while I'm willing to die, Doctor. And only while he believes it. I might not be so willing tomorrow."

He heard Sonnenberg take a breath that sounded impatient.

"You're being foolish, Jared." The voice was almost scolding. "Abel never controlled you. Abel simply survived when his survival was threatened. He may be cunning, he may be aggressive, he may have all the other predacious qualities, but he's no more capable of scheming or deceit than a lizard. Nor would he be capable of wanton killing unless he needed to eat what he killed. Abel does no more or less than what is necessary for his survival and he . . . Oh dear." Sonnenberg's voice became faint, as if he'd backed away from the microphone. Baker could hear the sound of switches being thrown. "Oh dear," the voice repeated, still distant, "here comes Connor Harrigan."

Harrigan was well inside the main gate when Sonnenberg noticed him. He stood partially hidden behind a small yew, considering how best to cross the open expanse of real estate to Sonnenberg's front door, which stood open. He stepped away from the shrub, revealing a pistol held close against his thigh. Baker was inside. Of that he was reasonably sure. The Hertz car he parked behind was almost certainly Baker's. Who else might be inside was another question entirely. And who indeed might be watching through the little scanner that his trained eye saw mounted on a drainpipe under a spray of ivy. As for the open door, he knew an invitation when he saw one. He also knew that this was not a house that could be furtively entered unless Sonnenberg wanted it entered. With a small sigh, Harrigan mounted the stone steps and followed his revolver through the doorway.

Inside he waited, with more a sense of anticipation than of danger. The house, if the main hall and living room were any sign, had an abandoned look. It was furnished well enough, rather like a model home is furnished, without the detail that spoke of habitation. He saw wall spaces where frames had recently hung, shelves with holes that lacked the symmetry of spaces that had been planned. All the contents of this house, Harrigan was sure, all the things that had been left behind, would provide no useful clue to Marcus Sonnenberg.

Harrigan felt the flash of anger that was now familiar. Baker was near, all right. Well, what now, Jared Baker? Do I walk through the rooms shouting your name? Or do I stand here like a dummy until you and Sonnenberg decide to show yourselves? Instead, if you don't mind, I think I'll take a little tour. Upstairs, for a start. Let's see if one of Sonnenberg's beasties comes leaping at me from an attic room like they do in horror movies.

Sonnenberg's bedroom was the first he entered. Harrigan flipped a light switch without effect. A burned-out bulb? He tried a table lamp. No power. Then what do we suppose made that scanner move?

The bedroom in its way was like the rooms below. The closets were full, the furniture all or mostly there, yet the room was curiously lifeless. Harrigan stepped to a curtained window and looked down on a tangle of ancient rhododendrons and to the golf course beyond the stockade fence. He could see several golfers in groups of twos and threes, not moving much. Harrigan noted the lack of activity but did not dwell on it. His attention fell instead upon several dim impressions in the carpet at his feet. Three of them formed a triangle. A three-legged table? A tripod? What for, Dr. Sonnenberg? What game did you play here?

The next room had the look of a guest room. No, a servant's room. Two starched maid's outfits hung in the closet. And two nurse's uniforms of the same size. The right half of the closet was empty. On the floor, a shoe rack built for six pairs of shoes held only three, all on the left side. On the right side, his eye picked up something small and white lying flush against the wall. A collar stay. Harrigan never realized women wore them.

There were five more rooms on the second floor as well as a stairway leading to the attic. The attic could wait, he decided. Perhaps forever. There was probably no way to enter it except head first, and to hell with that.

Of the remaining rooms, three were guest rooms, only one of which gave much feeling of use. He scanned the contents of a small bookcase near the bed. Books on sailing were among them. And a textbook on multiple personality. Baker's old room, he thought, turning back into the hallway. The last two rooms were a surprise. One was clearly a sickroom, the other a treatment room and pathology laboratory worthy of a small-town clinic. "A bloody hospital," Harrigan whispered. He looked for instruments that would offer a clue to the kind of surgery that had been performed there. The instruments had been taken.

Harrigan returned to the stairs and descended, not bothering to be quiet this time. He peered into what he took to be Sonnenberg's study. More missing items and sparsely knickknacked shelves. Another flash of anger. Oh yes, Baker. Why am I here, you're wondering, and where is Tina. She's well and happy, Baker. Don't you see the picture in my mind of Tina well and happy? If you'd like to know more than that, I'm afraid you and Dr. Sonnenberg are going to have to show yourselves."

Harrigan passed through the dining room and into the kitchen, where his eye fell upon a sliver of light coming from beneath the basement door. Once more he descended, his weapon leveled. He stopped at the sight of a white cabinet swung three feet or so out from the wall.

"Put the silly thing away, Mr. Harrigan." Sonnenberg's voice shocked him into a crouch. "And shame on you for strolling into so obvious a trap."

The words seemed to come from just above his head. A speaker, he realized at once. Also an alternative power source. But where was Sonnenberg? The white cabinet opened farther and Jared Baker's face appeared, his eyes cold and furious. Harrigan backed up a step.

"Easy lad." He squinted. "You are Baker, aren't you?"

"Where is she, Harrigan?"

"I'm afraid they've taken her, lad. Tanner Burke too. But I don't think they're in any danger."

"Who, damnit? Who took them?"

"You might ask your friend the doctor."

"Sonnenberg?" Baker snarled the question toward the speaker in the ceiling.

"Speaking of friends, Jared," the voice answered, "it appears your confidence in your two recent choices is not entirely well founded."

"No games, Sonnenberg. Who took her?"

"Stanley Levy." Harrigan directed his reply more to the speaker than to Baker. "A strange little man who gets stranger by the hour. Can I assume you know that perfectly well, Dr. Sonnenberg? An answer would be the polite thing."

"Hmmmph." Sonnenberg sniffed. "I detect a certain smugness, Mr. Harrigan. Can I in turn assume that you've experienced an epiphany of some sort?"

"I think so. More than one, in fact. For openers, I believe I know who you used to be."

"A modest achievement, Mr. Harrigan. Similar in usefulness to finding a pair of socks I once wore."

"Sonnenberg!" Baker shouted.

"Tina is well and safe, Jared. So is the woman. I feel I can assure you of that."

"You had her taken?"

"Not precisely, no," Sonnenberg answered. There was a vagueness to his voice, as if he were trying to remember something. "Harrigan is quite right about Stanley Levy. But Levy is Domenic Tortora's man, not mine. And I can promise you Tortora would not act against my interests. Those interests do not embrace harm to Tina Baker. She's in protective custody, Jared. She is quite safe."

"Safe?" Baker raged. "How the hell can she be safe with the father of someone Abel tore apart last night?"

"Oh dear, yes. There is that."

"Where is she, damnit?"

"Well now, that is a complication, Jared." The concern in Sonnenberg's voice sounded sincere, even to Harrigan. More than concern, Harrigan thought he heard confusion. "He'll want to speak to you about that, of course. As will I when we have time to chat. But it cannot be now, Jared. I must ask you to please trust me and believe that I would not let Tina be harmed. I've kept her from harm before under similar circumstances. And we've met, you know. We became great friends when she was in the hospital. She called me Grandpa. And my visits helped to ease her pain. They did, Jared. Truly."

Grandpa! Baker spat the word beneath his breath. Grandpa! He should have known when Tina told him about her visitor. Baker balled both fists and squeezed them white in an effort to control his fury and frustration. The bastard, he thought. The bastard has been working on her head too. Right from the beginning. By God, even if he lives to try it he'll never get another chance. Tears streamed from Baker's right eye. He shook them off.

"Charley, where is she?"

"i don't know." Even Charley sounded worried. *"Sonnenberg must know. Listen to him."*

"he doesn't let me listen. he fixed it that way. all i hear is he's all mixed up. but i hear other men. we have to go, baker."

"We're not going anywhere until—"

"it's the same men, baker. the same men are coming."

"Jared, you must go." Baker heard the rapid clicks of switches again. "Rats!" Sonnenberg growled. "It's too late. Assorted golfers seem to be converging on the house. They also seem to have automatic weapons where their mashie-niblicks ought to be." There were two more clicks. "Rats again! There are two more at the front gate."

"baker." It was Abel.

"Not now."

"they've come killing, baker. call me or leave."

"Jared, I make you a promise. Save yourself now and I will take you to Tina. You have my absolute guarantee of her well-being."

Harrigan checked his revolver. "Where the hell are we supposed to go unless you got a tunnel down here?"

"In fact, quite so, Mr. Harrigan. There's a vent in that room behind the air conditioner. It leads to a tunnel that leads to a covered well. Use it when you must. In the meantime, if you and Jared remain in this room and listen, you'll be entertained by the comeuppance of Mr. Duncan Peck. Take Jared, Mr. Harrigan, and retire now. You'll both find this encounter to be most instructive."

Baker hesitated. He knew he could do little except wait. But not knowing about Tina and Tanner Burke was more than he could bear.

Sonnenberg understood. "Remember my promise, Jared. Go inside. You'll know when it's prudent to leave."

"I'll come looking for you, Doctor. I'm going to find you."

"Indeed, Jared, indeed. Sooner than you think. Go back to the city, Jared, and wait. Go back to Central Park. Interesting things happen to you in Central Park."

Tanner was somewhere in the East Eighties. She knew that much. The neighborhood was German, judging by the names of the stores and restaurants they passed. All the numbered side streets looked about the same, stunted trees on most of them, a scattering of apartment buildings dating from the twenties, and between them rows of brick townhouses and brownstones that were much older.

Stanley tapped her arm and pointed to one of them, a brownstone painted red, its first floor occupied by one of those antique shops that never seem to be open. "By the hydrant," he said. "Go ahead and park by the fire hydrant."

As she shut off the ignition, Tanner noticed two young men carrying tennis rackets walking briskly along in her direction. Stanley followed her line of sight. He touched his ice pick once more to her ribs. She winced and looked away.

"You been good so far about not calling for help," he told her, his voice gentle, "and about not jumping out at some stoplight. I don't know if I would have stuck you if you did, but I would have stuck whoever came to help you, and then I would have been all alone with the kid. You don't want that, do you?"

Tanner shook her head.

"That's good because now you got another temptation. We have to bring the kid upstairs holding her between us. You get a chance to run again, but if you do I got no choice this time. I gotta hurt you. If I can't catch you, then I throw the kid back in the car and we drive someplace else, just her and me. You don't want that either, do you?"

"I'll stay with her," Tanner promised. She reached behind her and stroked the cheek of Tina Baker, who sprawled unconscious across the rear seat. Stanley took the ignition key and opened his door to the sidewalk, then crossed to Tanner's side and waited for her. With difficulty, they pulled Tina to her feet and struggled up a narrow flight of stairs, holding her erect between them.

The apartment had a musty smell of disuse. Yet Stanley called a greeting as he entered, announcing cheerfully that he was with friends. Tanner heard no re-

ply, although Stanley smiled and nodded as if a welcome
had been spoken from another room. He motioned Tanner forward through the entry hall and a long, high-
ceilinged living room into what appeared to be the only
bedroom. Its furnishings had a look that was old-
fashioned before Tanner was born. An old woman's bedroom. Antimacassars were draped over two embroidered
chairs and held in place with pins. The headboard of the
double bed was heavy mahogany and its design matched
that of a bureau and two end tables. A black-and-white
Dumont television, almost three decades old, rested on
one end table over a stack of magazines arranged on a
lower shelf. There was a copy of *Soap Opera* magazine,
several *Reader's Digests*, and the yellow spine of a single
National Geographic. On the bureau, backed by a tilting
mirror suspended by two heavy uprights, there was a silver menorah and two framed photographs of Stanley
Levy, one perhaps five years older than the other. These
sat on a runner of yellowed Belgian lace along with a tarnished brush and mirror set and a small glass tray that
held bottles of colored liquids. Three paintings hung on
the walls, all pastoral scenes, all in need of cleaning.

Stanley excused himself after placing Tina on the
tufted pink bedspread, then walked toward what Tanner
presumed was the kitchen. She heard a soft voice mur-
muring and the sound of cabinets opening and closing.
She hurried to Tina's side, shaking her without effect,
and then to a single large window, which faced an over-
grown garden in the rear. A rusty but solid grille covered
the window from the outside. Tanner turned from the
window and crossed once more to the bed, almost trip-
ping over a telephone wire. A dated black receiver
crashed to the floor from the shelf of the other end table.
Tanner grabbed it, praying Stanley had not heard. She
dialed the operator. Nothing happened.

"It don't work." Stanley's voice came from the doorway. He stood watching her with a fabric-covered ice bag
in one hand and tape and scissors in the other. "I'd get
it fixed, but she'd right away start asking how come I

never call her. You want to sit down over there?" Stanley pointed to the chair farthest from the bed.

"I don't want you to get nervous about this," he said, stripping several lengths of tape from the roll and guiding Tanner's arms behind her with a touch. "I mean, nothing bad is going to happen, like Tortora's kid tried to do. What about going to the bathroom? You have to go or anything before I put this tape on?"

Tanner blinked and shook her head. "What are you going to do with us?"

"Nothing bad," he repeated. "Tortora just wants Baker. He don't want to hurt the little girl. Anyhow, I wouldn't let him."

"But you'll let him hurt her father?"

Stanley shrugged and wrapped the first length of tape around her wrists. "I think the question is how come Baker wants to hurt Tortora and did a number on Tortora's kid. Not that the kid was that big a loss. It's like when they say it's the thought that counts. It's very disrespectful, what he did. Like a dare, you know? Tortora don't like that. He also wants to know how come. How's that feel, by the way? Not too tight?"

Tanner shook her head.

Satisfied that the tape would hold, Stanley picked up the ice bag and walked to the bed, where he placed it carefully against Tina's ankle. Then he folded back the bedspread and tucked it around her body. Tina gave a small moan.

"A little while, my mother will fix some lunch," he told Tanner as he moved toward the door. "I don't know if the kid can eat by then. Later, I come back, maybe I'll bring some Chinese."

She listened as he walked to the kitchen again and spoke some muffled words. Tanner thought she heard the front door click shut, she wasn't sure. The sound was lost in the clatter of utensils and the soft shuffling of slippered feet. He was gone, she decided at last. His mother would be coming soon. Perhaps Tanner could talk to her. Get her to cut the tape or at least go down to the street for help. She'd have to. How could any old woman,

Stanley's mother or not, allow this to happen in her home? Fear, maybe. Maybe she was just as frightened of her strangely gentle but lunatic son. Or maybe she was just as crazy as he is. Tanner shook her head sharply, regretting even the thought. The last thing she wanted to imagine was that the little old woman out there rummaging through drawers filled with carving knives was as mad as Stanley Levy. Tanner began to shiver.

Tina was dreaming once more. It was the halfway sort of dream, she knew, when you're partly awake and partly asleep and it's hard to know what's real and what isn't. Tanner Burke was here. That part couldn't be real. *Can it, Daddy? I mean, she's sitting right here in a chair. I should wake up. But I mostly don't want to and find out I'm dreaming.*

Daddy? Are you getting angry? About what? You think she's here too? She is. She really is. Right here in my bedroom.

Daddy, I can't hear. You're yelling. What do you mean, where's my room. You know where my room is. And she's here. Her real name is Liz. Did you know that? She wants me to call her that, and she says only her most special people all her Liz.

Baker snarled aloud, startling Harrigan, who was listening to the sound of moving feet on the floor above. Like a caged animal, Baker paced the few feet of the small room—back, forth, back again—then with another angry snarl reached for the ventilator cover and tore it from its clasps.

"Hey," Harrigan snapped, keeping his voice at a whisper, "what the hell are you doing?"

"Getting out of here." Baker ducked his head into the narrow opening. Harrigan snatched at his coat collar and jerked him back.

"What's the matter with you? You stick your head out of that well, you're going to get a hole in it."

"They're in New York someplace." Baker's eyes were flaming." "Get out of my way, Harrigan."

Baker never saw the punch coming. He saw a burst of light that flashed from his temple and felt his knees crash to the floor. Harrigan saw his eyes glaze over. They blinked as if confused, and tears came from one of them. They were clearing. Harrigan thought he saw the beginnings of a grin as he hit Baker again and a third time. He caught Baker as he fell forward.

"Sorry, lad. We have things to learn here first." Harrigan peered anxiously into Baker's face, a Hail Mary on his lips that the three blows had been enough.

In Tina's half-dream, she saw her father falling. First he was angry, really angry, then he sort of melted down. Floated down. Not angry anymore. Just kind of lost and calling out for people. For her and for Tanner. For Liz. And for someone else whose name sounded like *Abe*. Like he was trying to say the name and he couldn't.

He was floating down now but she was floating up. She could see a woman there, right there in the chair, like in her dream. Same hair. Same face. Oh gosh, it's really Tanner Burke. It's Tanner Burke right here in my— Wait a minute. This isn't my room. And there was that man. With the needle. And there was someone who tried to choke the man with a cord. No, wait. That was a real dream, that last part. Tanner? I mean, Liz?

"Wake up, honey," Tanner whispered urgently. "Look. Look at this tape." She'd pushed her chair closer to the bed and half-turned so Tina could see her wrists. "Tina, honey, try. See if you can reach this tape."

Tina raised one hand, searching toward Tanner's wrists with her fingertips. The hand hovered two feet short of its mark and then fell lazily to the bed.

"Try, Tina. Scooch over closer and try again. Tina, try . . ." She froze at the sound of the door opening.

Tanner could not see at first. The knob turned and then the door swung in. First a tray appeared with plates and glasses on it, all balanced on one hand while another grasped the edge of the door to close it. Now, by twisting her neck, Tanner could see the woman out of the corner of her eye. She wore an old, ragged bathrobe that reached all the way to slippered feet. Her ill-kept hair was drawn back in a wiry bun the way Golda Meier wore her hair. Golda Levy? Tanner saw at once the resemblance between the woman and her son. But she was young. Too young, Tanner thought, to be the mother of anyone the age of Stanley Levy. The woman smiled gently at Tanner Burke and brightened further when she saw that Tina was rousing.

"You like egg salad?" she asked. "There's some nice soup also."

Tina answered with a sleepy smile. It was a dream after all, she realized, at least the part about the man with the needle. There wasn't any such man at all. Just this old lady. And I'm with Tanner Burke and we're going to have lunch.

The old woman placed the tray on the bureau and smiled at one of Stanley's photographs. "While we eat we can watch the television. *General Hospital* is almost on." She shook out a napkin and laid it across Tanner's lap. "Then after, maybe you'd like if I read to you. You like from Sherlock Holmes? I could read *The Adventure of the Sussex Vampire* if it ain't too scary for the girl here."

Tanner swallowed back a sob. Tears of exhaustion and helplessness appeared in her eyes and a dull, sinking horror throbbed in her stomach. The gentle old lady holding a spoonful of soup toward her mouth was not Stanley Levy's mother after all. It was Stanley Levy himself. And the person smiling sweetly before her chair seemed to have no idea in the world that she was Stanley Levy.

16

Ed Burleson was the first through the door left ajar by Connor Harrigan. Two more men followed, snapping the safeties off their automatic weapons, and fanned out inside, directed by a wave of Burleson's hand. Burleson, like Harrigan, knew at a glance that the house was unoccupied. He touched one man's shoulder and pointed to the sliding patio doors at the far end of the living room. The man crossed and opened them, allowing Michael Biaggi and the man called Peterson to enter.

Behind Burleson, in the driveway, Duncan Peck sensed it too. He brushed off the restraining hand of an agent stationed near the gate and walked slowly toward the door, disappointment keen on his face. Ed Burleson heard his footsteps on the gravel and turned to intercept him.

"It's not safe yet, sir," Burleson told him quietly.

"Our friend has flown the coop, I take it?"

"It would seem so, sir. The house looks abandoned, but I suggest you wait until my men secure it. It could easily be boobytrapped."

Peck allowed himself a sigh. "Your men couldn't secure this house if they had a week and a fleet of minesweepers to do it. No offense, Edward, but I know this man." Peck walked past Burleson and through Sonnenberg's front door.

Peterson, with Biaggi following, was already on the

second floor. The two moved quickly from room to room, opening doors and bursting through in a crouch, or trading hand signals that argued over who would be the first to turn a blind corner. Peck heard the stomping sounds above him and the crack of a lock being kicked open. He winced at the damage being done to so fine an example of Colonial architecture. And as he winced, he was struck by the clear and certain feeling that he was not alone in his reaction. Peck folded his arms and let his eye wander along the walls and ceiling of the center hall. He smiled and raised a hand toward Burleson.

"Clear them out, Edward," he ordered.

"The search isn't completed, sir. Sonnenberg may have left some sign of where he's gone."

Peck waved aside what he knew to be an idle hope. "A message doubtless awaits us, Edward. We'll find it without enriching the local plasterers and painters."

"Well said, Duncan." Sonnenberg's voice seemed to float in front of them.

Burleson's gun barrel snapped up at the words and trained on the ceiling. Peck patted his shoulder and gestured the weapon away. He pointed toward a smoke detection device that seemed more than a bit overlarge and had a slit two inches square cut into it.

"I take it, Dr. Sonnenberg, that we're to play hide-and-seek for a while." He spoke directly to the smoke detector.

"If that amuses you, Duncan. However, you may correctly assume that I'm out of harm's way, even if my woodwork isn't. Please do as your master asked, Mr. Burleson. Send away your various androids so my friend and I can chat."

Burleson looked questioningly at Duncan Peck, who was busy scribbling a few lines on a piece of paper. This he tore off a pad and handed to Burleson. Burleson read it and, still doubtful, placed two fingers against his teeth and whistled. Peterson appeared at the top of the stairs, followed by Biaggi, then two more from the kitchen and study. Burleson huddled briefly with the four, brushing aside their questions, and directed them to positions outside the doors they'd originally entered. Biaggi left more reluctantly than the others. Burleson remained.

"This one is to stay, I take it?" Sonnenberg asked.

"If it's quite all right."

"I'm delighted," said Sonnenberg expansively. "Welcome, Mr. Burleson. Your invited presence suggests either that Mr. Peck would trust you with his life or that he fully intends to take yours when all is said and done. I suspect the latter. What was on the little note, by the way?"

Burleson folded his arms over his Uzi but offered no other expression.

"Gentlemen don't read each other's mail, as they say, Doctor," Peck answered. "Obviously, however, it contained instructions. What to do next, where else to look for you, that sort of thing."

"Well, if you'd asked, I'd have been more than happy to give you a hint. But you've been rude, so I won't. And as for this Dr. Sonnenberg business, you know perfectly well who I am. Or was. Back then, at least. One of these telescanners, incidentally, is installed in my study. By all means choose a comfortable place to sit and we'll have a long and frank discussion about old times and new. And I shall be frank, Duncan. I shall even be Blount."

Peck shook his head wearily and turned to Burleson. "That was a pun, Edward. Blount. It's the man's name. He was Ivor Blount when he worked for me."

"I'll bet you're just breathless to hear the story, aren't you, Edward?"

"Ivor—"

"Call me Marcus, Duncan. Less confusing."

"Marcus, is there a point to this? Not that I mind listening to your demented chitchat while my people search for you, but what exactly do you expect me to contribute? You hardly expect me to bare my innermost thoughts for the benefit of your recording devices."

"Not a bit of it, Duncan. There are no such devices. My word on it." Unless we count Connor Harrigan's own notepad, he thought, upon which he too is doubtless be-

ginning to scribble downstairs. Sonnenberg decided he'd
forgive himself the small lie of omission. "In any case, I
won't ask you to admit a thing. I do, however, have a surprise for you in just a short while. Do you mind if I pass
the time telling Mr. Burleson a story or two?"

"Would this surprise involve a lethal device, old
friend?" Peck began to envision being blown up or elec-
trocuted if he sought comfort in the wrong chair.

"Absolutely not!" Sonnenberg's voice seemed ap-
palled at the suggestion. "You're a guest in my home,
Duncan. I intend merely to annoy you. But there will be
compensation, I promise, in the coin of useful and valu-
able information."

Duncan Peck smiled. "We'll see who annoys whom,
Marcus." Peck strolled toward the study as he spoke, deciding to take Sonnenberg at his word. Burleson followed
and, after Peck was seated, chose a lesser seat for himself.

"Where to begin?" The speaker in the hall clicked
off and another beneath the study's mantel clicked on. "I
suppose, Edward . . . May I call you Edward? Thank
you. I suppose the tale begins in 1944, Edward. Back
when war could be fun. Bond rallies, patriotic songs,
winning—that sort of thing. Spying, too, had a certain
grandeur to it then. The espionage game attracted every
sort of person. Patriots, humanists, swashbucklers, and
most reliable of all, those who did it for the money. This
was before we learned to homogenize our spies and turn
earnest young Fordham and Georgetown graduates into
sociopaths like yourself, Edward.

"But I digress. Duncan here, and yours truly, were
once what a chronicler of the time described as the
young lions. We fought and dared. Dared mostly. My job,
under Duncan, was to train American agents for assignment to occupied European countries. Others taught
them how to spy, to kill silently, to kidnap, and to otherwise make mischief. I taught them how not to get caught.
I taught them how to blend with any populace and how
to convincingly live whatever identity they assumed. I
could, immodestly perhaps, turn a shoe salesman into a

pastry chef or a yachtsman into a truck driver. If I am boasting, Edward, it's not entirely without cause. No one placed in my charge was ever caught, save two women who were deliberately betrayed by Duncan here in order to have false information torn out of them through their fingernails. It was then that I began to suspect that Duncan's loyalties and personal ethics were less than rigid."

Duncan Peck glanced at Burleson and shook his head sadly. Burleson nodded that he understood the occasional need for reluctant ruthlessness. He understood further, his eyes said, what a trial it must have been for Peck to work with such a pansy. Peck glanced out the window. Peterson was near the front gate now. He held a device with a large circular antenna in one hand and a transceiver in the other. A direction finder, Duncan Peck knew. Perhaps he would not have to endure this very much longer. But long enough to fill in a gap or two.

"After the war ended," Sonnenberg continued, "I lingered on, performing a similar service but in reverse. People who were then in need of new identities included defectors, certain witnesses, agents who'd committed capital crimes more or less in the line of duty, and the like. Since the management of such an operation requires a certain indifference to truth and convention, Duncan Peck was naturally put in charge. The terribly secret Relocation Service was off and running.

"As it grew, Duncan found it convenient to use more and more of these people for his own ends. I mean, what's the use of having a political assassin on hand if you're going to let him lie fallow? Or a skillful forger. Or an extortionist. You understand this, don't you, Edward? You see it as a perfectly sensible alternative to leaving the power in the hands of the flighty electorate. I, however, was one of the flighty ones. I thought he was wrong and said so, even threatened to make my views more broadly known. So here you see truth and convention rearing their ugly heads again. Having heard me voice such alien concepts, Duncan reasonably concluded that I was deranged. From his point of view I probably was. It was not long afterward that others in government, including an honest man here and there, began to share his conviction. In truth, I was a bit of an eccentric. My public behavior became increasingly bizarre, thanks to certain controlled substances that found their way onto my luncheon plate whenever I dined with Duncan. In a matter of weeks, Duncan managed to do such violence to my credibility that my every pronouncement was seen as the raving of a lunatic. It remained only to put me where lunatics go. You're familiar with St. Elizabeths Hospital, Edward? It's where we entombed the poet Ezra Pound during the war. It seems that he recognized a random good quality in Germans and Italians before the rest of us were prepared to embrace a similar notion. Ezra was allowed to rant on for years, but in my case that simply wouldn't do.

"Two attempts were made on my life. The first involved an accidental overdose of drugs, which failed only because I'd learned by that time to palm half of every dosage as a matter of course. As it was, the remaining quantity left me in a coma for ten days. For the second attempt, I was slashed in the dead of night by a deranged inmate. I survived, as you see, but my assailant was never identified. He was a portly fellow, like myself, but with a bent nose, and he smelled of cheap cigars.

"Well, enough was enough. Feeling distinctly unwanted by this time, I decided to leave. Christmas was fast approaching. You remember Christmas, Edward. Good will toward men, gaily wrapped gifts, a goose spitting in the oven? No, I don't suppose you do. In any case, it was the one time of the year when Duncan's security was somewhat relaxed. I had several plans in mind. The best of a bad lot involved setting a fire in the common room and escaping in the smoke and confusion. They allowed us to work with paints for therapy, you see, and my ward contained no end of combustible materials. A fire would get me off the floor, but the gates outside were another matter. My salvation came indirectly from Duncan here in the person of Santa Claus himself."

* * *

In the basement room, Connor Harrigan put down his notepad at the sound of a grunt from Baker. He snatched up the yellow dart he'd kept in readiness and rushed to the cot where Baker lay. With the point of the dart against the muscle tissue of Baker's neck, Harrigan watched his eyes as he stirred.

"Sorry, lad," he said softly. "And I'll be sorrier still if you blink and I see the beastie looking back at me."

Baker filled his lungs and winced, his fingers moving tenderly against his jaw. Frowning, his eyes still closed, he reached inside his mouth and probed a tooth that had been loosened. Harrigan relaxed and drew away the dart. The soft green eyes opened. There were no tears.

" 'Twas for your own good, lad. You're no good to your daughter dead or in irons."

Harrigan didn't see the blow coming either. Baker's fist caught him high on the cheek and smashed him backward against the Morris chair. Harrigan rolled and kicked, trying to regain his legs, but they would not hold him. He covered his face with his arms and waited for Baker's attack. None came. Cautiously, he peeked through his guard.

Baker was ignoring him. Baker for sure. He sat on the edge of the cot, his head still clearing, focusing now on the familiar voice coming over the small speaker. Harrigan climbed onto the Morris chair and sat.

"Harrigan?" Baker asked, not looking at him, "you won't hit me anymore, will you?"

Harrigan touched his eye. "Not if this is how I'm thanked for it."

"I'd appreciate it."

Harrigan leaned forward. "There's an interesting tale being told up there. How much of Sonnenberg's history do you know?"

"Not much. Just what he told me. Probably none of it's true."

"Why don't we listen together now that we're friends again. Do you have any notion of where Sonnenberg might be lurking, by chance?"

"Probably on his boat. It's all rigged for this kind of stuff. He's probably talking from the middle of Long Island Sound."

"If that's the most logical guess, I suspect that it's exactly where he isn't. Hush, lad. We're about to learn of his adventures with Santa Claus."

"Sure enough," Sonnenberg's voice was saying, "on Christmas Eve the jolly old elf appeared, distributing presents from room to room. My Yuletide gift was a jar of Beluga caviar, Iranian, of course, which I presumed to be teeming with botulism. That presumption was based largely on the fact that Santa happened to be a portly fellow like myself who had a bent nose and smelled of cheap cigars. We chatted for a while of the joys of the season, and he sampled some fudge that I'd made in another of my therapy electives. The fudge was double chocolate with walnuts and, I'm afraid, most of my unused sedatives. Poor old Santa went to sleep in the middle of a swallow. Then, not wishing to deprive the other inmates of their Christmas goodies, I took up the baton, to say nothing of Santa's costume, and went about distributing gifts until a fire alarm cut short my rounds. It seems the portly fellow was smoking a cigar in a bed on which he'd carelessly spilled a can of paint thinner. A dreadful accident. Went up like a dried-out Christmas tree, they tell me. In my room. In my bed. The authorities could be forgiven for assuming that poor old cracked Ivor Blount was no more.

"But you ask, Edward, why no positive identification was made. Dental work and the like. The answer is that Duncan here was entirely convinced that his assassin had done his work. Duncan had even come by St. Elizabeths to make sure this time. How do I know? Because after a helpful orderly escorted me to the courtyard and I approached the main gate, whom to my wondrous eyes should appear but Duncan Peck, his face fairly glowing with anticipation behind the rolled-down window of a car parked at the curb. He questioned me with a look and I reassured him with a wave. He then drove off with the peace of the season in his heart. Sadly, his good humor lasted only a matter of a week or two, when it became clear that his bent-nosed Santa had vanished like the Spirit of Christmas Past. How long, Duncan? How long did you endure the nagging thought that something had gone seriously askew? How many more Christmas Eves went by without a visit from Santa before you gritted your teeth and exhumed your overdone assassin?"

Peck looked at his watch and made a show of yawning.

"Oh dear me, I'm boring you. But it won't be much longer. How long can it take your men to triangulate these radio signals? Indulge me, Duncan. It's been such a long time."

"I'm afraid you really are becoming tiresome, Ivor."

"Marcus."

"As you wish." Duncan Peck pushed to his feet and wandered to the window facing front. Peterson was still in the driveway, a radio at his ear. He saw Peck watching him and signaled that he needed more time. Peck turned and faced another smoke detector that was mounted above a corner cabinet. "Your self-righteousness, Marcus, is tedious most of all. You sit at what I presume to be a safe distance mocking me and mocking Mr. Burleson here. You mock men who have purpose to their lives while you play at yours. You escape from a mental institution in which you assuredly belonged and then for the next two decades you send me Christmas cards signed "Santa" with a little smiling face. It was a childish and arrogant act, Marcus. It was also the act of a man who is really quite mad. Whether or not I later chose to put you out of your misery, the papers committing you to that institution were entirely legitimate."

"Hmmm," the voice answered. "Duncan, I don't suppose you see an ethical paradox in that last sentence? Never mind. Perhaps we are a bit bonkers, both of us. I think I'll hold to the view that my form of lunacy is more engaging than yours. And a great deal more fun. You're quite right, Duncan. I play at it. I've had wonderful times and I've done some quite wonderful things with the human mind, as I hope to demonstrate shortly. And it's all quite to the good. So many of my people are now so much more than they were before. Your people invariably become less. Look at this pathetic robot, Burleson. You took a bright-eyed collegian and did this to him. Show me the joy in his soul, Duncan. Show me the pleasure he finds in this lofty purpose of which you boast."

"Jared Baker is hardly a barrel of laughs, Marcus."

"True enough," Sonnenberg acknowledged. "Jared is troubled. Jared is in turmoil. But the best evidence of Jared Baker's humanity is that he has the capacity for inner turmoil. He'll sort it out with my help or without it. You can't have him, by the way."

"We'll see about that, Marcus."

"We will, Duncan. We will indeed."

"I don't suppose you'd tell me whether there are more like him. Perhaps even how you plan to use these people who are so much better than we are."

"Don't mind at all," Sonnenberg answered agreeably. "I gather the triangulation process isn't going very well."

"We can't expect too much from robots, Marcus. What about the other Bakers. Do I assume there are more?"

"Nope. He's one of a kind. I have a near miss or two running around, but Baker is my first real success. As for my master plan, the truth is that I really didn't have one until you showed signs of mucking things up. Oh, granted I had all sorts of schemes in mind from time to time. Real mad-scientist stuff. A race of supermen and women. Government within a government. An army of Jared Bakers. Tomorrow the world, that sort of thing. But as you perceptively suggested, I play at it. I have neither the heart nor the low boredom threshold necessary for a sustained conspiracy. And in any case, my people have an irritating way of thinking for themselves at inconvenient times, unlike your doomed innocent here. In my loonier states I suppose I've teetered on the brink of a Messiah or Napoleon complex, but I really think I lack the power drive that would have made me sally forth from my little

Elba here. Hmmph." Sonnenberg chuckled. "A pun leaps to mind. Elba was I ere I saw Abel. Hmmph. That's really quite apt. Sorry, Duncan. Inside joke."

Harrigan listened in fascination, his attention punctuated by short periods of unreasonable fury that subsided before the anger could express itself. Even Baker was listening intently now, no less worried about Tanner Burke and Tina, but calmed past the point where he would have rushed uselessly and recklessly to find them.

"It sounds like the girl was right," Harrigan whispered appreciatively. "If you can believe Sonnenberg, all this time he's just been bumbling along enjoying himself." He motioned toward the pins on Sonnenberg's map. "Is it possible that all those people out there are sitting around waiting for a signal that Sonnenberg doesn't ever mean to give? And why, by the way, is he letting me see where they are?"

"They're not Sonnenberg's people," Baker answered. "The pins are in the wrong places."

Harrigan raised an eyebrow. "He wouldn't have gone to that trouble just to mislead anyone who saw a map they wouldn't even know about. Why wouldn't he just take the damned thing down? And what're those two pieces of crepe over Denver and Kansas City?"

"If you want a guess"—Baker shrugged—"I'd say they're Peck's people. Sonnenberg wouldn't have much trouble finding anyone Peck hid."

"I know. He wrote the book. What about the crepe?"

Baker suspected but he did not know. For reasons he wasn't sure about, he thought of Howard Twilley. Gifted, frustrated, angry Howard Twilley, who, Baker knew, was convinced that a purpose existed behind the talent Sonnenberg had developed in him. A purpose he was eager to fulfill and a talent he was impatient to use in a way more significant than in the suppression of barroom troublemakers. It would have been only a matter of time before Sonnenberg could no longer contain him. In a way, Baker thought, Peck might have solved a problem by becoming a nuisance when he did.

"I think it might be the demonstration Sonnenberg mentioned a few minutes ago. I think he means to teach Peck a lesson."

"How, lad?" Harrigan's brow darkened.

"Just listen." Baker pointed to the speaker.

"Another question. You haven't asked about all that happened at the Carey house. Would you like to be briefed or can I assume from the swings of my mood that my brain has already been picked clean?"

"Thank you," Jared answered absently. "It's not necessary."

"Screw you, Baker."

"Sorry, Duncan. Inside joke. Where was I, by the way?"

"You were escaping from a psychiatric ward," Peck answered dryly, "committing a murder in the process."

Sonnenberg clucked his tongue. "Ah yes, Duncan. You have had legal training, haven't you. Someone once wrote that no poet has seen in nature the variety a lawyer sees in the truth. We were discussing, in any case, whether or not I had a master plan. The plain truth is that since I paroled myself from St. Elizabeths, one thing rather led to another. First there was a need to create a new me, and I thought I might enjoy being a doctor this time. Something bearded, perhaps, and faintly Viennese. A Viennese accent and beard are usually all that is needed to set oneself up in the field of behavioral psychology. Still drifting, however, I drifted into my local butcher shop, where I sought to purchase a rack of lamb. The butcher was Ben Meister, who, speaking of lawyers, thought he would enjoy that profession, although I can't think why. But a lifetime of carving flesh turned out to be superb elementary training. Simulated regression—you recall the technique—helped do the rest. He thought he was Louis Brandeis for the twelve months it took him to prepare for the bar examination. Benjamin is in a Melvin Belli phase at the moment.

"Moving right along, Meister then defended a woman named Melanie Laver, who was charged with manslaughter. Unhappily, due to Meister's inexperience, to say nothing of Melanie's guilt, he failed to win an acquittal. Nice woman, though. We contrived a satisfying alternative to ten years in a Massachusetts state prison."

Peck looked at his watch, then winked at Burleson. Sonnenberg saw it.

"May I continue, Duncan?" he admonished. "Here's your quarry, 'fessing up to all at last, and you're being rudely inattentive."

"I'm terribly sorry, Marcus." Peck affected a somber expression and sat erect in his chair. "It's just that I've sat through this scene in every grade B detective movie of the thirties and forties. The protagonist pieces together all the loose ends in a tiresome chronology and then points an accusing finger at the surprise villain. Since there are few surprises here, Marcus, I wonder if we might vault ahead. To the modern era, perhaps."

"Well." Sonnenberg sniffed. "I suppose we needn't catalogue all the Ben Meisters and Melanie Lavers. Or the Roger Hersheys, the Howard Twilleys, and the Luther Dowlings. That's your complete list, isn't it, Duncan? It was the cause of your smirk to Edward a moment ago. Your wink was saying, 'Let the old fool ramble on, never dreaming that we're having these five people rounded up even as he prattles.' Well, they're not at home, and you can't have them either."

Peck flushed but held himself under control. He glanced at the phone and restrained himself from rushing to it to ask whether his roundup of Sonnenberg's known subjects was as futile as Sonnenberg suggested. "Perhaps there are surprises after all, Marcus. Please continue." He needed time to rearrange his thoughts.

"Along any particular avenue, Duncan?"

Duncan Peck shrugged. "I'm rather interested in the Chimera phenomenon, if you wouldn't mind."

"Ah yes." Sonnenberg picked up his thread. "It's instructive, first, to understand how we got there. It was really a sort of on-the-job training. As we went through the Ben Meisters and Melanie Lavers and on to the others, every new technique, every success at radically altering a personality or developing a new talent, led to whole new areas of inquiry. In some cases, we even succeeded in tapping genetic memories. I'd been fascinated by the subject for some time. I've always suspected that an 'idiot savant,' for example, who can hear a Beethoven piece once and then play it faultlessly without even a lesson, is actually displaying a skill that was mastered in a prior generation by a biological antecedent. All of us, in fact, possess skills and aptitudes that were actually learned by blood forebears generations, even eons, ago and retained in the genetic blueprint of later generations. A simpler example concerns animals. What we call instinct in a dog is actually behavior that was learned for the purpose of survival by an ancestor low on the evolutionary scale. Dogs and idiot savants don't spend a great deal of time thinking about what they can and cannot do. They just go ahead and do it. I simply began helping subjects to identify those talents, to believe in them and to focus on them.

"We were well along this road, Duncan, identifying deeply hidden knowledge and aptitudes, when we learned of experiments elsewhere that permitted a quantum leap. Several research centers, notably Cal Tech, had successfully taken memory-bearing brain tissue from one rat and injected it into the brain of another rat. The first rat, in one experiment, would be taught to run a difficult maze or learn a complicated feeding sequence, and then the tissue bearing that knowledge would be directly transfused into the skull of another rat. It worked. The difficulty, of course, was that the donor rat either died or was left impaired, so Cal Tech never got to try it on people."

"You, I assume, had no such reluctance, Marcus."

"Within certain limits, Duncan, but yes. In the past, I've restricted my experiments to terminally ill volunteers who, in return for the donation of their brain tissue within hours of their anticipated deaths, lived out their days comfortably and left handsome legacies to whomever they designated. They're all still quite alive, you know. Beyond providing nutrients to my rhododendrons out back, each is at this moment sharing productively in another human consciousness."

"Including Baker's, I gather."

"Oh goodness, no," Sonnenberg answered quickly. It wouldn't do at all, he thought, to have Jared wondering if I'd squirted bits of someone else's neocortex into his head. He's miffed enough already. "One does not create a Chimera, Duncan, more's the pity. One must find a Chimera. As I assume you recall, I've been looking for one for almost forty years. Oh, the Chimera potential is common enough if you know what you're looking for. Much more common than multiple-personality disorders, which themselves are a dime a dozen. First, it's a matter of understanding that a distinct personality exists within the limbic system of every human brain. Primordial man, basically. Something like old Bridey Murphy but far more elemental. The next step is to find the right subject, an individual whose primoridal or reptilian personality has slipped to the surface. What remains is to discover whether this phenomenon can be isolated and controlled. There's the rub, I'm afraid. One produces some very odd results along the way and far more failures than successes."

"The failures, I assume, are also gracing your garden."

"Not at all, Duncan. The procedure involves no danger to life." Sonnenberg reminded himself again that Baker was listening. "It's only that the subject must be stable, balanced and emotionally healthy. Lord knows what you'd find if you started digging into Edward here. Possibly nothing at all. Possibly, however, a great humanist and lover of mankind. After all, the nobler instincts you've managed to breed out of this surface creature must necessarily have found a home in some remote lobe or other. Speaking of lobes, one must also be certain, Duncan, that a chosen subject is not schizophrenic to any important degree, or all you'll end up with are creatures of your subject's emotional needs. I'm afraid I've made that mistake at least once in the past."

Duncan Peck leaned forward in his chair, deeply fascinated, his mind searching in several directions at once while absorbing the information so freely offered by Sonnenberg. Lunatic though he may be, Peck thought, he's far from foolish. Yet he's providing information that might be useful. Why? To keep me here until his friends from the police arrive? Hardly. A show of credentials will turn them away with even less inconvenience than Edward experienced with the Greenwich police. To detain us while his own people fly to his aid and our extermination? Not his style. To play cat and mouse? Obviously. But why? And as for these discourses he's enjoying so much, they have a curious quality, some of them. Almost as if he's speaking not so much to me but to . . . whom else, Ivor? You said there are no recording devices, and I think I'll take you at your word. Nor have you tried to elicit an incriminating admission from me, although you've made several such admissions yourself. For whose benefit, Ivor. Certainly not Edward's. Could Connor Harrigan be within earshot, Ivor? And Jared Baker?

"While you're being so generously discursive, Ivor—"

"Marcus."

"—Marcus, I don't suppose you'd share with me how one goes about identifying a Jared Baker."

"Actually, Duncan, we're running short of time," Sonnenberg answered. "You'll be getting a phone call in a very few minutes."

Peck stood up and motioned Burleson to his feet. "A disagreeable phone call, Marcus? I trust I'm not about to learn that the President of the United States is a former mechanic who once repaired your transmission."

"I try never to diminish, Duncan. Only elevate. Where are you off to, by the way?"

"I'm afraid I must rescind my early concern for your woodwork, Marcus."

*   *   *

"Charley?"

"peck thinks you're here. he hopes you're here. he thinks sonnenberg is talking to you and harrigan more than him."

Baker repeated Charley's message to Harrigan.

"Like the man said, lad"—Harrigan pointed to the shaft above the air conditioner—"we'll know when to leave. It sounds like things are about to get nasty."

"Jared?" It was Sonnenberg's voice coming from the speaker.

"Yeah?" Harrigan answered for him.

"They can't hear this speaker, Mr. Harrigan, although they will when they reach the basement. Do two things for me, please. First, make sure you haven't fiddled with the setting of the air conditioner. In fact, turn it up to its loudest setting. Next, go at once, but wait in the covered well at the end of that shaft until it seems prudent to take your leave."

"One more time, Doctor." Baker spoke to the microphone. "Where are they?"

"To the park, Jared. And you, Mr. Harrigan. Off with you both. Truth and justice await you there."

"Report, Douglas." Duncan Peck stood in the driveway, Burleson at his side, addressing his man Peterson. Michael Biaggi stood near, looking furtively into Peck's eyes for some sign of what might have been said.

"Sonnenberg's people are all gone, sir. The five our men tried to pick up, anyway. And they're all traveling light from the look of their apartments. Most personal effects are still there. I have a two-man team covering each location for when they return."

Peck turned to Burleson. "A probably useless measure, Edward, but leave them. If their homes are like this one, the remaining personal effects have been shed like the skin of a snake. A pity. I'd almost have been tempted to bargain all five for one Jared Baker."

"We're also having a difficult time with the direction finders, sir," Peterson continued. "He's set up a series of signal relays somehow. We've triangulated five different locations as the signal source, and before we can check out one he switches to another. Some are very close. One's coming all the way from a boatyard down on the Sound."

"A boat, you say?"

"I assume so, sir. I have a man checking to see if there's a berth in Sonnenberg's name."

"There probably is," Peck mused. "And boats have radio equipment. Although I can't think why he'd ensconce himself in anything so minimally mobile. On the other hand, Sonnenberg is nothing if not perverse. Send a man, Douglas. Have a second man prepared to place an immediate trace on a telephone call it appears I'm to receive here. With the rest, seal off this house and let us begin pulling it apart."

In a small lunchroom in Greeley, Colorado, two thousand miles west, Moon Huggins looked up in distaste at the black man slowly stirring coffee at the far end of the counter. Moon knew this was one of those smart-ass niggers the second he laid eyes on him. A three-hundred-dollar suit he probably paid for by selling his wife's black ass or peddlin' drugs to decent white folks. Even a vest, for Christ's sake. Walkin' in here and askin' for coffee and a sweet roll like he had all the right in the world, ploppin' down that briefcase on the next stool just like it was his. Ain't even drinking. Took one sip and he just sits there stirrin', happy as a hog because he got a white man waitin' on him.

Things just ain't the same no more. At least not here in Greeley. But it ain't changed all so damned much down in Tupelo. Not that I could ever go back there, likely. Picture him walkin' into a white man's place in Tupelo with his big flat nose in the air sayin', "Good morning, my man. Coffee and a pecan roll, if you please." Shee-it. Sumbitch probably never had a pair of shoes until some Jew commie got hold of him and filled his burr head with liquid shit. Speakin' of which . . .

"Hey, Ira?"

A heavyset man wearing laced boots and a red hunting jacket looked up from a newspaper. He was dressed too warmly, even for an early Colorado autumn. But hunting clothes told people he was a mountain man and summer clothes didn't. Ira hated summer. He didn't much like niggers either.

"Yo, Moon," he answered.

"You hear the one about the nigger who had diarrhea?"

Ira chuckled to himself. A third white man, a salesman according to the sample case at the base of his stool, glanced sorrowfully at the black man and lowered his head.

"Can't say I have, Moon." He closed his newspaper and pushed it aside. "What about the nigger who had diarrhea?"

"He thought he was meltin'." Moon Huggins slapped a palm down on the counter and guffawed. Ira chuckled again and winked his encouragement.

The salesman bit his lip. He reached into his pocket for a bill, which he waved toward Moon. Moon was glad to see that. If that ham and egg salesman was to leave, maybe him and Ira could have some fun with the nigger, providin' of course he wasn't smart enough to get his black ass out of here. Which it appears he ain't. Look at him. Just sittin' there with one of them superior eye smiles, too dumb to know what's in our heads to do to him if we get half an excuse. What's that he's doin'? Rubbin' up and down the sides of his cup with a handkerchief as if his damned snot rag was cleaner than my cup.

"Somethin' the matter with that cup, boy?"

"It's just fine, sir. Thank you." The black man lifted the cup to his lips and sipped, still holding it with his handkerchief. "I had the impression you'd rather not have me touch any of your fine china." Next he dampened his cloth in the coffee and began buffing away smudges on the counter itself. Ira stood up from his table, his eyes shifting between Moon and the black man. Moon's good humor had faded.

"Are you tryin' to be smart with me, boy?" He reached under his cash register and pulled out an old bung starter he kept there for troublemakers. Moon rested it on the counter a few feet from the black man.

"Not at all, sir. In any case, I'll be leaving shortly." The black man turned on his stool and flipped open the briefcase that had been sitting there. His politeness irritated Moon all the more.

"Don't go settlin' in here with that." Moon gestured toward the briefcase. "It ain't no readin' room. You want to read, you can haul ass down to Denver, where they got one of them black studies places with books all about where niggers come from and how one of them figured new ways to use peanuts. Hey, Ira. Don't that tell you somethin'? White folks can send TV cameras to outer space, but all the niggers are good for is figurin' out that if you mash down peanuts real good you got peanut butter. You ought to go look it up, nigger. You won't be so ignorant."

"Thank you just the same, Mr. Boley, but I've been there."

The color drained from Moon Huggins's face. "What was that, boy? What did you call me?"

"I called you Mr. Boley. You're Raymond Boley from Tupelo, Mississippi." Howard Twilley slid a hand over the open briefcase and then returned it, no longer empty, to the edge of the counter. Moon Huggins stared down across the length of a large-caliber pistol. Fitted to its muzzle was a dull black cylinder six inches long and as wide as a half-dollar.

"What the hell?" Moon's voice rose several notes. He pressed backward, crowding a stack of dishes. Ira took a step, snatching up a catsup bottle by its neck. A patient sidelong stare by Twilley caused him to think better of it. Ira put back the bottle.

"Mr. Boley," he said softly, "would you step out from behind that counter, please? Thank you. Just move toward those washroom doors if you will." He waved the foot-long weapon toward the hunter. "You first, Ira. Get on in there, please. The ladies' room."

"Is . . . is this a holdup?" It was the salesman.

"No sir," Twilley answered. "You and your property are perfectly safe. But I have to ask you to follow Ira there for just a little while." The salesman slid from his stool and backed toward the door Twilley indicated, glancing at his sample case only when Twilley looked away. Ira hesitated. Then, with a snort of contempt, he turned his back on the gun and fell in slowly behind the salesman. Twilley stepped to the front door, which he swung shut and bolted, drawing a grimy curtain over the glass and turning a plastic Dr. Pepper sign to the side that read CLOSED.

Boley entered the ladies' room last. With a guiding touch from Twilley, he took his place next to Ira against the far wall. There was no window. Twilley motioned to the salesman and directed him to a stool in front of a cracked and peeling mirror.

"Sit here?" the man asked, a deep shudder in his voice.

"If you don't mind, sir." Twilley turned toward the hunter. "Ira," he asked, "did you know Mr. Boley down in Tupelo by chance?"

"I got nothin' to say to you."

"Don't you mean, 'I got nothin' to say to you, nigger'?"

"You know what you are."

The pistol spat once and Ira's right leg whipped backward. It struck with such force that his boot smashed a hole in the plaster wall. A spray of blood traced a crescent on the plaster and on the white tile floor. Boley's eyes went wide and the salesman yelped as Ira crashed to the floor. Twilley stretched a calming hand toward the salesman but kept his eyes on Ira.

"Do you recall my question, Ira?"

Ira nodded but seemed unable to speak through his tightened jaw. Twilley pointed the pistol toward his other leg.

"Don't!" he gasped. "No, I didn't . . . I never been to Tupelo."

"You became acquainted for the first time here in Greeley?"

"Yeah . . . No . . . We met near here. On an elk hunt."

"And your friendship blossomed, based on a mutual distaste for us niggers?"

"Wha . . . ?"

"I'm asking whether you're both white supremacists of any sort."

"Well . . . No . . . Yeah . . . It ain't . . ." Ira was close to retching from the pain and shock of his wound. "It ain't personal. . . . We just . . ." He dropped his head, unable to deny his beliefs in front of his friend and even less able to articulate an expression of his philosophy that an armed black man might find acceptable.

"I guess it won't surprise you too much, Ira, to learn that this man is in fact Raymond Boley, Ray-Ray to his friends. Or that Ray-Ray was a Klan member." Twilley waved his pistol toward the transfixed restaurant owner. "Mr. Boley? Ray-Ray? Would you care to tell him the rest?"

Huggins-Boley could only twitch his head to one side.

"Mr. Boley is a modest man. The fact is, he's one good old boy who really knows how to handle us niggers. He personally castrated a fifteen-year-old black child." The last word was a hiss when Howard spoke it. But for that, his tone and manner remained icily polite. "Among his many other heroics, Mr. Boley also took part in the shotgun murders of an elderly couple who sought to file criminal charges against him. Quite a man, wasn't he, Ira? I bet it's hard to imagine that this quaking coward was that same avenging knight of the South."

Twilley turned toward the salesman, who was also trembling. The salesman thought he saw a wave of sympathy, even kindness, cross the black man's face. Then it was gone.

"Mr. Boley," he said, approaching the terrified counterman, "did you hear the one about the Klansman who had diarrhea?" His face was now within inches of Boley's. The pistol was somewhere below. Absurdly, the Klansman tried to smile. Twilley smiled with him.

The gun spat again. Quieter this time. Boley felt his body lifting to his toes. A curious look of relief came into his eyes as his brain argued that because the sound of the shot was different, and since the pain was not great, perhaps he had not been shot. Perhaps it was only a knee that smashed into him. Boley stood for a long moment flattened high on the wall before his legs began to melt beneath him. He felt the wetness on his legs, and his fingers reached to discover its source as he slid down the wall. And then he knew. Boley crumpled over, his mouth sucking air like a landed fish.

"You have to wait for the punch line, Mr. Boley," said the black man, stepping back. "You remember. About the Klansman who had diarrhea."

Boley made a choking sound.

"It was because some nigger shot off his balls, Mr. Boley."

The gun spat twice more. Before he fainted, Ray-Ray Boley watched both his kneecaps exploded through his trousers.

The salesman too looked as though he would fall. Twilley stepped over Boley and placed a steadying hand on his shoulder.

"Sir, it's the truth you won't be harmed," he told him. "Do you think you can get hold of yourself for a few minutes?"

The salesman jerked his head.

"My name is Ben. Ben Coffey." The black man's manner was now relaxed and friendly. "Would you mind telling me your name?"

"T-Tom. It's Tom Peebles."

"Do you know these two, Tom?"

"No. I'm . . . I'm from Boulder. I just wanted breakfast."

"Traveling salesman, huh? What do you sell, Tom?"

Peebles's lips moved, but he seemed reluctant to speak.

"No matter, Tom. Just making conversation." The black man looked at his watch and jerked his head to indicate that the subject was changing. "Tom, I'd like you to make a phone call for me."

A lamp on the desk in Sonnenberg's study had switched on. "That will be your call, Duncan," Sonnenberg's voice told him. "Just pick up the receiver. I don't like phones that ring. They have a certain rudeness to them."

Peck considered denying Sonnenberg whatever prank he'd planned by ignoring the call. But that petty satisfaction might deny him knowledge he could use. He reached for the phone and gave his name.

A man, a frightened man, identified himself with a name Peck did not recognize. Peck could hear another voice speaking softly, instructing the man Peebles who placed the call. "Just tell him what happened here, Tom. Tell him everything you saw."

Duncan Peck flushed as he listened. He covered one ear against the din made by Michael Biaggi, who was in the study, kicking out some paneling that sounded hollow. "Michael!" he snapped. Biaggi stopped and Peck waved him from the room.

"The man, Boley. Is he dead?"

"No sir. Um, I'm to tell you that he's been slowed down considerably. Sir, you understand I have nothing to do with this?"

"Perfectly, yes," Peck answered. "Who is the man telling you what to say, Mr. Peebles? Did he give a name?"

"Ben Coffey, sir. He wants me to be sure you know that. He says you can't plan on Boley to run any more errands for you and that he'll be slowing down one or two more just to make sure you get the message."

"What message specifically, Mr. Peebles?"

"He says Dr. . . . Sonnenberg? . . . He says Dr. Sonnenberg will explain everything. He says I have to

hang up now, sir. I really have to. He has this gun—"
The connection was broken.

Peck, his jaw tight, pulled out his notebook and
again began scribbling furiously. With a wave, he sum-
moned Ed Burleson and handed him the result.
Burleson's eyebrows rose, but Peck shut off further conversation with a light shove toward the door.

"I bet I know what it says, Duncan." Sonnenberg's
voice was pleasant. "Get thee our men to Greeley. Seal
off this. Cordon off that. FBI men to the airports and bus
stations. It all sounds very exciting. I think, however, that
Benjamin will anticipate a certain amount of hostile activity."

"There is a point to this, I suppose, Marcus?"

"I should think it would be obvious. You're being offered a lesson in humility, Duncan. I hope you'll profit by
it. Once I've painfully demonstrated that you can't hide
anyone I can't find, my hope is that you will curtail certain of the tawdry activities of your people in the field.
Another will be punished today and occasionally in the
future just to let you know I'm paying attention. Benjamin needs the exercise. I'm afraid his situation in Dayton
was beginning to pall. In truth, he has you to thank for
providing a timely outlet for his energies."

"I'll have your head, Marcus," Duncan Peck hissed
through his teeth. "I will have your head or you will have
mine. There will be no other way."

"One never knows, does one, Duncan." Peck heard
the clicking of switches. "Oops! Here comes one of your
worthies dashing breathlessly from the basement. He
seems to have found something exciting."

Ben Coffey took a dishtowel and used a carving knife to
slice it into several long strips.

"Tourniquets, Tom," he said. "Let's go back inside
there and you can tie up old Ray-Ray's legs. We don't
want him bleeding to death."

The salesman blinked. "Why . . . why did you do
this then?"

Ben steered him toward the ladies' room, indicating with a nod that he'd explain while Tom ministered.

Boley was unconscious. The man called Ira sat gripping his own leg high on the thigh, his eyes staring hatred toward Ben as he entered. Peebles began with Boley.

"You see, Tom," Ben said, glancing at Ira to make sure he had his attention as well, "Ray-Ray here got caught for what he did down in Tupelo. The FBI caught him and they had him cold. They decided, though, that Ray-Ray would be more useful as an informant than as a celebrity prisoner in some redneck jail. It ended up that a bunch of his friends got sent to the federal prison in Atlanta for violating the civil rights of the two old folks I mentioned. The specific violation was blowing their faces off with shotguns. Now, there's a few black people, me included, who'd like to have found Ray-Ray after that, but there are a hell of a lot more good ol' boys who also want him dead. They'll have an easier time catching up with him now that I've slowed him down some. Do you follow all this, Tom?"

"Yes."

"I don't believe a goddamned word of it," Ira croaked.

"Yes you do, Ira. Or you will when you read the papers. You just don't want to believe that a straight-thinking American like Ray-Ray here would turn on his straight-thinking, like-minded friends. You especially don't want to believe you got shot for a turd like that, but there it is, Ira."

"You go to hell."

Coffey shook his head in resignation. He thought of suggesting that Ira take one of those strips and tie up his own squirting wound before it pumped his life away, but what does a nigger know about anything? He turned his attention back to the salesman.

"Tom, the FBI will be having a long talk with you," he said, his voice low and confidential. "Would you remember to give them a message for me?"

The salesman nodded.

"You see, they turned Ray-Ray here over to the fellow you spoke to on the phone. He's supposed to hide people like Boley. That's his job. He hides them all right, and he keeps them hidden as long as they do as they're told and keep doing whatever they're good at whenever Duncan Peck wants. What Ray-Ray here is good at is shooting niggers, and he also doesn't mind doing that when Peck thinks a need arises, so everything works out fine. Peck has all kinds of experts. He has fellas that rob banks, that do kidnapping, fix elections, do extortions—just about any helpful little specialty Peck could need. You'll tell the FBI to take a look-see, won't you, Tom? Tell them I'm going to make a couple of other stops like this just to drive the point home."

Coffey rose to his feet. The revolver hung casually at his side.

"I'll be going now, Tom. I'm going to close this door, and I have to ask you not to open it for five minutes or so. If I see it move before I leave, I'm going to have to shoot through it. I'm also going to tear out the phone. After I'm gone, you find a filling station, call the police, then come back and pour yourself a cup of coffee until they come. Boley won't mind."

Tom Peebles nodded. He was beginning to sweat. There was something new in his eyes. Confusion, Coffey decided. Wondering why the Greeley police weren't here already after he'd told that man on the phone what was going on. But he knew Peck wouldn't have called the police. He knew he had time.

Coffey patted Tom Peebles on the shoulder and stepped through the door of the blood-splashed ladies' room, closing it behind him. He walked to his briefcase and laid the gun inside. He paused, thoughtful. Tom Peebles's expression still lingered in his mind. More than confusion, he thought. That was a fella trying to make up his mind about something. Coffey shook his head, dismissing the notion. Time to just get away from here. He closed his fingers over the briefcase lid.

"Ben?" came the frightened voice from a three-inch crack in the ladies' room door. "Please don't move, Ben."

Tom Peebles pushed through the doorway, a plated automatic pistol held tightly in both hands at shoulder level. Its line of sight stuttered nervously across Ben Coffey's chest. Coffey stared at the small chromed weapon for several seconds, making a disgusted face and shaking his head at his own carelessness.

"Oh, Tom," he said sadly, "now why would you be carrying a gun?"

"It's . . . I have a license."

"I should have guessed that when I saw you keeping your sample case close by. Jewelry salesman?"

Peebles hesitated. "I . . . call on doctors. Ethical drugs. There are addicts who'd . . ."

"That's fine, Tom. Now, instead of waving that gun around like you meant it, why don't you take your sample case and go pour a few pills into Ray and Ira back there."

"Ben, I can't. I can't let you shoot people and just walk out."

"You'd shoot me, Tom?"

"Please. I don't want to."

"You got your gun on him?" Ira's voice shouted from inside. "Shoot him, goddamnit." Ben could hear him struggling to stand on his one good leg. He would have to work fast.

"Look what's happening to your little gun, Tom. It's getting hot in your hands, isn't it? Hot and wet."

"No. No, it's—"

"I'm sorry, Tom. I'm terribly sorry you had to be put in this position. You don't want to be here. Lord knows you don't want to be holding that gun. And now that you are, you can't even shoot it. It's too hot. So hot it's starting to get soft."

My God, Peebles thought. My God, it's true. He could feel it. The gun was hot and soft and his hands were pressing right into the metal. He tried relaxing his grip, but that only made the front sight droop downward. It stiffened when he squeezed again, but now the butt was oozing out between his fingers. It couldn't be true but it was. The gun, he knew, would never fire. It would just fall apart if he tried to fire it. Even if the slide and firing pin still worked, the trigger would just bend back like putty if he put any pressure on it. He could feel it almost that way now. Hanging there. All limp and flaccid.

"Drop the gun on the floor, Tom. It won't go off. You'll see. It will bounce on the floor like a dead rubber ball."

"No . . ." The salesman stared helplessly at the mass in his hands.

"Just try it, Tom. You may as well. You're beginning to look pretty silly trying to scare someone with a gun that's dripping through your fingers."

Peebles parted his hands. The gun stuck fast to one of them. A look of revulsion contorted his face and he brushed frantically at the gun, as if it were a repulsive living thing. It fell away. Peebles watched it as it fell away and bounced crazily between his legs. Half in shock, he stared at the black man.

"Thank you, Tom," Ben Coffey said easily. "Now I think you were going to wait inside that ladies' room, weren't you? Why don't you tack on an extra five minutes for good measure."

Peebles nodded. He backed through the door, letting it close behind him.

And thank you, Dr. Sonnenberg. Coffey smiled to himself. You do teach some dandy things. And now, Benjamin, it's time to sneak your way down to old K.C. and visit some with another Pecker—hey, that's not bad— who puts bombs in cars for Mr. Peck when he's not off campin' and cat fishin' all by his lonesome along the big muddy, which is where me and him are going to . . .

His hand was on the bolt latch when the warning pulsed from the back of his brain. It came even before the *click* and *clack* of a slide opening and slamming home a cartridge. It came as the front door creaked open and its sound seemed to echo within him, like two doors opening at the same time. The ladies' room. Tom Peebles's gun. It bounced backward when he dropped it. It bounced backward into the ladies' room.

Ben Coffey never heard the shot. But he knew. He knew in those milliseconds when the world turned white in a flash so bright it made his head hurt. Then a blackness came in waves, as if a stone had been tossed in the middle of a pool of light, exploding its center and washing it away with a cooling, spreading darkness. It was much better dark. So peaceful. And it didn't hurt his eyes any longer. Ben Coffey knew he was dead. Sorry, Doc. I **know** what you'll say. Such a waste. And how I should **have** been patient. And about how I talk too much. But who'd have thought? Who'd have thought a nice fella like ol' Tom would . . .

Ira Teal hopped clumsily across the lunchroom floor, making his way from stool to stool, paying no attention to the stream of arterial blood that marked his route. The gore-slickened pistol slipped from his grasp and he fell on it, crawling now to the body of Ben Coffey slumped against the door.

"Goddamned nigger," he roared. Thrusting his arm out along the floor, he fired again, uselessly. "Goddamned smart-ass nigger!" Ira emptied the pistol into what remained of Benjamin Coffey and Howard Twilley.

Ira would bleed to death in the next five minutes.

At the base of Sonnenberg's cellar stairs, a blond young man named Sarsfield pointed out the wooden cabinet. "It's there, sir," he whispered to Duncan Peck. "The voice came from inside."

Burleson stepped from behind Peck and motioned Biaggi forward to a position at the cabinet's edge. Peck did not move closer, nor did he bother to lower his voice.

"What do you think, Edward? Are we to believe we have Dr. Sonnenberg trapped in his lair?"

"He'd be pretty stupid," Burleson said with a shrug, "but it's worth a look. I suggest you wait upstairs, sir."

Peck tilted his head back and casually examined the ceiling, seeing nothing, but certain another audiovisual device was hidden there somewhere. "What's it to be, Marcus?" he asked. "Are we to rush blindly to the sound of that voice, our better judgment blunted by your taunts?"

There was no answer. He turned and began climbing the stairs. "Have your men fire through the cabinet, Edward," he said over his shoulder, "and then enter if you feel it useful. Otherwise, let us withdraw from this house and put our alternate plan into action."

"You're no fun, Duncan." All but Peck tensed at the sound of Sonnenberg's voice, which came from inside the cabinet. "And as for your alternate plan, I trust one will come to mind before Edward here thinks to ask about it."

Peck paused near the top step, his drawn and taut face beyond the view of the others. Dignity, Duncan, he reminded himself. Dignity. He had no doubt, of course, that Sonnenberg planned yet another humiliation. Perhaps a fatal one this time. His choice was to walk away beaten or to endure it in the hope of salvaging something from it. Sonnenberg was quite right. There was no alternate plan worth the name. He turned slowly and lowered himself to a sitting position on the riser with what he hoped was the right touch of insouciance. "And what, Marcus," he asked wearily, "can I suppose I'd find behind that cabinet? A blank wall, perhaps? A witty message scrawled upon it?"

"Alas, Duncan." Sonnenberg chuckled. "You know me too well. Indeed, some thoughts of graffiti did cross my mind. 'Catch me before I clone more' was a particular favorite until a new notion replaced it. Come ahead, Duncan. The door swings open from the right."

Peck leaned forward, folding his arms across his knees, and languidly motioned Burleson forward with his fingertips. Burleson nodded and turned to Biaggi, who had chanced to be positioned at the end that swung open. Using hand signals, he ordered Biaggi to throw open the cabinet and enter low, indicating his own weapon as covering fire. Biaggi blanched and hesitated. Burleson showed teeth and signaled again with an impatient snap of his arm. Biaggi cursed to himself but could not refuse. He braced one palm against the cabinet's side and heaved it outward, then threw himself back against the protection of the wall. Peck scowled, noting Biaggi's imperfect response to Burleson's order, but put it aside as the glow from a small furnished room cast a corridor of light across the basement floor. He pushed himself erect and eased himself once more toward the lower stairs.

Peck could first see a thick Oriental carpet as he descended and then a bed. An old Morris chair and a floor lamp sat at the far end near an air conditioner. Now a row of cabinets came into view on the opposite side.

"On the wall, Duncan," Sonnenberg's voice told him. "My witty message is on the wall."

Burleson saw it first and gestured with his chin. A map of North America. Colored pins were well distributed across its surface. Peck's eyes went at once to the pins marked with black ribbon.

"Sonnenberg's people, sir?" Burleson asked.

"Hardly, Edward." Peck stared for a long minute. As much as he'd prepared himself for whatever slap of the face Sonnenberg had arranged, the sight of the map almost sickened him. Each pin was one of his own. His people. All of them, including the now-useless man marked by the pin just north of Denver and a soon-to-be-useless operative in the vicinity of Kansas City.

"Well done, Marcus," he said softly. "Very well done indeed."

"Gracious of you, Duncan. My files are rather impressive too. Poke about in them if you like."

"Marcus." Peck ran his fingers over the top of the nearest cabinet as if inspecting it for dust. "Should not the prudent man assume that the contents are either useless or misleading or that they'll blow up in our faces?"

"The prudent man certainly should, Duncan. One or all of the above. In fact, they're packed with thermite charges." A clicking sound came over the speaker. "Hear that, Duncan? It's a remote control device. The thermite charges are armed by the present setting of the air conditioner. They'll go off if the drawers are opened or if I set them off from here. Alarming, isn't it?"

Young Sarsfield stepped between Peck and the row of cabinets without hesitation, shielding Peck with his body. Burleson's hand closed over his shoulder, guiding him firmly toward the safety of the door. Biaggi too moved toward the cellar, but Burleson blocked him with a stiffened arm.

"My goodness, Duncan," Sonnenberg marveled, "where *do* you keep finding these people? These two at least seem absolutely convinced that their devotion to your well-being will be matched by your vaguest interest in theirs. It's so much easier to understand a sleazy wretch like Mr. Biaggi here."

There was more than fear on Biaggi's face. He had the look of a man waking from a nightmare only to find it had been real. It was the voice. Beneath its flippant rhythm and an accent that swung between faintly Brahmin and faintly European, beneath even its insults, Biaggi began catching the modulations of still another voice he'd heard. A voice that answered when he called a special number. A voice that caused money, large sums of it, to appear each month in a brokerage account he held under a Waspish name. A voice he'd first heard over the public phone of the Mobil station three blocks away. The phone that would begin ringing the moment he took up his post to watch and wait for Jared Baker. It was the same voice. The same and not the same.

"But not to worry, Duncan." Sonnenberg's voice was soothing. "I intend no harm to any of you. You'll begin feeding on yourselves soon enough."

Peck stopped in the doorway, resisting Burleson. "Then do I assume, Marcus," he asked, "that there's a point to this business about the thermite?"

When Sonnenberg answered, the easy, genial manner was gone. "I should have thought it was clear, old friend. I'm demonstrating that I can kill you if I choose, and I'll prove it if Mr. Burleson causes you to take another step. In letting you live, I am demonstrating my utter contempt for you as a man and as an adversary. You are also witnessing my capacity to teach you a lasting lesson."

Sonnenberg left him standing for a long moment as the message sank in.

"Go ahead, Duncan Peck," he urged. "Open any

cabinet you wish. Choose any pin you see on that map and pull the file that matches it. I have another set, of course, so you needn't worry about being tidy. Better yet, open the drawer marked A through F and pull the file on Mr. Biaggi here. Fascinating reading. But in fairness, naturally, you should allow him to riffle through yours."

Biaggi's knuckles went white against the grip of his weapon.

"Decisions, decisions, Mr. Biaggi. Do you bluff or do you shoot? Do you mow these three down and then set off the thermite to cover your tracks? But what if there isn't any thermite, Mr. Biaggi? What if there isn't even any file?"

Biaggi's eyes were wide. They darted around the room as if looking for an exit other than the one blocked by Ed Burleson and Peck.

"I'd bluff if I were you," Sonnenberg's voice offered. "Perhaps Duncan won't even open the drawer. Then, except for that stricken look on your face, you'd be able to deny knowing what batty old Sonnenberg is talking about."

Burleson shifted his position slightly. His Uzi's sights were now lined up on Michael Biaggi's chest. "Put your piece on safety, mister," he ordered.

"The feeding begins, Duncan. Big fish eats little fish. That will settle Mr. Biaggi's hash, but then there's the matter of your own file. Big Burleson fish and tiny blond fish here would have to be eaten too lest they nibble you to death. Next in line would be young Douglas Peterson, who even now is bounding across my kitchen floor. Welcome, Mr. Peterson. The more the merrier. In fact, bring all the rest. We'll have a community read followed by a feeding frenzy."

Peterson thundered down the basement stairs, then stopped abruptly, startled by his first sight of the revealed room and the frozen tableau inside. Peck raised a hand, warning him back.

"Sir?"

"It's all right, Douglas," Sonnenberg said, welcoming him. "No one here but us fishies."

Peterson blinked away his confusion. "Sir, I have to speak to you."

"Can it wait, Douglas? We have a situation here."

"No sir. I don't think so, sir."

"Can it be written down, Douglas?"

"Yes sir."

"Then do so, Douglas. Hand me a note and then return upstairs."

"Spoil sport," Sonnenberg muttered.

Peterson pulled out his notebook and scrawled a message, then left a space and scribbled another. His face shone with pleased excitement as he tore off the leaf and handed it to Peck.

"Duncan," Sonnenberg said, "I don't suppose you'd share the good news with me, considering the thermite and all."

Peck tried to read without expression. But the first item caused his lips to part involuntarily. By the time he reached the second item, a smile was tugging at the corners of his mouth.

"I'm afraid the second part is confidential, Marcus. But I'm more than delighted to share the first. Your man is dead."

There was a moment of silence. No one moved.

"Pray, what man, Duncan?" Sonnenberg asked.

"This one, you insufferable old lunatic." Peck reached the map in two steps and tore away the ribbon that hung near the city of Denver. "The one as black as this piece of crepe. Ben Coffey, Marcus or Ivor or whoever the hell you think you are. Ben Coffey is dead."

"How am I to believe that, Duncan?" Sonnenberg's voice was low and hoarse. Biaggi swallowed hard. Now he was sure he knew that sound.

"Dead, damn you." Duncan Peck's face was wild. A near-hysterical glee swept aside any thought of guns or fish or thermite. "He died of arrogance. He died of a very hard bullet from a very soft gun. Can I assume that has meaning to you, Marcus?"

"Duncan . . ."

"If you hurry, Marcus, you might salvage something

yet of your creation. If you rush out to Greeley quickly enough and can scrape enough brain tissue from the door of Boley's lunchroom and then scurry back to the street corners of Harlem, perhaps you can find another—"

"Goodbye, Duncan."

Ed Burleson heard the click. He dropped his weapon and flung Duncan Peck toward the doorway in a single motion. Biaggi's reflexes were just as fast. Slapping Sarsfield aside, he dove at the door and was airborne as the second click sounded. The room exploded into light. It seared the hair on the back of his head and came down like a lash across the back of his legs as he landed heavily on the body of Duncan Peck.

"Jesus!" Harrigan jumped at the funneled blast of heat that slapped him back against the wall of the well. He gasped, choking on the smoke that followed it. Half-blinded, he punched Baker's arm. "Let's go." He pointed upward.

Baker reached for the wooden grid above his head and heaved against the weight of the potted plants it supported.

"*baker.*"

"*Shut up, Abel.*"

Baker boosted Harrigan to the surface and scrambled up behind him, rolling to the grass out of reach of the toxic fumes. Harrigan, gun in hand and wiping tears from his eyes, crouched behind the well, his weapon trained first upon the sliding doors of Sonnenberg's living room. He saw men on their hands and knees below a rolling black curl. One crawled to the door and began smashing at it with a chair. He'd be busy awhile. Harrigan punched Baker again and pointed to the door cut on the stockade fence. Half-crawling, Baker reached it, but stopped at the sound of feet running on grass and the clacking of wood against wood.

"*baker.*"

"*No time, Abel.*"

The running man came into view, a golfer, his clubs

dancing wildly in the bag on his shoulder. Attracted by
the fire, Baker thought. He pushed past him and moved
onto the fairway. The golfer spun around, startled, then
slipped the golf bag from his shoulder and groped inside
as if selecting a club. A wooden clubhead exploded at his
touch, and the golfer slammed backward into a towering
rhododendron. Its branches seized his arms and hung
him there half-standing. Baker stared at a spreading stain
on the golfer's chest until Harrigan seized him and threw
him into the sparse cover of a boxwood.

"What just happened?" Baker blinked.

"I was about to shoot him. Someone else did."

"For what?" Baker flared. "For running to see what's
burning?"

Harrigan grunted in disgust. "I'm beginning to appreciate the beastie more by the minute. Where the hell
is he, by the way?"

"I can handle this, Harrigan."

"In a pig's ass."

Another running golfer rounded the fence at the far
end of Sonnenberg's property line, a short shotgun in-
congruous against his Izods. His eyes met Harrigan's and
seemed to widen in recognition. Then they winced, and
the golfer pitched forward soundlessly onto the turf.

"We got covering fire," Harrigan scanned the
treeline on the far side of the fairway but could see nothing. He pointed to an elevated green near the clubhouse
parking lot and shoved Baker in that direction. "Low and
fast." He rose into a runner's stance. "Let's get us one of
those cars."

"Roger?" In a grove of pin oaks partly hidden behind the
thirteenth green, Melanie Laver placed a hand on the
thigh of the man sitting on the golf cart next to her.
"Roger," she repeated, "you're all right, aren't you?"

"Sure," he answered. Hershey broke apart his rifle
with the turn of a screw and slipped the two halves
under the windbreaker on his lap. His eyes, Melanie
saw, were fixed upon Sonnenberg's house, but they were

dulled as if their focus was inward. Her hand stayed on his leg.

"It's right what you did, Roger," she told him gently. "You know they were ready to shoot Jared."

"I know."

"But it bothers you."

"Yes."

"You killed a lot of men when you were Captain Berner. Was that so different?"

"I can kill like he killed. But I can't forget like he could forget."

Melanie leaned over and kissed his cheek. "You're a much nicer man than he was, Roger."

Roger Hershey nodded. "I'm a nice man who kills people. There's something so wrong about this, Melanie."

She took his hand. "It'll be over soon."

Duncan Peck, singed and shaken, clung unsteadily to Sonnenberg's front gate as Ed Burleson dabbed a handkerchief against a cut on his forehead. He heard sirens, police sirens, close by and the klaxon of a fire truck not far behind them.

"Burn," he muttered.

"Sir?"

"Let the house burn, Edward. Keep them away."

Burleson frowned. "I can probably keep the local police out, sir, but I'm afraid even your credentials won't stop the firemen. They'll drive their hook-and-ladder right over this gate. My suggestion is we don't interfere with the firemen but otherwise quarantine the property."

Peck considered Burleson's suggestion and nodded. "The quarantine will include the press, of course?"

"Yes sir."

"What are our losses, Edward?"

"Two men shot, sir, presumably by whoever was hiding in the well. The cover's been thrown off, and there's a tunnel leading from the basement room. And Sarsfield died in the blast."

"The bodies?"

"In our van, sir. Except Sarsfield. The thermite probably won't leave anything of him at all."

"A pity." Peck sighed. "A brave young man."

"Yes sir. May I ask what you intend about Biaggi, sir?"

"He did save my life."

"Respectfully, sir, it's more likely that you got in his way."

"Hmmm." Peck acknowledged the possibility. In fact, he had no doubt of it. Nevertheless, a person of Biaggi's . . . flexibility . . . could occasionally be more useful than, say, an Edward Burleson, whose loyalty was beyond doubt but who would be just as loyal to a more senior government official should one choose to question him in the future. And one certainly would, particularly if the gunman in the well turned out to be the unendurably tiresome Connor Harrigan. Who else? Certainly not Sonnenberg, who'd have trouble climbing out of an automobile, let alone a two-foot tunnel and a six-foot well. And probably not Baker, at least where the shooting is concerned. Baker strangles, pummels and impales but he doesn't shoot. That's neither here nor there, however. The subject at hand is Michael Biaggi.

"I choose to take the charitable view, Edward," he answered finally. "Even if it's misplaced, our losses are such that Biaggi's value even as cannon fodder should not be minimized."

"Yes sir."

"The other business, Edward." Peck dropped his voice. "The subject of Peterson's most welcome note. Our people in New York are certain they have their man?"

"Yes sir. Our people report that he's uncooperative, but I've authorized questioning with prejudice."

"You're a very good man, Edward."

The smoke from the house stayed low. It rolled over the stockade fence like curls of dirty cotton and settled just above the close-cut grass. A growing ring of bystanders, neighbors and golfers, gathered at the edge of the property. A shame, Melanie thought. So many lovely things inside.

"Will he be coming soon?" she asked.

"Sonnenberg? Yes," Roger answered. "Soon now."

"Which house? It's that big gray one, isn't it?"

"The Dickerson house, yes. They're away. They're opening their Palm Beach house this week."

Palm Beach. She smiled. Palm Beach would be nice. In some ways nicer even than St. Croix, except that the people wouldn't be as much fun or as happy. In Palm Beach she could be a youngish socialite divorcée and learn to snort lines from silver trays with one pinkie in the air. And douche with Dom Perignon. Well, maybe not. Maybe Seattle would be better after all. A clean city. Clean and cold. At least too cold for a legitimate year-round tan. And running the bookstore Sonnenberg bought for her would be exciting in a gentle kind of way. She'd miss writing her column for the St. Croix newspaper, but she could always write a bookstore newsletter. Every month. And someday a nice, quiet, good-looking man would come in to find a book and he'd like her, and he'd start finding excuses to drop in more often. That was another nice thing about bookstores. Lots of reasons to drop in and stay awhile. Her name was going to be Molly. Molly Barrett. Hey! How about Wimpole Street for the name of the bookstore? Molly, the Barrett of Wimpole Street. What a gas!

"Roger?"

"Umm?"

"Are the Dickersons real? I mean, have they always been the Dickersons?"

"They're real." Hershey grinned. "Sonnenberg says only a vengeful God could make an Allison Dickerson. The house comes in handy, though. Doc went in to set up an intercom security system for them, and their kitchen ended up looking like Mission Control."

"It's good to see you smile, Roger."

"Yeah." The smile faded.

"Nuts! I made you self-conscious, didn't I?"

Hershey touched her hand reassuringly, but for several minutes he didn't speak. Then, "Melanie?"

"Yes, Roger?"

"Do you ever think you're crazy?"

"No." She turned to look into his face. "I'm not crazy, Roger. Neither are you."

"You never feel as if you're not real? Like you asked about the Dickersons?"

"Oh, Roger." Melanie slipped an arm around his shoulder. "All that happened is we took different names and changed a few habits. And we learned to use our minds a little differently than those people." She gestured toward the men and women who stood watching the fire's progress. "Look at them, Roger. What do you see?"

"Just people."

"Ordinary people, Roger. Bored people. Quiet desperation people. Most of them are miserable and half of them would leap at a chance to be like us. To be almost anything they could want to be. To start whole new lives without ever looking back."

"Melanie?" Roger Hershey gave her a squeeze.

"Yes?"

"You know that's a bunch of bullshit, don't you?"

"Yes."

17

It was almost five. Manhattan's homebound traffic crawled northward in fits and starts while the southbound lanes were nearly empty. Connor Harrigan drove slowly nonetheless, unwilling to risk being stopped for a speeding violation in a car lately stolen from the parking lot of the Westchester Country Club. Two hot-wired ignition cables swung freely below the dashboard. He eased the accelerator further at the warning sign for the Ninety-sixth Street exit and allowed the car to drift into the right lane of the FDR Drive. Baker, peering forward from the passenger seat, had pointed in that direction.

"You got any particular destination in mind?" Harrigan asked.

"Just the park." Baker answered with a squint of annoyance, as if his concentration had been interrupted. "Go down York Avenue and then cut crosstown to the Seventy-second Street entrance."

"While you're talking to your pals, ask them whether Peck got his ass blown off in that fire back there."

Baker shrugged, indicating that he didn't know and they wouldn't either. Nor did he much care. He had Tina on his mind. Tina and Tanner Burke.

"What about the message Peck got that made Sonnenberg decide playtime was over?"

"Ben Coffey?" The sadness of that news had barely struck him in the rush to escape the smoke and the guns.

It was hard to imagine that Howard—Ben—was dead. So much talent. So much torment. So much waste. So little in common between them and yet so much. He was the first, perhaps the only one until Tanner, to whom Baker could talk. The only one who understood the loneliness that came with the talent. The sense of being apart.

"No," Harrigan answered, "I mean the second part. Peck read that and acted like he had something big going for him."

"What about it, Charley?"

"i don't know."

"I . . . Charley doesn't know," he told Harrigan. "All that means is that it wasn't about me or Sonnenberg. Charley would have heard."

"You're sure?" Harrigan raised an eyebrow. "How could it not be about Sonnenberg?"

Baker shrugged again and returned his concentration to Tina. They were on York Avenue headed south but barely moving. A sewer maintenance crew at Ninetieth Street caused a bottleneck that brought traffic almost to a halt.

"Baker, stop with the shrugs," Harrigan snapped. "I'm trying to anticipate the guy if he's still on his feet."

"I don't know, Harrigan," Baker answered patiently.

"Then help me figure, for Christ's sake. What did you do, give up thinking when you got Charley and the beastie?"

"I happen to have something more important on my mind, Harrigan."

Connor Harrigan ignored the answer. "It's not you, it's not Sonnenberg, and it's not Coffey because they covered him in part one. Could Peck's people have nailed whoever helped you down at the Plaza?"

"No." That was Roger and Melanie. Baker wasn't sure whether Harrigan knew their current names or what good the knowledge might do him. But there seemed no point in volunteering it. "It's the same two who were covering us on the golf course. They're probably safe. They won't go back to the lives they had before."

"Okay, scratch five. Who does that leave?" The car

moved forward into the intersection. A line of buses blocked most of the next street.

"Isn't there a faster way to get to the park? Turn right here, Harrigan. Try Second Avenue."

"Where in the park, by the way?"

"Sonnenberg only said the park."

Harrigan heaved a sigh and swung onto Ninetieth Street, headed west. "That park is five miles long, Baker, and maybe two miles across. What do you say we get a little more specific."

"I told you. Seventy-second Street." Baker said this as if he had a reason. There was none. Only that the Seventy-second Street entrance had led him once before to Tanner Burke."

"tanner burke."

"What about Tanner, Charley?"

"go slow, baker."

"Charley says slow down." Baker tapped Harrigan's arm.

"What for? The wimp sniffs out radar too?"

"He's not a wimp, Harrigan. He's my friend. Slow down. I think he hears something."

Harrigan rolled his eyes but slowed the car to a jogger's pace.

"Charley, is it Tanner?"

"i think so. keep thinking tanner, baker. i think she hears when you think tanner."

"What about Tina?" Baker's fingers dug into the padded dashboard.

"i don't know. there, baker. i heard tanner. she's calling you, baker." Harrigan turned left onto Second Avenue. He watched Baker, fascinated. Baker's eyes were open but they seemed sightless. The car reached Eighty-sixth Street.

"no, baker. she's behind us now. she was on that street with trees."

"Harrigan." Baker blinked. "Take your next right and go back. Tanner's here someplace."

"You're shitting me."

"Just go right."

Harrigan signaled onto Eighty-third Street toward Third Avenue. His eyes closed, Baker directed two more right turns and then, with a waving motion of his hand, told Harrigan to slow and then stop. He opened his eyes to see a red brownstone with a closed antique shop on the first floor. Baker's face brightened.

"She's here," he said, reaching for the door latch. Harrigan grabbed his shoulder.

"Wait a second." Harrigan's face was disbelieving. "You mean she's here? Right here in this red dump?"

Baker nodded and shook off his hand. "Let's go," he said.

"Hold it," Harrigan insisted. "I don't want to sound negative or anything, but don't you think this is a little bit incredible? I mean, we drive into a city this size looking for a dame we're not even sure is here and we go almost straight to her address?"

"*What about that, Charley?*"

"*you mean what i think?*"

"*Please, Charley.*"

"*i think sonnenberg knows where she is. sonnenberg knows we can hear if we get close enough. sonnenberg knows when he says go to the park there's only this way.*"

"Thank you, Charley." Baker understood.

"*thank you, baker. it was nice what you said about how i'm your friend.*"

"You're welcome, Charley." Baker turned to Harrigan. "It's not so incredible. I'll explain later. *Charley, is she alone?*"

"*she doesn't know. she thinks so. there's a thing on her eyes so she can't see, but she knows you're here. she's yelling 'jared' but not out loud in case someone's there.*"

"Let's go." Baker stepped to the street.

Harrigan, his gun drawn, followed Baker up the narrow stairs leading to the only apartment on the second floor. "Shit!" he muttered, noting the heavy metal-clad door with three different locks cut into it. "Half this goddamned town is like a fort these days. That bottom lock is for a cane bolt on the other side. Your friend Charley got us this far, see if he can dig up a set of keys."

"Abel?"

"i can open it, baker."

"If there's no one inside to hurt us, Abel. I want you back before Tanner sees you."

"she saw charley. now you like charley."

"It's not the same, Abel. Just open the door. No more."

Baker looked at Harrigan and then at his revolver. "Don't get nervous with that," he told him. "Abel's going to let us in." Harrigan's lips parted and he shook his head. He understood Baker's words, but their meaning was slower to penetrate.

"Abel. Come out, Abel."

Harrigan fought his impulse to move out of Abel's reach. At last he was seeing it. All of it. And still his mind could not believe it. He watched as a man he'd come to know, even like, was changing before his eyes into something else in steps that were impossible to describe because they were so very small. Nothing changed, yet everything changed. The effect was staggering. Now there was a different man, a man Harrigan neither knew nor liked, a man who made Connor Harrigan wish he could turn and run. The man smiled at him and nodded once. A greeting. Harrigan shivered.

Abel turned from Harrigan and placed both hands over the tarnished doorknob. He lifted slowly. Harrigan heard a grinding sound above the door and looked up. The lintel was buckling. Splintering. Thick chips of layered paint came away and fell over Abel's shoulders. A growing strip of light appeared at the base of the heavy door. Abel released the knob, now half-crushed and bent on its spindle toward the ceiling. Stepping away, he smiled again at Harrigan, then raised one foot and smashed it against the door. It reeled inward under the blow, tearing loose from its hinges.

Abel bowed toward Harrigan, still smiling terribly, and with a sweep of his arm invited Harrigan to enter. Harrigan returned a show of teeth and stepped past him. As he looked away, he felt a small sting on the fingers of his right hand. Harrigan glanced down. The fingers of his gun hand met. The hand was empty. Harrigan crouched and spun, his arms raised in a defense he knew was futile against the hands that had snatched away his weapon so quickly that he'd sensed no motion. But there was no attack. There was only Abel smiling at him, the revolver held out on the flat palm of one hand. Harrigan swallowed and took back the weapon Abel offered, then stepped through the door, struggling to ignore the chill on the back of his neck.

A room on the left, the kitchen, was empty. A short hallway, dark with faded beige paint, led to an even darker living room and a series of doors at the other end. The first one Harrigan reached was a walk-in closet. Harrigan noted a curious mixture of clothing inside but turned away. The second door was a bathroom. The light from a small opaque window showed fixtures stained by years of dripping faucets and pink tiles cracked by the building's settling. He found Tanner Burke behind the middle door.

She was taped to a chair. More packing tape, with a folded washcloth underneath, covered her eyes. Another strip covered her mouth. She cocked her head fearfully at the squeak of the floorboards under Harrigan.

"It's Connor, miss. I'm with Jared." He reached first for the blindfold.

"get back, abel. quickly."

"Mmmph!" Tanner's head bobbed up and down. Her chest heaved in relief. Harrigan pried loose a corner of the blindfold, enough to grip. "This'll sting, lass. Hold on."

"abel!"

Harrigan tore at the tape. Tanner's eyes winced at the pain and the light but flashed gratefully at Harrigan. Now they found Jared Baker and struggled to focus on his face.

Abel moved forward. With one hand he reached for the remaining tape that gagged her and stripped it brutally from her mouth. He grinned at her. He grinned until Baker was far enough back to cover his face with his hands.

                    *   *   *

Tina Baker wondered dimly where they'd taken her this
time. She knew she should be concerned, and that Tanner . . . Liz . . . got all upset when she was being carried
out, but it was just too hard to keep her mind on anything. It was fairly far, across a bridge and back partly
toward Connecticut. Westchester someplace. A big stone
house at the end of a long driveway. A big couch in a
room that was too cold and too dark. Stanley knew she
was cold. He'd put his jacket over her, and now he was
trying to start a fire in one of those big carved fireplaces
like they had in castles.

     He wasn't good at it. He just used logs and a lot of
newspaper, but the fire was catching anyway. Its light
flickered upon the shape of another man who stood in a
doorway, watching her. He was dressed all in black. The
man wore one of those old-fashioned Hombergs low on
his forehead and a black coat with a big collar turned up
around his cheeks. She couldn't see much of his face.
Only that he was staring at her in a way that began to
make her afraid. Like that judge. The one in the hospital
who stood staring at her and wanted to know why his son
screamed and she did not. It wasn't him. She knew that
the judge was dead. It was just that this man reminded
her of him and that there was something familiar about
him. She didn't know what. After that last needle it was
hard to think about anything for very long.

     "Stanley," the man said. He spoke, she thought, like
something was wrong with his throat.

     "Yes, Mr. Tortora."

     "Is everything attended to, Stanley?"

     "The kid's ready." Stanley pointed. "She ain't under
too deep. Two of Dr. Sonnenberg's associates are bringing his boat down to the Seventy-second Street Basin,
then they're gonna meet us. If the alarm systems are off,
we're all set."

     "That has been attended to, Stanley. And the five
guards and their dogs have been relieved."

     "Mr. Tortora." Stanley looked into his eyes. "You're
sure you want to go through with this?"

"It's quite necessary, Stanley."

"How about Sonnenberg? I mean, with him being upset about his guy Coffey, maybe he should get more rest first."

"He's resting now, Stanley. He is gratified by your concern. Does the child know where we're going?"

Stanley shrugged. "I ain't told her."

"Then we'll observe her powers of deduction as well. Come, Stanley. It is time to go to the park."

It was less than an hour since the sun had set, yet the night seemed deeper where they were. Baker chose the place where they would wait and listen. It was along the low path that led to the zoo, not far from where he'd first heard Tanner's scream.

He heard many sounds and voices now. Too many. Like an untuned radio, they crossed and fought each other. There were the zoo sounds. The grunts of nocturnal hunters frustrated by the bars of their cages. Smaller animals, their natural prey, bleated alarms as if doubting the security of their own enclosures. From the roadway overhead he heard the occasional hum of homebound cars. From Tanner, who shivered on a rock nearby with Connor Harrigan, he heard thoughts of Tina, a gun, something about a gun, and of Abel. It was the thoughts of Abel that made her cold. Harrigan too had thoughts of Abel but mostly about a man called Stanley. Satisfied thoughts. Thoughts of a man who'd solved a puzzle. Baker could not follow exactly. It was about Stanley Levy, and Tortora, and Sonnenberg, and the woman Tanner told about who looked like Stanley. The pieces were there, but they would not come together in Baker's mind the way they seemed to be assembling in Harrigan's. Something blocked them. Nonsense nursery rhymes all garbled up and walls of brick. It was even more confused when Charley listened. Baker stopped trying. He tried to push his thoughts of Tanner and Harrigan aside like so many cobwebs in the dark and focus instead on Tina.

Tina. He could see her in his mind, but he knew

that what he saw could not be happening. Tina was drifting through time. Through history. He saw her first in the land of the Egyptian kings, floating over flat deserts lit by stars, past ancient tombs and limestone carvings. Now she floated forward in time, vaulting over centuries. It was the age of Ivanhoe. There were jousting knights with lances thrust forward. Weapons that cut and flailed. Foot soldiers in visored helmets standing stiffly at attention when she passed.

He was hearing Tina, he was sure, but he was hearing her in a dream she must be having. She was asleep. Still drugged, more likely. And dreaming about places she had read about but never seen. She did not seem troubled. She was smiling. There was a new place now. A place that was real. They'd been there once together. Where? Charley? Do you know where that is?

"Jared." Tanner touched his shoulder. Then her arms hugged each other against a chill that was not in the air.

"Take my jacket," he said. Baker slipped off the suede coat that had covered her a night earlier and put it over her. She placed an arm around his waist before he could step away and steered him back toward Connor Harrigan.

"We'll find her," she whispered, leaning into his chest. "I'm so sorry, Jared."

"Sorry?" He looked down at her. "What could you have to be sorry about?"

"A lot, I guess," she said softly, not caring that Harrigan could hear. "For not being able to look at you on the way over here. For not having met some other way. Especially for not taking care of Tina."

"That wasn't your fault at all," Baker told her.

"That's the truth, lass," Harrigan added. "I didn't do so well against Stanley myself."

Tanner gripped the leather purse slung over her shoulder and held it out toward Harrigan. "I have the gun you gave me," she said. "I had it all the time. I just couldn't bring myself to use it."

"Stanley would have pinned it to your hand, lass, before you even had a chance to point it."

"I had the chance," she insisted. "Before he tied me up he left us alone for a minute. It's not that I was afraid to reach into my purse for it. There's just been so much blood and dying that I . . ." She began to cry. Baker stood looking helpless until a glare from Connor Harrigan encouraged him to hold her.

Tanner tensed at his touch. It was only for the smallest moment, but Baker felt it and Harrigan saw it.

"It's the beastie, isn't it, lass."

She shook her head but changed it quickly to a nod. "I'm trying not to let it bother me."

Baker loosened his hold around her body. There was despair on his face. He looked as if he would drop his arms and walk away. Don't you dare, Harrigan's eyes told Baker.

"It bothered me," Connor said to her. "It scared the bejaysus out of me, himself standing and grinning like a maniac about to pounce. And if it scared a tough old horse like myself, I'd have expected you to swoon dead away. But you're made of good stuff, lass. So is Baker here. If there's a way to put this other business aside, the two of you should look for it. The beastie wants Baker to himself, Miss Burke. We knew that in your hotel room. He wanted us to see him because he wanted to scare us off, especially you. It's up to you whether you let him."

Baker, through his sadness, almost smiled. Harrigan saw it. Why is that funny, Baker? he asked in his mind.

Baker looked away. Harrigan was sincere, he knew, in his fashion. Harrigan liked him. He liked Tanner. He liked them both together. Together best of all. Baker would be so much easier to find after tonight if they were together. But it wouldn't work. Not as long as Abel was around. Even the memory of Abel. And you're wrong, Harrigan. Abel wasn't trying to scare you back at Levy's place. He wasn't trying to scare you at all.

"I don't think . . ." Tanner shut her eyes and then opened them, blinking. "I don't think he was trying to scare me," she told Harrigan. "He wasn't trying to scare you either." She looked up at Baker as if asking him to complete the thought. "I think he was trying to be . . ."

"Nice." Baker supplied the word.

"Nice?" Harrigan recalled the grin he'd seen only on Halloween masks and Cheshire cats.

"He wanted you to like him." Baker looked at his shoes.

"That was Abel's idea of being engaging?"

"More or less. What he really wanted was to show me I didn't have to hide him away. While he was at it, that gun business was to show you he could have hurt you if he wanted."

"Nice." Harrigan chewed upon the word. The expression on his face was a mixture of relief and bemusement. "You'll tell the beastie for me, Baker, that he could use an hour or two with Dale Carnegie."

"*baker.*"

"Yes."

"*i hear her, baker. she's in williamsburg. it's where she went a long time ago with you and sarah.*"

"No, Charley. Williamsburg is too far. It's in Virginia."

"*yes. yes. williamsburg houses and williamsburg rooms, where they have candle things on the walls and pictures of dead people and big high beds that have roofs on them.*"

"I saw Williamsburg too, Charley, but it's because she's remembering it and dreaming it. Where is she having the dream?"

"*williamsburg,*" Charley insisted.

Tanner cocked her head. "Williamsburg?"

Baker stared at her. "You can hear him?"

"Who?" She shivered again.

"Charley. Could you just hear Charley?"

"No." Her eyes opened wide. "I was thinking about Tina. Suddenly I imagined her in Williamsburg, Virginia. I've never even been there."

"Well, she can't be there," Baker repeated, passing over Tanner's astonishment at having the thought at all. "If we hear her, she's someplace close."

"*williamsburg, tortora. sonnenberg.*"

"*Wait a minute, Charley. You're hearing Sonnenberg and Tortora too in Williamsburg?*"

"*tortora. williamsburg. sometimes sonnenberg.*"

"*How come you can hear Sonnenberg all of a sudden?*"

"*just a little. i don't know, baker.*"

"Well, I know, damnit," he said aloud.

"You know what, lad?" Harrigan's concentration was intense.

"It's Charley." Baker's eyes darted about the darkness of the park. "Tina's here somewhere. He also hears Tortora and Sonnenberg and he's not supposed to."

Both of Harrigan's brows went up. "Tortora and Sonnenberg together?"

The question, and Harrigan's surprise, meant nothing to Baker. "He hears them both at different times. They're near here. It's in a place Tina thinks is Williamsburg or Egypt or . . . damn!"

"The museum." Tanner jumped. "The American Wing of the museum."

"Fools rush in, lad." Three times now, Connor Harrigan had to restrain Baker, guiding him north by west in a wide swing around the perimeter of the rambling complex that was the Metropolitan Museum of Art. They reached the circle where the obelisk stood. Cleopatra's Needle. From that spot, well inside the park, most of the darkened rear of the museum was in view. Harrigan stood sniffing the air.

"There's no one else out here." Baker scowled. "I'm going in."

"Patience, lad." Harrigan raised a hand. "It leads to a long life for you and for Tina as well. The way to a short life is to play by the other fellow's rules."

"I know I'm being set up," Baker admitted. "I don't know why, but Sonnenberg is setting this up. It's more than just a question of Tortora getting even for his son. Sonnenberg is playing me like a flute."

Harrigan and Tanner exchanged looks. Tanner's expression was one of surprised confusion, as if Baker had just said something he should have known was false. She started to speak, but Harrigan silenced her with a shake of his head.

"Can I ask, lad, what's so remarkable about Charley hearing Sonnenberg?"

"He's not supposed to. That's why you got all that gibberish in Tanner's bathroom when you tried to ask about him."

"Then you and Charley have been programmed, I take it, not to eavesdrop on the man."

"It's not hard to do," Baker told him. "Any stage hypnotist can suggest a block like that. If Charley hears him now it's because Sonnenberg wants to be heard. The old bastard is still manipulating me." Baker paced several steps toward the obelisk's base, restraining himself from kicking over a waste can. He stalked back to Harrigan. "You wanted to know how we found Tanner so easily in a town this size. The answer is we didn't find her. Sonnenberg gave her to us. From where we drove into Manhattan, there's no practical way to get where Sonnenberg told us to go without passing within a few blocks of Levy's building." He turned to Tanner. "Sonnenberg knew that if you had anything at all on your mind, it would be me or Tina and Charley would hear you. Now I'm about to walk into that museum, not just because I want my daughter, but because Sonnenberg wants me in that museum up against Tortora."

"Could all this be a test of some kind, lad?"

"What for?" Baker threw up his hands. "After today, Sonnenberg has to know I wouldn't cross the street for him."

An excellent point, Harrigan thought, and yet . . . "Think, lad. The man's a behaviorist. Everything he does is an experiment of one kind or another. He manipulates you, you saw how he manipulated Duncan Peck and his people, he probably even tested Tanner's ability to send and your ability to free her . . ."

Baker waved off the discussion wearily. "I just want my daughter, Harrigan." He rubbed his eyes and rocked momentarily with the loss of vision balance. "Tanner, I'd like you to wait here."

"Like hell." She stepped toward him. "You're so tired you can hardly stand."

"We'll go together, lad." Harrigan touched his shoulder and steered him toward the museum. "We'll find your little girl together."

On the north end of the museum, where the glass wall of the American Wing borders on the Eighty-fifth Street transverse, Harrigan spotted the outlines of a car partly hidden in a stand of junipers. One car, he nodded to himself. Not an ambush fleet. And Baker seemed to feel no other presence. But Harrigan could not shake the feeling that there was more to this night's danger than whatever Sonnenberg and that crowd had in mind. It was the museum itself. Something about the museum. The buzz in the back of his head had not stopped since they'd fled from Sonnenberg's well. There was an answer there. He'd almost had it, he thought, in the car with Baker before the Tanner Burke business started. But it fell back, just out of reach.

Simplify, Connor. See first to the business at hand. "There's a door." He pointed. It was set belowground, to be reached by a short flight of steps. "My old eyes can't read the sign on it."

"Staff Only," Tanner told him.

"The administrative section." Harrigan clapped his hands. "As quiet a route as any."

"How do we get in?" Tanner asked. "Won't there be an alarm?"

"Not tonight, lass. I think not tonight."

Tina was close, Baker knew. After all this time, a distance he could count in yards. Tanner slipped her hand into his. It kept him from kicking in the door that Harrigan was quietly forcing. It squeaked open. Harrigan entered first, a penlight in his hand, and cast its dim glow on a clutter of desks and card files, rows of binders and catalogues. On the far wall he found what he was looking for. A floor plan. A visitor's map mounted and framed. He stepped closer, beckoning Baker and Tanner Burke to follow.

On the map, the administrative section appeared only as a general gray mass. Harrigan tapped a finger against a spot that approximated their position and traced a route to a narrow set of stairs that led to the Great Hall on the floor above. He moved off in that direction. Tanner tightened her grip on Baker's hand and fell in behind.

The Great Hall, the immense high-ceilinged chamber that greets visitors from the main entrance on Fifth Avenue, seemed all the more cavernous in the darkness. No light reached it from the streetlamps outside, but a dim glow washed over the marble walls and columns. It came from pairs of small, recessed bulbs that marked the sides of portals and corridors at the edges of the hall. They cast no beam but reflected off the ornamental gilt of the ceiling and off the glass of the information booth and the display cases of the gift shop. Baker followed the pair of lights nearest the quiet breath of his daughter. She must have come this way, he was sure. Floated this way, she said. That meant carried. He wondered vaguely who could have carried her if Stanley Levy was as small and weak as Tanner remembered.

Baker saw the Egypt that Tina had passed. Hooded figures carved in stone. A sarcophagus, several of them, some the size of a child. The smell of death was long gone from them, but the sight made Baker move more quickly. More recessed lights were set high in the walls. Those would be the desert stars Tina saw. Harrigan stopped at a standing sign and flicked on his penlight. The Temple of Dendur, it said, a larger tomb brought intact from the Nile's flooding banks, was ahead of them. The Hall of Arms and Armor was to their left. Knights. Baker nodded. Yes.

"*Yes, Daddy. In through where the knights and swords are.*"

She was dozing, Baker knew. Her eyes were opening in fits. But through the fog of drugs she could hear him. She knew he was there and she was not frightened for him. Even Abel seemed to feel no sense of danger. He was quiet. And Harrigan. Baker looked at him. His gun was in his hand, but it dangled carelessly at his side. He looked not at all like someone about to face a man who'd almost killed him. To say nothing of Domenic Tortora and whatever help he'd brought.

"Daddy? Come on, Daddy."

The Hall of Armor was still more dimly lit. A single set of night-lights glistened faintly off the polished steel of the weapons and suits of armor that lined the walls. In the middle of the floor a mounted knight was frozen in midcharge upon a horse also clad in steel from head to flanks. Ivanhoe. Baker moved past it, Tanner with him. Harrigan took the opposite wall. On Baker's side, his fingers brushed over a display of halberds, long poles with spear points and axes at their ends. It crossed his mind to choose a weapon. An ax would not help against guns if guns were waiting. Let Abel choose what weapons he might need. Still no warning came from him.

Near the end of the Hall of Armor, Harrigan stopped and waited. There was a smaller room off to the left, Baker saw. The room was short, more like a foyer. Rifles and pistols, long useless, were displayed on its walls in glass cases. Beyond it was a much larger space bathed in a soft bluish light. Now Baker could see potted trees outlined against the high glass wall and backlit by the park lamps outside. Harrigan padded quietly to one side of the entrance. He motioned Tanner back and Baker to the other side. Tanner ignored him.

"Williamsburg, Daddy."

The huge room looked like a garden to Harrigan. An atrium. Park lights brighter than the moon filtered through tinted glass and spread over shrubs, sculptures, and stone benches placed against marble planters. He tensed at the sight of a human shape, then another. The pistol in his hand crept up and swept the room as his pupils opened and found a focus. Statues, he realized. Naked guys with swords reeling backward like they'd just been belted. A woman, also naked, drawing a bow against another figure in a tall stone carving that looked like a church pulpit. A preacher, maybe. Dressed in black. Or a judge. A Cotton Mather type.

Baker's eye too was drawn to the sculptures, but they were familiar to him from Sunday visits long ago. Rimmer's *Falling Gladiators*. Saint-Gaudens's *Diana the Huntress*. Only the pulpit was new to him. To his right, covering a full wall, was the two-story stone façade of a nineteenth-century bank. The Federal Gallery, he knew, would be behind it. Williamsburg. Baker had already taken a step in that direction when Harrigan reached to touch his arm and pointed.

The figure in the pulpit, the man all in black, had moved. He was standing now. Another man, smaller, appeared at the pulpit's base. Harrigan recognized Stanley Levy. A small startled cry came from Tanner. Harrigan, his eyes now accustomed to the light, allowed them to sweep the room. In the far corner he saw a third man, barely visible against a potted shrub. Harrigan could make out a scope-mounted rifle across his lap. He knew the man. Notre Dame. Harrigan touched his fingers to his head in an acknowledging salute. Notre Dame answered with his own.

Baker saw him too. Roger Hershey, he was sure. The small man would be the one who took Tina. And the man in black would be the man who ordered her abduction. But why Hershey? he wondered. Why would Roger Hershey be with them?

"Come closer, Mr. Baker." The man in the pulpit leaned forward, his voice high and rasping. And Connor Harrigan smiled at the sound.

"Tortora?" Baker squinted.

"Mr. Tortora," the man corrected. His hands clutched his lapels, making fists against his cheeks. "Come, Baker. It is time that you gave an account of yourself."

"Jesus Christ!" Harrigan swore softly through a set of his mouth that began to look like a grin. The grin reached his eyes and then, in an odd response, he folded his arms in the attitude of an amused spectator. Baker glanced at him, confused for a beat, then shook it off and took several steps toward the pulpit.

"I'll take my daughter now, Tortora."

"Hold it a minute." Harrigan raised a hand and took a step closer, again stopping Baker. He looked up at the man in the black hat. "I bet I know your next line. It goes something like, 'First you have my son to answer for.' How's that? Pretty close, right?"

The man in the pulpit blinked rapidly. Bewilderment clouded Baker's face as well. Stanley Levy straightened, his expression one of stunned disbelief at Harrigan's insolence. Only Tanner, though clearly frightened, seemed to know the meaning of Harrigan's behavior. Harrigan saw that.

"You want to tell him or should I?" he asked.

She shook her head, hugging herself against a new chill. Baker stared at Harrigan uncomprehendingly.

"What's the matter?" he asked Baker. "Not enough light for you in here or are you as batty as he is? Look." Harrigan pointed. "Look real close and tell me if you see anyone you know."

Baker, with Tanner Burke holding his elbow, moved across the marble floor to a set of four steps that led into the atrium's center pit. He took them past the Diana, whose arrow seemed aimed at the heart of the man he approached. At a distance of several yards he slowed and stopped, his head cocked to one side, in utter confusion as he peered up at the man now turning away from him slightly.

"That's close enough." Stanley Levy drifted into Baker's path, his right hand fingering the ice pick at the other wrist. He too seemed befuddled. Baker barely glanced at him.

"Doctor?" he asked softly.

The man in black shook his head.

"Dr. Sonnenberg?" Baker repeated.

"How the hell would he know?" Harrigan stepped up behind Baker, one eye on Stanley Levy. Roger

Hershey hadn't moved. "Ivor Blount, Marcus Sonnenberg, Domenic Tortora, and Christ knows how many others. If you want to figure out which is which, Baker, don't count on him to help you. The guy's been so many people, there isn't any *him* anymore. I bet you the old bastard couldn't tell you what name he was born with."

The man in the pulpit began blinking rapidly again. Tanner was fascinated. He had the look of someone waking up from a nap. She was stunned at what was happening but something less than surprised. The answer had been there all the time. It was there last night, when Charley came out in her room at the Plaza. Harrigan began to get it then too. What was it? What was it Charley had said that started Harrigan thinking so hard? It was that Abel found Tortora's son because Tortora's son was thinking about his father. But then that Charley could only hear thoughts that were about Baker, or of Tina lately, or of Sonnenberg. The puzzle had stewed in her brain as it had in Harrigan's. All the time, the solution had been there. The simple answer. The idea that was too crazy to say aloud. It had to be that Sonnenberg and Tortora were the same. Charley had as much as said so. Almost. But not quite, as if even knowing the pieces of a truth, he'd been kept by Sonnenberg from putting that particular whole truth together. It was the block Baker mentioned outside. It explained Baker's surprise. It explained why Baker, who knew so many things, could not know this.

"Sonnenberg!" Baker roared at him, the knowledge sinking in that it *was* Sonnenberg who had taken Tina. The head of the man in black snapped up. He pinched his face shut and shook his head violently, grabbing the pulpit's railing for support.

"Look at this." Harrigan pointed. Stanley Levy was also blinking. He stepped uncertainly away from the pulpit's base far enough so that he could look up as if to confirm the identity of the person standing there. Stanley's mouth moved, but he seemed to have trouble speaking.

"See anyone else you know?" Harrigan gestured toward Stanley with the muzzle of his gun.

Baker stared stupidly.

"What do you need, hints?" said Harrigan. "Okay, try this one. Stanley Levy is to Domenic Tortora as blank blank is to Marcus Sonnenberg. You fill in what's missing."

Dumbfounded, almost entranced, Baker looked at Stanley. He looked into the softening eyes of a little man whose body seemed to be shrinking and bending as he watched. Rearranging itself more than changing. Baker could not believe it. But for a gray head of hair tied into a careless bun, he was looking at Emma. Mrs. Kreskie.

"Emma Kreskie." Harrigan said it for him. "What about you, Miss Burke? Who do you see?"

Tanner had seen it even before Harrigan. If anything, having seen Stanley dress up as his own mother, she was less surprised. She knew nothing of Emma Kreskie. She was seeing Mrs. Levy again. Except this Mrs. Levy seemed unable to speak. Stanley had mentioned an Emma. A cousin. "My God," she mouthed, the full horror of it dawning on her. "There are three of him too."

"The lady wins a prize," Harrigan answered. "More exactly, this mess is another one of those Chimeras Duncan Peck is so hot to find." He looked up at the teetering figure in the pulpit. "Except what, Sonnenberg? What was Stanley here? Practice? A near miss? What?"

The name, Harrigan saw, seemed to jerk at the man in the pulpit each time it was spoken. And each of these tugs in turn appeared to cause an equal reaction in the man who was now only on the edge of being Stanley Levy. Emma is to Marcus, he told himself, what Stanley is to Domenic. Domenic goes back to Marcus so Stanley goes back to Emma. And vice versa. What did Sonnenberg call it back at the house? His connection with Tortora, I mean. A symbiotic relationship, he called it. Symbiotic, my ass. The guy's a skitz for the record books.

"Sonnenberg!" Harrigan had one more hunch to

play. "Sonnenberg!" He called the name again. Both times, the man in the pulpit twitched as if jerked by a string inside his brain. He seemed caught halfway. He was trying, Harrigan was sure, to be Tortora now. The man in black would be almost there, almost believing it, almost slipping into the persona of Domenic Tortora, but Harrigan could prevent it, he realized, simply by speaking the wrong name. Sonnenberg's name. While Harrigan reminded the man he was Sonnenberg, it seemed, the man could not believe he was Tortora.

"Mr. Hershey!" the man in black croaked. He staggered against the side of the pulpit nearest Roger Hershey. "Shoot this man," he rasped, his voice high again. And then at once he appeared to reconsider. Looking away as if to capture a thought he'd lost, he flitted a hand toward Hershey, erasing the order. Harrigan half-turned toward Roger Hershey, ready to crouch and fire if Hershey raised his rifle. Hershey met Harrigan's eyes. His head shook slowly, sadly. In slow motion, he took both his hands from the grip and stock of his rifle and folded them across his chest.

"Sonnenberg." Harrigan looked up again. "It's time we cut the godfather bullshit." His tone was firm but less rough than the words he chose. "You're Marcus Sonnenberg now. Dr. Marcus Sonnenberg. You can be whoever the hell else you want after we leave with the kid. Right now you're Sonnenberg. Sonnenberg is who I want to talk to."

The man on the pulpit swallowed. He'd begun breathing heavily. "First . . ." He squeezed his eyes shut once more. "First you must answer for my son. Baker. Baker must answer for my—"

"That's my line, Sonnenberg," Harrigan interrupted. "Anyway, you don't have a son. That son was Tortora's and even that was probably faked. By Sonnenberg. You can't stand up there being a Maf because there isn't any Maf. There's only Sonnenberg."

"The hell with this," Baker snapped. He slipped loose the arm into which Tanner's fingernails had been digging and moved off toward the bank façade.

"Wait," Harrigan called. "The guy's almost Sonnenberg again. You want to talk to him or don't you?"

Baker turned his head but kept walking toward the Greek Revival building. "Talk to who, Harrigan? Sonnenberg? Like you said, there's nothing left in there." Baker climbed the steps of the bank.

"Jared!" It was Sonnenberg's voice. Pleading.

Baker hesitated. He did not want to stop and turn.

"Jared!" Sonnenberg's voice choked again.

Reluctantly, Baker turned to face him. "Doctor?" He spat the word.

"I'm . . . sorry, Jared."

"Tina's all right?" His eyes were blazing.

"She's well, Jared. Sleeping. I'm sorry, Jared."

Baker took a single step closer. "Why, Doctor? Why did you take her?"

Sonnenberg raised both hands to his oversized hat and took it off. Removing it seemed to help him concentrate. He opened the buttons of the heavy black overcoat, paused as if feeling for the effect, then shrugged the garment to the pulpit's floor. It did help. It was easier for him to be Sonnenberg now. He did not answer Baker's question. But there was an answer. Harrigan, watching closely, could see it in his eyes. And he could also see that a full understanding of his actions was beyond him. Absently, sorrowfully, Sonnenberg ran his fingers over the detail of the pulpit's stonework.

"Bitter pulpit," he muttered to himself. He raised his eyes to Jared Baker. "Named after Karl Bitter," he added. "The man who carved it." Sonnenberg paused to take a long breath. "I intended no play upon his name, but I suppose there's a metaphor in there someplace. What words does one speak from a bitter pulpit? Does one preach repentance and regret? Or do I preach tolerance and understanding to one who despises me? Understand yourself, Jared, and you'll understand me. Understand me and you'll understand yourself. There's truth to that, Jared, although I suspect you're not of a mind to listen."

"No, Doctor," Baker answered. "As a matter of fact,

I'm not." He turned once more and stepped through the doors of the bank façade. Tanner Burke followed him.

"I'll listen." Connor Harrigan remained at the base of the pulpit. A few feet away sat Stanley Levy, or what remained of him, staring indifferently at the floor, shoulders hunched, back bent, looking old. He reminded Harrigan of bag ladies he'd seen around Grand Central Station.

Sonnenberg did not look at Harrigan. His sorrowful face stayed fixed upon the doors that Baker had entered. But he responded.

"To what purpose, Mr. Harrigan?" he asked.

"Like you said. Understanding."

"I doubt you'd profit by it, sir. Nor am I of a mood to endure the snorts of a cynic such as yourself. You view the capacity of the human mind only in terms of corruption and venality. I fear its grander potential is beyond you."

"We're talking grand all of a sudden?"

Sonnenberg ignored the question.

"Grand as in what?" Harrigan pressed. "Grand theft auto? Grand larceny? Grand juries? What?"

"I rest my case, Mr. Harrigan."

Harrigan reddened. "You're a patronizing old screwball, aren't you. Where do you get the balls to feel so superior?"

Sonnenberg bit his lip. A reply had begun to form, but he seemed determined not to discourse with this man or be distracted by him.

Okay, Harrigan thought. Let's try sticking the needle a little deeper.

"I mean, you spend maybe twenty years bouncing between two different people, each as phony as the other. One's a second-rate Dr. Strangelove and the other thinks he's Don Vito Corleone. One carves up people's heads and the other breaks legs if people don't pay off his loan sharks. Plus which he causes ice picks to be stuck in the bodies of people who inconvenience either one of them. And now crude old Connor Harrigan learns that there's a nuance to all this that's too delicate for a dope like him to understand." Harrigan stepped closer. He began to slide his revolver into his belt but glanced at Stanley, Mrs. Kreskie, whoever, and thought better of it. Sonnenberg turned his head still farther from Harrigan and kept it locked upon the bank building.

"Okay." Harrigan shrugged. "So I have to guess. But you'll tell me if I happen to hit it, won't you, Sonnenberg?" He held up his left hand and began ticking off his fingers. "You create Domenic Tortora for these reasons. One. Cultivated nice guy Sonnenberg needs a cultivated bad guy Tortora who is willing to behave in ways that nice guy Sonnenberg considers indelicate. Sonnenberg, for one thing, doesn't like to kill. He hardly kills at all except for an occasional lapse like knocking off Santa Claus down at St. Elizabeths. Tortora doesn't like to kill either, but he'll always come through in a pinch. Us unrefined types call that schizophrenia and you a psychopath. But what do we know about grander potential?

"Two. It occurs to you that anyone with an upper-class dago name, as opposed to Mario Greaso for example, plus a black hat and coat, a fat wallet, a big house in Bronxville, and lots of mysterious absences, can function very nicely on the edges of the dago underworld. Automatically, that gives you the dago Brylcreme set looking to do you favors. It gives you cops looking to get on your pad, judges looking for you to get them elected to the Appellate Court, where the real money changes hands, and it makes everybody else afraid to fuck around with you.

"Three. It gives you a place to go if the shit hits the fan like it did today up in—"

"Hardly, Mr. Harrigan." Sonnenberg stopped him with a wave of his hand. "Being Domenic Tortora full time would be more than I could bear. I happen to loathe oregano, tomato paste, and the entire expatriate population of Sicily. Tortora will vanish forever before tomorrow comes, doubtless leaving rumors involving cement overshoes and the like."

"What happens to your kid?"

"Tortora's kid," Sonnenberg corrected, "assuming you refer to the bad seed ravaged last night by our friend Abel. In any case, his care has been provided for. If he survives, I'm sure we may count on him to carry on the more sordid traditions of the Tortora family name."

"Which is not the name he was born with."

Sonnenberg leaned forward. "So that it's clear, Mr. Harrigan," he said, sighing, "I'm speaking to you not because you've so cleverly drawn me out but because you prove to be a perceptive man in your own vulgar fashion. I'll retain that favorable impression only as long as you avoid asking the obvious."

So, Harrigan realized he'd guessed right about the kid. He was a prop. Picked up someplace along the way by Tortora or Sonnenberg and used to create the illusion of a life history. An orphan, maybe. Abandoned, more likely, given what a shit he must have been even as a baby. You'd think Tortora would have picked a foundling with a better disposition if he knew he'd have to look at him for the next twenty or thirty years. Which probably meant that Sonnenberg hadn't figured on needing to be Tortora that long. So what happened? Try a simple answer, Connor. Try one thing led to another. Like Tanner Burke says. The guy doesn't so much plan as he gets caught up in his own momentum. Which makes him a bitch to anticipate. And which starts to explain how he gets caught up in these lives he leads.

"You want perceptive and vulgar? You got it." Harrigan nodded. "Tortora's kid was a central casting prick. If he wasn't any loss, why did you go through the whole charade of having him order Tina Baker's kidnapping? Back at your house, as I recall, you acted like this was news to you."

"It was," Sonnenberg admitted. "To a large extent, it was."

"Which makes you a certifiable wacko." Harrigan couldn't resist it. "You know that, don't you?"

*   *   *

Baker found no bank behind the stone façade. No brass teller's cages or roll-top desks. Federal period, the sign said. He stepped into a large drawing room seven decades farther back in time than the bank that housed it. Not quite as far as Williamsburg but close enough. The age of Duncan Phyfe and Hepplewhite. Cabinetry that was light and graceful, chairs and settees with soft curves to their woodwork. It looked like Sonnenberg's home.

"Daddy?"

Baker's head turned and Tanner's with it. The silent call came from a chamber off the drawing room. As Baker moved toward it, his eye twitched. It was not yet a stab of warning, only alertness. Like a dozing watchdog who lifts one ear at a sound too faint to cause alarm.

There were several chambers. Bedrooms, mostly, that could be entered off the central parlor. They were all period rooms, Federal style more or less, all reproductions of rooms found in fine homes of the era. Baker saw the name Haverhill. The Haverhill Room. A waist-high glass barricade had been moved away from its entrance. And he saw Tina.

She lay curled and uncovered on a canopied bed. A candle burned steadily on a washstand at its side. Her eyes were closed, but a smile stretched across her mouth when she felt him there. Baker froze at the sight of her, not fully believing that it was Tina, that she was within his reach. Tanner's hand against his back urged him forward. In steps he would not remember taking he was at her side, bending over her, not yet touching, doubting even then that she was real. Very softly, he touched his fingertips to her forehead and brushed away a strand of hair that lay across her face. Tears streaked Baker's face. His own tears. They spotted her T-shirt at the shoulder and ran across her neck. Only a bit more boldly, he ran his fingers through her soft hair and down along her cheek. He caressed it tenderly.

"That's not a hug," she whispered. A sob convulsed Baker. He threw himself into arms that opened for him.

Tanner held back, smiling, wiping tears of her own. Tina Baker's eyes opened with effort and found Tanner. A hand reached out and Tanner took it in both of hers, but she did not otherwise intrude upon the moment.

"Hello, Jared." A woman's voice made Tanner flinch. Baker tightened but barely moved. Tanner reached a hand to the embroidered red bed curtain that hung from the canopy and tore it open. A woman sat in the darkness of the far corner, swaying quietly on an upholstered rocker. There was a Gucci purse on her lap, and against it Tanner could see the gleam of a small plated pistol. Slowly, Baker drew back his head from Tina's cheek, kissed it once more, and turned toward the voice.

"Melanie," he acknowledged. Odd, Tanner thought. His manner showed neither surprise nor concern. She stepped around the bed, moving, she hoped, within range of a kick should the woman lift her weapon. But the muzzle shifted in her direction before Tanner could pass the last bedpost. Not aiming. Not threatening. Rather warning her away by its presence. Tanner took a defiant step closer and waited.

"Melanie." Baker saw the pistol. He gathered his arms under Tina's body and lifted her from the bed. "I feel like killing someone tonight, Melanie. I'd just as soon it isn't you."

"... makes you a certifiable wacko. You know that, don't you?"

Sonnenberg sneered with just his eyes. "That's one conclusion, Mr. Harrigan, witless though it may be. Rather than waste time volleying insults, however, I will point out that actors, whether on the stage or in your government's undercover activities, quite commonly become absorbed in their roles. When the news reached me of young John's destruction, I was Tortora. I reacted as Tortora. The death of a son was real to me then. The Domenic Tortora I created would never have permitted such an event to go unavenged. Sonnenberg would of course have been more pragmatic. But his influence had its limits while the reins were in Tortora's hands."

Harrigan whistled to himself. Did I say he's a skitz

for the books? The guy's world class. Yet Harrigan knew there was a certain demented logic to what Sonnenberg was saying. It had to apply to Stanley as well. Getting lost in the role. Except there were three Stanleys. Stanley himself, Emma Kreskie who he thinks is his cousin, and Mrs. Levy who he thinks is his mother. At least the three Bakers know who the hell they are. What was it Sonnenberg told Duncan Peck back in his study? You have to be careful, he said more or less, that the subject you pick isn't a skitz to any great degree already. Make that mistake, and all you end up accomplishing is to give form to personalities that were already the product of your subject's emotional needs. What needs?

Sonnenberg's attention had wandered back toward the façade. "What do we suppose is keeping Jared?" he asked.

"It's been a year and a half." Harrigan shrugged. "They're catching up."

"I suppose." Sonnenberg nodded.

"As long as we're passing the time of day, you mind if I ask about Stanley here?"

"Hmm?" Sonnenberg asked distractedly. "Such knowledge would be quite useless, Mr. Harrigan."

"Just curious. What happened? He was real close to his mother and she died on him?"

"Hardly close."

"So why's he off the wall about mothers?"

Sonnenberg shook his head wearily and leaned toward him. "Purely in the interest of enhancing your sensitivity, Mr. Harrigan, I will tell you that Stanley did in fact have a cousin and obviously a mother and that they treated him disgracefully. He retreated into books, the mysteries of Sherlock Holmes specifically, which they delighted in tearing into shreds whenever they found them. Their abuse was ended through the agency of an ice pick. Stanley was institutionalized as a young man. Therapy was characteristically useless, so he provided his own. He invented a mother and a cousin whose devotion would remain total as long as Stanley lived. They're quite real to Stanley and he to them. The earlier agony has been totally suppressed. In fact, he thinks all mothers are quite wonderful. That's a useful hint, Harrigan. The proper mention of your own mother could save your life someday should you otherwise upset Stanley."

"You knew all this going in?" Harrigan frowned.

"Only his history. Emma and his new mother were something of a surprise when they appeared. It might have been quite a mess, but happily I was able to keep the three from randomly revealing themselves by associating one with myself, the other with Tortora, according to their talents, and retiring the third to the quiet life of an urban senior citizen. Is that disapproval I see on your face, Mr. Harrigan?"

"As a matter of fact I think it stinks, yes."

"Do you indeed, Mr. Harrigan?" Sonnenberg smiled patiently. "Can I assume you have an alternative to suggest?"

"Leaving him where he was, for openers," Harrigan snapped, "where they could have helped him properly."

"Where he was, Mr. Harrigan, was in a dry cleaning establishment on Tremont Avenue. He was released, quite unhelped, to a future of slipping polyethylene bags over laundered shirts by day, sleeping on the premises by night, and being entirely unable to function in society beyond regular morning visits to a neighboring butcher shop, where he swept the floor in return for being decently fed."

"Ben Meister's place?"

"Very good, Mr. Harrigan. I'd ask you now to consider what Stanley has become. He kills, yes, but no more indiscriminately than you. I daresay he's a kinder man. Infinitely more loyal, I think. No longer terrified by a world that had no place for him. Now, as you've seen, he's quite capable. Perhaps more than a match for even the storied Connor Harrigan. The same might be said of Emma Kreskie."

No easy rebuttal sprang to Harrigan's mind. The original Stanley, he knew, was one of thousands released to the streets of New York City alone each year by overcrowded mental institutions. Some actually lived on the streets. A lot more got numbly through each day doing menial jobs like Stanley's with the plastic bags. At least Stanley was living. And he had an anchor. But what was going to happen to him when the anchor wasn't there anymore? Sonnenberg himself said that he was going to deep-six Tortora.

Well, Harrigan thought, he couldn't worry about that. Or how crazy Stanley actually was or whether Sonnenberg belonged in a rubber room or running the President's Commission on Human Resources. Simplify, Harrigan. Do what you came here to do. Get Baker and his daughter out and keep them on a nice long leash until you figure out how to use him. Which Sonnenberg knows damn well you plan to do, judging from that loyalty crack. And which he damn well plans to do himself unless Baker can stash himself better than Sonnenberg can find him. Get on with it. Except there's something untidy here. There's something about this museum that bothers the shit out of you and it keeps dancing just out of reach. And there's something else. The point of all this. I mean, here we have Sonnenberg, who set up the snatch on Tina Baker—forget all that Tortora and his kid crap for a minute—then orchestrated getting us all down here. Then we get here, and almost nothing is going the way Sonnenberg could have wanted it to go. He stands up there answering questions he doesn't have to answer. Hershey sits over there in another world watching the show. Stanley, or whoever, sits rocking back and forth. And Baker's in there getting his kid. Which is taking a little too long, by the way. Anyhow, wacko or not, Sonnenberg's no dope. And he's definitely not acting like a man whose plans fell apart. So what is it? A test, like I asked before? Baker says no. Besides, what's to test? Sonnenberg knows everything Baker can do. But it *is* a test, damnit. An experiment. Everything the guy does is an experiment. So ask him, Harrigan. The guy's in a talking mood, right? On the other hand, the hell with it. Let's just get Baker and get out of here. Like I said, something about this place bothers you.

"What do you say we take a walk and move things

along in there?" Harrigan cocked his head toward the bank façade. With the barrel of his revolver, he motioned Sonnenberg down from the pulpit.

"We'll wait here, Mr. Harrigan." Sonnenberg sat back against the pulpit's rim.

Connor raised his weapon higher and gestured again.

"Be nice, Sonnenberg," Harrigan said evenly. "I won't kill you, but you could lose some skin."

Sonnenberg smiled. A patient smile. "Please throw that thing away, Mr. Harrigan. There's a trash receptacle on your left."

Harrigan took a step toward the pulpit. The hell with it. He'd drag him off.

"And while you're looking for the trash can, Mr. Harrigan, I suggest you consider Mr. Hershey's argument for doing as I ask."

Harrigan turned his head slowly. Roger had shifted his position and the rifle was no longer on his lap. The cross hairs of its scope were now squarely upon Connor Harrigan's chest. Harrigan looked up at Sonnenberg.

"Roger's had a change of heart? A little while ago he took himself out of the game."

"Out of Domenic Tortora's game," Sonnenberg corrected. "I'm afraid Roger has had doubts about Domenic's stability. The gun please, Mr. Harrigan."

"Please, Jared." Melanie turned her hand and opened her fingers so that the small automatic rested harmlessly across her palm. "He's your friend. Please don't leave without talking to him."

Baker shut his eyes wearily at her use of the word.

"I know, Jared." Melanie's voice was gentle. "Friends don't kidnap little girls. But he had no choice, Jared. I swear he didn't."

"Right." Baker adjusted his grip on Tina's body, then directed Tanner toward the door with his head. "The devil made him do it. Tortora, right? Don't waste your time, Melanie."

"Jared." She raised her voice, a note of desperation at its edges. "It's not Tortora. It's true Marcus has a problem with that sometimes, but he always controls it. Just like you with Abel and Charley. Please talk to him, Jared. He took Tina for her own good."

"*baker.*" It was Charley's voice. Baker ignored it. One of Tina's eyes popped open.

"Jared, wait." Tanner placed a hand against his shoulder. "What about Tina's own good?" she asked Melanie Laver.

"Duncan Peck would have taken her." Melanie answered a bit too quickly, then looked away.

"*baker.*"

Tina's other eye opened wide.

"As a hostage?" Tanner asked. "There's more, isn't there?"

"I . . . I don't know." Melanie looked down again.

"Let's go." Baker swung Tina's body toward the door.

"Damn you, Jared." Melanie's voice stopped him. "We're going way out on a limb for you," she said, angry now. "Peck is using everything he's got to round us up. None of us are safe until we get into our new lives far away from here. Roger Hershey is out there close to a breakdown because he killed three men today who would have killed you, and he's too sweet a man to do that anymore. A fourth who was guarding Marcus's boat almost killed him because he hesitated. Marcus and Stanley Levy both kept Tina safe when Tortora might, just might, have harmed her. You can mock that if you want, but then I'll ask you how obedient Abel's been, starting with the day Sarah was killed. We're your friends, Jared. Marcus is your friend. He couldn't go without seeing if he was right about . . ." Melanie chewed her lip. Her eyes dropped to Tina, who was staring intently at nothing. One of Tina's hands had clawed at the wool of her father's sweater and was stretching and twisting it.

Baker felt a stiffening of Tina's body and looked down at the fist. The blood was draining from his face when he looked up again. "Finish your thought, Melanie," he said, his voice a bare whisper.

Melanie hesitated, working her mouth soundlessly. Then her chest heaved once and her body sagged. The hand with the pistol dropped to her side.

"BAYYKKERRR!"

"Something went wrong, Jared. It's Tina."

"It's Sonnenberg all right," Michael Biaggi whispered into his transceiver. He crouched low in the dew-dampened shrubs that lined the glass wall of the American Wing. The figure on the pulpit had just shed his hat and overcoat and was leaning over its edge toward Connor Harrigan. He'd almost missed Roger Hershey, who lounged listlessly some fifty feet away. "If Baker's here, I don't see him."

In an apartment over the Castelli Galleries on Seventy-seventh Street near Fifth Avenue, Ed Burleson straightened at the sound of the doorbell and handed the transceiver to Doug Peterson, who stayed by the open window. A third man, in his fifties, sat slumped against an art-filled wall. He'd fainted. Fingers on both his hands were broken and bleeding. At his feet were the torn remnants of the canvas and frame of an oil painting. Burleson reached the apartment door and tapped it once from the inside, opening it only at the sound of Duncan Peck's voice.

"Sonnenberg's there, sir." Ed Burleson gestured in the general direction of the museum. "Just like Poindexter said he'd be."

Peck glanced disinterestedly at the broken man curled near the wall. "Philip Poindexter." He nodded. "This man was Luther Dowling before his reincarnation as assistant curator of the Metropolitan?"

"Yes sir. We're unable to confirm that through the identification bureau, but he acknowledged as much under interrogation. Luther Dowling, Junior. In fact, he was once the owner of Sonnenberg's house."

"Hmmm," Peck reflected. "Rather sloppy of Sonnen-

berg to tell us the name Dowling instead of Poindexter.
It shows the folly of allowing oneself to be diverted by a
compulsion to taunt."

"With respect, sir," Burleson replied, "we were still
lucky. He says Sonnenberg reached him at the museum
and told him to make sure the place was unguarded and
unwired tonight and then bail out immediately without
returning to this apartment. He disregarded that last in-
struction in order to pick up some paintings he especially
valued. Poindexter was in the act of packing when our
people made their sweep."

"Some sweep." Duncan sniffed. "It's yielded one
small fish unless we count the cadaver of Howard
Twilley. It will serve little if it fails to result in the taking
of bigger fish. Whom do you have observing the museum?"

"Biaggi, sir. He's on the north end, and one of my
men is covering the door to the museum offices through
which they forced entry. Biaggi just confirmed seeing
Connor Harrigan with Sonnenberg. As a bonus, Roger
Hershey is in the same room."

"No sign of Baker?"

"I'm afraid not, sir."

"More's the pity," Peck muttered. "Have we an idea,
by the way, why Sonnenberg would set up a rendezvous
with Connor Harrigan in so exotic a location? Or why he
wouldn't choose a meeting place both more conventional
and more simply arranged? Or why Connor Harrigan is
suddenly not in the company of Jared Baker and the
Burke woman?"

"We have no information on either point, sir."

Peck refrained from rolling his eyes at this sluglike
response to his presumption that Burleson possessed an
imagination. Marcus, Ivor, whoever, had made a valid
point, he thought, about Edward and his ilk. Ah, Marcus!
If only you'd been a reasonable man. And ah to you too,
Connor. One must give the devil his due. How terribly I
shall miss you. How desperately I shall wish that I might
have had one of you rather than ten of these. If it were
you and not Edward, for example, you would ask why

there was a need to force entry into the museum. You would answer that the person who entered in that fashion, doubtless yourself, was an unwelcome guest.

"Mr. Peck," Doug Peterson called from the window, his transceiver at his ear. "Biaggi says that Roger Hershey has a rifle pointed at Connor Harrigan and is disarming him."

Voilà! thought Peck. Who, therefore, is the welcome guest? Jared Baker? The rest of Sonnenberg's assorted clones? If so, Sonnenberg will soon notice that Philip Poindexter is not among them and begin to sniff the wind. And what of Baker's kidnapped daughter? An event of doubtless major significance and doubtlessly arranged by Sonnenberg, since I know, alas, that I was too late to that table. There, now. There is reason for a confrontation and a broken door. If so, Baker would hardly assign Connor Harrigan as his daughter's rescuer. Baker's there. He's there or he's coming.

"Tell Mr. Biaggi," Peck ordered Doug Peterson, "that in five minutes we'll be at his side. He is to take no action." Peck turned to Burleson, satisfaction on his face. "When thieves fall out, Edward." He smiled.

"Sir?"

"Never mind, Edward. Have you considered a plan of attack?"

"Cover the probable exits and observe, sir. When they start to come out, we can redeploy and take them."

"That was your plan at the Plaza, Edward. This time we'll go in." Peck noticed the torn and shattered painting at Poindexter's feet. "What is that, by the way?"

"It's one of the pictures he returned to get, sir. I believe he said it was a Bernard Buffet."

"An original?"

"Yes sir. We tore it a strip at a time to encourage his cooperation. It brought faster results than physical coercion."

Peck closed his eyes. "We'll go to the museum now, gentlemen. Acquit yourselves well and perhaps you can smash a Cellini cup or two."

"Sir?"

"Never mind, Edward." Peck waved a hand toward what was left of Luther Dowling. "Bring that with you. The van is at the curb."

"Yes sir."

"You're a very good man, Edward."

"Holy shit!" Biaggi swore aloud, tossing his transceiver to one side and crouching deeper into the bush. The doors of an old-fashioned building had slammed open, kicked from the inside, and there was Baker. Holding the kid. Screaming at Sonnenberg. Biaggi couldn't hear. He could only see the face and the teeth. And the actress, Tanner Burke, trying to quiet him. And some other dame.

He was screaming about the kid, Biaggi knew, from the way he kept looking down at her. But the kid wasn't listening. She was just looking around. Staring at walls. Staring now at him, Biaggi thought. He pulled back farther. Easy! There's no way she could see. She's yelling something. She's pointing. Jesus! Now they're all looking. Harrigan's running for a garbage can and Hershey's waving him off. And Sonnenberg is staring. Sneering, the son of a bitch! Take no action, huh. So the bastard can set me up again? Bullshit.

Biaggi leaped to his feet, snapping the safety off his Uzi, and smashed its butt housing against the safety glass of the window wall. Nothing happened. He stepped back, in panic, and fired a short burst that cleared a ragged eight-inch hole. Out-of-focus figures scattered on the other side. A woman near Baker crashed backward, her hands clutching at her abdomen. Hershey whirled toward Biaggi as the woman cried out. He snapped one shot that missed by inches, then backed away, finally turning and running toward Melanie Laver. Biaggi ignored the retreating back. He jammed the short Uzi muzzle through the hole and sighted low and left on Sonnenberg's pulpit. He fired. Explosions of stone danced upward amid an echoing roar and sprayed showers of sparks and granite when they reached the railing below Sonnenberg's chest. Sonnenberg, arms flailing, staggered backward and slammed hard against the pulpit's inner wall. Biaggi squeezed again as he hung there. Nothing. Empty. He fumbled at the pocket of his gray raincoat for another clip. Baker was running now, the other woman with him, the girl Baker carried shielded by their bodies. Biaggi found the clip and jammed it in place. Too late. Baker was inside a doorway to the right before Biaggi's front sight caught him. To Biaggi's left there was a blur of movement. A man. Running toward him. Running like a woman runs. His mouth moving soundlessly, his eyes full of hate.

"Levy!" Harrigan screamed his name. Stanley Levy, Biaggi realized. He hadn't seen him. Must have been behind Sonnenberg. Take your time, Michael. Nothing in Levy's hands. Biaggi shifted his position for an insurance burst into Sonnenberg, who was fast sinking out of sight.

"Levy, get down!" Harrigan yelled again. The running man faltered, glancing back at Harrigan, who was furiously waving him out of Biaggi's line of fire. Indecision slowed Biaggi for no more than a second. Sonnenberg was gone. He swung his weapon onto Connor Harrigan. A short burst and Harrigan dropped. Was he hit? Biaggi wasn't sure. Once more he hesitated before swinging the barrel back to Stanley Levy, who looked different now. He seemed more agile. The mincing step was gone and the eyes were filled with a cooler kind of hate. An ice pick was in his left hand and he'd sidestepped so his approach was just at the edge of Biaggi's field of fire. With both hands Biaggi wrenched the Uzi toward Levy and against the constrictions of the hole he'd cut. Biaggi fired, then coughed in pain. Christ! The Uzi's recoil raked the back of his hands against the ragged glass. Jesus! He was hung there. Relax your hands. Straighten them. Easy. Biaggi saw only the blur that was Stanley Levy diving at his gun barrel. And then the ice pick. It arched low and wide, and its thin spike seared into the knuckles of Biaggi's right hand, raking through to the Uzi's grip. Biaggi screamed.

Levy's right hand gripped the Uzi's sight and his face pressed flat against the glass, his teeth bared and biting as if they could chew through to Biaggi's throat. Levy twisted and ripped with the ice pick, then pulled it free for another thrust. Again Biaggi screamed. Desperately, he braced one knee against the glass and hurled himself backward, scoring his hands and stripping the flesh from his knuckles. But he was free. In agony, he cradled his hands. The Uzi had fallen to the ground three feet beneath the bloodied hole. He reached for it but pulled away in horror. Stanley's arm was coming through the hole, the ice pick in his fist, slashing, sweeping, forcing Biaggi back. Measuring the arm's arc, Biaggi crouched lower, his torn fingers stretching for the weapon. Now Stanley was snarling insanely, his shoulder slamming against the glass for an extra inch of reach. Biaggi lunged for the Uzi. He had it. Hands trembling, he found the trigger and fired. A three-foot slab of safety glass exploded inward at Stanley's beltline.

Headlights. Splashing on the museum's north wall as their vehicle mounted the roadway's curb and climbed up on the grass. Biaggi stood up, waving, directing the van toward him, toward the shattered glass. Burleson leaped from one side, his weapon ready, while the van slowed.

"Hit the wall," Biaggi screamed at the driver. The man at the wheel hesitated but Burleson understood.

"Make a door," he called, pointing with his machine pistol and waving the van forward. "Put a hole in it and back away."

The van surged forward, grinding over the shrubbery until its bumper was flush with the wall. Then it surged again. There was a screeching, wailing sound as the glass resisted and stretched, then the crack of a giant bullwhip as an eight-foot section collapsed. Duncan Peck was out of the van before it could back away.

"Michael?" He glared.

"Baker's in there," he said quickly. "Baker's daughter, the actress, Harrigan, everybody. I got Sonnenberg. I got Sonnenberg and I just got Stanley Levy."

Peck wanted to slap him. He wasn't sure why, but he wanted to thrash Michael Biaggi.

"Baker's loose in there, sir," Biaggi said quickly.

"Where's Chuck Graves?" Burleson asked. "The man on the other door."

Biaggi shook his head. "He didn't come to the sound of the gunfire. I guess he's holding his post."

Burleson jerked a thumb at Peterson. "Get back with Graves and go in from that side. Take him with you." He pointed to the van's driver, a balding, long-armed hulk named Gorby. "Are you able to function?" he asked Biaggi, noting his hands and remembering those of Philip Poindexter.

"They still shoot," Biaggi answered. He worked the action of his Uzi as if to prove it.

"Darts, Edward," Peck snapped. "I want Baker alive."

"If he'll cooperate, sir."

"You cooperate, Edward. I want him alive."

Baker stopped inside the small dark foyer where the firearms were displayed. Breathing heavily, his head pounding from the raging inside, he lowered Tina to the floor. Tanner Burke dropped beside her, her hands over Tina's cheeks.

"Oh, Jared, look." Tina seemed to be in spasm. Her eyes flashed excitedly and her body trembled. "She's terrified."

"No she's not," he hissed. Baker wiped at a well of tears that had formed in his right eye. He pushed to his feet and stepped back to the atrium entrance. Connor Harrigan, hobbling but moving quickly, almost knocked him aside.

Harrigan glanced at Baker but did not speak. Taking his weight off a punctured and bleeding leg, he fished into the pockets of his trousers. Grunting, he pulled free a handful of change and keys. In their midst he found three spare cartridges. Penlight and cartridges in hand, he hopped to the nearest display case and played a small beam on the cards describing the exhibits. Finding the caliber he sought, Harrigan half-turned and brought his elbow against and through the glass of the case. He seized a Walker Colt, .36 caliber. Close enough, he hoped. Harrigan thumbed the cylinder free and forced in the three cartridges, first lubricating their jackets with oil from the sides of his nose. "Let's go," he told Baker. "Out the way we came."

Baker shook his head. "They have three men coming that way."

Harrigan didn't bother asking how he knew. He waggled the Walker Colt. "Three bullets," he said.

Baker reached into the case and withdrew another pistol, which he cracked, holding the barrel up to the light. "Plugged," he said simply. "It's an art museum, Harrigan."

Harrigan checked his Walker Colt and cursed. He hefted it, weighing whether to discard the pistol, then jammed it into his belt. Good for a bluff if nothing else, he decided.

"Wait a minute." He brightened. "Your gun, Miss Burke. The one in your purse."

"Out there." Tanner pointed. "Oh, my God!"

She saw her purse where she had dropped it when the first shots were fired. She saw it at the marble stairs leading into the Federal Gallery and she saw Melanie Laver.

Melanie was slumped against a ceramic urn at the bank façade's entrance. Her face was ashen, and she was looking down at blood-smeared fingers that she kept pressed against a spot low on her belly. Roger Hershey was holding her, rocking her. His rifle lay several feet away, across the atrium steps. To her left, the corner of her eye caught movement and she ducked back, it registering only then that the movement was more of a drunken stagger. She looked again. Harrigan saw it too. It was Stanley Levy.

He too had been shot, it seemed. Harrigan remembered the distant chattering sound the Uzi had made, a sound like the first the Uzi had made when it punched its gunport through the glass and unlike the booming roar that meant its muzzle had been thrust into the echoing room. Stanley had been shot from outside the window, he knew, which meant flattened tearing slugs like the single stray that had found Melanie Laver. Stanley had to be ripped apart inside and yet he was standing. Staggering. Reeling away from the jagged hole some vehicle had made and stumbling toward Sonnenberg's pulpit. He'd reached it now. He was groping blindly at its sides as if searching for an opening that would take him to its core. To where Sonnenberg had fallen. Sonnenberg was inside it someplace.

Harrigan heard voices now. Back toward the hole where the slaughter had started. He heard his own name. And he heard Michael Biaggi's voice. Harrigan cursed Biaggi in his heart but he cursed himself more. Now he knew what troubled him about entering the museum and what eluded him when he tried to question Baker about what Duncan Peck might have going for him. Peck knew something or he'd made a collar. Of either or both Harrigan was sure. The collars he was trying to make, the ones he'd identified from the numbers in Hershey's wallet, were all accounted for by the time Peterson ran down to the basement and wrote out his note. Baker was with him and Coffey was dead. He didn't know it then, but Notre Dame and the Laver woman were waiting up above on the other side of the fairway. That left the museum guy. Poindexter. Stupid. He was too goddamned Irish thick to remember the connection. And so goddamned cocky about figuring out this Sonnenberg and Tortora business that he waltzed everybody right into a trap an amateur should have smelled.

"We have to get out of here," Harrigan said, his brain recalling the visitor's map he'd scanned when they entered.

"How?" Tanner asked, her horrified stare still fixed upon the carnage in the atrium.

"There are towns that are smaller than this place." Harrigan looked over his shoulder toward the Hall of Armor. "We get out of this wing and there are more rooms than Peck's crowd can cover. We can hide out or take them one at a time."

"Can you carry Tina?" Baker asked quietly.

"Me?" Harrigan asked. He looked down at the puncture wound in the flesh of his thigh. Better tie that up, come to think of it. He stripped off his necktie. "Maybe. Depends how far. What do you have in mind?"

"baker." It was Abel.

"Take my daughter, Harrigan, and take Tanner. Back past the stairs we used you'll see a bunch of English and French period rooms. It's like a maze. Hide. there, Harrigan. Hide there and keep them safe until I come back for you."

"Jared," Tanner protested.

"What are you going to do?" Harrigan's face was skeptical. "Take this bunch on by yourself?"

"yes, baker. yes."

"No," Baker answered. "Go now, Harrigan."

Tanner Burke started to shake her head in refusal but stopped. She stared into Baker's eyes, blinked, and then looked toward the pulpit. "No, Jared," she whispered. "You don't even know if he's alive."

"What the hell is this?" Harrigan asked.

"Get moving, Harrigan," Baker said again. "I'm going to get Sonnenberg."

"Who is?" Harrigan asked. "You or the beastie? Because even if it's him, he better damn well be bulletproof, which he damn well isn't. The only reason Peck hasn't busted in here already is because he thinks we're armed. But if you make for Sonnenberg, you have to cross a clear killing ground. Even if you make it one way, odds are you'll find a stiff."

Baker turned away without answering. He lifted Tina from the floor and carried her back to Connor Harrigan, who hesitated, scowling at Baker, then reluctantly took the weight that Baker held against his chest. Baker looked once more into her eyes. He had to look away. "Take care of her," he said to Tanner. "Take care of yourself."

"i won't let you, baker. i won't."

"Stuff it, Abel." Baker lowered his head and charged into the atrium.

*   *   *

"It's Baker." Biaggi tapped Burleson's arm and winced at the pain in his hand. He brought the Uzi to his eye.

"No." Peck stepped from behind the safety of the van's open door and snatched away the weapon. "Darts, Michael. Darts, Edward. I want the man alive. Now, Michael." He pushed the shoulders of both men closer to the breach the van had cut.

Baker was running almost blind. Thirty feet into the atrium's perimeter, he had to stop behind a planter and wipe away the tears that flooded his eyes. His head was pounding.

"why, baker? why are you doing this? i'm better at it, baker. i'll help you."

"Will you help Sonnenberg?"

"yes, baker. i'll crush the men who hurt him. i'll crush the men who want to hurt tanner burke and tina. go back, baker, and we'll wait for them in the dark."

"That's what I thought."

Baker wiped his eyes once more. The pulpit was still twenty yards away. Closer, at half that distance, sat Roger Hershey, his arms around Melanie Laver, both bodies fully in the open.

"Roger," Baker called.

Hershey did not react. Melanie's eyes opened at the sound of Baker's voice.

"Melanie?" Baker whispered. "Can you move? Can you get back inside those doors?"

She shook her head, a sad smile on lips drained of color. "I was going to have a bookshop, Jared." She reached to pat Roger Hershey on his arm but pulled her hand back when she saw the wet blood on her fingers. "That would have been something, wouldn't it?"

"It still can happen, Melanie," he said, not believing it. "What's wrong with Roger?"

"One killing too many." She tilted her head and kissed him lightly. "He's just too sweet a man, Jared. You're both sweet men."

"Yeah." Baker crawled toward her and up the steps of the Greek Revival façade. He pulled open one of the double doors. There was a whistling sound, an insect sound, as a feathered dart thunked against the other. Baker grabbed Hershey, who held fast to Melanie Laver, and dragged him inside. Once there, he drew his hand back to slap Hershey sharply across the face but he couldn't. Instead he shook him. Roger blinked up at him.

"Pick a room, Roger," Baker told him. "Can you get her to a bed?"

Hershey nodded slowly.

"I'll be back, Melanie," Baker promised.

"Get away from here, Jared. Don't let them take you."

"They won't shoot me, Melanie. I heard them."

"Shooting's better than what they'll do with you, Jared. They'll take you apart piece by piece. Get away, Jared. Take Tina, Jared, and get away."

"Like she is? What's wrong with her, Melanie?"

Melanie didn't answer. Perhaps she couldn't.

"I'll be back," Baker said again.

Baker opened the door a crack. A shadow moved off to his left. Biaggi. Baker heard him. And he heard Burleson, the other one, moving low along the glass wall in the direction of the pulpit. He saw Stanley there, still standing, moving, trying pathetically to climb the pulpit's side. Baker couldn't watch. He dropped his eyes and they fell upon Roger Hershey's rifle. Baker flung himself through the door and dove for it.

"Freeze, mister," Burleson's voice called. Baker swung the rifle and fired blindly at the voice. Something stung his shoulder. Baker tore the dart loose and ran to the narrow, winding steps of the pulpit.

Sonnenberg was lying there, eyes closed, his black Tortora hat crushed beneath him. Blood from a dozen wounds covered his face and chest. Baker's stomach fell. With his rifle covering the steps he'd taken, Baker felt blindly for a pulse at Sonnenberg's neck. "Come on,

Sonnenberg," he muttered, seeing Tina's half-wild face in his mind, "come on."

A hand closed over his wrist. "You do choose the poorest times to chat, Jared."

"Hold it." Harrigan stopped near the far entrance of the Hall of Armor, just past the mounted knight and charger at its center. He'd heard a sound. A scraping of feet on bare marble. "The three guys," he whispered to Tanner, easing Tina to her feet between them. "Sounds like they're moving in."

The scuffing sounds were vague and he could not gauge their distance. Maybe far off. Maybe plenty of time to reach the period rooms. On the other hand, his leg was having enough trouble carrying his own weight without Tina's hundred pounds on top of it. Bet with the smart money, Harrigan. The smart money figures your handicap and gives three to one they'll nail you if you go gimping together in these halls.

"Can you keep the kid quiet?" he asked Tanner.

"I guess. Why?"

Harrigan hobbled to the armored horse and lifted a scarlet parade skirt that reached almost to its fetlocks. "Get under here." He reached back for Tina to abort any discussion and eased her under the fabric. "Just stay quiet," he told Tanner, who followed. "Stay there all night if you have to, no matter what you hear."

"What are you going to do?" she asked doubtfully.

"Cut the odds a little, maybe."

Harrigan backed away from the mounted knight, flicking on his penlight once to see that no hands or feet were too apparent. They'd be safe, he thought. The eye of anyone coming in would go up, startled by the lance, and then go past it once the guy relaxed. He kicked off his brogans and hid them on top of a display case before making his way into the darkest part of the corridor. They'd fan out, he knew. They'd have checked the same map and have seen at least three ways into the Garden

Court. Harrigan chose the most direct route, the one he'd taken through the first Egyptian rooms.

Chuck Graves, the man Burleson stationed at the door Harrigan had forced, also picked that route. Peterson would take the Hall of Armor. The van's driver, Gorby, was assigned a passage through European Decorative Arts.

Graves picked his way slowly but not cautiously, his mind on the place with the glass wall and on blocking escape. With the barrels of pistols held in either hand he probed the first dark nooks he passed, but there were too many. Move. Keep moving. They're ahead of you, not here.

He reached a long, narrow hall where the lesser tombs of middle kingdom gentry were arranged among island cases that showed the minor treasures with which they were buried. Chuck Graves paused at one case, his eye attracted by a gleam inside. He wanted to ignore it. But a part of his mind wondered what would shine with hardly any light. Gold, maybe. Like the King Tut stuff. The opportunity tugged at him. Graves laid his dart pistol on the case, then fished for a Bic lighter and struck it.

"You want to die, kid?"

Graves went rigid, more surprised than fearful. He judged the voice to be ten feet behind him. His first instinct was to release the butane lever and roll to one side while the night-blinded gunman fired at nothing. But he also knew that the voice was probably Connor Harrigan's. He wouldn't be fooled. Harrigan would use one muzzle flash to spot him and the second to kill him. But maybe Harrigan didn't want the noise. Stay cool. Remember your training, he told himself. Remember Harrigan can't see the gun in your other hand. Talk to him. Get him thinking. Let him know that even if he makes the street he can't get out of the city. Tell him Duncan Peck's still willing to deal if he takes this last chance to come home.

"Harrigan?" He kept his voice even. "I think we better talk, Harrigan."

"Bullshit!" Harrigan's breath was suddenly at his ear. The heavy Walker Colt came down behind it.

Sonnenberg would be hurting, Baker decided, but his wounds did not look serious. Chips of stone, perhaps a bullet fragment or two from Biaggi's second burst. But they appeared serious and Sonnenberg knew it. A quick inspection, he gambled, and they might let him lie harmlessly while they rushed in pursuit of fleeter game. Which might surprise them nastily if they ran into Mrs. Kreskie in one of these dark hallways. To say nothing of friend Abel.

"You're not using him," Sonnenberg whispered.

Baker waved him to silence. With his index finger he marked two positions flanking the pulpit. Sonnenberg understood. But that was all the more reason for leaving him at his game of possum and loosing Abel among them. But there was more. He saw it on Baker's face. Tina. Ah, yes. Tina. Sonnenberg resisted only slightly as Baker, rocking momentarily as if seized by a passing vapor, took Sonnenberg's arms and gathered them over his shoulders in a fireman's carry.

"They'll shoot us," he said into Baker's ear.

"Just darts." Baker hushed him. "I'll pick them out of your butt later." Sonnenberg bit back a groan as he felt his lacerated chest pulled tight and hoisted against Baker's back. Your butt, no less. Marcus Sonnenberg a shield, no less. Jared Baker was spending entirely too much time in the company of Connor Harrigan.

Biaggi saw them first. Baker and Sonnenberg. Two clean shots. He shifted his dart pistol into his left hand and drew out his service revolver with his right.

"Michael!" Duncan Peck's voice boomed from the rear of the room.

Maybe one shot. You want darts for Baker, you got them, but I want one insurance shot through that old bastard's ear.

Baker whirled as if he'd heard and raised his rifle in one hand, jerking the trigger. Nothing. He'd forgotten to chamber another round. A dart, Burleson's dart, struck him high on his chest. Unable to work the bolt without dropping Sonnenberg, Baker hurled the useless rifle toward Biaggi's head, ruining the aim of another dart that whistled harmlessly between his legs.

"Edward," Peck's voice sounded, "shoot Michael if he raises that revolver again."

Baker tore loose the dart that sprouted from his collarbone, glancing up along its line of flight. He saw Burleson, a reloaded dart pistol again leveled at his chest and a revolver aimed at a right angle in Biaggi's direction. Burleson hesitated, distracted.

"BAYYKKERRR!"

Move, Baker urged himself.

"Stanley?" Sonnenberg's shout startled him. He felt his burden shift as it struggled for a better look at Burleson. Baker looked again and saw Stanley this time. The little man had staggered up from the pulpit's bloodsmeared base and was reeling drunkenly toward Burleson, his hands forming outstretched claws. Burleson saw him now, too late. Fingernails dug into Burleson's face and tore at it before Burleson could throw up his arms in defense. He clubbed furiously at Stanley's head with the barrel of his dart pistol.

"Stanley!" Sonnenberg's anguished cry came again. He kicked at Baker, wrestling him, twisting wildly at Baker's grip. Baker struggled for his balance and against a second assault now pounding from inside his head. He fell backward, tears flooding his eyes, grasping desperately at Sonnenberg, who had shaken free and was starting to crawl toward Stanley Levy. A heavy door crashed open, and three fast shots thundered near Baker's ear. Behind him, Baker realized. They were behind him now too. He felt an arm pulling him to his feet while a hand with a gun in it reached past him and seized Sonnenberg by his collar. Baker opened his mouth to shout Abel's name.

"yes yes baker."

He took a breath, but his tongue slipped over the word when he tried to form it.

"On your feet, lad," Harrigan's voice barked. "Help me with Sonnenberg."

"Stop this, Connor." Baker heard another, more distant voice. "On my word, Connor, no one need be hurt."

"Your ass," Harrigan growled, snapping a shot toward Duncan Peck and another at Biaggi, who was diving for cover behind one of the gladiators. Baker felt himself moving, driven by Connor Harrigan toward the guns and armor, Marcus Sonnenberg somehow between them. More shots. A spray of stone that made Harrigan grunt. Baker felt the dark doorway swallowing him and the marble floor rushing up toward his face.

Harrigan, himself almost spent, dragged Baker and Sonnenberg through the firearms foyer and into the deeper blackness of the Hall of Armor. At the far end he thought he saw a shadow ducking quickly out of sight.

"We're in a mess, lad." He'd found Roger Hershey while working through the bank building from the rear. No help there. Not much here either, by the look of it. Harrigan put a hand on Baker's shoulder and shook it. "Come on, Baker. We're dead meat if we sit here."

"Tina?" Baker whispered distantly.

Harrigan slapped him sharply across the face and was relieved to see a flash of anger. "That's what we need, lad. We need the beastie."

"No," Sonnenberg barked, straightening to a sitting position against an island display case. "The darts. They'd work much faster on Abel. His metabolism, it's too efficient."

Harrigan glared at him. "Let's hope no one else heard that, bucko." He flipped open the cylinder of the gun he'd taken from Chuck Graves before cramming him into a half-open sarcophagus and shouldering the stone lid back in place. One cartridge left. He remembered the three in his Walker Colt. Christ! Wrong caliber again. Harrigan held up the two revolvers for Sonnenberg to see.

"Two guns," he said quietly, "and one useful bullet

between them. The three of us are a mess, and they have five trained men all armed and mostly healthy. Don't start with theory, Doc."

"It's not theory. Abel won't even last as long as Jared."

"What about Charley, then?"

"Much slower metabolism," Sonnenberg answered, shaking his head, "but he'd be quite useless in a physical situation."

"Tina," Baker called.

"she's sleeping," Charley answered. *"liz rocked her and kissed her so she's all quiet and sleeping."*

"Charley, where are they?"

"under the horse."

"Horse?"

"big fake horse."

Baker turned his head and saw where Charley meant in the dim outline against the far portal lights. He nodded, the small motion making him dizzy.

"Charley, I don't think I can help her. I think I have to call Abel."

"abel's getting drunk now. i'll try to help her, baker. i'll be scared but i'll try."

"Drunk?" Baker asked. Oh! Yes. The drugs. Oh God, Tanner. Liz. Liz, I'm so sorry.

In the Garden Court, the big man, Gorby, had worked his way to a small door at the end opposite the bank façade. Burleson, from the position he now held at the entrance to the firearms foyer, saw him and waved him forward.

"Where are Peterson and Graves?" Burleson whispered.

Gorby glanced around to get his bearings. "There's a big room through there with suits of armor. By now they should be at the only other door to it." He couldn't help staring at the womanlike scratches that raked Burleson's face.

"Okay, stay here," Burleson ordered. "I'm sending Biaggi in first to draw fire. We go in behind him from both sides and Peterson will move in from that end. He turned toward Biaggi, who stood several yards away with Duncan Peck. Peck seemed to be scolding him. He raised a palm toward Burleson, keeping him at a distance.

"Michael," he was saying softly, "I want Baker alive and I want Sonnenberg alive. Do you understand that, Michael?"

"Yes, Mr. Peck."

"This part is equally important, Michael. I want only Baker, you, and myself alive when we leave these grounds. Sonnenberg is to die by no hand but mine. Do you understand that, Michael?"

Biaggi blinked as if it were too much to absorb.

"Richard the Lion-hearted, Michael, died at the end of a siege from a crossbowman's dart. On his deathbed, King Richard forgave the man who killed him. Even so, the hapless archer was tortured to death by Richard's officers on the ground that only a king should kill a king." Alexander the Great, Peck recalled, took a similar view of the murder of Darius, but he considered his point adequately made. It was unthinkable that an adversary such as Ivor Blount had become would die at the hands of an insect like this.

"It's a question of respect, Michael," Peck continued. "My respect for the man's genius is such that I'm prepared to forgive any lesser man who might have been temporarily subverted by him. Is my meaning clear, Michael?"

His meaning was clear. Biaggi nodded. He was nuts. He was as screwy as Sonnenberg and as fucked up as Baker. But if there was a way out of this, Biaggi was ready to take it. "Just tell me what you want, sir."

"I want no one alive, Michael, who might compromise me if questioned, except one whose silence is ensured by a profit motive. These people"—he gestured toward Burleson—"will nobly answer any question asked by a higher authority. You will not, Michael, because I'm going to make you rich. You will become steadily richer with each subsequent service. Your greed, you see, is your salvation."

Peck looked for the light in Biaggi's eyes that would tell him that venality had won its battle over suspicion and doubt. The light came. And then an even greater glow of relief. Good, thought Duncan Peck. Let us hope that it glows a beacon to us all until it is convenient to extinguish it.

Nuts, Biaggi repeated to himself. But nuts wrote checks. And the checks would go into the same bank as the tapes he'd make, with copies sent to Peck so he'd remember who had who by the balls.

"Sir?" Burleson approached partway. "Sir, Gorby's had an idea. We might be able to turn on the emergency lights in there."

Harrigan crouched as he sensed another movement near the far end of the hall, near the armored charger. The horse's skirt, he realized. It was moving. Harrigan squinted through the darkness. He saw a shadow moving silently near the mounted knight. Tanner Burke, he decided from the size and shape. Now he heard a dull popping sound, as if something fastened had been pulled free, then a faint scrape of metal against metal.

"Oh, damn!" he heard Baker mutter.

Harrigan reached out to silence him and then brought the same hand cupped to his ear.

"Harrigan." Baker pushed to his hands and knees. "It's Tanner. She heard me."

"What's she doing?" Harrigan wondered if anything would ever surprise him again. "I told her to stay put."

"She has a mace." Baker struggled for balance to rise to his feet. "One of Peck's men is down there. She's going after him with a mace. And outside they're saying something about these lights. She'll be wide open, Harrigan."

"The beastie, lad. Does he have enough left to take out that one man before he wraps the mace around the lady's neck?"

"Abel?"

"*i can, baker. only now. last chance, baker. only now.*"

"He says he can handle it."

"Let's do it, lad." Harrigan pulled Baker and Sonnenberg erect. "Take out the man and get me his gun. If we reach those narrow stairs we used, I can hold them to doomsday while you lose yourself in the park."

"No," Sonnenberg rasped. "He'll never . . ."

"*Abel. Only that one. Only get us safely out of here. Do you understand, Abel?*"

"*safe. yes, baker. i'll make you safe.*"

"*Come out, Abel.*"

"Jared, don't!" Sonnenberg's voice rose. "He won't run. He'll never run."

Even in the darkness, Harrigan could see the grin. And he saw Abel's hand as it reached for the wall. And then the crunching sound of a war ax being torn from its mounting.

"You're first in," Burleson told Biaggi. He stood with his dart pistol in his right hand and a revolver in his left. The revolver was leveled at a key-operated light panel on the wall near the foyer's entrance. "I fire at this as soon as you dive through. When it shorts, emergency lights go on and we follow."

Biaggi glanced at Duncan Peck.

"Gorby first," Peck whispered. "He's healthiest."

Gorby took a breath and stepped into the doorway. He hesitated. Biaggi stepped forward and shoved him headlong into the darkness. Then, pistols leveled, he and Burleson dropped to a crouch and waited for the first muzzle flash or movement.

Instantly, something was wrong. Gorby had stopped with a muffled grunt, as though striking a wall Biaggi knew was not there. The dim outline of Gorby's shoulders stood motionless for a long moment, then rose slowly as if floating and began to drift backward toward the Garden Court. Biaggi saw Gorby's legs now, twitching, quivering, the toes half a foot off the surface. He lifted his eyes, his brain asking what could dangle two hundred and twenty pounds that high, and he looked into the grinning face he had seen in the park. Gorby, his head lolling sickeningly to one side, hung at the end of an outstretched arm. A spiked medieval war ax bobbed carelessly from the other.

"Darts!" Peck gasped an order. Burleson's pistol spat at Abel's chest, and Biaggi, stumbling backward, fired another that lodged in Abel's cheek. Abel rocked and blinked but the grin remained. Burleson swung his revolver toward the switchplate. Four quick shots roared until it answered with a spit of flame and smoke. Emergency fixtures, mounted high in corners, instantly flickered and began to glow amber, their light glancing off a metal thing that bobbed up sharply and arced toward Burleson's head. Burleson's reflexes saved him. He threw himself under and away from the whistling blow and crashed into a tangle with Duncan Peck. Peck thrashed himself free. He ducked under Gorby's body, which had swung like a counterweight under the force of Abel's blow, and scrambled on his hands and knees out of Abel's field of vision. That took him into the firearms foyer, but Peck was beyond fearing any lesser threat he might encounter there.

Harrigan saw him. He saw Peck's face in the faltering, growing amber light, crabbing frantically toward him. Peck paused to pat awkwardly at his waist as if a weapon had been lost, finally wrenching a small aerosol can from a loop on his belt. Chemical mace. Good luck, Harrigan muttered to himself. He raised his pistol with its one remaining bullet. What the hell, he thought. It's as good a shot as he'd get. But another gun cracked first, and a bullet whined by his face with a rumbling roar that swept the length of the Hall of Armor. Harrigan whirled toward its source. Peterson! He faced Harrigan, in a combat crouch, near the flanks of the mounted knight.

Harrigan swung his revolver, his sights dropping on
Peterson's breastbone, but in that motion he saw Tanner.
Damn, he couldn't shoot. She had appeared from behind
a display of thrusting weapons and was padding quickly
toward Peterson, a real mace poised at her shoulder like
a baseball bat. Peterson saw Connor's surprise and spun,
dropping to one knee as the mace came down across his
raised gun arm. Harrigan heard the bone crack, and a
wild shot blasted a cloud of plaster from the wall. The
muzzle blast stunned Tanner.

Before she could raise the weapon again, Peterson
snatched at the mace's shaft with his good left hand and
pulled. The two of them crashed backward against the
leg of the mounted knight. Come on! Harrigan wanted to
shout. Get clear! The horse's parade skirt flipped up. Two
arms, small arms, wrapped around Peterson's neck and
squeezed. "No!" Tanner screamed. Then her long hair
flew as Peterson's fist caught her high on the temple. Harrigan fired. The shot, aimed too safely and too
low, ricocheted harmlessly under Peterson's splayed legs.
Peterson tensed, awaiting the impact of a second bullet
he could not avoid. None came. He saw that Harrigan's
sights had him cold and that the line of fire was clear, yet
there was no shot. Peterson faked to his left. Still nothing. He knew then that Harrigan's gun was empty.

Abel threw Gorby aside. He seemed confused by
the number of men. The old one. Where was the old
one? Biaggi, his face white with fear, fumbled another
dart into the gun chamber and fired. Abel slapped it
away with the blade of his ax.

Duncan Peck was near Harrigan now. Peck glanced
at him, his exhausted enemy, his face bright with excitement. If he saw the gun in Harrigan's hand, he ignored
it. "Look at him," he whispered. He cast his eyes about
the Hall of Armor as if looking for a greater audience
with whom to share what he was seeing. He saw
Sonnenberg, slumped against a wall, glaring at him
through hooded eyes. "Look at him, Ivor. He's magnifi-
cent."

Abel turned at the voice, reeling, barely balanced.

He swiped once more at the men, who danced out of reach, awaiting the drug's effect. Abel almost fell. Recovering, he staggered toward Duncan Peck. He's had it, Harrigan was sure. Even Duncan Peck's fear seemed to wash away under a shine of excitement. A look of clinical interest on his face, he raised his CN aerosol and released a ten-foot stream. Abel blinked and shook his head, reacting no more than that to the chemical burn at his eyes. A fifth dart struck his back. Abel flailed the ax wildly. Burleson stepped under it and into the Hall of Armor, kicking the useless gun from Harrigan's hand in his stride and sweeping the room with one turn of his head. His mind photographed Peterson, his one good arm shoving the dazed actress forward and then dragging a small figure from beneath a stuffed horse.

Abel saw Duncan Peck now and lunged drunkenly toward him. Burleson leaped. A flying kick glanced off the side of Abel's head. His hand snaked to the knot of Burleson's necktie and caught him in midflight. Burleson's cheeks swelled red and his eyes went wide. From arm's length, Abel brought that florid face closer and peered into it, trying to focus through eyes that would not function. Strangling, Burleson punched at Abel's face. Vicious karate blows above and beneath the feathers of the dart still lodged in his cheek. Abel shook them off. He seemed to realize that this was not the man he wanted. He swung Burleson to one side and let him fall.

"Bring her," Peck shouted. "Bring the daughter."

Abel's head whipped toward his voice. Peck backed away, first dangerously close to Connor Harrigan, then quickly shifting his direction. His back struck something soft but firm. Marcus Sonnenberg had struggled to his feet and moved unnoticed into Duncan Peck's path, blocking Peck's retreat with his body.

Before Peck could react, Abel was upon him. His fingers gathered Peck's lapels and lifted him, bending him backward over a display of pommeled daggers. Abel raised the war ax and grinned again.

"Daddy!" Tina called. She too was trying to focus on

the man who seemed to be her father. Peterson knocked Tanner Burke aside and placed his muzzle against Tina's head.

"Don't make me kill her," he barked. "Let him go or she dies."

Abel snapped his head toward the voices and the small, stumbling figure being propelled toward him by Peterson's knee. The sudden motion of his head made him reel, but still the ax stayed poised.

"Baker," Peck sputtered. "It's your daughter. Your little girl. They'll shoot her if you hurt me."

Biaggi had entered the hall cautiously. Seeing Harrigan unarmed, he jigged to an angle that would give him a maiming shot at Abel's raised elbow, then cursed as a recovered Burleson leaped into his line of fire. Burleson dove at the raised ax, wrapping his full weight over Abel's weakening arm.

Peck saw the ax quiver and start to sink, first away from him and then out of sight behind Abel's shoulder. Good man, Edward. Such a very good man. Abel's eyes were glazing over. The hand gripping Peck's chest trembled and seemed to slip a bit. He was going now, Peck knew, from the effects of drugs that would have left three ordinary men unconscious by now. Fantastic. But Peck knew what was really stopping this Chimera. The daughter. Chimera or no, he was still a father who would not risk harm to his daughter. She's everything to him. She's what brought him here. She's why we have him now. We'll keep her, he decided, his mind racing with hysterical clarity. I'll tell Michael. The daughter can live. She must be kept alive to control this one. But only for that purpose. And only the daughter. Not these others. Not Ivor. Surely not Harrigan or the girl.

Baker. Baker understood this, Peck saw. The glazed and distant eyes were staring back at him. Nodding now. Except there was the smile. The smile was back. Why was he smiling?

"I have no daughter." Abel hissed the words almost patiently, his tone that of a man explaining a misunderstanding. "The child is Baker's daughter." The grin widened. Peck heard a woman scream. He saw Baker's shoulder roll and twist once more and the ax rose up again. Duncan Peck shrieked. Past Baker's shoulder he saw the ax, now running with blood, and he saw Burleson's face where the long sharp spike should have been. He was impaled there. Peck wailed in despair at the sight of Burleson's dead eyes staring back at him. One eye moved, then bulged to the side. A gleaming piece of steel slowly pushed its way out of the socket behind it. Kill him! Peck screeched in his mind. Why don't they kill him? Michael? Where are you? Douglas? Never mind what I ordered. Shoot! Shoot, for the love of Christ! Don't let him do this to me!

Peterson wanted to fire. He wanted to lift his gun from Tina's head and blow that grinning maniac away, but he wavered. The actress had moved close. She'd go for his arm, he was sure. And then Harrigan, down but still dangerous, would be on him. Biaggi too was frozen, his line of fire blocked by Burleson's gibbeted body. The only clear angle would bring him too within Harrigan's reach.

Peck was fainting. But through a gathering white haze he felt a sudden stiffening of the arm holding him. As if shot. Yes, shot, his brain cried out in hope. Biaggi must have shot him. Good, good man. Now he saw pain in Baker's eyes. Anguish. The mouth still grinned cruelly, but the eyes were pleading, wincing, disbelieving. The grin faded and the lips moved. Trying to form words. A great breath . . .

"*No!*" Abel roared into the face of Duncan Peck. "*No, Baker! The darts. You can't live with the darts, Bayykkerrr!*"

The shout, the desperate plea, shocked Peck out of his swoon. Baker's face! The face was almost melting. Burleson's devastated face fell slowly away, slipping off the war ax with a sucking sound and folding to the floor. Peck felt his own body slip. The grip was easing. The face Peck saw was softer now. Soft and sad. Jared Baker slid weakly to his knees.

* * *

Baker knew at once he'd made a mistake. But there was no real choice he could live with. He'd stopped Abel from killing again. He had to. Maybe he could make Tina believe that Burleson had caused his own death by leaping on the ax. Maybe Tanner Burke too. But there would have been no explaining what they would have seen Abel do next. Abel would have cleaved the face of Duncan Peck in half. Baker had to stop that. He would have been shot a half-second later by either of the two men with guns, but that was not his reason. He just had to stop it. But at what cost? Because now his body was like jelly and his mind was a swirl of fog. Abel might have been right. Maybe he couldn't live with so many tranquilizer darts. The first two already had him stumbling. Then Abel took . . . how many more?

He heard Sonnenberg. What was he saying? Say it out loud, Sonnenberg. I can't hear. Charley? Yes. I know. Charley can live. His body works so slowly. But Charley can't help. Sonnenberg? What can Charley do?

Baker felt his body being dragged.

"Charley?"

"abel's asleep," Charley whispered. There was a quality of dull wonder in his voice.

"Charley, can you help me?"

"abel?"

"Never mind Abel. Charley, you have to come out."

"sonnenberg is calling you. sonnenberg says help him. sonnenberg says help mrs. kreskie too. and melanie."

"I can't Charley. I can't even help myself."

"sonnenberg says tina can help."

Now he could hear Tina calling him. And he knew Tanner was with someone. They both were. They were telling the men not to hurt him. To stop dragging him. Baker also knew that one was dragging Connor Harrigan because he was weak from loss of blood and he couldn't put weight on his leg anymore. But Harrigan wasn't weak. He was pretending. Baker knew that. Maybe Harrigan could help. Sonnenberg? Tina can't help anybody, Sonnenberg. She can't even if I'd let her, you son of a bitch, because of whatever you pumped into her.

He felt the hands let go of his shoulders and his head cracked against the marble floor. Baker barely felt it. Through a half-opened eye he could see he was back in the atrium. Near the steps to the bank. Baker saw Harrigan there, slumped on the bottom step. Sonnenberg too. His face was turned sorrowfully toward the pulpit's base, where Stanley lay curled in a tight ball. Tanner was behind Sonnenberg. She was cradling Tina in her arms.

Peterson stepped through the doors of the bank from inside, his arm splinted with slats broken off a Federal chair. He stopped near Tina. "Hershey's handcuffed to a stair rail," Baker heard him say. "The woman's dead."

Melanie. Poor Melanie.

Now Harrigan was saying something. Inside his head. Reach out your right hand, Baker. There's a purse just by your fingers. Feel it? There's a gun in there, lad.

I can't.

"Don't even blink, Harrigan." It was Biaggi's voice. He stepped toward Harrigan and reached inside his jacket. Connor saw the torn flesh on the back of Biaggi's hands.

"Did someone smash the cookie jar, Michael, while your hands were in it?" Harrigan asked.

He was taunting him, Baker knew. Why?

Biaggi found what he was reaching for. He paused, looked into Harrigan's eyes, and tore it away roughly. It was the Walker Colt. Its hammer raked painfully across Harrigan's ribs.

"Hey, look at this." Biaggi smiled. "What do you think this is, Harrigan? The OK Coral?"

Biaggi faked a fast draw from his hip, cocking the old Colt and pointing it at Harrigan's forehead. Harrigan cleared his throat and spat full in Biaggi's face.

Biaggi stood frozen by the insult, his eyes flaring. "That, fat man," he said in quiet rage, "is going to cost you one set of balls." He lowered his aim to Connor Harrigan's groin. Harrigan threw his arms across his face.

"Connor is about to kill you, Michael." Duncan Peck

reached for the revolver in Biaggi's hand as he spoke. Biaggi hesitated, the force of his angry grip squeezing new blood from his hand.

"Did it strike you as odd, Michael," Peck asked, "that a man would cover his face when his private parts were threatened?"

Biaggi, flushed, found the cylinder release and looked down the barrel. It was plugged. The shot would have taken his hand off.

"Excellent try, Connor." Duncan Peck bowed slightly. Harrigan acknowledged the compliment with a nod. Peck took the Walker Colt from Biaggi. "For another thing, Michael, we must learn from Connor what became of our man Graves or of his remains. It wouldn't do to leave him behind, credentials and all. Even then, I suggest you spare Connor's life long enough for him to walk out to the van. You and Douglas have enough dead weight to carry as it is."

"christina, help me."

Baker heard Charley's voice calling her. On his own. He'd never done that before. Wait. Yes, he had. He said so that time in the car, when he spoke about himself and Tina being friends. But *Christina?* Did he call her *Christina?*

Baker heard a grunt nearby and a shout of protest from Tanner. It was Harrigan's grunt. Biaggi was kicking him. Trying to get him up. Harrigan was still acting like he couldn't. He just lay there. Why did he let Biaggi kick him?

"Charley? I think I have to call you out. There's no one else, Charley."

"christina, help me. help me now."

Baker tried to move his lips to form Charley's name, but they only quivered and sagged against the cold marble. He felt a hand on his face. Plucking out the dart still imbedded there. Now the fingertips were on his eye, pushing back the lid. It was Duncan Peck's hand, Baker saw. And behind Peck someone else was moving. There was a yelp that sounded like a cane-whipped dog and Peck's head turned. Baker couldn't see. But through

Peck's fingers he could feel a current of sudden fear. Harrigan must have tried something. This, though, was more than fear. It was terror. Baker strained to look through Duncan Peck's trembling fingers. He saw only a shadow. But it was dancing crazily in the flood of an emergency light, like a giant puppet gone wild.

Peck saw his man Peterson and he saw Baker's daughter, but everything about them was terribly wrong. His brain tried to sort the picture. Moments before, Peterson had been holding the girl, lifting her to her feet. But now the girl was holding him. One hand had taken him by the throat. The fingers seemed buried to their second joint in the flesh around his windpipe. And Peterson, this grown man, was being tossed and flopped like a large stuffed toy. Peck watched his man for what seemed like minutes as his legs flew from under him and his head and trunk slammed again and again on the marble floor. The slats of his splint flew broken through the air. His good arm, once desperately clawing, now flapped as brokenly as the other. His eyes were flat and dead.

The girl could not be doing that, Peck's mind insisted. Then he looked closely at her face. Her eyes were shining, almost black. The skin of her face seemed stretched across it and her teeth were bared in an animal's snarl. He watched, transfixed, as Baker's daughter threw away the man she'd been smashing to the ground and, grinning, advanced toward him on legs that were straight and strong. He wanted to scream Biaggi's name. Help me, Michael. You'll be rich. Anything will be yours if you'll help me.

Perhaps he managed to shout the name. Because Biaggi had been ducking and weaving past the flail of Peterson's legs, his eyes wide in disbelief, his revolver bobbing in his hand as he sought a clear shot. At last, when Peterson's body crashed to the floor, he had one. Biaggi stepped aside as Tina moved toward Peck, then raised his sights to the back of her skull.

"Watch out." Peck found his voice. "Watch out for Harrigan."

Harrigan was scrambling across the floor like a dart-ing spider, ignoring the girl, lunging at Biaggi's gun. Biaggi sidestepped and kicked him. Harrigan took the blow, catching Biaggi's shoe under the wrap of his arm. Biaggi hopped in a frantic attempt to tear himself loose, his own motion preventing his aiming his gun. Harrigan suddenly loosed his hold and snatched at the revolver's barrel while driving Biaggi backward. The pistol flew from Biaggi's hand. Off balance, he reeled into the path of Tina Baker.

Peck saw Biaggi lurching at her. He saw the girl reach one hand sideways to meet him, but the shining eyes stayed locked on his. Wrestle her, Michael. Throw her down. Yes, throw your arms around her neck and crush the life out of her. Yes, Michael. That's good. You have her, Michael.

For a moment, Peck couldn't see the girl. He saw only Biaggi's back and his straining legs. And he saw Connor Harrigan struggling with the Burke woman, pulling her away, turning her face from the girl and Biaggi. Why wasn't Connor helping the girl? And why was Sonnenberg just quietly watching, neither fear nor surprise on his face? Biaggi shrieked. His legs stopped straining and collapsed under him, the point of one shoe beating a tattoo against the hard floor. Now his torso was bucking like Peterson's and the shoulders were in spasm, as if he were a springbok caught in a leopard's jaws. For a hopeful moment Biaggi's head wrenched free, but something snatched it back. The body stiffened once and went limp. Peck watched it slide slowly to the ground once more, revealing the wild, shining eyes of Tina Baker. Peck realized to his horror that those eyes, Michael Biaggi or no, had never left his own. He saw her hands, both drenched with blood, now reaching out for him. Almost petrified, Peck reached to cover his throat. But she wasn't reaching there. The wet hands reached for his head, holding it, caressing it. They felt hot against his temples and they hurt. Between them he could see Connor Harrigan watching. The woman's face was held pressed against his chest. A gun in Harrigan's free hand.

Stop her, Harrigan. Shoot her, for God's sake. Connor, please. Don't let this happen.

Peck dimly thought he heard a shot. Oh God, yes. A shot. Oh, good man, Connor. You're such a very good man.

But there was no shot. Just as there was none before when it was her father who gripped him. What Duncan Peck heard this time was the sound of his own skull cracking.

The Garden Court was quiet. Tanner Burke, weeping softly, sat on the floor with her arms around Jared and Tina. They were both in a deep sleep.

Harrigan, his wounded leg dragging, shuffled over to them. His foot struck Tanner's purse where she'd dropped it earlier. With a grunt he bent to pick it up, then offered it to her. Tanner shook her head. Harrigan placed it back on the floor near her knees. Reaching over her, he felt for a pulse at Baker's neck. Then Tina's. They were weak, especially Baker's, but they were steady.

Roger Hershey, freed of his handcuffs, wandered vacantly through the room, wiping blood from exhibits and straightening those that had been disturbed. He picked up Baker's war ax and sat down with it across his lap, wiping it clean with a handkerchief and polishing it with his sleeve.

Sonnenberg was near the pulpit, where Stanley Levy lay dying. He called softly to Roger twice, three times, before Roger put the ax carefully aside and went to him. The two men lifted Stanley and carried him into a better light, where Sonnenberg set about examining his wounds.

Harrigan limped over to Duncan Peck and looked down at him. Peck rested where Tina had released him, in a broken heap against the *Diana*'s pedestal. His legs were splayed, and one of them still twitched. Alive. Harrigan could hear Peck's breath coming in short, bubbling sobs from a head that was oddly misshapen. He studied him for a long moment, hefting his revolver thoughtfully in his hand, then turned and studied the face of Tina Baker. It was soft again. And sweet. A gentle kind of pretty. He felt Sonnenberg watching him. Harrigan raised his eyes, his brow forming a silent question. No words were spoken. No minds were probed. There were only the thoughts of one man understood by another. Sonnenberg nodded. Harrigan nodded back and took several steps toward the body of Douglas Peterson.

Tanner assumed at first that Harrigan was searching him. He unbuttoned Peterson's jacket and began stripping it off. Confusion shone on her face when he folded it neatly in half, then laid it across Peterson's head so that it was covered fully. Confusion turned to disbelief as Harrigan bent to place the muzzle of his gun near where Peterson's temple would have been. Harrigan pulled the trigger.

"No!" she screamed at him. Harrigan turned toward Michael Biaggi and undid his jacket in turn.

"Goddamn you, *no!*" she screamed again. Her eyes swept the room, searching for help. Hershey had glanced up at the shot's report, but his attention returned at once to Stanley. Sonnenberg's eyes were on Harrigan. His look said he understood what was happening and thought it proper.

"You bastards," Tanner raged. Frantic, she lunged across the broad chest of Jared Baker and snatched at her purse, fumbling at its clasp. "Harrigan," she shouted, finding the pistol he'd given her, "Harrigan, you bloody bastard." She aimed it at his stomach. The weapon seemed huge in her hands.

"Put it down, lass," he said gently.

"That's enough killing, damn you," she choked out.

"Yes, Miss Burke," he answered, motioning her pistol to one side, "I'd say more than enough." He put away his own weapon and stepped toward Tanner, his hand outstretched. Tanner drew back, hesitating for a long moment, then with a cry of disgust she hurled the gun to the corner farthest from Connor Harrigan. He turned from her. Back toward Michael Biaggi. Once more Tanner screamed helplessly as Harrigan threw the jacket across Biaggi's face and fired almost before it settled. The body bounded once and was still. Tanner, half in shock, fell back sobbing.

Sonnenberg did not look up from his work on Stanley Levy as Harrigan eased to a crouch at his side. Stanley's eyes were open but unseeing. There was no sign of life but for a slight, rhythmic pulse of blood from a gash cut by Burleson's gun barrel. The crueler abdominal wounds were packed with fabric torn from Sonnenberg's heavy coat.

"He's got balls," Harrigan said softly. "I have to give him that."

"I think he'd return the compliment." Sonnenberg nodded.

"Will he make it?"

"Not entirely," Sonnenberg answered. Harrigan noted the choice of words but didn't question them. "What of you, Mr. Harrigan? What will you do now?"

"Clean this up, for openers." Harrigan scanned the carnage. "There are people I can call now that Peck's out of the ball game."

"What of Jared?"

"Baker walks. When he can, anyway. We had a deal. The kid and Tanner Burke too."

"He's really quite something, isn't he?"

"Yeah." Harrigan made a face.

"Although I don't think he'll be much use to either of us for a while."

"Not to you, anyway," Harrigan told him. "Get it straight, Doc. That party's over."

"Perhaps." Sonnenberg shrugged. "It certainly is as far as Baker himself is concerned. But he'll never serve you, Harrigan. He'll surely never unleash Abel again if he can help it. Perhaps not even to save his life."

"Maybe." Harrigan flicked a look toward the one or two lives that Baker might think were important enough. Sonnenberg followed his glance.

"The daughter won't remember, you know. She'll

think it was a dream unless one of you tells her differently. The dream will quickly fade."

"How did it happen, Doc? The kid's another one, isn't she?"

"A Chimera," Sonnenberg answered. "Yes. I'm afraid she is." Sonnenberg craned his head at the sound of a motor outside the glass wall. It was Roger, he knew, bringing his car closer to the window. Roger had already carried the body of Melanie Laver there.

"What happens to her, Doc," Harrigan pressed, "or don't you know?"

"It's hardly a well-traveled road, Mr. Harrigan," Sonnenberg reminded him. "I can know more about the Chimera phenomenon than any man living and still know almost nothing. I know that the potential among human beings is quite common, that in Jared's case the primal Baker had already worked its way close to the surface before the first traumatic stimulus released it, and that the result is two distinct and quite opposite personalities plus the original conglomerate. Certain of the physical and mental capabilities of Abel and Charley, however, were an utter surprise."

Harrigan gestured toward Stanley. "No matter how it turned out, Stanley here was practice. You must have had some idea of what you were getting."

Sonnenberg shook his head, running a hand gently over Stanley's cheek. "Stanley would not have prepared me for Abel's strength, to choose just one example. But even that is common. Documented stories abound, such as the mother who looked out her window and saw that the jack of her son's car had slipped while he was working beneath it. She panicked, flew through the door, and lifted the car off him, realizing only later that she'd done something physically impossible. But it clearly wasn't. And isn't.

"Everyone has a triune brain, Harrigan, which means everyone has an Abel. Everyone also has a hemispheric cerebral cortex, which means everyone has a Charley as well. And everyone who's ever had an extrasensory experience, even feeling that a telephone is about to ring, has had at least a nodding acquaintance with his own Charley. Where extrasensory messages are received, they have obviously been sent. It should come as no surprise, therefore, that Charley is quite capable of communicating with other Charleys. What has not been understood before now is the mechanism. A formed and developed Charley communicates with latent or incipient Charleys by literally calling their parts together. One potentially unhappy result is that the residue amounts to an unassembled Abel."

"That's what happened with Tina?"

"That's my guess, Harrigan. Underline guess."

"So Tina's not a Chimera?"

Sonnenberg straightened. "You're not paying attention, Mr. Harrigan. Everybody is a Chimera. Baker was simply a better subject than most and Tina was simply closer to the source. As, incidentally, was Tanner Burke. What Tanner Burke is is an unusually perceptive woman whom you've begun to imagine has psychic abilities. She has nothing of the sort. What she has is a Charley and an emotional affinity toward the prototypical Charley. There is a danger, Harrigan. The danger is not what Tanner Burke is or what Tina Baker is. The danger is what Jared Baker's now irreversible Charley can now call into existence. This, Harrigan, is what I had to see for myself. And this, sir, is why I've sought to keep those three apart."

Roger Hershey lifted Stanley in his arms and carried him toward Sonnenberg's car.

"We'll be leaving shortly," Sonnenberg told Harrigan. "May I assume you've no objection?"

Harrigan let out a breath. He cocked a thumb toward Baker and his daughter and Tanner Burke, who would not look at him. "I've got all I can handle, Doc. Maybe we'll have a talk some other time."

"Perhaps." Sonnenberg backed away from Harrigan. His hands came from behind his back, one of them holding a stray pistol he'd picked up unseen. "At the moment, however, I'm going to solve at least one of your problems. What's left of Duncan Peck will be coming with me."

"Peck is mine." Harrigan stepped toward him.

"Prior claim, Mr. Harrigan." He raised the pistol level with Harrigan's belly. "Justice will be done, however. I promise that." Sonnenberg reached a beckoning hand toward the revolver in Harrigan's belt.

Harrigan placed his hand across the butt and held it there. "See you later, Doc."

Sonnenberg took him at his word. "A favor, Mr. Harrigan? Duncan has clearly taken the assistant curator of this museum. Philip Poindexter. I suspect he's been abused and is under guard someplace. He's really a very good curator, Mr. Harrigan. Knows his pre-Columbian."

"I'll take care of it." Harrigan nodded. "But Peck likes his packages neat and tidy. If I was you, I'd look in that van on the way out."

"I'm obliged, sir."

"Good," Harrigan replied. "You can settle it now. How does Baker keep the beastie from rattling the bars every time some drunk spills a drink on him?"

"You flatter me that you think I know."

"Then who the hell do I ask? Dear Abby? Guess, Doc. If you don't know, then give me the way to bet."

"Tranquilizers," Sonnenberg answered. Perhaps.

Harrigan spat. He kicked at a dart gun that lay on the floor near his foot. "Now who's not paying attention?"

"There's a drug called Reserpine. Once before it seemed to affect Abel much more than Charley. Used lightly, it should also help to subdue any normal hostilities that this overall experience may leave with him. Reserpine is common enough. In fact, it's been used in the Far East for centuries in the treatment of the mentally ill. Its properties are—"

"I'll look it up." Harrigan stopped him. "Here comes Roger."

*   *   *

Sonnenberg limped to where Tanner Burke sat with Jared and Tina in her arms.

"Goodbye, miss," he said.

She ignored him.

"You're all quite remarkable, you know. You as well. I shall miss you."

"You make me sick." She looked up at him. "You all make me sick. My God, doesn't the damage you've done bother you at all?"

Sonnenberg only sighed in response and surveyed the scene around him. His eye fell upon the Karl Bitter pulpit, now scarred from Biaggi's bullets but at least wiped free of gore. He regretted that, to be sure. And he would weep for Melanie Laver. And for Ben Coffey. But what else could she mean? Surely not the fate befalling Duncan's people. Could she mean Jared? What else should he have been? A convict? How much time would have passed before the other prisoners ventured a homosexual gang rape or any other violence against his person and then watched their arms being torn from their sockets? Baker would still have been what he is while understanding none of it. At his best, even avoiding jail and retreating back into his world of lawns and white houses, he would have been like a billion others puzzled by their occasional rages and ashamed of them, hearing inner voices but denying them, sometimes clearly knowing the thoughts of others but finding a curious comfort in the local psychiatrist's quack verdict of a treatable neurosis brought on by the pressures of modern living. Damage indeed. Let us hope that the passage of time may bring with it a less hysterical view of events.

"And what of your life, Miss Burke?" he asked as Roger Hershey hoisted the unconscious form of Duncan Peck upon his shoulder. "Mr. Peck, depend on it, can hope for a long and useful existence after an appropriate period of penance. But what will you do with yours? Mouth inane dialogue for the cultural enrichment of the nation's bowlers and waitresses? Smile prettily at cameras for the betterment of the hair coloring industry?"

She watched him limp away behind Roger Hershey. By the time he reached the cut in the glass wall, Marcus Sonnenberg wasn't limping anymore. Harrigan saw it too. He had a further sense that once Sonnenberg passed through it, he wasn't Marcus Sonnenberg anymore either.

18

Most of a winter had passed.

A northern California winter. The snow, when it came, fell gently on earth that crusted but never quite froze. The ground here, unlike Connecticut's soil, did not yield to winter and then timidly send up its hardiest buds, like scouts, to report back on winter's retreat. Rather, the soil here rested placidly between growing seasons. And when the day came that the rest was ended it would burst into life as if on signal, a carpet of yellow poppies leading the way by hours.

The place was Clear Lake, a hundred miles north of San Francisco and fifty miles inland. The home was made of pine logs cut from a forest not a mile up the road. The balcony, or raised deck, Baker had built himself. From it he could see the full expanse of deep blue water and the peak of Snow Mountain against the far horizon past softly rolling hills. That view, done in oils, already hung over the massive stone fireplace that Baker and Tina had built together.

Baker stepped away from the window and picked up his palette. He stood for a moment, admiring the half-finished canvas in the crisp afternoon light. Tina's face. A portrait. Smiling at him. Not bad, he thought. Not Delacroix. But not bad. It was the best thing Sonnenberg had given him. The phone rang.

"I'll get it, Daddy," Tina called. He heard her footsteps skipping down from the loft bedroom she'd chosen. It was the third call that day. Two from a young man named David, whose family was taking a ski vacation at Lake Tahoe, except he wouldn't have a bit of fun unless Tina came with them. David's father, a small local vintner, had already asked Baker's permission and gotten it, but Baker would say nothing until Tina herself asked. A part of him hoped she would not. They had not been apart since Harrigan had half-carried them across Fifth Avenue, where he stole another unlocked car. But the less selfish part wanted her to go. The leg was strong. Strong enough. It was time to test it and use it beyond her daily, mile-long walks to school, forsaking the school bus in favor of the exercise, or her weekend hikes into Lucerne with Sam, the stray dog she claimed to have found.

The other call was a hangup. It troubled him as all such calls did. But Charley said he felt nothing. Not to worry. But while he thought of it, would Baker mind some cherry sauce for a change on the duck he was planning to roast for dinner? Next time, Baker promised. Connor Harrigan would be stopping by in an hour or two, and he didn't have time to run down to the Safeway in Lucerne.

Charley or not, the hangup stayed on Baker's mind. He couldn't shake the thought that it might have been Tanner. It wasn't, though. She didn't have his number. She didn't even know they were in the same state. For all Baker knew, she'd blocked those two days out of her mind by now. Five days, counting the next three in a motel near Kennedy airport waiting for him to be able to stand up. And when he could, when he could look into her eyes to see if she saw Abel when she looked into his, he remembered almost grinning with relief when he saw that she did not. But then he caught her staring at Tina. Tanner didn't see Abel there. No one could. Not in that face. That was what made it so terrible for Tanner. That there could be an Abel there. That a sweet, happy child could tear the throats out of two grown men and crush the skull of another. That's when Baker left her. For all their sakes. Tanner couldn't get away from Harrigan fast enough anyway.

"Daddy?"

"Yes, Vickie." Victoria. Tina's middle name. They kept Baker. It was common enough. And Tina understood. Baker knew that she'd have preferred Liz if she had to have another name, but she'd seen the sadness in her father's face when she brought it up.

"David Torrence asked if I could go skiing next weekend with his family. Or do you already know that?"

"Fathers know everything." He smiled. "Do you want to go, honey?"

"I think."

Baker shrugged. "You like David. You like skiing. What's to think about? Personally, I'd enjoy the peace and quiet."

"He wants to go tomorrow. It's a whole week."

"A whole week of peace and quiet is even better." But Baker saw she was doubtful. It was something more than leaving him alone that long. "Babe, do you want to tell me what's bothering you?"

Vickie waved her hands to show it was nothing. Then, "Do you ever get feelings?"

"I've been known. Yes."

"I've got a feeling that I should be here tomorrow. That I'll really want to. Sounds dumb, doesn't it?"

"It'll sound a lot dumber tomorrow when you're here cleaning your loft instead of cutting slalom gates."

Vickie nodded. She knew he was right. Probably. All the same, though. "I'm going to say thanks, but maybe next time." She heard a crunch outside and stepped to the window. "Anyway, here comes Mr. Harrigan."

Vickie excused herself once Connor Harrigan settled next to the fire and took his first long sip from the Scotch Baker offered him. Sam followed her onto the terrace, where she slipped on a pair of Walkman earphones and began dancing with the half-Husky mongrel.

Baker returned to his easel and pretended indiffer-

ence while he waited to hear whether Harrigan brought
news this trip or whether he'd finally ask the favor that
Baker knew would be coming one day. He would refuse,
no question. But he'd listen. He owed Harrigan that
much.

"Are you going to tell me?" Baker asked. "Or do
I . . ." Do I have to ask Charley? he almost said.

"Good Scotch, Jared." Harrigan had something on
his mind, all right.

"The name's Paul. Try to get used to it."

"Yeah." Harrigan stood up and walked to the
counter, where he poured another two inches. "Well,
that's the first piece of news. You're Jared Baker again.
The Connecticut charges are all quashed."

Baker had expected that. The charges had no real
substance anyway. Wiping them off was easy for
Harrigan, especially with a phone call from Duncan
Peck's replacement, who owed his appointment to
Connor Harrigan as much as anyone. Still, Baker
thought, he'd leave things as they were for a while.
Things were good, mostly. And if it isn't broken, don't fix
it.

"Anything on Sonnenberg?" Baker tried to sound as
though his interest was casual. He hoped it would be
someday.

"Not a thing," Harrigan answered. "Not him, not
Levy, not Peck. Levy and Peck figure to be dead. Levy
for sure. He didn't have enough gut left to string a banjo.
No word on Roger Hershey either. You want my own
opinion, I think the guy deep-sixed himself. You can't be
Mr. Nice Guy Who Kills People without something
cracking sooner or later."

Baker knew better, although he wasn't sure how.
Roger was alive. His name was Barrett now and he ran
a bookstore up north someplace. Probably the bookstore
Melanie had mentioned. Barrett's of Wimpole Street.
Melanie had never said all that but he knew. Maybe
Charley heard her talking about it once. Whatever. Why
don't we all just leave Roger alone as long as he's quiet
and happy. Baker hoped he was both.

"Selling any paintings?"

"A couple." Baker nodded. "I have a gallery in San Francisco that said they'd like to do a show this summer. Tina . . . Vickie also talked the high school into setting up an exhibit and getting me in to teach adult education classes."

"Sounds like a nice life."

"Your exact thoughts"—Baker smiled—"were 'Boring as shit' and 'When is this turkey going to start looking for some action.' "

"Charley's a pain in the ass."

"That was strictly Baker, Harrigan."

Harrigan stood up and strolled to the window facing the lake and the road that wound past it. "You know," he said, "if I ever did ask you to do something, it would be strictly a Charley deal. No beasties."

"Nice of you to drop in." Baker's good humor faded.

"Just so you know." Harrigan reached into his pocket and pulled free a thick envelope, which he handed to Baker. "Here's a present."

"What is it? My arrest record?" Baker held up his fingers to show he had paint on them. Harrigan slipped the envelope into Baker's pants pocket.

"Paper," he answered. "Good paper. It says you're really Paul Baker, San Diego birth certificate, matching records down there. Also job history, education, military, the works." Harrigan saw his face darken. "Relax. No one knows but me. A friend of mine at the Bureau of Engraving does this for me once in a while if I get him tickets to Redskins games. This makes it easier for you to move around, like when you go to your show in San Francisco. Who knows, you might want to drive all the way to Hollywood someday."

"You've seen her, haven't you?"

"I've seen her."

Baker put down his brush and wiped his hands on a stained towel. "How is she, Harrigan?"

"She still hates my guts pretty good, in case that news brightens your day. Aside from that, she's not working too much. Spends a lot of time sailing her little boat by herself. Long walks on the beach. That's where I caught up with her. Beats the shit out of me why, but that lady cares about you, Baker. Taking off like you did busted her up some. For which I think you were an asshole, by the way. I mean, it's not like you had a whole hell of a lot left to hide from her."

"It's a different world, Harrigan. It wouldn't have worked."

"If you're in hiding," Harrigan agreed. "But I keep telling you you don't have to hide. Or is it me being an asshole?"

Baker didn't answer.

"It's the kid, right? Tina."

Baker nodded. "And Abel." It was possible, just possible, that over time Tanner could have forgotten what she'd seen Abel do. It was terrible to see, but sometimes the violence of a plain man who's out of his head with anger can be just as awful. Almost. But it would never work that way with Tina. Like Sonnenberg said, Tina didn't remember a bit of what happened in the museum, but Tanner surely did. And someday, if she were around Tina, someday she might slip. She might overreact to a normal display of anger on Tina's part. Or to a nightmare Tina might be having. Or to a distant and dreamy look. Or to Tina knowing through ordinary intuition what was on Tanner's mind. It was better the way it was.

"Why didn't you tell her the truth about what you did at the museum?" Baker asked.

Harrigan knew what he meant. He meant the bullets fired into the heads of Peterson and Biaggi. The coats dropped over their faces so bits of brain would not spray over the woman and the girl sitting near them. Dead brains. The life torn out of them by the hands of Tina Baker. Bullets fired for the record. So that the record would show it was Connor Harrigan who killed them, whatever ridiculous story might be told one day about a little girl ripping them apart.

"Leave well enough alone." He shrugged. Besides, Baker—and you can hear this if you want—that's one hell of a favor you owe me.

Harrigan dug into his pocket again and pulled out two plastic pill bottles. "Here's your refill," he said, offering them to Baker. "Reserpine. Down to a quarter grain, like you asked. How's it doing?"

"It works fine." Baker nodded. "Of course, I haven't really been exposed to anything out here that might make me angry. And I'm not about to risk calling Abel. But I think he's slipped pretty far back down. Not much from Charley either. Even Charley's become more of a thought than a voice. More of a well-developed intuition than a separate person."

"That's great," Harrigan said, not meaning it. "You're almost Joe Normal again." He looked at his watch. Let's just see, he thought. We'll see how good that intuition is working.

Harrigan settled back and watched as Baker painted, drinking in the feel of Baker's new surroundings. A nice life, he thought. A little boring, yes, but for Connor Harrigan and probably not for Baker. Technically, of course, it sucked as a relocation identity. I mean, the guy keeps his own last name, he has a blond daughter with him even if she doesn't limp anymore, he keeps all his hobbies, which include painting, skiing, and putzing around in boats on that lake out there, and he doesn't even wear those tinted aviator glasses now. Me, I'd find him in a week if I didn't already know where he was. Of course, no one's really looking for him as far as either of us knows. Except possibly Sonnenberg, who could also find him in a week. Baker's no dummy, so he has to know that. Which means he has something going for him that makes him not worry about it too much. Which means, if I was a betting man, which I damn well am, I'd lay very nice odds that old Charley is just as sharp as ever.

Harrigan checked his watch again. Almost time.

He made small talk about his drive up through the California wine country and the little yellow flowers that seemed to be everywhere this trip, all the while watching Baker's expression. A small wrinkle of concentration now, but Baker shook it away. Another one a minute later. This time he kind of tilted his head to one side like he was listening. What do you hear, Baker? Just some intuition, right?

The deck door opened and Tina ... Vickie ... entered the high-ceilinged living room. Funny look on her face. Like something was wrong. Not bad wrong, just wrong, and she couldn't quite figure out what it was. They looked at each other. Their eyes met. Same look on Baker's face. Shit, Harrigan thought. The kid still had it. He hadn't figured on that. He'd hoped, at least, that Sonnenberg was right. That it would all be like a onetime dream.

Vickie touched her father's arm and walked past him to the window facing the road. She was still there when Harrigan heard the distant sound of a small truck grinding into a lower gear. Harrigan watched her face.

"Liz?" The word formed silently on her lips. Harrigan looked out the window. A pickup truck. Two hundred yards away. Could be anyone.

Baker laid down his brushes and wiped his hands once more while crossing to Vickie's side. He saw the truck. His mouth falling open, he turned and shot a look at Connor Harrigan. Harrigan wasn't sure whether he saw more of joy or anger on Baker's face.

"Merry Christmas," Harrigan said, rising. "If you don't mind, I don't think I'll stay for dinner." He buttoned his coat while walking to the door opposite the approaching vehicle.

"Liz!" Vickie screamed. She whipped open the door and took the porch steps in a single leap. Tanner jumped from the cab, her arms opening wide, a beam of astonished pleasure on her face at the ease with which Vickie ran, then she stumbled backward under the impact of a hundred leaping pounds. Tanner buried her face in Tina's hair, tears dampening it, trying to wipe her eyes dry on the collar of her ski parka so she could look up at Jared Baker, the dope, who just stood there on the porch trying to look serious with his mouth while his eyes were grinning like an idiot.

Vickie stretched to look past Tanner into the cab of the truck. She saw a large blue duffel, a western hat sitting on top of it.

"You're staying?" she asked excitedly. Now Vickie could see into the bay of the pickup. Another duffel. And a pair of skis in an Olin bag. "How long?" Vickie cried. "How long are you staying?"

"A weekend?" Tanner asked, looking up at Baker. She wiped once more at the tears, then stopped, not caring whether Baker saw them or not. "A weekend," she said more firmly. "Maybe longer."

Baker, his face softening, hesitated for just a moment before stepping off the porch and slowly descending the stairs. He wanted to run to her, to hold her, to tell her how sorry he was that he'd hurt her, to try to make her understand. But he couldn't think of a thing to say that wouldn't sound stupid or that couldn't wait. His own eyes moistened. He didn't wipe them because he was afraid that when he looked again she'd be gone. Even seeing her, it was almost too much to believe that she was really there. That she cared about him like Harrigan said. That she cared enough to swallow back whatever pride a jerk named Baker had left her and drive all the way up here, not knowing whether he'd welcome her or turn her away.

"Your hair," he said. He knew at once how stupid the first words he spoke sounded. Of all the things he might have said. Like, "I'm glad you're here, Tanner." Or, "I missed you very much." Or, "I'll never know what you see in me, but God, I'm grateful for it, and oh, how I love you."

Her free hand, the other hugging Vickie, went self-consciously to her hair, which remained full and thick but cropped at her shoulders. And beneath her red parka she was wearing faded jeans. And western boots, the working kind. And she wore no makeup.

"Liz Burke," she told him, sweeping her hand down the length of her body as if presenting it. "This is Liz Burke. Tanner Burke won't be coming."

"Maybe longer." Baker nodded, reaching toward her. "Maybe much longer."

Epilogue

On the campus of San Jose State University, some forty miles south of San Francisco, a gaunt, silver-haired man struggled to pull a wheelchair through the exit of the building housing the faculty lounge. His movements were stiff, and he appeared to stagger with each sudden movement.

The man seated in the wheelchair looked up as the sky came into view. It still threatened rain after a morning squall that had left the streets and sidewalks slick. In one hand he held papers he'd already begun to grade. Better to wait, the professor decided. He stuffed them into a leather portfolio, straightened his lap robe, and tamped a green Tyrolian hat more snugly over his head.

His face, like the hat, had a robust Alpine look about it. His cheeks were a vigorous pink, and his intelligent eyes had the lines of a man who smiled easily. The man guiding his chair, in contrast, had eyes that only stared distantly. But they seemed to brighten a shade when the professor spoke his name and whispered encouragement to him. He pulled the wheelchair clear of the doors and turned it into position to descend the three stone steps to the sidewalk. He was tall but frail, and he moved with the uncertainty of a recovering paralytic learning anew the functions of his limbs. He braced himself against the weight of the chair as its rear

451

wheels eased over the uppermost step. One foot began to skid on a wet surface. He moaned aloud.

"Hold on," a female voice shouted from nearby.

There were two young women. Students. Their flats slapped against the pavement as they ran to assist Professor Lehrmann and his faltering aide. Each grabbed an armrest of the wheelchair. Together they held it balanced as the thin man lowered the chair over the remaining steps.

"Thank you." The professor smiled. "You are both very sweet. Very sweet indeed." His voice was deep and strong, his accent German.

"Our pleasure, Professor Lehrmann," one answered.

The tiniest wince behind his smile reminded them that he was in pain. He was always in pain, the students had heard. Something about being beaten by Nazi thugs when he was a graduate instructor at Leipzig. And yet there was always that good humor, always time to stop and chat. In no time at all, it seemed as though he'd been teaching there for years.

"Miss Lindsay Rollins, isn't it? And Miss Carol . . ."

"Carol Burns, sir."

"Yes, certainly. Forgive me."

Carol brushed the apology aside, pleased that he remembered even part of her name. "I loved Tuesday's lecture, Professor Lehrmann. Early German Renaissance. You sure do make that stuff come alive."

"Stuff indeed," he snorted good-naturedly. "But of course it *is* alive. Since childhood you've been singing about good King Wenceslaus, and now you know the fellow was real. There were two, in fact, in the Luxembourg line. However, I'm afraid the second called for flesh and wine once too often, and the electors threw the drunken rascal out. I trust you'll stay tuned, Miss Burns. Johann Gutenberg is about to start tinkering with movable type, and Martin Luther is brooding about giving the pope a piece of his mind."

The thin man fidgeted as the two freshmen laughed. They looked up into his eyes. He seemed uncomfortable. Eager to leave. A very strange duck, they thought, this silent man with the oddly misshapen head. And yet his twin sister, Professor Lehrmann's housekeeper, was very nice. Carol had met her when she returned a book. The housekeeper seemed to have the same motor control problem as her brother, hereditary probably, but her mind was quick, and she had a really funny New Yorky way of expressing herself.

"Well"—Carol tapped Lindsay's arm—"don't let us keep you, Professor."

"Yes." Lehrmann hefted his leather folder. "Off to my study for more fascinating excursions into the undergraduate psyche. The two of you must come visit me one day. I shall offer you a glass of hot spiced wine and promise not to bore you too terribly."

Their faces split into grins. Half the kids in their dorm would give anything for such an invitation. He was fun, the conversation was always wonderful, and then there were all those precious things. Pre-Columbian, mostly. All museum quality.

"We'd be delighted, sir. Anytime you say."

"Four o'clock today then?" He touched the brim of his hat. "And come in good appetite. My housekeeper's rumaki is to die for."

Professor Lehrmann watched as the two pleased and flattered young women fairly bounced toward the next corner and turned left out of sight.

"Quite charming, aren't they?" he said to his companion.

The tall man nodded indifferently.

"The Burns girl is a National Merit Scholar, you know," Lehrmann continued. "Also fluent in two languages, well traveled, an adequate cellist, a competitive skier—although I've had enough of those for a while—and captain of the freshman girls' lacrosse team. An impressive list of accomplishments for one so young."

He chortled to himself as if enjoying a private thought. "So many, in fact"—he looked up, grinning—

"that I hardly know what to make of her. That's a pun, old friend."

The silent man answered with a trace of a smile, then turned the wheelchair and pushed it forward. At the curb he had trouble again. The wheels came down hard upon the macadam, and the professor's leather portfolio slipped from his lap. He moaned an apology. Stiffly, he bent to pick up the folder from the wet street. An ice pick slipped from his sleeve as he stretched. It rolled against the curb, where a runoff of water twice pushed it beyond his awkward reach.

"Leave it, Stanley." Professor Lehrmann reached a hand to his shoulder. "If the need should again arise, your sister always keeps an ice pick in her kitchen."

Stanley Levy's eyes cleared for a flickering moment at the sound of his name. They would clear for longer periods, the professor knew, with the passage of time and with the growth of new neuron chains that would link Stanley's brain tissue with that of his host. Before long, he would catch up with his less damaged sister. Before long, there would be more Stanley. And there would be less of the dull and distant expression that was once the face of Duncan Peck.

"Let's go home, Stanley," Professor Lehrmann said gently. "There is much to do."

ABOUT THE AUTHOR

JOHN R. MAXIM lives in Westport, Connecticut, except when he's in Europe. He won't tell us what he does there.

The author has written six previous books, including *A Matter of Honor, The Bannerman Solution* and *Time Out of Mind*, and is published in ten languages. He is currently at work on a new novel.

DON'T MISS

TIME OUT OF MIND

BY

JOHN MAXIM

AVAILABLE IN FEBRUARY, 1994
WHEREVER BANTAM PAPERBACKS
ARE SOLD.

AN 451 11/93